STUCK WITH YOU

STACY WILLIAMS

Cover art by Rebekah Hamersley
Edited by Olivia Winston

ISBN: 979-8-9890449-7-9 (ebook)
979-8-9890449-8-6 (paperback)

To those seeking new beginnings and fresh starts.
Those hanging on by a thread of hope, believing things can be different.
Keep fighting. You're still standing.
Sometimes, we have to walk through hell to appreciate all that comes after.

AUTHOR'S NOTE AND CONTENT WARNING

Dear Readers,

I am truly honored and humbled that you've chosen to spend time with Slade and Sarah. While this story will bring you laughter, heartwarming moments, and make you swoon, please be aware that it also addresses heavier topics and themes, such as grief, infidelity, and strained family relationships. I handle these subjects with significant consideration, sensitivity, and care.

It is very important to me to consider my audience's preferences. Please note this story contains adult language. If you prefer a fully closed door experience, you may wish to skip Chapter 53.

As always, thank you for your support.

XOXO,

Stacy

CHAPTER 1

SARAH

Poop. There is poop eve-ry-where.

I hold my breath as my eyes trace over the small, confined space.

"No!" I throw my hand out like a stop sign.

Frankie's bottom lip puffs out, and she starts to cry, holding her arms out for me to pick her up.

Ok.

I quickly untuck my silky blouse and strip it off, setting it on the rocking chair. I tie my freshly dried waves back with a hair tie and grab the wipes off the top of the dresser, ready to enter the danger zone. I need elbow-length gloves, but alas, I'm diving in bare-handed.

"All right, Love Bug." I scrunch my nose, carefully inspecting the damage. "I guess we're getting a bath this morning." *Which I do not have time for.*

I tug one arm out of her sleeve and then the other, delicately lifting the soiled shirt over her head.

"Ma-ma," she whimpers, reaching for me, and I curl my spine, pulling my clean body away from her grasp.

"Hold on." I rip a thousand wipes from the container to attempt to scrub away some of the dried mess stuck to her back and sides. She jolts at the cold and cries louder.

Her soaked bottoms sag, and I toss the handful of wipes into the pool of sewage spread over the crib sheet, then work to remove her pants.

One side of the diaper hangs open, the cheap tab having come loose in the night. Store-brand diapers are my number one enemy today. I'll draft a letter to the company on behalf of all of mom-kind.

I hold her arm with one hand while trying to inch the sticky and stinky fabric over the bloated diaper. My nostrils flare as I suck in air through my mouth, which might be worse.

Ulk, yuck!

Frankie whimpers as I try to free her from the abhorrent mess. I release one chubby foot and then the other, letting the diaper fall to the sheet that will likely find its home in the trash.

I stare at it, holding her by the arms. "Ok. It's ok. One thing at a time."

I grip her under the armpits and hold her away from me, quickly moving to the bathroom, hoping to avoid getting poop on my skirt.

"Mama, I'm hungry," Ollie whines from the couch as I scurry across the hall with a smelly baby. "In a minute, bud."

She stands along the side of the tub while I turn on the water, needing it to warm quickly.

"Ma-ma-ma-ma." Fat tears drip onto her cheeks.

"Shhh. It's ok. We'll get you all clean." *As quick as possible.* I run a hand over her hair, feeling the stiffness along the back. I can't even think about it.

Damn diapers.

I check my watch and blow out a breath. Frankie's cries turn to a fuss as the water pools around her squishy little feet.

After the quickest sanitizing bath of Frankie's life, I wrap her in a towel and head back across the hall where the morning Poopgate remains.

"All right, you little dung beetle, now that you smell fresh, let's get you dressed."

With a diaper and fresh clothes, I hurry to the living room and sit her beside the basket of toys. I check my watch again, knowing Helen will arrive any minute, and I'm only in my bra.

I stop at the edge of the couch and lean down to plant a quick kiss on the top of Ollie's head. He laughs as Bandit crawls across the screen, 'baaing' like a sheep. My little guy is snuggled up with his big-eyed, stuffed blue fish, giggling at Bluey. The giant fur ball next to him raises his head from Ollie's lap, cocking his head as if I'd forgotten him.

"M-mama. I'm hungry," Ollie whines.

"One sec, ok?" I rush back to Frankie's room, carefully removing the sheet and waterproof pad, folding it in on itself to carry to the washer. In the basement, I select the cycle with the hottest setting, then rush up to pull on my shirt.

My phone buzzes on the dresser. I swipe to answer, but—

"Ow! Shhii . . ." I bend at the waist, bringing my foot to my hand and cupping my toes, uncertain if they're all still attached. I hold my breath, hoping it will ease the pain and the desperate need for nothing to be broken.

Holy mother of . . . Piece of shii . . .

I wheeze, clenching my teeth and trying to keep myself upright rather than crumpling to the floor where my toe may be lying severed and in need of reattachment.

"Gooooood morningggg," my mom sings, but it's clouded by the pain.

I inhale and exhale, blinking tears from my eyes.

"Honey?"

"Yeah." I choke out. "I. . .stubbed my toe." I carefully rub my pinky, confirming it's still there, but I can't be sure it's still pointed in the right direction.

"Oh, ow. That hurts like a . . ." I hear her suck air through her teeth, and the long-distance sympathy does nothing to help the virtually vomit-inducing pain.

I lean my shoulder against the wall and inspect my tights, which thankfully are still intact. Not even a snag.

I release my foot and gently wiggle my toes even though the fiery ache is almost unbearable.

I limp down the hallway, clutching my phone to my ear. I peek at Frankie, working on pulling every toy out of the basket, hearing the *click, click, click* of dog nails on the old hardwood floor trailing me.

In the kitchen, I reach into the large tub next to the back door and dump a scoop of food into Grover's bowl.

"So, what did you do yesterday?" my mom asks in her typical cheerful tone, likely attempting to distract me from the pain.

I need a bit of my mom's peppiness. "Unboxed a few more things and then studied."

I tap the speaker button and set my phone on the counter next to the coffee pot. I pull my travel mug from the dishwasher, inspect it, and decide it's clean enough for the gas station-like sludge I'm becoming accustomed to drinking.

"Sweetheart, you need to get out and make friends. You're too young, smart, and beautiful to sit at home and have your nose in books."

My mom is the fun mom. The social butterfly. The one who marches to her own drum and right into the party. There's no room for bad days or wallowing. When things suck, you grab the bull by the horns and make it dance.

I dump in enough vanilla creamer to make the crappy coffee tolerable. "I'm going to work. Believe me, it's enough socialization these days."

I glance at the time and must be out the door as soon as Helen arrives.

"What about Kat? Why isn't she dragging you out of the house? She seems like a woman who wouldn't take no for an answer."

She's not wrong. From what I can tell, Katrina Dunn is a shark. The woman chews people up one side and down the other. Fortunately for me, she doesn't appear to view me as prey. Are we friends? That's probably a stretch, but for some reason, she's taken me under her wing, at least for now.

Two weeks ago, on my first day of work, Kat made herself at home in the chair beside my desk and gave me a rundown on all of my coworkers and the rules for sticking it out. She made it clear that if I wanted to last, I had to refrain from fraternizing, no matter how tempting it might be.

I still don't quite understand the last one since the list of candidates to possibly fraternize with is equal to none, but I noted it anyway. I never have and never will date or mess around with a co-worker, and that's before I was screwed all to hell by the one person who should cherish me beyond all others.

Kat smiled a quick, sly smirk and wished me luck as she left me with the twenty years' worth of marital assets my other boss designated as my first assignment. The same ones I'm still digging through and drowning in.

"Honey, you need a night out with the girls."

I used to have girls' nights filled with movies, laughter, and sharing new mom woes, but those days are long gone, and so are those friends. A night out would be fun. But one, I don't have any friends, and two, the list of what I currently need goes so far beyond a night out.

I throw some crackers and cheese in a baggie for lunch. "Mom, I spent all weekend cleaning and studying during nap time. There are still things to go through and boxes to unpack. Plus, even though she's not my direct boss, she's probably not someone I should casually hang out with. I have to prove myself and show I can do more than answer phones and create spreadsheets."

I unlock the back door, and Grover trots out to do his morning business.

"Well, maybe join a gym or something. I bet they have one that has childcare."

"Right. Like I can afford that."

"Yeah." She breathes out a mix of frustration and disappointment, which tugs on my gut that wants to ignore those same constant feelings.

"Did that ancient washer quit making noises?" Thankfully, she's moving on.

"Yes. Good thing because I'm out of underwear."

"Pfft. Just go without. It's the thing these days." I will not ask how she knows that. "Oh, did you get the box I sent you? There's a cute Kate Spade bag in there. I snagged it right before Cynthia got her grubby mitts on it. It's perfectly professional and in amazing condition."

I drop my lunch into the large, beautiful bag. "Yes. It's great. Thank you." I won't tell her I've considered selling it for the cash, but it's too perfect.

"It came in last week, along with the most exquisite gown. It made me think of . . ." I tune out the reminiscing, not having the energy for dreams long past, and am saved by the front door opening and closing.

"Mom, I gotta go. Helen is here."

"Ok, honey. Have a good day. Love you!"

"Love you, too." I step into the living room. "Good morning."

"I'm sorry I'm running late. I got stuck behind the train." Helen shivers. "It's turning into winter out there. All the leaves are frosted over."

The front yard is blanketed with gold leaves covered in a dusting of white frost. I make a mental note to see if there's a rake in the garage.

I snatch Frankie from the floor, and Helen places a worn hand on her back, smiling at Ollie. This woman is a straight-up blessing and the only reason this move was possible.

Two years ago, when my paternal grandmother died, I learned she'd left me this house. I'd considered selling, but after my life imploded, this place offered us a home and, by some miracle, a job opportunity I would've been an idiot to refuse. The best part: no one told me it also came with a Helen.

Helen had been friends with my grandma for years. They attended the same church, and she visited each week, checking on her more frequently as she weakened. Then, she watched over the empty house, and we connected after ownership was transferred to me. When she learned I was considering moving and had a job interview, she insisted on caring for my babies during the day.

But she doesn't just take care of them. She loves on them, and if I can't be here to do that myself, there isn't anyone better for the job.

"Looks like things are coming along." She surveys the room and the few remaining boxes tucked in the corner.

"I'm getting there. There's another load in the garage to donate. I only have a few more closets to go through and the basement."

"Stella liked to hold onto things, but she'd be so happy to know life is being lived inside these walls again."

From what Helen has told me, my grandma lived here for thirty years, and I'm fairly certain this small brick bungalow contains items she had when she moved in. I've been slowly sorting through cupboards, closets, and dressers. It's strange to sift through a lifetime of belongings of a woman I never knew. I won't complain. I love this cute little house and am beyond grateful for the chance at a fresh start.

I kiss Frankie's squishy cheek and hand her over. "They haven't had breakfast yet, and I had to wash Frankie's sheets. Could you put them in the dryer?"

"Sure thing, dear. I'll see if I can make a dent in the basement during naptime."

I lean down, blocking the TV screen, and hold Ollie's face. "Be good today, ok? I bet Miss Helen will read your new library books if you ask. They're in your backpack on the hook." My five-year-old's current obsession is birds. He blinks his big blue eyes, then gives me a soft smile. I kiss his sweet face.

Helen follows me into the kitchen, and I carefully slip my foot into my heel, trying not to wince. It'll be a long day for my swollen pinky toe.

"I removed the car seats. They're in the garage if you need them." I throw my bag across my body and grab my coffee. "Call me if you need anything."

"We'll be just fine. Have a good day." Helen gives a little wave, and Frankie's little fingers squeeze in and out.

I smile and wave back as guilt socks me in the stomach. If only I could be here, make money momming, and maybe change the sucky world at the same time.

I pull the back door open, and Grover lunges at me. Before I can stop him, the big dog's paw rakes down my leg.

He prances to his water bowl as I close the door with a fresh twelve-inch run in my tights. My last pair.

I close my eyes and breathe, shoring myself up for whatever is ahead because I have a feeling it's gonna be one hell of a shitty day.

I climb into my BMW, switching on the seat heater to help ward off the chill of bare legs and lack of coat.

Despite setbacks, I'm still extra early. Two weeks into the job, it might be a tad lame, but I don't care. I've worked since I was fifteen, when I'd had enough and decided to make something of myself regardless of whether anyone believed I could.

Fifteen-year-old me didn't have a clue what it would take to become something, but I knew what it meant. It equaled independence, freedom, and never having to depend on anyone. It meant escaping a small world and becoming part of one where I could be seen for more than my circumstances.

My young plan evolved, and I succeeded until I foolishly let myself be led astray. Now, it's up to me to regain all I lost.

I turn the corner, my car sounding like a garbage disposal as I accelerate. I'm pretty sure it's the same odd noise I heard when I went to the grocery store on Saturday. I lower the radio and listen.

As I ease into the parking lot, I hear it again and accept that I'll have to research mechanic shops to get it checked out. A broken washing machine is one thing. A broken car is entirely different.

I pull open the glass door that reads Macavoy, Dunn, & Chambers. The pristine waiting area resembles a living room with leather furniture and a fireplace. Two desks are tucked behind a short wall where Robyn and Marcie greet clients.

I head down the hall to my small office, knowing at least one of the partners seems to be here at all times. Their workdays begin before sunrise and run long into the night after a full day in court.

I log in to my computer and check my phone while it starts up.

ROXIE: Remind me to never drink again.
ROXIE: But you should be proud. I didn't punch any assholes in the face this time.
ROXIE: I kneed him in the balls! *Smiley face emoji*

I cover my mouth, trying not to laugh out loud. Roxie has been my best friend since sixth grade. Just two girls from opposite sides of the tracks that run through our small town.

It all started when a girl shoved my lunch tray and said mutts weren't allowed at her table. Roxie stood, announcing she was allergic to bitches, and moved to the other side of the cafeteria. She motioned for me to follow. We ate together every day after, except when she skipped.

I set my phone aside and flick open the lid on my travel mug.

Pop.

The released pressure shoots droplets of coffee all over my papers.

I exhale. *Of course.*

I mop them up with a Kleenex and peer down to be sure it didn't spray all over my shirt, then open my email to twenty-four unread messages. I click on the most recent one.

Hi, Sarah. I won't be in today. I did hot yoga and now I'm like so hot and have a headache. It could be from the wine I had last night, but I don't know. Plus, I think my cat's seasonal depression is already kicking in and needs some extra attention. Anyway, could you tell Cory? Pretty please.

Thanks!!!

Robyn

The law firm has three partners who share two assistants: Robyn and Marcie. I was hired by Griffin Macavoy, the head partner and one of the leading family law attorneys, as a paralegal. The other paralegal, Cory, has worked with Griffin for years. From what I can tell, Cory is smart and knows it. It's yet to be determined, but it's also possible he has a giant stick wedged up his ass.

On my first day, he ran through the computer systems and office protocol, then tossed a binder at me with instructions for each program, wishing me luck as if delivering a challenge.

My first legitimate assignment is asset valuation for a large case, a tedious process that requires significant time and extensive research. Cory has been monitoring my progress and workload as if he has authority.

I've helped Kat with a few small things, but the third partner, Seth Chambers, handles estate planning and wills. So far, we haven't interacted outside of staff meetings.

I draft a brief email to Cory, informing him that Robyn may not be in, and proceed through my inbox.

"Sooo . . ." I jump at Kat's sly voice.

The sole female partner steps in and plops into the chair, dressed in fuchsia high-waisted dress pants and a cute black top. The late thirty-something crosses her legs, her long black hair falling in delicate waves. Katrina Dunn is striking. She's tall, poised, and has a badass edge that tells you she'll back you into a corner.

"You scared me." I twist in my chair to face her with my hand over my heart, waiting for it to return to normal pace.

She smiles apologetically. "Did you get everything unpacked?" She inspects her perfectly manicured nails.

This woman is all fun and sass, but research shows she morphs into a barracuda when you get her in a courtroom. I can tell the men in this firm don't quite know how to handle her, and she loves every minute of it.

"It's coming along. Most of it is put away."

One of the best parts of this move is being out from underneath the frat boys and the constant scent of weed. Our six months in an apartment back home only made me more grateful for the house and this opportunity.

She pushes her lips to the side. "Now that the rosy glasses have been removed and you're settling in, you'll see how completely dull this city really is."

"I have a feeling nothing is ever dull with you around." I smile, resting back in my chair. "What about you? Do anything fun this weekend?"

She groans, her head falling back toward the ceiling. "I was preparing for the Ingram case. Reading through the notes, I contemplated shoving my head in a toilet and flushing it about a dozen times."

Kat is also a divorce attorney. Behind Griffin, she's making a name for herself as one of the best. Most of her clients are on the wealthier end of the spectrum, which she says rarely leads to an amicable separation.

"I had to read about Dr. Ingram's porn addiction and picture all of the ways in which . . ." She doesn't finish but shivers, her whole body reacting to the mental images.

"You should have called me. I would've helped."

She peeks at me under her long, thick eyelashes. "I like you way too much ever to do that. Plus, you have sweet babies that need time with their mama."

I glance at the picture of Ollie and Frankie. I miss slow mornings and all the snuggles. I halt the memories, remembering why I'm here.

"Morning, ladies." Griffin stops in the doorway. He's a tall, distinguished-looking man with salt-and-pepper hair and bright blue eyes. I've seen him in nothing but expensive suits and the occasional sweater on days he's not expected in court.

"How are the Connor assets coming along?" He rests his shoulder against the doorjamb.

"I've been working on the investments, and then I'll dig into the real estate. I can email you what I have so far."

He nods. "Very good." He smiles, displaying his straight, white teeth. "Did you have a good weekend?"

"Yes. It was quiet." I keep it short and sweet, steering clear of all personal matters.

He nods again. "Great. I'll let you ladies get back to it." He offers a small smile and winks, leaving us.

Kat's eyes roll to the ceiling. "Brilliant and charming is dangerous inside the courtroom and out." Something in her tone tells me she's witnessed both. "Just watch out when Junior strolls in."

"Junior?" I raise an eyebrow.

She raises an eyebrow right back and adds a smirk. "Griffin's son. He'll like you, so it's best if you set him straight from the beginning."

I stare at her, wondering if she gives this advice to everyone or just me.

"Have you met any of your neighbors? I don't know what I'd do without the old guy who lives next to me. He mows my lawn, scoops the snow, and brings me vegetables from his garden all summer long."

I take a sip of coffee, thinking how nice it would be to have someone rake the layers of leaves in my front yard that are turning soft and will eventually smell. "An older couple lives next door, but my nanny says they travel a lot. Ollie made friends with the cute, bubbly librarian."

Her shoulders roll forward. "That used to be me until this job sucked all the cute, sweet innocence from me."

Me too, although it wasn't a job.

She checks her watch and stands, straightening her pants and blouse. "I've got to gather my stuff and head to the courthouse to battle the porn-addicted slob."

"Hey, do you have a recommendation for a mechanic? My car is making a noise, and I should probably get it looked at." The possible expense makes my empty stomach roll into a hard ball.

"Stop by Cal's. It's only a few blocks down and the only place I trust." She turns to leave but stops and falls back. "Shit, Cory! If you're gonna float around here like Count Dracula, at least wear a cape. Women don't like to be snuck up on."

He steps to the side, watching her as she exits.

"Or micro-managed." She points at him.

His attention turns to me as his pasty pale cheeks turn just the tiniest bit pink. Kat, on the other hand, grins at me and disappears.

Cory remains standing, his long, bony body towering over me. He pushes his glasses up his pointy nose and shifts his weight to one foot. "Griffin said you're going through the files for the Connor case. I thought I'd take a quick look and make sure you're accounting for things properly."

I return to my computer, biting my tongue before I inform him that he should take into account his nose hairs curling around the other nostril.

I wiggle my mouse, pulling up the spreadsheets I've put together outlining each account and its activity. Cory leans over my shoulder, inspecting, his stale breath accosting me.

My phone buzzes, and I reach to click it off, but stop when I see the name on the screen. My breath catches as a chill runs up my spine, and my skin prickles.

It's been two months. I inhale slowly as my heart breaks out into a panicked race. My fingers shake with the urge to answer, but I can't while Cory takes his sweet-ass time double-checking my work.

My knee bounces, knowing what will happen if I miss this call. I grab my phone, praying it will keep ringing.

"So, these here," Cory points to the screen. "They're the only investment accounts you've found? Seems odd there aren't IRAs, or at least a 401k."

The buzzing stops, and I've missed it. I set my phone in my lap, my body deflating as my pits spew sweat, knowing what's to come. I try to pull my head from my phone and back to this job—the one I desperately need.

"Sarah," Cory's snappy tone pulls me out of it. "Where are the other accounts? There's no room for mistakes."

I roll my chair back an inch, needing his condescending tone and stanky breath to back up. I open the spreadsheet I've created for retirement accounts. "These are the only accounts we've been given." I scroll to the top. "I can double-check with Mrs. Connor, but this is all she listed."

Cory studies again while my fingers itch to tap out a message.

"Does Griffin know about this?"

I withhold rolling my eyes. "Yes. I discussed it with him last week. He's prepared to use this as further proof of their unwillingness to cooperate."

Cory crosses his arms over his chest, clearly dissatisfied. "When you finish, send it to me, and I'll review it before you send it to Griffin to be sure you've noted everything.

I nod, needing him to leave now.

His eyes drop to the phone in my lap. "I have a few administrative things you could help with if you have time on your hands."

I grip my phone, wanting to throw it at him so he'll leave me alone and I can hit call back. "Sure. I'll let you know." I force a smile.

He stares at me a moment longer and then exits my office. I tap the missed call, bracing my elbows on my desk. I press the phone to my ear as it rings. And rings. My exhale comes out in a whoosh when the automated voice picks up. *Dammit!*

ME: Call me back. It's important.

I stare at my phone, waiting for the ring that won't come. I missed my chance. Out of all of the days and all the minutes within, he calls the one time I couldn't answer. Not with Cory standing over me.

8:34 a.m. I close my eyes, wanting to go home and snuggle into the old couch with Ollie and Frankie and watch endless hours of Bluey, hoping that when I crawl back out, maybe just one thing might be a little bit easier.

CHAPTER 2

SLADE

I toss a banana peel in the trash and push the eggs around the skillet. The door to the garage opens, letting in the brisk morning air.

"How was your night?"

"Eh." Krissy tosses her keys on the table and sets her lunch bag beside the sink. "Guy came in complaining of abdominal pain. Turns out he hadn't crapped in two weeks. I had to give him an enema." She kicks her shoes off and yawns. "He shit a brick. Literally. Let that be a lesson to you if you don't poop after a few days."

"Kris, that's gross." I turn the burner off and scoop eggs into two bowls, handing her one.

My younger sister laughs, her dark hair spilling from her short ponytail. She takes her bowl to the small table.

"Did you hear anything about the day shift?" I reach into the fridge for the hot sauce and slide it to her.

Krissy works the night shift in the ER. With the stories she's told me about gunshot wounds, gang fights, and prisoners, I'm ready for her to help people during daylight hours, but also in a different unit of the hospital.

She shoves a forkful of eggs in her mouth. "Not yet, but a lot of other nurses applied for it," she says while chewing. "Somebody said a shift opened in Labor and Delivery. I'm going to talk to the manager. My experience at the clinic might help."

Krissy has volunteered at the women's clinic since she started the nursing program. It's important to her, and she's helping women who often wouldn't have access to care otherwise, but I worry about her safety.

I shovel the last bits from my bowl into my mouth and place it in the dishwasher. "I've gotta get to the shop. A tow truck has a drop-off. I'm going to the gym with Carson when I get off, so I'll be late."

She nods, holding her bowl under her chin. "I have a date tonight, so you two will have to fend for yourselves for dinner."

We take turns cooking, and it's her night.

I rest against the counter, crossing my arms over my chest. "With whom?"

She takes another bite. "One of the docs. He's asked me out a couple of times. I thought I'd give him a shot."

I groan. My sister may be twenty-four, but her taste in men sucks. I haven't liked a single one. They're either doctors or finance managers and look like complete douchebags.

"How old is he?"

Her head falls to the side, looking at me from under her long, dark lashes. "Calm down, Stone Cold. It's a date. If he asks me to marry him, I'll get you a copy of his birth certificate."

"Does he have kids?"

"Oh, for real." She stands, moving to the sink to rinse her bowl.

It's a legitimate question. Turns out the last one was married. "Do you know anything about this guy?"

She matches my stance. "No. That's why it's a date. I guess I'll find out tonight." She smiles and spins, heading out of the kitchen and up the stairs. "And don't wait up," she hollers as I hear her bedroom door close.

I run a hand over my face. "Don't wait up, my ass." I've been waiting up every night of my life with her boy troubles and girly drama. That shit was endless through high school.

I hear her door open. "Oh, and ask Trig if the apartment in his building is still open. I want to go look at it." The door closes again.

I grab my keys, knowing it'll be another sleepless night.

The car exits, and I push the button to lower the door as the impact wrench grinds.

"Shit!" Trig hollers.

"If you stripped another nut, it's coming out of your paycheck."

He flips me off over his shoulder and tightens the remaining bolts before rolling the next tire over.

Wind returns from the break room, toting his lunch box, and stops beside me. The man got the nickname from his uncontrollable flatulence and ability to drop bombs that would clear out an entire stadium.

His weight shifts from one foot to the other. "What crawled up your ass today? If this place is going under or something, you should just tell us."

I look at him. "Going under? Are you blind? The lot is full, and so is the calendar." Every appointment slot is filled and then some.

He shrugs, unmoving as if I have more to say.

It's been a year since I financed the three-stall garage, which I took over from Cal, who opened it forty years ago. Over the ten years I've worked here, I've only ever seen a handful of slow weeks. Now is definitely not one of them.

This place is my second home, and Cal is the dad I never had. When I needed it most, he gave me a job and, over time, showed me how to run his business. I'll do whatever it takes to keep it afloat. Currently, the only issues I'm facing are a lack of space in the parking lot and manpower to keep up.

There used to be five of us and Cal, but six months ago, my best friend and Cal's granddaughter, Alex, moved to be with her husband, the starting quarterback for the Colorado Big Horns. They have twin girls and are raising Mark's younger sister. Alex owns a small auto restoration business. Occasionally, I fly out to help her pull an engine and rebuild it.

She's the most gifted mechanic I've ever seen. Hiring someone to take her place would be impossible, but if the workload remains, I'll have to try.

"Is Krissy still talking about moving out?" Wind's question is soft, and Trig's motion stills. Carson remains bent over a hood, pretending to inspect a radiator cap.

I glare at him. "What do you know about Krissy moving out?"

His eyes flick to the Nosey Nellies across the room, then he clears his throat. "I just . . . I . . ."

I set the part requisitions on the bench, turning to him. "Spill it, Wind."

"She was talking about it during the game the other night, and she messaged Trig a bit ago, asking about the open apartment again."

My eyes roll to the top of my head.

"She knew you wouldn't ask." He shifts his lunchbox to the other hand. "You know, Millie and I are only a few blocks away, and Trig would be upstairs. It's a safe neighborhood."

Wind and his high school sweetheart reconnected at a reunion last year, and ever since, the man has been all sunshine and happy endings. He's now immune to real life and the shit that comes with it.

"I've talked to her about it. I'm not discussing it with you. Any of you."

"Fine." He turns for the door. "But she's a grown woman, Slade. She's made up her mind, and I don't think you're gonna stop her. It'd be best to know she's safe and has friends close," he hollers over his shoulder.

The heavy metal door bangs as he exits. Trig's eyes meet mine for a moment before he returns to work.

These guys look out for her, and each knows better than to ever think about crossing a line, but I don't want her living in the same apartment building.

I grab the stack of orders, double-checking part numbers and quantity.

Trig zips the last tire on and returns the car to the lot. He hangs the keys on the board and fetches his own, stopping to hand over the clipboard with the worksheet attached. “She’s all done. Do you want me to enter this?”

I take the clipboard. “Nah, I’ll input it when I’m done here.”

He nods. “I gave Krissy the landlord’s number. She’s been asking for days. I can’t just ignore her.”

Even though I know he’s right, I won’t be saying it.

I like Trig. He’s a good kid, but we call him Trigger for a reason. The wannabe racer has a need for speed and hangs with a rough crowd. One that Krissy doesn’t need to get mixed up in.

“I’ll talk to her about it.” That’s all I’m offering because Krissy and I will discuss it. Again.

He nods once. “Sure. I’ll see you guys tomorrow.”

Carson drops the hood of an SUV. “You know she can make this decision without you.” His voice comes over my shoulder. “She’s trying to include you. The more you ignore her, the more you’ll piss her off. She could end up in a place a lot worse.”

“I don’t need this from you, too.” I remain focused, ready to call it a day.

“She’s a grown woman, Slade. At some point, you’re going to have to let her go. You can’t protect her from everything.”

Like hell I can’t. I turn toward him as he wipes his hands on a shop rag.

“She doesn’t need to be living downstairs from Trig or his biker friends.”

His chin drops, unable to disagree. “Then maybe you should help her find a place. She wants your approval.”

I stare at him, needing him to drop it and wondering when in the hell he became so insightful. “Yeah, well. I might not have to. She’s got a date. I wouldn’t put it past her to run off and get married just to piss me off.”

"With whom?" Carson's hands move to his hips.

I bite back a shit-eating grin. Carson and I have been friends since Cal hired him years ago when he strolled in looking for a job. With Alex gone, he's my closest friend. I'd trust him with my life, and I know without a doubt he'd look out for Krissy.

"A doctor."

"Shit." It comes out as a mumble, but I heard it.

I cross my arms over my chest. "My sentiments exactly, but I have to think one of them won't be a complete dick and . . ." I shake my head. "If she ends up with a highly educated, successful, not-piece-of-shit, I'd be ok with that. It's what I want for her. I want her to have all of that and more."

I spin back to the computer. "I don't want her living in a crappy apartment when she comes in after working all night. Or with dates."

He makes some sort of grunting noise as I get back to scrolling. "I'm heading to the gym. You coming?"

"Yeah, but I need to input these part orders so we can get some of these vehicles moving. I'll meet you there."

He grabs his keys, and the door slams closed.

I flip through the pages, confirming part numbers and reviewing inventory.

The door opens and bangs closed again.

"Welcome back, asshole. What'd you forget?"

Click, click, click, click.

I lift my gaze from the computer. A woman stands with her hand wrapped around the straps of a large leather purse. Her long, dark hair is pulled back in a high ponytail, and she is wearing a white, silky-looking button-down shirt tucked into a black, knee-length, fitted skirt and heels.

"Not sure I've been called that before." She surveys the space. "Although I seem to recall a relatively recent low-class bitch reference."

Her amused gaze spears mine, and even across the space, I force myself not to react—her eyes: one brown and one blue. My gaze flicks between them, subconsciously examining the shocking difference and wondering if it's natural.

She stares at me, her arms folding across her chest.

"Umm, I thought . . . Sorry, we're closed."

Her eyes drop to her watch. "You're closed?"

I think it's a question. "We wrap up at five."

Her arm drops to her side, her shoulders rolling back. "It's two 'til."

I rest my hands on my hips. "Not much we do here can be solved in two minutes."

Her head falls to the side an inch. "Great." She pushes out a breath as her eyes roam around the space again, and then she turns for the door.

"Did you need something?"

She twists back, the look on her face telling me she's debating reiterating my statement about being closed, but decides to forgo it. "My car has a whirring sound, like a garbage disposal. Katrina Dunn said you all were the best."

Stiff posture, confident stare, and a large, expensive bag. Lawyer.

I've seen Kat Dunn in action. She's not someone I'd ever want to oppose in a verbal sparring match. If my instincts can be trusted, I'd venture this woman might be the same.

"A garbage disposal?"

Her shoulders roll back, and her arms cross over her body again. "Yes. I need it looked at to be sure it's nothing significant."

Shit.

I'd like to tell her to come back tomorrow, but she won't be back, *and* that's not the way we do business here. Even when it comes to lawyers.

"What make and model?" I grab a clipboard and a pen. I have a distinct feeling I'm going to regret this.

When she doesn't respond, I find her staring at me.

I raise an eyebrow. "Do you just want to show me?"

"2021 BMW X3." It rolls right off her tongue.

I lower the clipboard. "I don't carry parts for imports."

Her shoulders ease down. . .barely. "So, you can't help me?"

Can I help? Yes. Is it most efficient? No. Does this information allow me a huge excuse and save me from dealing with this woman, who most likely thinks the rest of us are all just minions? Hell yeah.

"I send all imports to the dealer."

Her hand grips her purse strap, and her hip juts out to the side. "Just take it to the dealer?"

She needs to stop asking me questions and making it sound like I'm incompetent and incapable.

"Dealers have direct connections to suppliers. If you need parts, they'll get them faster."

"You can't get parts if they're needed?" One thin eyebrow raises, waiting for my answer.

I inhale and let it out slowly, knowing I'll want to punch myself in the face for being baited, but I think that's exactly what's happening.

I shove the pen into the clipboard and grab my keys. "Do you have an issue letting me hear this 'whirring' sound?"

She doesn't move, but I feel her watching me.

"Go for a drive? With you?" Her confident tone downshifts into something a touch softer.

I turn to her. "Yes."

Those eyes run over me for a long, silent moment. "Uh. Sure."

I step around her, reaching for the door, and she hurries out. I follow, her heels clicking against the pavement as we cross to her BMW. I might be wrong, but it looks like she's limping.

She climbs in while I press the button to move the seat back.

She drops her bag in the back, keeping a grip on her phone while she watches me work to fold myself into the small space. It smells like sunshine, and just registering that has me wanting to plug my nose.

Instead of starting the car, she swipes her phone, her fingers flying over the screen.

"What are you doing?" I don't have time to sit here while she conducts business or whatever the hell it is.

Her brown eye peeks at me from the corner. "Texting someone. I don't make a habit of getting into a car with borderline rude men." She glances at me, a slight smirk pulling at her lips, all self-assurance returning. "If I end up on an episode of Unsolved Mysteries, at least they can't caption it with 'It was her own damn fault she'll never be found.'"

She misses my eye roll. "Borderline?"

She smiles and finishes tapping out her message with a little shrug. "The scale is fluid. We'll see how our cozy little test ride goes."

She sets her phone in the door handle and starts the car.

I exhale, already completely sassed out, and I need this to be quick. "When do you hear the noise? All the time?"

She backs out of the spot. "I'm not sure. It seems to occur when I'm slowing to turn or accelerating from a stop."

She stops before exiting the parking lot.

"How long ago did you first notice it?"

She turns right. "A few weeks ago, maybe, but it's becoming more frequent."

I point. "Take a right here, and two blocks down we'll try a couple of things."

"Yes, sir." She flexes her hands on the steering wheel, and my gaze skirts over the space where no ring resides.

I want to jab my eyes out for unconsciously noticing, but I grunt instead.

"Forgive me, I'm having anxiety-provoking flashbacks of my driver's test." She slows through a two-way stop.

"Trouble passing?"

"No, I had this scary old dude who barked orders and sucked his teeth so hard I started to panic one might come loose and pop out on the dash."

I glance at her, wondering if this is some kind of tactic she uses to defuse situations or if she's for real. Her eyes remain focused, dead ahead.

She follows directions, taking us to the quiet streets behind the garage.

"Come to a full stop up here, and then accelerate slowly," I direct.

She brakes, bringing the car to a halt. I listen, watching the odometer as she presses the gas. When the needle just passes the twenty-mile-per-hour mark, I hear what she might describe as the grind of a garbage disposal.

I hold my hand out. "Stop, and do it again."

"Did you hear it?" Her tone holds a hint of excitement, as if she were doubting herself, which I find incredibly interesting.

"Maybe." I'm not confirming anything, but I definitely heard it.

She pulls to a stop again. "What is it?"

"Shhhh." I hold out my hand as she eases off the brake. I lean over the center console, squeezing between the seats toward the back to hear better. My chest bumps her shoulder, and she shifts closer to the door, giving me room.

I listen for the sound, but my dumbass senses identify that the smell of flowers and coconuts is her. Rather than being suffocating, it's light and nice, but *definitely* not what I should be taking note of.

There's a distinct grinding, and it sounds like her left back tire might roll right off.

"That's it. Did you hear it?"

I resituated myself beside her. "Yeah. Go right here, and it'll take us back to the garage."

"What is it?"

I run a hand over my short beard. "I'll have to get it up on the lift to be sure, but it sounds like the wheel bearing."

Silence carries us back to the garage, and she follows me inside.

I set the clipboard down next to the computer, waking it.

"Sooooo, what does that mean if it's a wheel bearing?" She stands on the other side of the counter, watching me.

I pull up the vehicle specs. "I need to look at it, but that's what it sounds like. Could be a rotor getting stuck, but—"

"What does that mean? What will it take to fix it?" The questions fly at me with a hint of frustration.

I cross my arms. "You'll have to leave it, and let me take a look to see what parts are needed. Then, I'll be able to give you a timeline."

Her gaze turns to the truck sitting over the pit. "A timeline? So, you're saying this will take a few days?"

"If you're lucky."

She nods slowly. "And how much will this cost?"

I pull up our schedule.

"Not sure. I need a parts list before I can tell you that, but you'll need an appointment for me to look at it first."

She swipes at her phone, her fingers tapping away, then stops as she scrolls and reads. She presses her finger to her lips, then scrolls some more and stops to read.

Is she googling it? Shit, she's probably researching the process to install a new bearing.

I brace my arms on the counter. "What are you doing?"

Those eyes peek up at me from underneath her dark eyelashes, and I have to be careful not to stare awkwardly.

Her gaze moves back to her screen. "I need a few minutes."

"The shop closed at five."

She ignores me, slowly scrolling and zeroing in on whatever she's investigating.

"How long will this take? You fact-checking me?" That gets her attention, and her head comes up to meet my stare. "If I want to rip you off, I'll break five other things in the process of just fixing the one. At some point, you're gonna have to trust me, or you can take it to the dealer and see if you like their answer better."

The hand with her mini research engine falls to her side, and her eyelids droop. It's clear that trusting me isn't something she's inclined to do.

"Thank you for your time. What do I owe for the listen?" She reaches into her massive purse, digging inside.

Why the hell do women need to carry around suitcases? How much shit can they possibly need? All. The. Damn. Time?

"You shouldn't be driving it. It's not safe."

Her hand stalls, and her eyes spear mine. "Yeah, well, I appreciate your time, but—"

"The wheel could fall off while you're driving. You can't drive it like that."

I see her chest expand and then slowly retract, like she's seeking patience, which makes two of us.

"I need a car."

"Get a rental. It's what most folks do."

She huffs out a laugh. "Just get a rental," she mumbles, her lips curling into a vague smile.

She starts to sway back and forth, her lips pushed to the side, thinking. "What's the percentage chance of my wheel actually falling off?"

I scratch my beard. I know this woman isn't dumb. "Is that something you're really willing to gamble on?"

She presses her eyes closed and runs her fingers over her forehead.

I have no idea what I'm doing, except I think of Krissy and how I'd hope someone would help her. "You leave it, and I'll see if I can fit it in tomorrow. I can let you know what I find."

She stops rocking. "I can't. . .just leave it." She wraps her arms around herself, her eyes falling away. She pushes out a long breath. "Is it possible to drop it off tomorrow before you close?"

I don't even have to look to know the schedule is completely full. I also don't know what it is about this woman that has me considering exceptions.

"Fine. We close at five. If it's after that, you can drop the keys in the drop box."

She watches me for only a second before nodding. "All right, I'll have it here tomorrow." Her weight shifts to her other foot, and her brow furrows, but then it's gone.

"Ok."

She turns, and I definitely see her limp as she tugs the door open. I wonder what happened.

It bangs closed, and I run a hand over my face. What in the hell is wrong with me? I shake my head, knowing the guys will give me nothing but shit for this when they find out.

I log off the computer and lock up, ready to get to the gym to burn off the flustered annoyance running through me. It's uncomfortable and irritating as hell.

I don't make exceptions and push other jobs aside.

I don't like lawyers.

I shove out a breath as I climb into my truck and start it. I have a feeling I just agreed to something I'm really going to wish I hadn't.

CHAPTER 3

SARAH

ME: Call me back, Miles. It's important.

"What are you gonna do?"

I rinse a stinky sippy cup, trying not to gag, and put it in the dishwasher. "I don't know. He said it wasn't safe to drive, so I'll have to figure something out."

"Do you believe him? Cause I'd have serious doubts about Ron's ability to advise when anything is dangerous."

Ron owns the small repair shop in the town where I grew up, the place Roxie still calls home. He's toothless and heavily sedated all of the time. I wouldn't trust that viable neurons are still firing.

I don't think Ron and the grump that climbed into my car have much in common. From what I could see behind his tight-lipped exchange, he had teeth. I also got the feeling that, despite his big, burly, tattooed gruffness, he knew what he was talking about.

"He was nothing if not blunt, so I have no choice but to believe him." The tall, scowly man was direct in a brutal way that was both refreshing and irritating as hell. "Although he called me an asshole."

It almost made me smile, but then he turned that broad, towering body toward me, and the intense gaze that followed felt like I'd intruded on his private property. For some reason, the pinched expression from underneath his ball cap made me want to pick at that rough, rugged, intimidating exterior.

"What?!" Roxie's voice inclines. "Did he lose a nut?"

I laugh. "Not yet. I need him to fix my car first. I think he thought I was someone else. But I can't really blame him for being irritated. I walked in two minutes before they closed."

I curse the car I never would've chosen in the first place. I'd sell it, but getting another reliable vehicle would likely require financing, and that's not currently an option.

I hear Roxie take a bite of an apple. "He sounds like a jerk. Maybe you should get a second opinion."

"I thought about it, but I read reviews. They all rave about their experience."

Am I defending him or my decision? Dammit. I'm not sure.

"What if this joker spends his nights and weekends crafting elaborately shining reviews to lure hot pieces of sophisticated ass like yourself into letting him fix your car, but really he's dropping bricks of coke in your undercarriage, and you then become the mule for his trade." She breathes. "Sarah, I love you, but you won't survive in the clink."

"You're insane." I laugh.

"Ha! And don't forget it. I got your back, babe." She takes another bite and talks as she chews. "Did this mofo get all weird and ask about your eyes? I'll bug out for the night and run over to drop an elbow on his ass."

"Actually, he didn't even seem to notice. He was too busy maintaining his Pissy Pants to notice or care." The man crossed his elaborately tattooed arms over his chest and stood there like I was supposed to know they closed *before* five—their listed closing time.

It's a rarity for people not to stare or ask if my eyes are real, as if I have fake eyeballs. I used to wear contacts to even out the color, but not anymore.

"Well, that's one small tick in his favor. Is he attractive? Why do all guys who act like complete dicks usually have to be good-looking? There must be some genetic code that combines handsomeness with a depressed social IQ."

"Can broody and bitter be attractive?" I will never say it, but the grouchy Neanderthal was amazingly handsome underneath all that gloom. Deep green eyes that seemed to infer far more than I wanted him to, and hair that curled out from underneath his cap just long enough to twist around a finger. He should wear a warning that reads prickly with a sour mood and may roar.

I smile, thinking about it.

Roxie snorts. "Do pretty assholes shit?"

"Rox!" I laugh, holding my stomach and missing her so much.

I close the dishwasher and start it.

"Have you heard anything from Miles?" Her question is soft, as if she knows to tread lightly.

"No. He called today, but I couldn't answer. Cory was in my office."

"Of course that scrawny little snitch was. Let me guess. Miles hasn't called back."

When I don't confirm it, I hear a long string of curses under her breath.

"You need to take his ass to court and invite every news outlet in the country."

I lean against the counter, knowing even if I could afford it, I'd worry about dragging Ollie and Frankie into a public mess again.

Dealing with Miles is like walking a tightrope. It's a balancing act of carefully requesting that he follow the court order without triggering him and causing him to lash out or retaliate when I don't meet his demands. It's allowing him to believe he's still in control, while convincing him to do the right thing.

It's exhausting and self-loathing to let someone have that kind of power over you, but right now, it's all I can do. No matter how badly

I wish I didn't, I need him to pay up without destroying me in the process.

Our divorce was quickly finalized when I agreed to shared custody with monthly child support, which my lawyer advised was the best-case scenario given my circumstances. A year later, he hasn't once asked to see the kids, and I haven't seen a dime. Payment would require submitting to his absurd requests, which would involve me resorting to being his emotional crutch or verbal punching bag.

I wish I could take him to court and demand he pay up or alert the world that he's too busy attempting to manipulate me to help his children. But I learned the hard way that this man doesn't play nice or fair, and I can't risk going down that road again. Not when I'm trying my damnedest to start over and build a life for the kids and me.

I let Grover in the back door and lock it, then head into the living room and sit on the floor. Ollie is playing with his airplane while Frankie gnaws on the head of one of the Little People. She drops it and crawls into my lap.

"You want me to pay him a visit?" Rox asks, and I know she's contemplating it.

"Nah. I know you'd do just fine behind steel bars, but I love you too much to see that happen. I need you to stay on the outside. We'll just have to get used to the bus for a little while."

Ollie's head pops up, and I smile. "What do you think, Ol? Should we see what the big, blue buses are like?"

He nods, a slight smile appearing.

"Ugh. Sarah. I hate this for you. I mean, I'm so glad you're there and not here, but. . .I wish I could be there to help."

"I know. Me too. Come see us soon. Ok?"

"For sure."

"I gotta get these little stinks in the bath so I have time to study."

"Ok. I have to get to work. I told Micah I'd take his shift tonight."

Roxie manages the pub that serves as the local hangout despite her parents' distinct objections. Sometimes I think she only continues to work there just to piss them off.

"Make sure you're sleeping," Roxie commands.

"You be safe. And no punching people."

"Ha. You're no fun. Some people really deserve it. Give Ollie and Frank kisses for me."

We hang up, and I kiss the top of Frankie's head as she attempts to shove Ariel into a small plastic car.

"C-c-c-can we go on the bus?" Ollie steers his small biplane through the air.

"I think so. We might have to ride it for a little while. Think we can do it?"

He nods, his bright eyes meeting mine. "It'll be f-fun."

"It'll be an adventure." I slide my arm around him and pull him to my side as he makes buzzing sounds, his plane doing a flip before swooping low to the carpet. "Five more minutes, then it's bath time."

The plane zooms past my face as I reach for a book and open it. I read while Ollie puts on an air show and Frankie munches on plastic princesses with drool running down her arm.

After two books, I throw them in the bath while washing my face and brushing my teeth.

With both kids wrapped in towels, Ollie runs and jumps onto my bed. I lay Frankie down, and she flips over, trying to crawl away. I grab her ankle, and she squeals. I blow on her belly, causing her to erupt with giggles as I strap a diaper on her, then confine her to footie jammies.

I rub the towel over Ollie's wet, dark hair. "One, two, three blast-off." He jumps, pulling his bottoms up, and lands back on his butt, bouncing as he reaches for his shirt.

We gather blankies and stuffies, and I chase Ollie down the short hallway to the living room. He screams, and Grover barks and prances, protecting his boy.

I drop into the plush rocker-recliner beside the brick fireplace I've been too scared to light. With the temps falling close to the freezing zone, I may just risk it at some point and pray the chimney is clear.

"Two books, big guy, and grab *The Barnyard Dance* for your sister." Frankie twists in my arms, hearing the name of her favorite book.

"We always read that one. It's b-boring."

"Better not dance or laugh then." His speckled eye peeks at me with attitude. "It'll cost ya, and fines are high tonight. Smiles are extra hugs, and laughs are kisses. As many as I want." He looks at me, his mouth held tight, giving it his all. "And the slightest wiggles . . . Dude, you can't even begin to afford what that will cost you."

He climbs into the chair next to me with a stack of books, and I poke his side. Noises come from his little throat as he curls up.

With Frankie on one leg and Ollie on the other, we rock, making all the animal noises and hand gestures before moving on to the next. Halfway through book two, Frankie's head begins to bob, and I shift her to my chest while Ollie turns the pages.

He snuggles into my side with his fish. "Can we ride the bus t-t-tomorrow?"

"I'm not sure, but I need to leave our car with someone so they can look at it."

"Like a doctor?"

"Kind of. If something is broken, they'll fix it." *At least, I hope so.*

"Can he come on the b-b-bus, too?" He squeezes his sad stuffed fish.

"He should definitely come with us. All fish need to go on a bus ride."

He giggles, his fish clutched to his chest as his little fingers run over the worn blue material.

I slide a hand up and down Frankie's back, her squishy face tucked into my neck. I breathe in the smell of clean babies, wondering how in the hell I'm going to do this.

I will do it. One way or another. I'll figure it out.

I close my eyes as we rock back and forth. Grover moans as he rolls his furry body, warming my aching foot. I force myself to stay awake. I have a list of things I need to complete before it's my turn to go to bed.

"Mama, I'm thirsty."

I peek down at the sweet face that needs to be sleeping. I should deny all hydration requirements, but dammit, I can't. "Let me put Frankie in her bed, and then two sips, sir. That's it."

He smiles.

I lay Frankie in her bed along with her Lambie and turn on the white noise machine. I find Ollie and Grover waiting for me in the hallway, both looking emaciated from lack of water.

"Go climb into bed, and I'll get Grover's water bowl."

He snorts and runs to his room on the other side of Frankie's. I fill a sippy cup and tuck him under the covers of the queen bed. I replaced the gold-framed landscapes that were hung on the gray walls with photos of the Blue Angels and a wooden shelf lined with Hot Wheels.

Grover's tail thumps against the quilt.

"All right, buster. Lap it up. You need to get to sleep."

Ollie takes two long swigs and hands me the cup. I set it on the night table and sit on the edge of the bed, leaning over and resting my arms on each side of him.

"It's a big day at preschool tomorrow. You're making Halloween slime. Maybe it'll have eyeballs in it." I widen my eyes.

He grins. "Maybe it'll have b-b-boogers in it."

I wrinkle my nose. "Eww. That's gross." I tickle his stomach. "Better not be any real boogers."

I kiss his forehead. "I love you, little man."

"Wove you, Mama."

I kiss his cheek and turn off the light as his projector displays stars and planets on the ceiling.

I leave the door open, heading to the kitchen and hoping answers lie in there somewhere because I've got nothing. I stop at the thermostat. Sixty-eight degrees. I punch the down arrow a few times, needing every bit of savings I can get.

I scan the sparse shelves in the fridge, then open the pantry and grab a box of Frosted Mini-Wheats. I sit at the small table where my computer and books await.

Popping a flaky rectangle in my mouth, I pull up my checking account. I release a slow breath, and my hope deflates with it. My next paycheck won't hit until next Friday.

I close my eyes, letting my head fall into my hands, feeling like I could puke. The list of expenses continues to climb by the second, and now I have to figure out how to make it work without a car for who knows how long. That painful fact doesn't even include how I'll pay for the repairs.

I pull up the city bus schedule, knowing there's a stop two blocks down. I jot down times and routes, seeing that I can catch a bus in the morning that will drop me off four blocks from the law firm. I'll have to be sure to leave work on time to catch the ride home, which will get me back in time for Helen to leave.

I drop my pencil while depression and anxiety challenge my ability to map out grocery store and library trips. I need the big man at the garage to tell me this is a brake issue and a quick, affordable fix, but that won't be my luck.

First, I need to arrange a ride home so I can drop off my car. I hesitate, then realize I don't have another option and grab my phone.

ME: Would you be able to give me a ride home from Cal's Garage tomorrow? I have to drop my car off after work.

KATRINA: Sure thing. I got chu.

KATRINA: And tell that little crackerjack our date for Happy Meals will be collected.

I rub my temples, needing to focus on something I can control—my grades. I open my syllabus and then my book. I highlight and make notes until my eyes begin to droop. At some point, I lay my head down, remembering to pray for just one thing to turn in my favor.

CHAPTER 4

SLADE

I loosen the bolts and remove the valve cover.

"New rotors and brakes are done, and the car is back in the lot." Carson leans up against the side panel.

"Did you text the owner?" I shove the ratchet into my back pocket and pull the cover off.

"Yeah." He pushes off and turns, but I stop him.

"Can you stay late today? Something is supposed to be dropped off later, and I could use your help to take a quick look."

"Sure. I've gotta run out quick, but I'll come back. What is it?"

I inspect the seal, avoiding eye contact. "BMW X3."

"We're taking on imports now? And after hours?"

I don't answer, pulling off the seal and reaching for the brake cleaner. I know what's coming, and I don't need it. I'm not sure why in the hell I'm making exceptions, but I agreed. Now, I'll pay for it over the next few hours.

He rests his muscular build against the side panel again. "Who is she?"

I hear the shit-eating grin in his tone.

I don't react. "Can you help later or not?"

"You can fess up now, or I'll find out later. I'll consider taking it easy on you if you just tell me."

"Tell you what?" Wind stops next to Carson.

These guys like to roll into drama like a pig in shit. They are my employees, my friends, and I'd call them family.

"We've got a late arrival. BMW." Carson crosses his arms over his chest.

"We're taking imports now?" Wind frowns.

I straighten. "Would you busybodies get back to work? The garage needs to be cleared out."

Carson's head cocks to the side. *Shit.* "She needs the entire garage, too?"

I clench my jaw, knowing he's just trying to get under my skin.

"She?" Wind holds up his hand. "Wait." He looks at me. "This is a favor for a woman?"

There's silence as Trig tunes in from the next stall over.

Wind huffs in disbelief. "You gotta be shitting me." His hands fall to his hips. "When in the hell did you step out of your emotional isolation long enough to attract a woman? How did I miss this?"

I glare at him. "Emotional isolation?"

Carson grins ear to ear, deeply proud of his ability to stir shit up.

Wind shrugs. "Millie's diagnosis."

Millie is a shrink, and I need her to stop psychoanalyzing me.

Wind runs a hand down his beard. "She says that you're emotionally unavailable because it gives you comfort. You push people away so you don't have to risk getting hurt."

I want to punch something. Maybe him. I spent all my emotions years ago, and ever since, maintaining moderate annoyance is all I can handle.

I groan as Trig joins the gossip girls crowding me with their suffocating attention. "You all can shove your head and emotional intelligence up your asses."

They snicker.

I exhale slowly, gathering patience I don't have. "She stopped in last night, a few minutes before closing. Kat sent her over. I told her she should take it to the dealer, but she wasn't fond of my suggestion."

"Katrina Dunn?" Trig grins with that slick, boyish smile.

I'd like to see Kat chew his flirty young ass up one side and down the other. Just the thought makes me almost smile.

"So . . ." It's Carson's dumb voice again. "This is a favor to Kat." He sounds amusingly skeptical, but he can think whatever he wants.

I wouldn't call it a favor, but Kat has helped me out a time or two, so I owe her. I'm also smart enough not to be on her shit list.

I cross my arms over my chest, staring these jokers down. "It's a job, and this is how we do business. Would any of you idiots point to the door if a woman needed help?"

I know the answer, but I want to see them squirm because every one of them would do exactly what I did.

Silence. All eyes are everywhere but on me.

"Damn straight. Now get to work before I fire your asses."

Trig is the first to depart our little sharing circle. "You won't fire us. We clear cars out of here faster than anyone else would. Besides, if you have any shot at a date with this woman, you're gonna need us."

I hear snorts from Carson and Wind's throats, holding back laughs.

I let my head fall back toward the ceiling, my eyes rolling with it. They are going to beat this to death and then beat it some more.

That's all I hear for the rest of the afternoon. The comments and jabs are tossed across the space as they take aim at my preferred relationship status. Single.

Do I date? No. Have I slept with a woman here and there to scratch the itch? Sure, but it's been a long time. It never ends well, and I don't have time or any desire for that kind of drama in my life.

Eventually, Wind and Trig head out for the day, and Carson hollers that he'll be back. The quiet that follows is nice. I print the specs for the BMW and check my watch. 5:10 p.m. Maybe she won't be back after all.

I take a stack of invoices to my office and lay them on the desk when I hear the door bang closed. There's shuffling and the click of heels, which tells me it's her rather than Carson.

I head back out, and the woman stands on the other side of the counter, just inside the door, with her back to me.

"Do you always ignore business hours, or is it just my time you seem to discount?" I mean it as a joke, but she spins, appearing flustered as she blows her long hair out of her eyes. "I wasn't sure you'd be back."

She adjusts the large purse draped across her body, and the corner of her mouth twitches. "I seriously contemplated it, but then I realized if my car is broken, I need someone who'll get. It. Done. You seem just King-of-the-Pride-Lands enough to make it happen."

She waits for a response, all unease slipping right under the satisfaction of her sarcasm.

I cross my arms over my chest. "King of the Pride Lands?"

She shrugs one shoulder, her chin tipping up slightly. "Felt fitting. You're. . .a lit-tle liony."

The sparkle in that one blue eye stirs something within me I can't quite identify, but I need it to knock the hell off.

I hear noise as I step up to the counter. She twists, dropping down to—

"I have to get your car seat, ok?" she says softly. "Don't move. I'll be right back."

She straightens, and behind her is a little boy, four or five, maybe, sitting in one of the three chairs beside the door. My eyes flick to the carrier beside him, holding a baby dressed in an outfit with pink dinosaurs.

It starts to fuss, and she bends to rock it. "Shhh. I'll be right back, Love Bug."

"Do you need help?"

She turns, wobbling on one heel tucked somewhere underneath her high-waisted dress pants. "Uh. . .no. I just need to grab his seat and her base."

Her phone rings, and she searches her large bag. The little boy stares up at me, his legs gently swinging back and forth. She finds her phone and checks the screen, her lip tucking between her teeth. Her eyes flick to mine and then to the boy.

She swipes and takes five steps away, answering.

No longer able to see her, the baby's lips curve down and quiver as she starts to cry.

I glance over, and the woman is pacing, her hand on her forehead and whispering in forceful tones. I can't help but wonder who's on the other end of the line, getting an earful.

I lift my ball cap and run my hand through my hair as the baby's cries build. I roll my neck and step out from behind the counter, squatting in front of the boy. The girl's lower lip juts out further.

Well, shit.

I rock the carrier gently. "What's your name, partner?"

The boy stares at me, and up close, just like his mother, his eyes are unique. Both are blue, but one has a large brown slice. His eyes run over my face, watching me closely.

"Who's this guy?" I point to the tattered stuffed animal with bulging eyes, wondering who gives a kid a stuffed toy that looks like a bloated, dead fish. The crying ceases as if the fact that I can speak shocks her into silence.

The boy's legs swing a little faster, his gaze dropping to the ugly fish and then bouncing back to me.

I glance over my shoulder at his mom, charging one way and then the other, her dress pants flowing around her as if she's stalking the prey on the other end of the phone. Her voice is low enough that I can't hear her, but her face and gritted tone tell me this isn't a friendly chat that could be postponed.

I continue to push against the edge of the carrier. The baby's gray eyes track me despite the movement, gripping a raggedy, floppy lamb.

The boy wiggles in his seat, tucking the fish closer to his side.

"Does it have a name?" I point to his companion, and he stares at me, his eyes growing wide.

"You're not familiar?" The voice comes over my shoulder, and it's the return of that confident sass I experienced about this time yesterday. She leers over me, arms at her side, looking like she just went three rounds in the ring. "He's Pout-Pout."

My gaze returns to the boy, a slight smile creasing the corners of his mouth. I stand. "Pout-Pout? Interesting name."

She drops her phone in the great abyss slung at her side, her hands moving to her hips. "Funny, I'd think you'd make great friends. Pout Pout Fish spreads his dreary wearies all over the place."

I face her and her amusement, but hear a muffled giggle from below.

I definitely won't get paid enough for this.

"I need your information." I round the counter and log into the computer, helping this along. "Name." I keep my eyes trained on the screen, but when she doesn't immediately reply, I find her staring.

"So, once you verify the issue, you'll call me before you do anything?"

I straighten, crossing my arms over my chest. "It needs to be repaired. I just don't know the specifics yet."

Her head falls to the side slightly, her shoulders rolling back. "If this issue is serious or requires parts, will you send me a quote before proceeding?" She rephrases her question.

This woman and her distrust are grating on my very last nerve.

"Yes. I'll note not to touch anything without discussing it with you."

Her eyelids drop a few millimeters. "Thank you. That would be so kind." She checks her watch as if I'm holding things up.

"Your name." I return to the forms, wanting to get out of here sometime tonight.

"Sarah Atwater, and that's Sarah with an 'h.'"

I get her phone number and then her address.

"237 North Edgewood."

I stop typing, glancing up from the keyboard under the bill of my cap. She twists to check on the kids, patiently waiting as my reserve dips a little lower.

"Excuse me." I must not have heard her right.

The door opens and closes, and Carson strolls in. "Hey, sorry. That took longer than . . ." He stops, his eyes transfixed on Sarah's, but only for a second before he catches himself and surveys the rest of our after-hours guests. He nods at the kid. "I'll toss dinner in the back." He holds up a brown paper sack.

Sarah's attention returns to me.

"Come again," I ask, needing her to repeat herself to be sure I heard what I thought I heard.

She repeats her address, and I see Carson's steps falter as he passes, some kind of noise coming from his throat.

My fingers stiffen as I try to type, jabbing the keys like a gorilla.

The door opens again, and in steps Katrina Dunn, a woman ready to bust any man's balls at her whim. If only the rest of the guys were here.

"I made it." She runs a hand over her long, wavy black hair. "Those imbeciles took three hours to argue over who gets the prize-winning dog sperm."

The woman I now know as Sarah and I look at her.

She waves a hand. "It's a long story. I'll spare you the brain-infecting details." She eyes me, one hand moving to her hip. "Slade, it's been a while. How's Krissy?"

I hired Kat when I took guardianship of Krissy.

"She's good. Working at the hospital and still making me want to lose my shii . . ." I glance at the boy behind Sarah. "Mind."

Kat grins. "Attagirl. She and I should get drinks. You tell her to call me."

I nod. I will absolutely *not* help arrange that. Krissy doesn't need any assistance in driving me to an early grave. On one hand, I'm proud of her independence and ability to speak her mind. On the other hand, I'm pretty sure she's determined to pay me back for every strict rule by making it her adult mission to bulldoze each one with flair.

I hear boots behind me announcing Carson's return.

"Who are you?" Kat's gaze shifts to over my shoulder.

Carson removes his backward cap, holding it to his chest. "I'm Carson, ma'am." He leans against the counter. "Here to help Slade not fall into something he can't handle." The ass grins, his pearly whites shining against his tan skin.

I will punch it right off his face as soon as we're alone.

Sarah peeks over her shoulder at her kids while one of Kat's thin, dark eyebrows perks.

Thankfully, rather than taking the bait, she spins, her trench coat fanning out around her.

"Crackerjack! I didn't see you back there." She moves toward the little boy.

"I'm not J-j-jack." He grins.

Both of her hands jet out to the sides. "No?" she feigns surprise.

"I'm Owiver."

Kat slaps a hand over her forehead. "Are you sure you're Oliver? You seem pretty smart and excellent to me." His dangling legs swing as he smiles. "Are you ready for our date?"

He nods and hops off the chair. "I thought we'd let your mom and sister tag along, too. You're a little young to be out late on your own, Jack."

He giggles, taking her extended hand.

Sarah cuts in. "I need to get the seats from my car."

"I'll help." Carson jumps on his white horse and charges toward the door. He glances back at me with that smirk as if he's confiscated a secret he'll use to his advantage until the end of time.

"Now, you're not one of those guys with low self-esteem who won't let a woman buy his Happy Meal, are you?" Kat asks Oliver. "Because I'm not sure this will work if you are." She leads him to the door, and Carson holds it open. "Look, Jack! Contrary to all evidence, chivalry hasn't kicked the bucket for all eternity."

The door bangs closed, and a wail erupts behind Sarah.

She turns, scooping up the carrier, and links it over her arm. "Shhh. It's ok." She puts her hand over the tiny girl's belly, then her focus returns to me.

I grab the forms off the printer. "I need a signature." I bypass the credit card information to avoid any further skepticism.

She pulls a pen from the tin can, twisting back and forth to keep the baby calm. "So, you'll call me as soon as you know something?"

I look at her. We've seriously been through this. What the hell? "Yes."

"And you'll not do or order anything without my consent?"

I straighten, crossing my arms over my chest. "Would you like a report notarized and delivered by a courier?"

Her eyes drift toward the ceiling as if she's contemplating it. "Is that an option you offer here?"

"Look, this is my business, and I don't run it by screwing people over. I will perform an inspection and let you know exactly what I find. If you want a second opinion, feel free."

The door opens, and Carson steps back in.

"You're all set." He smiles.

Sarah's peculiar eyes hit mine, her lips moving to the side, and the fact that she remains unaffected by this conversation makes my skin prickle and shrink two sizes.

She waves a hand. "That won't be necessary, but if the quote could come without the sprinkles of bitterness, that would be fantastic." She rolls her lips as her hair falls from behind her ear, but it's unable to mask her pure enjoyment of picking at my calloused layers.

This is where wanting to punch myself comes into play. I knew I should have sent her to a dealer, but no. My big mouth said I'd help, and now I'm stuck with whatever is happening that makes me want to peel off my skin to release the swell of foreign discomfort this woman is happily stirring within me.

Carson sniffs, and I know his dumbass is relishing this entire thing.

Her hand jets out, her key ring dangling from her finger. "Thank you, Mufasa. I look forward to hearing what you find." She bites the corner of her lip, and my jaw clenches.

"You want help." Carson jumps in, offering a hand to take the baby carrier.

"Thanks, but I've got it." She scans the chairs to make sure she hasn't forgotten anything. Carson holds the door open, and she disappears into the darkening night.

"Aren't you just Mr. Helpful?" I grumble.

Carson grins. "Southern charm, man. It's how we're bred. You've got a little in there. Especially when it comes to single moms." He pats me on the chest as he takes her keys from me.

Of course he'd note the absence of a ring. I'll be damned if I'll admit I'd already noticed.

"It's just difficult to see underneath the bitterness, Mufasa." He laughs as if it's the funniest thing he's ever heard.

I press the button to open one of the garage doors extra hard.

"And she lives across the street from you." He chuckles, covering his mouth with his fist. "I hope I'm there when she realizes it."

I'm going to have to move.

He pushes away from the counter. "I think you may have just met your match." He points at me. "Plus, she's a lawyer. You better guard your balls, man." He laughs harder.

"How about you shut the hell up and see if you can pull it onto the lift the first time. I don't want to be here all night."

He strolls toward the door. "You know, in the south, it's proper manners to welcome our neighbors with baked cookies or something."

The only thing I'm baking is his ass if he doesn't shut his mouth. "I'm not making any cookies or welcoming anyone. Up here, we mind our own damn business."

He snorts. "Go ahead and tell yourself that, bro. I can't wait to tell the guys."

I want to ram my head into a wall. Maybe I'll get amnesia, and this will all disappear.

I need this job to be over as soon as possible. Next time, the import is going to the dealer, where I don't have to deal with incessant sass and listen to the guys' constant shit-giving.

I sure as hell won't make even close to enough for this.

CHAPTER 5

SARAH

I check my watch. I still have an hour until I need to catch the bus.

It's day two of bus life, and it's not so bad, except for asking Griffin to adjust my work schedule, which he was fine with. There's also the creepy old man who believes he's a pirate and spends our morning ride filling me in on the government spies out to steal his treasure. Then, there's the little issue of my refrigerator contents being down to half a gallon of milk, two or three eggs, and a random assortment of condiments and fruit.

Bus life as a single mom of two kids doesn't afford easy access to grocery shopping, library visits, or taking the kids somewhere in an emergency. It all creates a new layer of planning and anxiety on top of what already exists.

I tap my phone—no missed calls.

I'm still hoping to hear from the garage today, and I need it to be good news—a quick and inexpensive fix. That won't be the case because that's not how my life works.

I tap out another message.

> ME: Miles, this isn't funny. The order is clear, and you're required to follow it. I'm not playing your games.

My brief conversation with Miles went as expected. The fact that I had to have it in front of the man who now holds my only form of independent transportation in his hands was the kind of suckfest that's fitting these days. Given that Miles actually called, there wasn't a chance in hell I would let a growly mechanic keep me from answering. It didn't matter what he heard. I'm pretty sure he made up his mind about me the minute I set foot in his garage.

Plus, it was only two minutes of the same damn thing. Me, attempting to be mature and rational, despite wanting to reach through the phone and rip his head off, and him, not giving a single shit about anything but himself. I did, however, survive another round of threats, accusations, and manipulation. Today, I'm still standing. Yay me.

I swipe my phone to check my email, scanning for a quote even though Slade said he'd call me. Slade. Such an interesting yet fitting name.

There's a light knock on my door. I don't even have to look to know it's Cory. It's like the skinny weasel waits until I have my phone in my hand to appear as if he's catching me in an office offense.

He clears his throat, and I set my phone aside, twisting in my chair.

"What's up, Cory?"

He pushes his wire-rimmed glasses up his nose with one hand, the other clutching a stack of files. "I wanted to review the Connor files. You haven't sent them yet, and the court date is tomorrow."

I square my shoulders. "Griffin has them."

His thin jaw flexes. "I wanted to review them when you finished compiling everything."

"I spoke with Griffin about a separate matter this morning, and he said that wasn't necessary." I refrain from smiling, and it takes effort. His eyelids droop a little lower. "Also, my schedule is shifting slightly. Griffin approved it." *And it will be thirty fewer minutes a day that I have to deal with you.*

If weasels could snarl, I'm pretty sure he would, but instead, he stands there swiping his hand underneath his nose.

"What are you working on now?" His beady, dark eyes flick to my phone and then back to me.

"Griffin received confirmation on the Sanders case and asked me to update the agreement. Kat is pulling me in on some research."

He sniffs, extending the file folders in my direction. "Client information needs to be updated in each of these. You can contact each and ensure we have the most recent information."

I glance at the files and then back at him. "Is it urgent?" I know it's not, and he needs to understand I'm not his assistant.

"You should have them completed by tomorrow afternoon." His arm wobbles, and he retracts the files when I don't take them.

I rest back in my chair. "Isn't that something Marcie handles?"

"She hasn't been at her desk."

That sounded a little defensive.

"Oh, don't worry. She had an appointment but said she'd be back. I bet you could leave them on her desk with a note or email her. If you want, I'd be happy to deliver them." It'll save her from having to deal with his overt condescension.

"An appointment?" He all but rolls his eyes.

I don't know if it's a question or a statement, but I'd like him to get out of my office. "Yes. She's taking care of a little feminine issue."

I would never divulge personal information, but Marcie's voice carried down the hall from the kitchen this morning, and the entire office was made aware of her IUD replacement.

"Who's got feminine issues?" Kat pops her head around the doorway. "I have cramps so bad, my uterus might actually drop out on the floor."

Cory's eyes drift upward, his cheeks turning red while I press my lips together to keep from laughing.

"Oh hey, Cor. You wouldn't happen to have any Midol up in that arsenal of meds you keep in your drawer, do ya?"

He tucks the folders under his arm and turns to leave. "Excuse me." He attempts to push past her, but she sticks her arm out, stopping him.

"Seth is looking for you. Something about a large fortune and a donkey sanctuary. He thought you might be familiar with jackasses." Her mouth pulls into a wide, fake smile.

Cory avoids eye contact as he slinks around her.

Kat's gaze follows him down the hallway, and then she grins. "He just makes it so damn easy." She crosses her arms over her chest, leaning against the doorjamb. "He's intimidated by you."

I raise an eyebrow, wondering what he has to be intimidated by.

Her shoulders drop an inch as if she can read my mind. "You're gorgeous, brilliant, and Griffin is loading you with the good stuff. He's threatened by you." She glances down the hall. "But if I catch him loitering in here one more time questioning your workload or wanting to review things, I will not only line his entire office with maxi pads, Griffin will be required to fire his ass."

As far as I've seen, Kat and Griffin only interact when necessary. They're business partners, but they don't appear to be friends. I haven't quite grasped why that is when they both seem to socialize with Seth.

The office calendar indicates that Griffin and Seth golf on Friday afternoons, weather and schedules permitting. Kat and Seth regularly meet friends for drinks and have invited me multiple times, but happy hours typically don't include kids.

"Have you heard from Slade?"

"Not yet. I'm not sure I want to know the damage."

"He's a little rough around the edges, but a good one. He'll shoot you straight and not take advantage."

Kat has only said she helped Slade a time or two, but never how. It's none of my business, and client-attorney privilege is real, so I haven't asked. That doesn't mean I'm not curious.

She glances at her watch. "I have a hair appointment at four, but if you want, I can drop you off at home." Her nose scrunches. "I hate that you're having to ride the bus."

She offered to pick me up in the mornings, but she lives on the opposite side of the city and is usually here before sunrise or heads straight to court.

"Only if it's on your way."

She waves a hand. "I'll grab my stuff and hopefully have time to squeeze those babies."

My phone buzzes, and I reach for it, hoping it's Miles and that, by some miracle, he's ready to be a decent human being. It's Slade Bennett.

"I'll meet you out front in fifteen." Kat throws a thumb over her shoulder and disappears.

I swipe to answer. "This is Sarah."

There's a moment of silence before the low, grumbly voice. "It's Slade."

My stomach squeezes tight, knowing this will be a blow to my bottom line that I cannot afford or easily recover from.

I brace my elbows on my desk, sending up a silent prayer. "Hi. It's nice to hear from you. I've been anticipating your call." They say kill 'em with kindness, and I wonder if that works with nerves.

I hear faint banging and what sounds like a drill in the background.

"I have an estimate prepared. Do you want to go over that or have it emailed?" His cordialness remains intact.

"Let's just rip the Band-Aid off. No need to sugarcoat it. Just give it to me straight, doc."

This man's severe seriousness makes me want to push every single one of his buttons just to see what happens. Life sucks enough, but to wear it as a coat of armor would be really heavy.

He releases an exasperated breath. "The wheel bearing is bad, which will require parts and labor. Your brake pads are about seventy percent worn, and I'd recommend replacing the rotors at the same time. I checked your tires, and they're nearly at the wear indicator. You probably have around 5,000 miles left, but with winter coming, it's best to replace them. Your oil and fluids are low. According to the sticker, it's about three thousand miles past due for an oil change. You're lucky your engine didn't burn up."

Of course it can't just be one thing. I rest my forehead in my hand as my stomach sinks to the bottom of the growing black hole. "What's the bottom line?"

His deep voice proceeds through an itemized list, and I slump back in my chair, feeling like I might drown underneath the weight of the numbers.

When he's done, it's my turn for silence.

"Sarah." He barks my name, and I snap to.

"Yeah."

"How do you want to proceed?"

I fill my cheeks with air and slowly let it out. "Do I have a choice in any of this?"

"Not on the wheel bearing. The brakes and rotors could wait, but you'll save on labor if we do them at the same time. You need your oil changed and fluids drained and replenished. Tires can wait, but I wouldn't recommend it."

I could puke and think about putting my head between my knees as my chest constricts to half its size. "You said you have to order parts. How long until those come in?"

"For the wheel bearing, about a week."

Nooooo. "Is it possible to drive it in the meantime?"

"Sarah." The way he says my name makes my skin prickle. "Your wheel could fall off."

I close my eyes. "Sooooo, you're saying no?"

He groans, and the sound brings me a millisecond of reprieve.

"Fine. Do you have any idea when you might have it fixed?"

There's a long pause. "Once I have the parts, I'll fit it in where I can, but it could be a few weeks. You'll need to tell me what you want me to do about the rest of it."

"Great." *Just freaking great.* "Will you let me know when parts come in?"

"I'll put you on speed dial."

My life is crumbling before me, but did he just make a joke, or was that sarcasm? I. Cannot. Tell.

"Ok, then. I guess I'll look forward to hearing your peppy voice with better news."

There's another grunt and grumble, and we hang up. My evening will be spent applying for a new credit card with a limit that will hopefully allow me to cover this disaster. One I'll be lucky to pay off within my lifetime.

I log off my computer, gather my things, and meet Kat in the parking lot. Her SUV is superior to the smelly bus, especially this afternoon.

Kat pulls out of the parking lot. "Getting my hair dyed and my eyebrows waxed shouldn't feel like a luxury, but these days, it comes close to a spa treatment."

I rest my lunch bag in my lap. "I don't think I've had my hair cut in over six months."

Her eyes drift from the road to my head, running over my sleek ponytail. "Seriously? What kind of shampoo do you use? It's so shiny, and you don't even look like you have split ends."

I smile. "The cheapest bottle I can find."

She gasps as if that's blasphemy. "We can't be friends." She raises her hand between us.

My phone buzzes, and I pull it from my purse. It's the invoice for the inspection Slade assured he would send.

SLADE: I need to know about tires and brakes.
SLADE: Oil and fluids are non-negotiable.

> ME: Anyone ever tell you that you're kind of like a large wild feline that stalks the tundra?

I just can't help myself. His bossy matter-of-factness makes me want to pick at every grouchy layer.

SLADE: I'll wait to hear from you.

ME: Ok. Shall I send you that information via text, or would you prefer a phone call?

SLADE: Text

ME: Yes, sir. I hope you have a pleasant evening.

I scroll, mentally adding the total of the things he said were required.

"Is everything ok?" Kat's voice is soft.

I inhale and let it out. "Yeah."

"You sure?" She glances at me. "You know if you need anything . . ." She lets it hang there.

I'd be lying if I hadn't considered seeking her advice about Miles and my pathetic situation. But it's messy, and she's my boss. Nothing good would come from dumping my baggage in the middle of the only thing putting food on our table, no matter how minimal it might be.

"Thanks. I'm good. Just hoping Slade can work magic, and my car will be fixed sooner rather than later."

She nods. "How are your classes going?"

I enrolled in two online courses to work toward a bachelor's degree. Achieving a paralegal certificate was a first step. It helped me get this job, but I added two classes when I found out I qualified for financial aid. Juggling work, mom life, and studying is a challenge, but I'm determined to do it.

"Statistics make me want to pull my hair out if I can even stay awake."

She laughs. "Ugh. I had the worst professor. He smelled like mothballs and had hair growing out of his ears. I couldn't even think with all of that going on. I don't know how you do it with kids."

It's my turn to laugh. "Lately, not very well." I barely passed my last test, but I keep that to myself.

She pulls into my driveway. "I gotta run. Kiss those babes for me."

I grab my things and climb out. "Thank you so much for the ride."

She waves a hand. "You call me if you need anything."

I enter through the back door, and the scent of onions and garlic welcomes me. A wet nose greets me, along with a bark and wagging tail. I carefully slip off my heels and flex my toes. The swelling around the smallest is finally starting to recede.

"Mama!" Ollie runs into the kitchen with Frankie crawling as fast as she can behind him.

I bend to kiss his face and squeeze him. I swing low, scooping Frankie up, and pull her to my chest, kissing her cheek.

She lets out a squeal. "Ma-ma."

"Mama, wook." Ollie holds out a large, orange paper letter F that's been turned into a fox. "It's a f-fox."

"It looks so good, bud. Did you make that at preschool today?"

He nods.

Helen rounds the corner, tugging on her coat. "We took a deep dive into fox territory today." Her eyebrows raise, and she winks at me.

"They eat rabbits and v-vegetables." His little nose crinkles.

I squeeze him against my leg as Frankie pats my cheeks and presses her face to mine. "I bet they eat broccoli."

He giggles. "No. Dat's gross. They're too smart to eat broccoli."

"I had to stop by the store to pick up a prescription, so I grabbed milk and a few other things," Helen says, zipping her coat and patting her pockets for her keys like it's no big deal.

"It's my turn for t-t-treats next week." Ollie spins, running off to the living room.

When Helen's smiling eyes finally meet mine, they turn soft. I suck in my stomach to contain my rolling emotions and the feelings of complete failure.

"Thank you," I offer softly.

She reaches for my hand and squeezes. "Your grandmother helped me when I needed it most. There's hamburger casserole in the fridge for you to pop in the oven."

I hug her tightly. I don't deserve to have a Helen.

She gathers her purse over her shoulder, and I walk her to the front door.

"S-see you tomorrow, Miss Helen!" Ollie hollers, sinking to the floor with Grover, his fox readying to take flight.

"His teacher mentioned a speech pathologist. She gave me her name and number and said getting Ollie evaluated might be a good idea."

My shoulders slump, and Frankie's arms wrap around my neck. Ollie used to work with someone when I didn't have to worry about bills and collection agencies. Since then, his speech has regressed, and his stutter has become more prominent. It's worse when he's nervous or unsure, and kids don't understand his struggle.

"She also said there's an early intervention program that offers scholarships you can apply for."

I clench my jaw, not wanting to think about scholarships. None of this would be an issue if Miles weren't a selfish prick and I weren't so stupid to believe his lies.

She pats my arm. "Ok. I'll see you tomorrow."

Frankie waves her little chubby fingers from the doorway.

Helen turns and blows a kiss. "Bye-bye, sweet girl."

I close the door and lock it, carrying Frankie to the couch. I sit in the middle with her on my lap, and she rests her head against my chest. The fox soars with Ollie and Grover trailing behind as it lands beside me. He climbs and settles into my side while Grover plops at my feet.

I take a deep breath, reminding myself that they are safe and we are together. My eyes burn, and my nose stings. I lower my chin to kiss the top of Frankie's head, breathing her in.

There was a time when I dreamed of making it out of the place I felt stuck in, adhered to based on circumstances. I worked my ass off and ticked off one goal after another.

I did it. I became what no one thought I could be. Then, I got caught up in a web of lies I never saw coming. But even now, I wouldn't change a damn thing. Ollie and Frankie are worth every single minute of heartache, struggle, and disappointment. They're all that matters.

So, I will do this. Whatever needs to be done. I'll work my ass off. I know how to do that.

I close my eyes, picturing what once was. The woman I was proud of.

"Are you guys hungry?"

"I want Goldfish." Ollie lays his fox down as Frankie's head pops up.

"Me. Me." Frankie pats her chest.

"Guys, we don't have Goldfish."

"Yes, we do." Ollie hops off the couch and runs to the kitchen.

Helen. Of course, we do. I strap Frankie into her booster.

I pour the fish and grab my notebook.

I make a list. At the very top is applying for a credit card and figuring out how to get groceries on the bus. Then, I'll look into speech therapy programs and somehow pass my classes. At the very bottom, I note: Regain the stability and independence I'd earned.

I picture the satin strips hanging in my room. The ones I really need to remind me that I did that once, and I can do it again. Only this time, I'll make it with two kids, and I'll never put myself in a situation where I lose it again.

CHAPTER 6

SLADE

"Owww." Krissy stumbles down the last step but catches herself on the railing.

"Morning, sunshine."

She grumbles, dragging into the kitchen. She bumps me to the side, trying to get to the coffee pot.

"If you have time this morning, I've got a full lineup at the shop. We could use some help with oil changes and rotations."

She runs the sleeve of her sweatshirt over her face. "I just got my nails done."

I hand her a clean mug from the dishwasher. "So."

She pours the steaming black liquid and returns the pot to the warmer. "I have a staff meeting and hope to talk to the manager of the labor department. They want to set up an interview."

I pick up the small box on top of an open bubble mailer lying on the counter. "What's this?"

Krissy turns, resting against the counter and bringing her mug to her lips. "It's a genetic testing kit. The girls at work were talking about them." She takes a careful sip.

"A testing kit?" I frown, setting it down.

"Yeah. They said it might show if I have any of the markers Mom had."

My eyes drift back to the small cardboard box. "You want to know that?"

We don't talk about our mom often. It brings back a tidal wave of emotions neither of us is comfortable getting close to.

She shrugs. "I feel like I should know." Her voice drops a level. "I mean, it'd be good for possible preventative care."

A tightness creeps over my chest with those words. "You sure? Would it change anything?"

She weighs her head from side to side. "Maybe. I'm still thinking about it."

I watch her, knowing she's already decided, or the box wouldn't be sitting on the table. She's trying to protect me, but she wouldn't do this behind my back. We don't hide things from each other. It's a rule.

I've been Krissy's guardian since she was thirteen, when our mom died. It was vital we didn't keep secrets if we were going to survive the teen years.

"Will you let me know?"

"Sure." One side of her mouth curls up. "I heard you met the new neighbor." She changes the subject, hiding her smile behind her mug.

Of course, those jackasses are yapping about it like it's breaking news. They seriously need more shit to do. I fill my travel mug with coffee.

"Cute single mom, huh?" she asks nonchalantly, like there wasn't a group message with every inconsequential detail they could conjure to create as much drama as possible.

When I don't take the bait, she tries again.

"It's nice of you to help her."

I screw the lid on my cup. "Her car needs repairing. It's business."

"You sound a little defensive, Stone Cold." She skews her tone, attempting to push my buttons.

"Are you available this morning or not?" I'm not engaging in their useless chatter.

"If my meeting doesn't run too long, I'll stop by and help for a bit."

I tug open the fridge and grab the container of leftovers for lunch.

"Or, I could go grocery shopping so we actually have food," she says as if I'm still supposed to stock the house.

"There's food in the pantry. You just have to make it."

She scoffs like that's a ridiculous concept.

"If you move out, you'll have to cook."

We trade making meals, but Krissy conveniently has plans pop up on her assigned nights.

"Nah. I'll just be strategic about lining up dates."

"Didn't go well with the doctor?" I ask, but I'm not really sure I want to know the details.

"I didn't say that." She pushes away from the counter and stops at the bottom of the stairs. "Will you go with me to look at apartments?"

I turn in her direction, thinking about what the guys said.

"Please," she begs softly.

"Not Trig's apartment."

"Deal." She smiles and climbs the stairs. "Good thing. Otherwise, you're gonna have to be cool with me bringing the hot doc back here."

I run a hand over my face. She wears me out.

I shove the plastic container of chicken and rice in my lunch box and swipe my travel mug from the counter. I grab my hat and coat, needing to get to the shop and sort out the schedule. If I have time, I'll run payroll, check inventory, and review statements to see if I can bring on another mechanic.

I back out of the garage, and Brandon stands in the middle of his yard, staring at me while his mini dog shits in his front yard. My next-door neighbor spends his days walking his wiener and watching what everyone else does.

When I moved in, he complained that my truck was too much for his noise sensitivity. Then, I caught him eyeing Krissy and told him if he didn't want to be blind, he should keep his eyes on his side of the fence.

At the end of my street, I proceed to turn right. As I approach the bus stop, I notice a woman sitting on the bench that's usually empty. I roll closer, and my head swivels, seeing—

My foot spontaneously stomps on the brake, sending my coffee flying off the center console. "Dammit." I rip the tumbler off the floor. Thankfully, the sliding lid was closed.

I stare out the window at Sarah sitting in a skirt, her long, slim legs covered with black tights and heels. It's forty-some degrees, and she's wearing a thin sweater with a collared shirt underneath. Her long, shiny brown hair hangs in waves, shielding her face. She's focused on the open book across her lap.

All common sense screams to roll on past, but my stupid ass finger goes rogue and pushes the button to lower the window. "What are you doing?"

Her head snaps up, and those tantalizing eyes spear me. One as blue as the morning sky. The other, like warm amber. Both are enhanced by a light layer of makeup.

She glances right, then left, looking up and down the street before focusing back on me.

"Did you look up my address? Are you stalking me?" Her head falls to the side, and she crosses her arms over her chest, her brow scrunching.

My shoulders slump as my eyes roll. I have lost my damn mind. Krissy has finally driven me to complete insanity.

A car approaches in my rearview mirror but proceeds around my truck. My gaze travels back to the woman on the bench as she shoves her book into her bag.

"Stalking you?" I have to hold back a scoff. "Has that been a common occurrence that would make you believe I'd spend my time hunting you down in hopes of catching you alone and off guard?"

One dark eyebrow arches as she zips her bag closed. "That question was a bit detailed, don't you think?"

I rest my wrist on the steering wheel, gathering my patience. "What are you doing?" My frustration builds at the annoying part of me that doesn't like her sitting here alone, where anyone could—

One foot starts to bob over her crossed legs. "Uh, as far as I know, this isn't a launch pad, but if a spaceship lands, I'll be sure to snap a pic before climbing aboard." Her eyes grow wide. "I might even send it to you."

My molars grind together. I will my leg to release my foot from the brake, but the damn thing doesn't move. I have things to do, and I don't have time for. . .this. "Where's your rental?"

Her shoulders roll back, and her neck lengthens. "I didn't reserve one." There's a momentary pause. "As you can see," she says, one hand extending before her. "I'm taking the bus."

I inhale long and slow, returning my gaze to my windshield and the road beyond. The sun casts an illuminating haze that must also be clouding my cognitive processing ability.

"You didn't reserve a rental?" I ask calmly and cooly, mustering all of my strength.

She ignores me, her eyes traveling down the street as if I no longer exist.

"Sarah."

Her bright blue eye peeks at me from the corner.

"Get in," I order, moving my stuff from the passenger seat to the back. I glance at my watch.

She doesn't move, and another car passes.

"Get in, Sarah," I say as delicately as possible, needing her to hurry up so we can both get to work.

She sets her backpack in her lap and wraps her arms around it, gripping her phone. A complete act of stubborn defiance.

"You're so kind to offer, but. . .no. The bus will be here any second."

I want to lift my foot off the brake and let my truck carry me away from the beautiful threat sitting before me on a cold ass bench. A vision of the little boy with the ugly, fat fish and the baby in the carrier flashes through my mind.

She stares at me, those hypnotizing eyes burning into me. Eyes I might be able to stare at all day.

Fuck.

My body temperature escalates. I run a hand over my face.

My damn boot stays put. "Get in the truck, Sarah. You're not riding the bus."

A smile tugs at her lips. The kind that tells me I just waged war.

"Do you get away with telling everyone what to do?"

My teeth grind together. "Sarah."

"Slaaaaade." My name rolling off her tongue shoots tingles up my spine in the most uncomfortable way. "I don't know you. I'm not getting in your truck or going anywhere with you. I don't know how you found me, but you need to leave. The bus will be here *any second.*"

If she thinks I'm afraid of her or this bus, she's out of her damn mind.

I yank my foot off the pedal and roll forward, drifting to the curb. I shove the gear shift into park and push my door open, letting it close behind me.

I march back and stop in front of her. "You are not riding the bus. Have you heard about things happening to people on buses? I have a twenty-four-year-old sister, and there isn't a chance in hell I'd let her sit out here. I live across the street from you. I saw you on my usual route to the shop, and given that you work with Kat, I know your office is just a few blocks from the garage. So, *please* get in the truck." I point to make myself clear.

She cranes her neck to glower at me. "Would you let your sister get in a truck with a strange man who ordered her to do so?"

I inhale, hoping a strong dose of patience is in the air. I let it out as the bus rounds the corner three blocks down. I have no doubt that if she had a chain available, she'd lock herself to this bench.

"We've met twice, spoken once on the phone, Kat was a reference, *and* you now know we're neighbors. You can call my sister if you need further background information."

She perks at the offer. Shit. No man would survive the two of them.

The bus engine roars toward us, and steam billows from my nostrils. "Get. Up. Sarah." I pause, needing her to listen. "Please."

She does not move.

My gaze tips up to the sky, seeking all composure and fortitude. When my eyes fall back to her, she's watching me.

"You have a daughter, no? Would you want her to ride the bus where people are regularly being followed, held at knife-point, robbed, and who knows what else, *or* would you rather she get in my truck where you know I would drop her off safely at work?" I grit out the last part as the bus's brakes squeal.

Her eyelids droop, and I see I hit my mark.

She springs off the bench as the bus eases to a stop. "Great. I'll probably lose my window seat away from the guy convinced he's Blackbeard." She stomps toward my truck, her backpack in her hand.

I shrug out of my coat and place it over her shoulders. "Where's your coat? It's freezing."

Her steps falter, surprised by the weight of it. She glares at me, but shockingly, she accepts it.

I reach around her, opening the passenger door for fear that she'll spin, run, and hop on the bus just to piss me off. Her eyes dart to me again out of the corner before she lifts her leg to climb in. Her narrow skirt constricts her movement, and she teeters, falling into me.

She braces her hand on the middle of my chest and stops, only for a second, eyeing the placement of her palm. Her gaze flicks to mine, and I offer my hand. A smile tugs at my lips at her unspoken need for help, but I keep that shit under wraps.

She lets out a little huff before placing her freezing hand in mine. I wrap my fingers around it, and the ice-cold contact creates a burning sensation that runs through me.

She uses it to boost herself into the seat, and I close the door.

I round the truck, shaking it off and shoring myself up for the next ten minutes.

I climb into the driver's seat and am immediately assaulted by the scent of sunny days on the beach. It smells like her car. Knowing that makes me want to stick my head out the window and roll it up to cut off all circulation and air.

The last time I knew and cared what a woman smelled like taught me enough to avoid being susceptible to such characteristics ever again.

I reach for my seatbelt, and Sarah does the same, maneuvering the belt around my coat.

Great, my coat will probably smell like her. I'll have to bleach it.

I put the truck in drive and pull away from the curb, completely ignoring Sarah's stiff posture.

I clear my throat. "Why didn't you get a rental?"

The woman is a lawyer and drives a BMW. The idea of her taking the bus is absurd.

Her upper body twists toward me. "Do you always address people with such a bossy tone?"

She answers a question with a question. Why am I not surprised?

I run a mechanic shop where the guys depend on a paycheck. I've taken care of Krissy since she was thirteen, which required a level of maturity and responsibility I was in no way ready for, but I did it.

Am I bossy? Maybe. Do I have to be? You bet your ass. It's how I survived, and Krissy made it to womanhood.

"Most of the time."

She stares at me as if she didn't expect my honesty. "Why didn't you say anything about living across the street?"

"You scare me."

She laughs as if I'm joking, but it's the truth. From the moment she set one heel in my garage, this woman has pushed buttons that have remained undetected for so long that they were corroded and impenetrable.

"Well, don't worry. I don't bite. . .often." So she says, but I'm not inclined to believe her.

I stop at a red light and glance at her. Her bottom lip is tucked between her teeth to hide a smile, and I avert my gaze to the road.

"I didn't know the house had sold."

She adjusts in her seat. "It didn't. It was left to me."

"Are you from here?" And the guys say I'm incapable of making small talk.

She doesn't answer right away. "No. I'm from a small town up north. We moved almost a month ago."

I notice she doesn't elaborate. "Do you have family here?" Even though it's none of my business, I'm curious what brought her here with two kids.

"No. Have you always lived here?" She turns the tables swiftly.

"Yes. My sister still lives with me, but she's looking at apartments."

"If she's twenty-four, she's probably ready for her own space."

I glance at her and her astuteness. "I think I might be ready for my own space, or she's gonna send me to an early grave."

She huffs a laugh as if she understands.

I pull into the lot of Macavoy, Dunn, & Chambers. My eyes snag on the sign, and my grip tightens on the steering wheel. This is a place I would never willingly set foot in, except in desperate times that call for desperate measures.

I stop in front of the door, and Sarah unbuckles.

She unzips her backpack. "How much do I owe you for gas?"

I stare at her as she pulls out her wallet. *Is she for real?* "Thirty-two cents, but a surcharge of three dollars for the unwarranted sass."

Her gaze tips up to mine, and her lips press together to prevent a smile. "Well, it's probably best to start a running tab. You can just add it to my bill."

She removes my coat, and I want to tell her to keep it, but I know she won't.

"Do you have a ride home?"

"Yep." She pushes open the door.

I study her as she grabs her backpack and climbs out, wondering if her ride is the bus. "Sarah."

She stops, and her head drops to the side. "Are you a worrier?"

This woman appears to have an innate ability to shift the conversation away from her.

"Thank you. . .for the ride." Those eyes linger on mine only a second more before she steps back and closes the door.

I watch until she disappears through the glass. She should come with a warning: Hazardous. Proceed with caution. Because she seems to be able to pick and pry at the calloused layers that were worked into place long ago—ones I like and wear comfortably.

I exit the parking lot far from comfortable and have a sneaking suspicion that it might not return for quite some time.

CHAPTER 7

SARAH

A buzzing sound filters through my sleepy fog, and I feel the vibration under my cheek. I yank my head up, wiping the drool from the corner of my mouth, and then use my sleeve on the streak left on my textbook page.

The clock on the microwave reads 2:32 a.m. I run a hand over my face and check my phone, expecting a text from Roxie on her way home after closing the bar.

MILES: I'll be in LA next weekend for an event. I'll fly you in, and we'll talk.
MILES: Don't forget, Sarah, you left.

I stare at the messages, not surprised he would text me in the middle of the night. It never changes. It's all a game. I inhale and let it out, wanting to ignore him forevermore, but I can't.

ME: We have nothing to discuss other than you following the orders. Don't drag this into something it won't ever be.

Even as I type, I know it's as good as talking to a brick wall—carefully crafted, solid, and self-secure, but completely hollow inside.

Miles is waiting me out—dangling the fruit before me to see how long I'll last before I break. He knows I can't afford to get my attorney involved, and I'll do anything for Ollie and Frankie. He's calling my bluff.

I squeeze my phone in my hand, wanting to throw it across the room. I don't want a single thing from him, but Ollie needs speech therapy, and I have to be able to pay for things like car repairs, doctor's appointments, food, and diapers. I've tried to get ahead and build some savings. But when you've been stripped of everything, including your friends and entire support system, that's difficult to do.

I stare at the black text in my book, knowing it's the end of the conversation for now. I attempt to read where I left off, but it's no good.

I stand, my body tense with exhausted frustration. I reach into the cupboard for a cup, but my sleeve bumps a glass.

"Shit!" I scramble to catch it, but it crashes to the floor. I stare at the shiny shards scattered around my bare feet, shimmering in the light—a visual representation of my life.

Grover trots around the corner, and I hold out my hand. "Stay. Sit." He stops and stares at me. "Sit." He plops his butt on the ground in the doorway and his tail thumps against the floor.

A muffled cry rises, and I grab the dustpan and brush from under the sink, quickly sweeping up the mess before Frankie wakes Ollie. I dump the glass in the trash and scan my feet.

"Come on." Grover follows, and I switch off the kitchen light.

Frankie stands in her crib, whimpering with her Lambie in one hand, two giant tears resting on her cheeks.

"Hey, Love Bug." I lift her and hold her against my chest. "It's ok." I kiss her cheek. "Let's change your dipe," I whisper into her staticky hair.

I change her diaper and carry her to my room. Grover reclaims his spot at the end of Ollie's bed as I lie down in mine. Frankie snuggles next to me, her face pressed into my neck.

I kiss her forehead, staring across the room at the array of ribbons glistening in the narrow beam of moonlight filtering through the blinds. "It's all going to be ok," I whisper.

I close my eyes, recognizing the patter of small feet followed by the click of nails.

"Mama."

I crack one eye, and Ollie stands beside the bed. "Come on." I move the sheet to the side and open my arm to him.

He climbs in, and Grover jumps onto the bottom of the bed. I wrap my arm around my little guy, and he burrows in.

"Let's get some sleep, guys. We've got a big adventure tomorrow."

I peel the small, sweaty hand from my face and am greeted by the soft morning light pouring through the blinds. I rub my eye with my free arm, noticing the foot wedged in my pit.

I carefully adjust the limbs sprawled around me. Grover's head pops up as I curl up to search the nightstand for my phone, but it's not there.

I wonder what time it is. My eyes flick around the room as I become aware of the golden glow and the fact that I couldn't hear my alarm. I wiggle out of the confined space as Ollie murmurs and stirs.

Grover follows me down the hall and into the kitchen, where my phone buzzes with soft, melodic tones. *Noooo.* It's seven fourteen, and the bus that routes to the grocery store will be at the stop in a little over an hour.

I rush back to my room, and Ollie sits up, rubbing his eyes. "We've got to get moving, bud, if you want to ride the bus today."

I grab jeans and a sweatshirt from my small closet, then quickly brush my teeth and hair, pulling it back into a ponytail.

"Frankie. We're going on b-b-bus today." He leans close to her face as her eyes drift open and closed. "Come on." He shakes her.

"Careful. Let her wake up."

He hops off the bed.

"Go get dressed, and then we'll have to eat a fast breakfast."

I wash my face and moisturize. My phone buzzes on the counter. "Hey, Mom."

"Hi, honey. I'm opening the store this morning and wanted to check in. It's been a few days since I heard from you."

These past few days have been a whirlwind. The kind that blows through and leaves everything in disarray. I wouldn't even know what day it is, except that the bus schedule has become my latest required obsession.

"It's been busy. I had to take my car to the shop."

"Really? It's not very old."

"Yep. Apparently, the wheel could fall off." I smooth a light layer of foundation underneath my eyes to hide the dark circles and bags.

She makes a clucking sound. "Luxury for an exorbitant amount of money, but the wheels fall off. Ha!"

My thoughts exactly.

"Well, what's this delightful surprise doing for you?"

I want to laugh because there really isn't always a bright side, at least not when the storms keep rolling in. "Nothing but make things twenty times more difficult than they already are."

"I'm sorry, honey." My mom loves drama, but she fully understands the struggle of being a single mom with minimal funds.

"I've been able to get a few rides to and from work, but I'm taking the bus."

When I say it, it doesn't sound so bad. The reality is it sucks ass. Like right now, when I need to get the kids ready and out the door, and also figure out how to manage groceries on the bus.

I thought about having them delivered, but that costs money I don't have, and unfortunately, every penny counts.

"Who have you been getting a ride with?" My mom's tone perks right back up.

Only my mom would look at this situation as a golden opportunity in disguise. I won't be discussing my morning rides with my grumbly neighbor.

We've ridden together a total of three times. The first was unexpected, to say the least. He commanded and groaned, but for some reason, the man's outward annoyance with life is amusing. There's comfort in knowing others feel the struggle, and it's clear he has some of his own.

Each day since, he's sat inside his truck, waiting for me. He's driven mainly in silence to the soft sounds of old country music on the radio.

"The neighbor across the street has been giving me a ride to work, and Kat has brought me home when she's not in court." I brush on a thick layer of mascara, seeing movement out of the corner of my eye.

"Oh, you met your neighbors? That's great, honey. I . . ."

Frankie crawls toward the edge of the bed, and I rush to her, leaving my mom's interlude about great neighbors. I scoop Frankie up, and she giggles and squirms as I carry her into the bathroom.

"Mom, I've gotta go so I can get the kids breakfast." I run the thin black brush over my other eyelashes again.

"Ok. Do you think you'll be home for Thanksgiving? We're organizing a potluck. I work Black Friday, but I'd love to see you and my babies. Russ's kids will be in town, but I hope you can come home. I miss you three."

My mom manages a boutique consignment shop that only accepts name brands and high-end items. Most items come from the big cities, and she constantly snags things I could never afford. It's what allows me to look even remotely professional every day.

Russ is my mom's current boyfriend. He's a nice guy, but spending Thanksgiving crammed into her trailer with his kids and pretending to be some happy family doesn't sound like a good time.

Also, the thought of going home makes me want to puke. My mom loves the small town she grew up in and is chairwoman of the mobile home community she delights in. She's the busiest of bodies and knows everything about everyone. If there's a function to organize, she's on it, but I couldn't wait to get out and never return.

The thing about small towns is that everyone knows everyone and everything about them, or at least they think they do. With my mom's loud personality and rotation of boyfriends, I never had a chance to remain under the radar.

When I left, it only got worse. She made sure everyone was aware of each achievement as any proud mom would. When I married Miles, I was suddenly no longer Susie's girl with different colored eyes from the other side of the tracks. My DMs were filled with townsfolk who'd never had a kind thing to say until they wanted a wedding invitation.

"I don't know, Mom. I'm taking it one day at a time."

"Think about it. I'm sending another box with some amazing items that arrived the other day. I found a coat for you. Kiss those babies for me!" she sings.

"Love you, Mom." We hang up, and I shove my phone in my pocket, shifting Frankie to the other hip. "Let's get you dressed and something to eat."

She claps her hands and bounces on my hip. "Eat. Eat."

"Ollie! Are you dressed, buddy?"

Ten minutes later, Ollie is eating cereal while Frankie attempts to get yogurt into her mouth with globs dripping onto her bib.

"Grover, let's go outside." I open the back door, and he trots out.

I check my watch again. "When you're done eating, get your coat on," I tell Ollie as I grab a handful of cereal.

"Ready!" He hops down from his seat to get his coat, leaving the last bits of cereal and milk in his bowl.

I pull the baby carrier from the hook by the door and set it next to my backpack. "You ready, Love Bug?" I wipe Frankie's mouth and carefully remove her soaked bib.

"Pout-Pout." Ollie takes off back to his bedroom to retrieve his fish.

"Go potty, too?" I holler after him.

I unhook Frankie from her booster seat, then open the door to let Grover in, but he's not there. I peek my head out and scan the backyard. "Grover! Come." He doesn't appear.

"Mama, I p-p-peed on the wall."

My body slumps. "Really?" I want to melt into the floor. "Hurry. I'll clean it later."

"Mama, can I take my p-plane on the bus, too?" Ollie holds out his small metal biplane, and I notice his shoes are on the wrong feet.

"Quick. Switch your shoes. We've got to find Grover."

He plops on the floor and un-Velcro's his shoes. I slip Frankie's coat and shoes on while she tries to grab a pink spatula from the utensil canister.

With her on my hip, I step outside, scanning the backyard again. The gate stands open a foot.

Shit! Of course this would happen today.

"Hurry, bud."

Ollie pops up, holding his fish and plane.

We circle the house with Ollie's plane doing loop de loops as we conduct our search.

"Grover!"

The crisp swish of leaves sounds as I trudge to the front yard. I stop, listening and glancing up and down the street. My stomach bottoms out at the thought of him being lost.

"Grover!" Ollie yells, standing on the porch steps.

I stop at the sidewalk, switching Frankie to the other hip.

"Grover!" *You little shit.* "If you get hit, I'll kill you."

"Everything ok?"

I spin, and a middle-aged man with short blond hair stands at the end of my driveway, holding a tiny brown dog with a long, pointy snout and floppy ears. The man's eyes are wide, like he's waiting with anticipation.

"Our dog got loose," I say, peering past him and hoping to see furry movement. I don't see his fawn fluff anywhere.

"Does he have an ID collar and chip?" The man takes a few steps closer, ready to assist, a slight smile showing off crooked teeth, while his dog snarls. His eyes flick to Ollie behind me, spitting plane noises and running in circles. "I'm Brandon." His hand pops out from under the dog. "I live—"

"Go home, Brandon!"

My eyes jet to Slade marching across the street.

Brandon twists at the growled command and takes two steps backward. "I was just offering to help."

"She doesn't need your help, so go home." Slade barges right past him, and his tall, broad body stops beside me on the sidewalk. He's a human barricade not to be crossed.

I stare up at him, and the thick hair curling out from under his hat, those fierce green eyes glaring at Brandon.

"Good morning, Rory." I just can't help myself.

His gaze flicks to me.

Brandon scoffs. "You know, you're a—"

"Careful," Slade warns, his eyes moving to Ollie, who's still as a statue.

"Guys, this is real fun, but I need to find my dog."

I leave them to their testosterone feud, holding out my hand for Ollie to take. I adjust my arm under Frankie to lift her a little higher.

"What about the b-b-bus?" Ollie asks.

"We've got to find Grover first."

I watch Brandon slug back across the street to his house, which I note is next to Slade's.

"Do you know which way he went?" Slade asks, and I turn toward him.

I shake my head. "The gate must have come unlatched. He never runs, but he probably chased after a rabbit."

Ollie stares up at Slade, his plane momentarily grounded.

"Does he have a name?"

"It's Grover," Ollie states.

Slade's bearded chin dips to look at Ollie. "Grover?" he asks as if he needs clarification.

Ollie nods.

"Like the furry blue Muppet?"

Ollie smiles widely and nods.

"He's a Goldendoodle. He's smart but not familiar with this area."

"You need a coat, so stay here," he orders me. His gaze falls to Frankie, who's leaning over my arm in an attempt to escape to the ground where she can practice walking. "I'll get my truck and see—"

"Anybody looking for this guy?"

A female voice comes from behind us, and I turn to see a woman being pulled by my dog. She's wearing leggings and a sweatshirt, and her short, dark hair is pulled back in a ponytail. She's young and beautiful, with blue eyes that sparkle.

"Grover!" Ollie runs toward him, and Grover pulls against her petite frame even harder.

The woman releases his collar, and the two boys meet. Ollie throws his arms around the massive furball's neck.

"He was down the street and around the corner, sniffing a light pole."

"Thank you." It rushes out along with my relief.

"I'm Krissy. This ogre's sister." She tips her head in Slade's direction. "I'm kind of bummed. I was hoping we could keep him." She grins up at Slade, who remains deadpan. "He never let me get a dog."

"I don't know. He seems like a cat guy to me." I glance up at him.

"Ya know." Her finger taps her lips, her eyes growing wide. "You're right. One of those long-haired fluff balls."

Slade's weight shifts, and I think I hear a soft groan.

I smile. "The kind that would drape itself all over him. I bet he's a big, cuddly kitty underneath that thick layer of detest for all happy, snuggly things."

Krissy's mouth falls open. "Yes, and—"

"Mama. The b-bus?" Ollie points, and I hear the puff of the brakes as it stops two blocks down.

I check the time on my phone, avoiding the giant's gaze beside me.

"You were taking the bus?"

I close my eyes, inhaling long and deep. "I was, but now . . ."

"Yeah. That's not a great idea," Krissy says softly. "I work in the ER, and there have been incidents lately. Usually at night, but still."

My shoulders slump, and I finally give in, letting Frankie down. I grip her hands as she wobbles, working one foot forward and then the other.

Grover barks at Ollie, kicking leaves in the air.

"What's the deal with Brandon?" I gesture across the street, distracting them from the bus conversation.

"Brandon was over?" Krissy rolls her eyes. "Did you tell him to take his wiener and go home? He sits in his driveway and watches everyone's comings and goings. If you need something, the guys are over all the time." She throws her thumb over her shoulder toward their house. "Come get one of them."

I glance at Slade out of the corner of my eye.

Krissy squats to Frankie's level. "How old are they?"

"Ollie's five, and this is Frankie. She's thirteen months."

She tugs Frankie's coat down and out of her face. "I usually work nights, but if you ever need a sitter, let me know."

"Thanks," I say, inching forward.

"Where were you going?" Slade's gruff voice cuts in.

Crap. He's still gnawing on the bus thing.

I glance at him over my shoulder, not needing a lecture. "I just needed to grab a few groceries," I offer confidently.

"Oh, that's perfect, then." Krissy stands. "Slade was heading to the grocery store to pick up snacks." She swats him on the shoulder with the back of her hand, smiling brightly as if she solved one of the world's problems.

Slade glares at her, but she only smiles, completely ignoring him.

"He's a real joy to shop with. Stops to chat with all the old ladies and swap recipes."

His head rolls back toward the sky as if begging for help.

"Oh, that's ok." I jump in, needing to stop this in its tracks. "I'm sure Slade has better things to do, like perfecting his scowl and working to breathe fire out of his nostrils."

Krissy's head tips back, and laughter tumbles out. "You know, when I was a teen, I caught him—"

"Krissy," Slade growls a warning.

She grins.

I need to tiptoe right out of this little situation. "Thank you for offering, but—"

"Oh no, he's going anyway. You can't take the bus." She glances at him, waiting for him to agree, but he remains silent. She continues unaffected by his apparent annoyance. "Careful, though. The idea of dropping a sugary treat in his cart sends him into a spiraling meltdown of how processed sugar affects your body."

She pats him on the shoulder. "He'll be glad to help out."

"Kris," he states as if daring her to say one more word.

"Ok, well, off to bed." She turns for their house. "I have to work tonight, warden, but meeting the doc for a quick . . ." She trails off, making her way across the street.

Slade runs a hand over his face as if he's pulling himself back from the brink of mass internal destruction.

"I really like her," I say, swinging Frankie back to my hip.

"She never stops," he grumbles.

"Hey, thanks for stopping over." I whip a finger pistol at him and start backing toward the house, needing him to get on with his day. The idea of grocery shopping with him makes my stomach quiver and roll. "Come on, bud." I wave to Ollie, saying a silent prayer that he comes willingly without mentioning the B-word again.

"Sarah." It's bellowed in that commanding way.

I have to bite my tongue to suppress the desire to ruffle his fabricated calm facade.

I halt my retreat, fully aware of those bright green eyes searing into me from underneath the rim of his hat.

"I'll be over in five to load the car seats." He turns, not giving me even a second to respond.

I watch his big body stalk back across the street while my own fills with absolute dread for what's ahead.

Frankie rests her head on my shoulder.

Ollie's hand slips into mine. "Mama, can we s-still ride the bus?"

I inhale and let it out. There is absolutely no bright side to any of this. It's just a dark, gloomy, never-ending suck fest.

I turn for the house. "What do you think about a big truck instead?"

CHAPTER 8

SARAH

If he follows me around this store, I will lose my ever-loving shit. My neck burns, and my armpits spew sweat as I slowly push the cart through the produce section.

Slade is at my six, creeping along behind me as if the bins of fruits and veggies can camouflage the big behemoth. I need him to get to shopping.

I scan colorful fruit, looking for the yellow sale signs. Frankie reaches over the edge of the shopping cart and pats the shiny apples.

"C-can we get these?" Ollie holds up a net full of clementines.

I eye the price sign, nod, and he drops them in the cart. I grab a bunch of bananas and a bag of apples, mentally calculating my running total, knowing milk and yogurt are a must.

I replace the coffee beans I'd thrown in back on the end cap and push forward.

"I'll meet you at the front." Slade's low voice pulls me out of my tentative mission.

I breathe in relief as he moves past me toward another part of the store. I stand for a minute with Ollie swinging off the cart like a monkey to gather myself.

Slade pulled his truck into the driveway while I scrounged for any possible excuse for why he didn't need to take us to the store, silently cursing when I came up empty.

He helped me load the car seats while I inhaled and exhaled, hoping to survive this little shopping adventure with a limited number of questions and my dignity intact. Ten minutes later, Frankie was strapped in the shopping cart with Ollie riding shotgun.

It's one thing to roam the store with your meal planner, searching for the best deals. It's entirely another when you have to decide between fresh fruit and a large pack of chicken breast that will last two weeks. The internal battle is bad enough. I don't need a witness.

I swipe open my phone and tap the app, double-checking the coupons. "Hang on, Ol."

He plants both feet on the end of the cart, and I push us toward the refrigerated section, needing to make this quick. We wander up and down the aisles, grabbing only the essentials. I spot Slade from a distance and keep moving.

Ollie hops off the cart. "We have to get the sssstuff for my cookies."

It's Ollie's turn to take treats to school. I check my list for the few ingredients we need to make his favorite, and park the cart in the candy section, looking for the Hershey's Kisses.

I squat, searching the lower shelves.

"Well, hello there."

A man's voice catches me off guard, and I peer up to find Griffin smiling at Ollie and Frankie. Rather than his usual suit, he's in a button-down shirt and jeans, holding a shopping basket.

From my observations, Griffin works around the clock seven days a week, except for an occasional tee time with his son, business acquaintances, or Seth.

I know he's married and has two grown children—a son and a daughter. Kat mentioned that his son is a piece of work, but I've yet to meet either of them.

"Hi." I stand.

"It's nice to finally meet these two." He smiles at Ollie.

"This is Oliver and Frankie," I say, resting my hands on the cart.

"I've heard a lot about you," he says.

Ollie only stares, and Griffin's gaze returns to me.

"It's a gorgeous day. Do you all have plans?"

Why is it strange to converse with people you practically see and speak to daily? Outside of the confines of the office, it's awkward. Or maybe it's just that I'd like to avoid discussing anything related to my personal life and what that currently entails.

One thing I learned long ago is that people immediately formulate a perception of you. You can be smart, capable, talented, and the most badass of all badasses in any field, but often, it will all go unrecognized if you don't have the persona to match. People like neat, organized, and uncomplicated—a nice tidy box they can place you in. It gives them comfort.

My box has a long history of layered duct tape over holes with labels that have been scratched out and replaced. Now, all the contents have been dumped out and are waiting for my careful examination to determine what remains true. I'm a little terrified there won't be much I recognize anymore, and beyond that, I just might need a brand new box. So, until I get it sorted out, I'd prefer to keep that mess under wraps for my viewing pleasure only.

"We're grabbing a few groceries, and then we might play outside this afternoon." I keep it short and general.

He nods, and I see Slade round the corner of the aisle. His cart stops alongside mine as his gaze drifts to Griffin.

I'm not sure what happens exactly, but there's a shift. It's like when barometric pressure drops before a storm. You can't feel it, but you know the atmosphere around you is different.

Griffin's weight shifts under the pressure of the big guy's expressionless stare. Uncomfortable doesn't even begin to describe the still silence, and my body temperature climbs again.

"Griffin, this jolly giant is Slade, my. . .neighbor." It stumbles out of my mouth because that's what happens when things are weird.

Griffin only nods, his eyes lingering on Slade. I contemplate easing my cart backward and letting whatever is happening continue without me.

"Well, I'll let you get on with your shopping." Griffin's gaze falls to the kids again. "It was nice meeting you." He dips his chin. "Sarah, I'll see you at the office." He turns and walks away.

My eyes travel to the unmoving, massive rock beside me. He stares down the aisle at my boss's back. "I'll meet you up front." His tone is flat and hoarse.

I watch him stop at the chips, tossing a couple of bags in before disappearing around the corner. I have no idea what just happened, but I'm ready to get out of here and go home.

I reach for a bag of Kisses and toss them in the cart, checking it off my list. I hurry down the remaining aisles and duck into the shortest checkout line. Ollie hops off the end, and I attempt to organize the items to place them on the revolving belt.

"Wook, Mama." Ollie points to a bouquet of balloons with a massive jet floating high above the rest.

"Those are cool, aren't they?"

Frankie twists in her seat to see, pulling one leg up to give herself a little leverage. I tug the cart forward and place my hand over her to ensure she doesn't go anywhere.

Ollie stays put, mesmerized by the helium-filled foil. "I want the j-j-jet."

"Not today, buddy," I say, reaching for the divider and setting it on the belt. I drop the milk jugs on the conveyor and then the canned items. "Come on, Ol."

He doesn't move. "But I n-n-need dat jet." His little arms rise and fall at his sides as if that balloon is mandatory for us to get home.

"Ollie," I warn softly, not needing a meltdown today.

Frankie wedges her leg and foot against the cart again and pushes up. I unhook her and place her on my hip as I unload the rest of the items. Heat and moisture begin to build underneath my sweatshirt like a sauna.

"Huh!" Ollie stomps his foot, crosses his arms, and turns his back to me.

"Ollie, come on. Another day, ok?"

He spins back around, his arms spreading wide. "B-but I need dat j-j-jet!" Tears fill his eyes, and I close mine for only a second, needing all sanity to hold strong for just a bit longer.

As I force them back open, Slade's cart rolls into our lane just behind me.

Of course.

I'd like to squeeze my eyes shut, wiggle my nose, and transport myself to a different place and time.

"Ollie," I say again as I drop my box of generic tampons and lotion on the belt.

"B-b-but I need it!" he yells, tears spilling over.

Slade stares at Ollie, who's planted in the middle of the lane, arms curled around himself, and his face scrunched with anger, pointed directly at me.

The cashier scans my phone and begins zipping my items across the scanner. I turn back to Ollie, watching as Slade squats down beside him.

"Hey, partner."

Ollie hunches his shoulders, his lower lip jutting out further, trying not to cry.

"That's a cool balloon, huh?" Slade nods, gesturing to the floating aircraft. "Where's that plane you had earlier?"

Ollie doesn't move an inch but eventually gives in and pulls his small metal biplane from his pocket.

Slade holds out his large palm, and Ollie hesitantly sets the plane in it.

"*This* is a cool plane. Way cooler than that one." He turns the plane over in his hand, rolling it. "They don't make many like this anymore. Did you know that?"

Ollie shakes his head.

"They don't. Want to know why?" Slade holds the plane out between his fingers. "Having two sets of wings actually slows the plane down, so they started making them with one set of wings. But, these guys are still the best at doing tricks." He races the plane past Ollie's face and into a barrel roll.

The corner of Ollie's mouth lifts. "You g-g-got to do it like dis."

Slade hands over the plane, and Ollie shows him a loop de loop. I stand in complete astonishment that the big, growly, tattooed man just talked my kid out of a full emotional stomp-fest and taught him something about one of his favorite things ever. I wonder what else the broody mechanic has jammed up his flannel sleeves.

He stands, his gaze shifting from Ollie to me. I avert my attention to the cashier ringing up my remaining items. I place Frankie back into the cart and pull my credit card from my wallet.

I insert the card and wait, keeping an eye on Ollie and the man behind me—the one I'm not sure what to make of.

The credit card reader beeps. Declined. I run it again while the cashier waits, organizing Slade's chips and beer.

The machine beeps again, and my gut rolls into a hard knot and drops to my pelvic floor with the feel of his eyes on me. *Shiiiiittt.*

The cashier taps something on her screen and turns to me. "Do you want me to try it over here?" She holds out her hand.

I glance at the total and quickly flip through my cash, knowing I don't have enough. A burning itch crawls up my neck, most likely along with red splotches, and a bead of sweat rolls down my side. I pull out the credit card I received in the mail for emergencies only. Right now feels like an emergency.

I insert the card, and in no time, the receipt prints. Thank God. I push my cart to the end of the counter, and Ollie follows. Slade moves down to help load the plastic bags into my cart.

"Ummmm . . . I think I missed these." The cashier holds my box of tampons in the air. "They got stuck to the side behind his beer."

And this is how my life goes. Why can't just one thing be easy?

"I got it," Slade tells her, motioning for her to place them in the bag with chips.

He quickly completes his transaction, and we push our carts toward the exit. The rush of cool air from the opening doors feels amazing against my hot skin.

Slade hands me my tampons. "This clearly isn't your full grocery haul, but I would've liked to see you try to get this on the bus, especially with these two."

I peek at him, and there's just the slightest tilt to his lips behind that short beard. My anxiety slowly dissipates.

"Ha. You just underestimate me." I stop the cart at the back of his truck and pull Frankie from it.

Those grass-green eyes move to the corner as he slowly turns his attention to me. He blinks once, twice, but doesn't move an inch.

My body begins to heat all over again. I have no idea what he's thinking, but something tells me it's probably best if I never know.

CHAPTER 9

SLADE

"Piece of shit!"

The ratchet clangs to the floor.

"If you broke the tensioner, it's coming out of your paycheck," I holler.

Carson groans. "What if I lose a finger? You gonna charge me for that, too?"

"Depends on how much of a mess you make." I pull my phone from my pocket.

ME: Parts have shipped. I need to know about brakes, rotors, and tires.

SARAH: Know what? Google provides in-depth information about each.

ME: If you want them replaced.

SARAH: Brb

ME: Are you Googling it?

SARAH: Nooooo! On hold to speak with a mechanic who delivers sucky news with a smile.

ME: Text me when they say you need new struts and calipers and strip your lug nuts.

"Hold on. What the fuck? Is that a smile?" Trig asks, pointing the impact wrench at me.

I don't move a muscle except for the ones that control my eyeballs to meet his smartass gaze. "What the hell are you looking at? I'm not paying you to stand around and make shit up."

"I don't know. That defensive tone raises suspicion." Carson leans against the fender of a Honda, inspecting his hand.

"Maybe it was a spasm. I get those sometimes." Wind opens and closes his mouth, working his jaw.

"Nah, I saw it. It was like catching sight of the white flag going 200 miles per hour." Trig taps his index finger to his temple. "Quick as lightning, but I caught it."

"My ass. The only thing you're gonna catch is the sidewall if you're not careful." I push away from the workbench.

Trig makes a noise like I'm ridiculous, but I've seen him race his motorcycle. Although he's diligent and smart, it can be dangerous.

Carson curses again, and I stroll over. "Want some help?"

"Well, aren't you in the giving mood?" He grumbles, attempting to stretch the serpentine belt again.

I hear a snort. "Seems he's turned over a new leaf. Been more than helpful lately." Wind runs a hand over his shaggy beard, amusement oozing from him.

"Yeah, next thing we know, he'll be scheduling free safety checks and handing out lollipops." Trig tries to withhold a smile.

These assholes like to give me shit, but they'd do everything I'm doing and more. Every lousy one of them. It's why they're still working here despite how much of a pain in the ass they are.

"Grocery shopping together is pretty intimate," Carson adds. "What's next, picking out furniture?"

I don't even have to see his face to know a smirk is riding across his mouth.

I've never grocery shopped with anyone other than Krissy, and I can't argue with Carson's statement. There's something about wandering the aisles with someone and having them witness the items you pull from the shelves that feels invasive.

As I followed Sarah, I watched her carefully evaluate and select items. At first, I wanted to roll my eyes and was tempted to ask her if she was going to Google every item and ingredient, but then I saw it. Something so familiar it socked me in the stomach. It happened so fast that I could've missed it.

Oliver held up a bag of tiny oranges and asked if he could get them. As he dropped them in the cart and returned to swinging off the end, Sarah casually removed a bag of Starbucks coffee grounds and placed it back on the display.

A memory flashed in my mind of my mother doing the same thing when money was tight. Krissy and I begged for the big box of brand-named cereal or the Lunchables that every other kid brought to school. But it was the first time I watched her pay with food stamps that returned clear as day. She slid them from her pocket and quickly handed them over, hoping no one would see.

Shame filled my belly at the flashback. I was fifteen and I'd waited for her by the entrance, fearful of anyone from school running into us. I was just a stupid kid with no idea of the kind of strength it took for her to do whatever she needed to take care of us, and that was before I learned she was sick.

"It wasn't like that." I grab a wrench and lean over the fender. "Krissy offered for me to take her. Besides, you tell me how she'd get two kids and groceries on and off a bus."

Carson releases the tensioner. "So, you wouldn't have taken them if Krissy hadn't offered?"

The door slams closed with a bang. "Taken who where?" It's that deep, forceful tone, and my shoulders slump.

We all turn to the stocky old man, strolling toward us.

I took this shop over from Cal, but the man doesn't leave us be for too long. He said he spent too many years worried about this place to see it go under.

Cal has always given me more shit than I've ever known what to do with. I suspect he misses this place, but I think it's more that he likes to be sure we aren't getting into mischief without him.

"Which of you dimwits has done what now?" He stands beside me, surveying the guys.

Carson clears his throat as Wind's gaze drops to the floor, but Trig squares his shoulders, raises his arm, and points his skinny ass finger directly at me.

Cal shifts his weight to the other foot and swivels so slowly to peer up at me. His arms cross over his chest as one bushy gray eyebrow raises in complete delight to join this roast fest.

The complete silence where there's typically mayhem makes my neck break out in an itchy sweat. The last thing I need is Cal's solid, sound advice wrapped in thick sarcasm that challenges me to think about Sarah in all the ways I don't want to.

"Slade went grocery shopping with a woman," Carson says plainly.

Trig sniffs. "He's trying to tell us he wouldn't have except Krissy *forced* him to."

This shithead is calling my bluff. "I think she's struggling for money," I offer softly, attempting to cover my ass.

Sarah's financial situation is absolutely none of my business and sure as hell none of theirs, but this conversation needs to be over pronto.

Cal's gaze tips up to mine. He scratches his chin, covered with white whiskers. "She's a lawyer and lives in a nice house. That's her BMW parked on the end, isn't it?"

My eyes snap to *them*. I will kill these tattletales and move into this shop to run it every day by myself.

As if they can see the rage building, these assgabs suddenly have tasks to do and scatter like mice.

Cal stares at me, waiting for an answer. He's like an old dog with a bone and won't be letting this go.

I inhale slowly to de-escalate my temper while I reevaluate each interaction with Sarah and everything I witnessed, questioning my instincts. I come to the same conclusion. She's struggling.

"Not everything is as it appears." It's all I'm saying.

I remember how my mom looked perfectly healthy and at the prime of her life when she told me she was sick. The CIA should employ moms. They can cover up shit no international spy would be able to pull off.

"Hmmm." His gaze fades back to the guys. "I always knew you were smart."

I turn to look at him, but he avoids eye contact.

"You adding tires, new brakes, and rotors when the bearing comes in?"

I exhale. "Yeah," I offer quietly.

"You're a good man, Slade. You're a blunt bastard who might not know how to get out of his own way, but you're one hell of a man."

He slaps me on the back. "Don't listen to these idiots. You're doing just fine. This isn't a race. You go at your own pace, son."

He drops his bomb of wisdom and leaves me to help Carson with the belt.

My phone buzzes, and I pull it from my pocket.

KRISSY: See you in fifteen for the first viewing.

"Shit. I gotta go." I holler over the noise. "I promised Krissy I'd walk through a couple of apartments tonight." And it gets me the hell out of here.

Carson's head raises. "Where?" His tone is stiff.

"One is not too far from the house, and there's a townhouse near the hospital."

He grumbles something.

"Can you lock up for me tonight?" I ask him.

He nods, snapping the cover into position.

My phone buzzes in my pocket again.

SARAH: Hey, Fluffy Kitty. Let's hold off on the brakes and tires for now.

I try not to smile at her constant nicknames, but it's difficult.

ME: Ok.

It's too bad I already ordered the replacements. What the confident, self-sufficient lawyer doesn't know won't hurt her.

When I look up, Cal's watching me. "You'd better be careful. Helping someone is one thing. Helping a smart, beautiful woman who lives across the street and is not inclined to roll over at your bark . . ." He whistles quietly, a grin spreading across his weathered face. "It might appear to some as if you *like* helping her." He winks.

The guys cackle as if it's the funniest damn thing they've ever heard. "Shut your asses up and get to work. I've got to meet Krissy."

They laugh harder, but Cal's words linger like pig shit on a hot day. I'm unwilling to admit that driving Sarah to work really hasn't been that bad.

I grab my coat and keys, also not wanting to think about when her car is fixed, she won't need me to do that anymore.

"Look at this." Krissy swings her arms wide and spins in the middle of the furnished living room. "Look at all this space."

The townhouse smells of fresh paint and carpet glue. I peek out the window, surveying the street and the falling sun. "Have you calculated the monthly utilities?"

Her arms fall to her sides, her shoulders drooping. "You're such a buzz kill with all your anal, mature questions."

I shove my hands into my pockets. "You won't live here long if you can't afford it."

She rolls her eyes. "I have a spreadsheet, Stone Cold. I can make it work if I'm reasonable with the thermostat and Starbucks, and watch the games at your house. I'll still be maxing out my 401k and have some left for savings," she says like she's totally annoyed by planning for the future.

"So, you're moving out but mooching off my sports packages?"

She shrugs, wandering back into the spacious kitchen. "If the guys can, I should be able to. I've put up with your strict sour ass far longer than they have."

"They pay me for a portion of the subscription."

She turns toward me, her jaw dropping. "What?! Really?"

"And they bring beer and snacks."

She huffs. "Uh. Those little suck-ups. Fine. I'll bring wine and maybe contribute a snack, but nothing homemade. You can nag Wind for all the fancy stuff he makes." She jabs a finger at me. "Besides, you're going to miss me."

I turn away, inspecting the cabinets. She's not wrong. I will miss her. It's been the two of us for a long time.

"You know it's time." Her voice turns soft.

She's right about that, too. It's just that I barely remember a time when I wasn't taking care of her.

"It'll be weird not having you just downstairs or knowing that you'll be waiting up for me when I get home."

"I don't wait up," I grumble, glancing at her over my shoulder.

Her blue eyes rise to mine from underneath her long, dark eyelashes.

How in the hell does she know I wait up?

"You know, it might be good for you to finally have the place to yourself and see what life has to offer."

I want her soft, tentative words to bounce off my back and drop dead, but instead, they stick like battery acid, corroding my calloused surface.

"Maybe it's time for you to start taking care of yourself and figure out what you want."

"I have everything I want." It comes out more forcefully than I had hoped.

The long beats of silence force me to look at her. She rests against the counter, arms crossed over her small body. I see the defiant thirteen year old all over again, unwilling to take a single ounce of solid advice until she comes to the conclusion on her own.

"I call bullshit, bro. I may have been young, but don't think I've forgotten Melissa and what that was like. What you were like before and after."

It's been twelve years, but just the mention of her name stirs a wave of remorse. I was twenty and stupid, having to watch my mom disintegrate to nothing right before my eyes. I was weak and vulnerable and had my whole life turned upside down, suddenly responsible for a teenage girl.

"And Mom wouldn't want you to spend all your days alone living in the garage."

"Don't bring Mom into this, Kris." I stare at my boots, my tank of patience depleting quickly with her choice of topics.

"It's true. I think we owe it to her to live out the happily ever after she never got."

Every muscle in my body constricts to withhold the jab about Mom's choices, not really being of the kind that leads to fairy tale endings.

I fist my hands, crossing them over my chest. "I was made a fool once. That won't ever happen again."

Her eyes meet mine, and she nods. "I know it won't, so Stone Cold, you need to quit hiding behind the sad, messed-up shit that happened in the past." She pushes away from the counter, swiping the keys with her hand. "If you don't, the best, most important things might slip right past you, and your salty, sour grapes ass will miss out on everything I think this life is supposed to be."

I stare at her back as she walks to the door, surveying the space one more time. I wonder how she got so wise with all that sass consuming her insides.

She stops at the door, turning to wait for me. "Oh, and you're welcome."

I meet her at the door. "For what?"

Her shoulders fall again like I'm new to Earth. "Uh, for helping you out with Sarah. I'm pretty sure that woman could serve you your balls on a silver platter, but instead finds your poor attempts to be cold and distant amusing."

I step outside and run a hand over my face, needing the cool evening air to shock some of the emotions from the last fifteen minutes right out of my body. "Kris, you need help."

She locks the door and turns to smile at me. "Well, therapy is a privilege I take full advantage of. You should try it. It might finally get you in touch with the feelings part of your soul and help you score with the neighbor lady."

She raises her eyebrows and skips down the three stairs.

I have no idea how I survived to get to this place where she's moving out. "Can you sign the lease now?"

She laughs, walking toward the office. "There's one more I want to look at."

I groan. "You're buying me dinner, then."

"Whatevs. Call the guys. We need to round up the troops to celebrate this momentous occasion." She spins, walking backward.

"What's that? Witnessing your last attempts to drive me to an early grave?"

"Ppsssh. No, you finally having an opportunity to actually get. A. Life. And my ability to finally bring guys home without worrying there will be a brigade of prison guards waiting to greet him."

"Prison guards?"

She turns back around. "Yeah. You guys, with all your tatted muscles, broadening and flexing to see how long it will take to make them tuck and run. You know, I should at least have a chance to find a nice guy and be able to slowly break them into the crew."

"Well, quit dating spineless jellyfish, then."

"You're gonna have to give one of them a chance."

"Good luck. I don't like many people."

"Ha. Don't worry, Stone Cold." She reaches up, patting me on the shoulder. "It's going to take someone pretty special. They're gonna have to be strong enough to put up with all of my shit." She grins.

She's one hundred percent right about that, and I'm damn proud.

CHAPTER 10

SARAH

I pull open the oven door and slide the cookie sheet in.

"Is that slimy ferret still sticking his pointy nose in all your business?"

I hear the clink of glass in the background and picture Roxie drying glasses and hanging them above the bar. I've filled her in on Cory and his incessant need to check everything I'm working on as if I'm completely incompetent.

"Griffin and Kat have started to pull me in on cases he's not involved in, so that's helped ward off his lethargic surveillance, although I'm pretty sure he silently curses when we cross paths."

"Has he been checked for rabies? It alters the mind, so if he begins to drool . . ."

I laugh, dropping a ball of cookie dough onto the cookie sheet. "Kat thinks he's intimidated by me."

"At least he's smart, then."

Cory is smart, he just needs to mind his own damn business. He's another reason I keep my personal issues and situation to myself. I have no doubt he'd use my stress and past against me in any way he could.

"Maybe he needs some Ensure and to get laid." I hear her shiver. "I might have nightmares just thinking about it, and I haven't even met him."

I pull another sheet of foil from the roll.

"So, you're making treats for Ollie? I could use a dozen cookies. It's going to be a long night. Declan is in town."

Declan is the bad boy Roxie dated in high school to piss her family off. She ended up falling in love with him, and when he left for the Army, she said goodbye, knowing it would never work long distance. The problem is, no matter what she says, I know she's still in love with him. Or maybe it's more the idea of him and how he goes against everything her parents deem acceptable.

"Declan's in town?"

"Yeah. I guess he's on leave. Jax said he was bringing him by as if I needed forewarning or something."

"Do you?"

She groans. "It's been years, but he's just. . .that guy. Ya know?"

I know. He's incredibly handsome in that rugged, dangerous way, but also charming.

"You need to be careful. I'm sure he's got that stiff military swagger and won't be sticking around for long."

"Yeah. Why do I have to be a sucker for all that?" she whines. "Maybe I should invite him to a family dinner. I could shock the actual shit out of my parents. That would be fun."

"But then, he'd be leaving."

"Maybe I should run away and live with you until he's gone." There's silence like she's contemplating it. "Anywho, Ollie's cookies?"

"Yeah, it's his turn at preschool, so I'm making his favorite. His teacher sent home pamphlets and phone numbers for speech therapists, suggesting he needs help." I unwrap the foil from the Kiss and place it on top of the raw dough.

"Have you heard anything from that balding dick yet?" The disgust in her tone makes me smile.

"Balding?"

"Look, I accidentally clicked on one of his reels. I'm just saying, he looks like a dick with hair, but it's definitely receding, and when it's gone, he's going to look like the actual thing."

I hold in laughter, threatening to burst out and likely wake the kids. "Rox!"

"What? I might have commented as much."

A moment of silence follows that extends long enough for my belly to feel it, and a small knot begins to form.

"Rox?"

"He's got a new agent," she spits out. "A woman. She's gorgeous, and fawning all over him like he's the next Barbara Walters. Although I wonder if she's aware he lacks class and intelligence." Rox knows Miles well enough to suspect he's up to something and likely using this woman to get it.

Miles is one of the top news anchors in Chicago. He's confident, strikingly handsome, and appears to have it all. I think he actually believes he does. He's also smart, deceptive, and knows what strings to pull, when, and how hard. The man has charisma and connections—together, they're lethal.

It's true what they say about fame, power, and pride. It changes people. He climbed the ranks and, along the way, became someone I didn't recognize, or maybe I just never wanted to see it. I married one man and divorced another.

Do I care what Miles does or who he's sleeping with inside a closet or out? Nope. Not even a little bit. Do I care that he muddied my name and reputation and stripped me of every possible thing he could? Not so much anymore.

The only thing I want from him is the support he's been ordered to provide for our children. If it were an option, I wouldn't even want that. But Ollie needs speech therapy, and I want to be able to sign him up for soccer without having to sacrifice something important. The list of things goes on and on. I'm not talking about extravagance or luxury. I just need my bank account to be at a minimal level so I can care for our kids without worrying that I won't have enough for food and diapers.

I also have to pay for the repairs on the car he bought, even though he knew I wanted a minivan. But I suspect the shithead left my name on the car as a spiteful gift. Now that I've seen Slade's quote, I have no doubt.

"I'm sure she's keeping him too busy to return my calls." There's another beat of silence that only tightens the knot in my gut. "What else is there?"

"He was being *coy* about a move to a new network." It comes out softly.

I pause my Kiss unwrapping. "A new network? Where?" It's Miles's goal to make it to New York City.

"He didn't say, but the dumbass look on his face told me it's a big move."

I want to hang up and start searching. My mind races with what this means. He either has no intention of being involved in Ollie and Frankie's lives, or he's gaining speed to do something crazy.

The timer goes off on the oven, and I spin to turn it off. I grab the towel to pull the cookies out and set them on the stove.

Nooooo. I stare at them.

"You ok?" I hear Roxie's tentative voice.

"Uh. Yeah."

"He can't do anything. He hasn't been involved, isn't paying child support, and flinging his ding-a-ling at every opportunity possible."

She sounds so confident, but my stomach is taking cover. I know better than to think he can't or won't do anything. Miles always gets what he wants, and most often, that seems to be to destroy me.

I hear someone hollering on the other end of the line.

"Hey, I gotta go. You sure you're ok?"

"Yeah. Thanks for telling me." I guess I need to start following what he's doing again because I'll be damned if he'll catch me off-guard.

"I was thinking I'd come visit for Thanksgiving. I need a break and an excuse to avoid dinner with my family."

"Ok. Sure." My gut aches with this new information.

"I love you." Roxie's soft voice hits me in the chest.

"Love you, too."

We hang up, and I stare at the cookies. They do not look like they're supposed to. It's quite fitting—a flat melting mess you no longer recognize.

I scoop up the foil and crumple it into the overflowing trash.

I put the next pan in and set the timer, praying they look like actual cookies.

I tie up the bag and tug it out of the trash can, then slip on my shoes and haul it out the back door to the bin. I lift the lid and drop it on top, suddenly wanting to kick the living shit out of something. Maybe the trash.

I catch a flicker of headlights out of the corner of my eye and see the neighbors' shiny trash cans at the end of their driveways.

I blow out a breath into the cold night air and tip the bin to wheel it to the street. I tighten my grip on the handles, wanting to strangle it along with the unknown rising around me.

I hurry down the driveway and almost make it to the end when the wheels catch on the raised edge of the sidewalk. I jerk to a stop, and the bin topples over, the trash bags tumbling out.

Of course! I stand fuming.

I give the large plastic container a hard kick and then another. "Mother fucker, piece of shit, no good, scumsucker. . ." I fist my hands, letting my head fall back to the dark sky filled with bright stars that feel like tiny specks of hope too far to reach. "Uuuggghhhh!" I stomp.

"Bad day?"

My body jolts, but it's that low rumble I've come to recognize. I twist, and under the glow of the street light is the big guy with his hands tucked in his coat pockets.

If I didn't know better, I'd think there might be a teensy bit of amusement underlying that two-word question.

I glare, even though he can't see it. "Careful. I'm in a shit mood."

"Really? I couldn't tell by the assault on the trash can."

It comes out dry, but. . .is there a joke in there?

I huff and place my hands on my hips, needing to get a grip as he strolls over. I shiver. My T-shirt and leggings are no longer enough for a late-night outdoor meltdown.

"Where's your coat?"

I bend, swiping one of the full plastic bags. "Oh, for the ever-loving—" I drop it, yanking my hand away. "Shit!" I grip my hand, holding it close to my body.

Slade sets the bin right side up. "You all right? Let me see." He moves in front of me, holding out his hand.

I tuck my hand close to my chest, squeezing with the other, feeling the warm stickiness coat my fingers. "I caught a piece of glass." I glance at the busted trash bag. *Dammit.*

"Let me see," Slade barks the order.

I release my fist over his large hand and uncurl my fingers. Blood oozes from a slash across my palm.

"Put pressure on it and hold it up." He carefully cleans up the mess and places it in the bin. Then he ushers me toward the house. "Let's get it washed off and see if I need to call Krissy."

I try to match his long stride, gripping my hand tight as the pain settles in. "Call Krissy for what?"

"To see if you need stitches and stay with the kids while I take you to the hospital."

"I'm not going to the hospital."

He peers down at me as he opens the back door. "We'll see. Let's get it clean and have a good look at it."

He waits for me to enter, completely unfazed by my direct opposition to going to the hospital.

"Has anyone ever told you you're severely bossy?"

"Every damn day," he says, oh so matter-of-factly. "Now, hurry up before you drip blood on my boots." He nods toward the inside.

I peek down and see blood running down my arm.

I step into the kitchen and I'm hit with the scent of baked cookies, so I'm sure the timer is about to go off. Grover hops to his feet and barks at the sight of Slade.

"Shhh! No barking. If you wake them, I will strip you of all your Poodle, and you will be an outdoor dog."

His head cocks to the side as his nose works to inspect Slade.

I hurry to the sink and turn on the water, uncurling my hand under the stream. The burn tears through my flesh, and I wince.

I hear Slade unzip and drop his coat on a chair behind me, and then his large shadow appears over my shoulder. "How does it look?"

Every time I pull my hand from the water, blood pools in the center.

"I don't know. It burns like hell."

He pumps two squirts of soap into his palm and starts scrubbing. I pull my hand from the water to let him rinse his and return it as he grabs a towel.

"Let's see."

I face him, holding it out, but blood floods to the surface. He rips off a paper towel, and I take it, pressing it to the wound.

The oven timer begins to chime, and Slade glances at it.

"Here." His large hands grip me around the waist, and he hoists me onto the counter next to the mixing bowl as if I weigh nothing.

Well, ok then. I stare at him.

"Keep it up and put pressure on it. We need the bleeding to stop enough so we can get a good look at it."

Grover, utterly unimpressed with our guest, drops to the floor to lick his paws while I watch the calm, assertive man turn off the timer. He folds the towel in half, reaches into the oven, and places the sheet on the stove. I lean to get a peek at the cookies, and my body slumps, wanting to melt to the floor and stay there until one damn thing goes right.

"Are those—"

"I knnooowww!" I whine, my head falling back into the cupboard. "They look like boobs! I'm going to send my kid to preschool with cookies that look like they belong at a bachelor party."

"How did you—"

"They were supposed to have chocolate kisses on top, but I accidentally grabbed the white chocolate." I hold my hand to my chest, pressing my thumb against my palm. "I thought it would be fine."

Slade stares at them. "Sarah, they really do look like boobs."

Why does he have to confirm it?! "Why can't you just say, 'It'll be fine, Sarah. Five year olds don't even know what boobs look like.'"

He twists, and his piercing green eyes meet mine under his hat. "Do you want me to lie to you?"

The seriousness in his tone grips my stomach while I contemplate his question. "No," I say in absolute defeat.

"You can't send those to school."

I groan. "Why can't just one freaking thing be easy?"

He taps the button to turn the oven off and then moves in front of me. "Let me see your hand." He holds his out, waiting for me to release mine. His long, calloused fingers extend toward me, and I notice his stained cuticles.

I peek up at him, and I find him watching me. Those emerald eyes run over my face. I let my hand fall into his warm palm, and his fingers curl loosely around it.

I pull the bunched paper towel away, and he raises my hand to carefully inspect it.

There's a clean two-inch slice across the pad of my palm, and it burns and aches open to the air.

Slade's thumb rests against my wrist. "It's a nasty cut, but it doesn't look too deep." His eyes flick to mine. "Do you have a first aid kit?"

"It's fine. See." I gesture to my hand, where the blood is finally starting to clot. He stares at me, a human boulder firm in place. "Above the refrigerator."

He releases my hand, and the warmth from his is immediately gone. It's strange watching my carpool buddy roam my small kitchen. He pulls the kit from the cabinet and sets it beside me.

"Were you beating the hell out of the trash can over these. . .booby cookies?" He rummages through the wrapped bandages.

"Booby cookies? Really?"

"What would you call those?"

He has a point, but I will not concede.

I lift my chin. "An experiment," I say with complete confidence because sometimes you've got to go with what you've got, and I've been doing a hell of a lot of that for some time now.

His eyes meet mine, and I swear I see his lips tilt upward the slightest bit despite his short beard attempting to hide it.

"So, what happened?" He finds an acceptable bandage and holds out his hand again, silently requesting mine.

I weigh keeping it all in and locked up tight, where I handle things on my own, but tonight, it doesn't seem like that's working so well.

I force my gaze to his as he delicately takes my hand again. The patience and gentleness I find there tell me it might be ok to tell him. He's completely unrelated and uninvolved, but then again, I saw how this man judged me when I first took my car in. He thought I was some rich bitch from wherever the upper side is in this city.

"You know how they say you win some, you lose some?" I slump as Slade grabs a tiny foil packet of antibiotic ointment.

He says nothing as he lifts my hand closer to his face.

"Well, I'm on a heavy losing streak."

He tears open the packet and squirts it along my cut. The silence lingers as he places the bandage, and my skin warms with being vulnerable.

"It just. . .feels like every damn thing is hard." I huff out a laugh, needing the blunt giant to *say something*. "Even making cookies for my kid's preschool class," I try to joke.

He smooths the sticky edges of the Band-Aid across my palm, and his thumb brushes back and forth across my wrist, inspecting his work.

Those mysterious eyes drift up to mine, but then he releases my hand before I can tell what's behind them.

He tosses the wrapper in the trash, and Grover's head perks up as if Slade might give him a scoop of food.

Slade moves to grab his coat off the chair but pauses. "You're studying statistics?" His brow furrows.

I glance at the textbook sitting on top of my laptop. "I don't think you can call what I've been doing studying." I hop off the counter, irritated that I laid all that out there, and he didn't say a damn thing. "I mostly use it as a pillow."

I grab the mixing bowl, carrying it to the trash to scrape out the cookie dough, but Slade takes it from me. He uses the spatula to clean the sides.

"You're taking a class on statistics?" I hear the confusion in his tone.

"Yeah. I mean, not by choice. It's a requirement. I can only handle two courses. I thought I'd get it out of the way, but with how things are going, I'll be retaking it."

He turns toward me, the bowl resting in his hand. "You're in school?"

Why does he sound so surprised? "Yeeeaaah," I say slowly, ready for all his questions to stop.

He glances at the book again and then at me. "You're not a lawyer."

I put my hands on my hips and then drop the sore one. "No. I'm a paralegal, but I want to be a lawyer. I was really lucky to be hired by Griffin Macavoy. He took a chance on me."

His eyes rest on the table again, and then he sets the bowl in the sink, fills it with water, and washes it. When he's done, he pulls on his coat. "Be careful with your hand."

That's it? That's the end of the questions and conversation?

I stare at him. "Got it." I salute, so completely unable to read this man, and it's frustrating as hell.

It's possible I see his lips twitch as he turns for the door. He reaches for the knob but stops.

"I think it's when we're held to the flame that we find out what we're really capable of. You're gonna be ok, Sarah." His eyes hold mine, and I see so much but also so little.

Something swirls in my chest that begs to know everything in between.

He nods once. "I'll see you in the morning."

He opens the door and disappears into the night. I stand there, not completely sure what to make of the deep insight he just dropped and left me with.

A tickle creeps up my throat, wanting desperately to believe him. I want to know that it really will be ok.

He said it so perfectly. I feel like I'm being held to the flame to see how long I'll actually be able to last before I crash and burn. All I know is that I just hope I'm made of strong enough stuff to withstand whatever might come next.

CHAPTER 11

SLADE

"What are these for? It's not one of the guys' birthdays."

I swat Krissy's hand away from the clear plastic grocery sack. "How was work?"

She yawns. "Fine. It was actually slow. I sat with a little guy with RSV." She reaches into the refrigerator. "But, I heard from the labor department. I have an interview. It's still night shift, but if I get the job, hopefully, a day shift will open up at some point."

I pour coffee into my travel mug. "That's what you want? The labor department?"

She nods, pulling two pieces of bread from the bag and placing them in the toaster. "Yeah. I want to specialize in women's health, and it will be great experience for the clinic."

"Did you decide on the townhouse or the apartment?"

The last apartment we looked at was just as nice as the townhouse, but with the lower rent comes upstairs neighbors and less privacy. I'm voting for the townhouse for safety reasons, but I'm doing my best to keep my mouth shut and let her decide.

She shrugs. "I'm going to sleep for a while and see if I can run through them one more time before I have to work tonight. They're repainting the townhouse and replacing some of the appliances, so the lease wouldn't start until December first."

I grab the grocery sack and my coffee. "If you want me to go with you, text me."

The toaster pops. "I might see if one of the guys will go and get their opinion."

"Not Trig." That shit will tell her the townhouse just cause it's bigger.

She smiles. "Fine. Maybe Wind and Millie have time."

"You should ask Carson. He'll tell you which one is built better and has the best finishes."

She only shrugs.

"I've gotta go, but if you have any time this week, I could really use you at the shop. I have to get some things turned over."

She unscrews the lid on the peanut butter. "You need to hire someone."

"I have to have time. See ya."

She pulls a butter knife from the drawer and waves it.

I pull into Sarah's driveway instead of waiting for her at the end of mine and push my door open just as she steps out.

"Hi." She frowns.

I extend the plastic grocery sack. Her eyes flick from me to the bag. Me. Bag. Me.

"What's this?" She slings her large purse across her body and slowly takes it. She looks inside and then at me, her head falling to the side. "You got cookies?"

"No kid can take treats that look like breasts to school."

One side of her mouth curls up. She glances at the cookies again and reaches into the bag. "What is this?" She pulls out the Starbucks coffee. She stares at it and lifts it to her nose, closing her eyes as she inhales.

She looks like she's experiencing a euphoric high, and it takes effort to keep from smiling.

Her eyes drift open, and she holds the coffee out toward me.

"It was buy two. I figured you probably could use the coffee."

Those eyes squint just a little as if she's considering calling bull shit, but then they fall to the coffee again. When her gaze meets mine again, her head falls to the side. She blinks quickly, her lips pressing together.

"Thank you," she says softly. "Helen was going to make something this morning before they had to leave, but Ollie will love these. And I . . ." She holds the coffee to her chest. "I owe you for every caffeinated buzz I get off these grounds." She smiles, blinking again, and it's breathtaking.

Her glossy, different-colored eyes have a way of making me feel defenseless, as if somehow she sees through all the layers I don't like messed with.

When she laid down the sass last night and told me everything was hard, I felt her overwhelming exhaustion in the way she said it. All the weight of what I'm beginning to understand that she carries.

So many questions that are none of my business shot off like rockets. One after another, wondering why she seems to be doing this all alone. It's not that I don't understand the struggle of single parenting. I do. I saw it firsthand with my mom and then experienced it to some extent with Krissy.

With Sarah, I get the impression that it's more than just financial strain and trying to care for two kids while working full-time and going to school.

"I'll set these inside and be right back."

I return to my truck.

She reappears and climbs in beside me, setting her stuff on the floor and fastening her seat belt. "Ollie is so excited about the cookies. Thank you for getting them. If you tell me how much, I'll—"

"Sarah, it was nothing. A boy deserves to have non-offensive cookies for school."

I back out of the driveway.

"First of all, boobs might not be appropriate for preschool, but they are not offensive. And second, you should know that I can actually bake. I was just . . .off my game."

"Hmmm. Ok."

She swats my arm. "You're a punk, you know that?"

"A punk?"

"Yeah, all blunt and bossy, but then you go and buy cookies for my son. You better be careful, or I might start to think there's a layer of sensitivity under all that . . ."

"Bitterness," I offer.

She bites her lip to hide her grin.

Her long brown hair is down in waves today, held back by a headband. I have the urge to reach over and tug a strand.

I shift my gaze to the road. *What the actual hell?* I run a hand over my beard and then place it firmly on the steering wheel, gripping it tightly.

"You know, you can keep your little disbelieving hum to yourself, sir. I can bake my ass off. I just need to not be in the middle of a meltdown while I'm doing it."

I glance at her out of the corner of my eye against my will. She finally has a coat on, but her legs are only half covered by a black pleated skirt, and I really shouldn't know that. I stab the rolling asphalt before me with my eyes, needing them to stay glued.

Sarah is beautiful. The kind of beautiful that's intimidating because she never flaunts it or expects attention from it, even though her eyes alone would stop traffic.

"How's your hand?"

"It's fine," she says plainly, gazing out the window at the crisp fall morning.

"It's cold this morning. It's nice to see you wore a coat today." There's an insane part of me that wants to push her buttons and watch her get a little riled up.

Out of the corner of my eye, I see her head swivel in my direction. I want to grin, but I bite it back.

I turn into the law firm parking lot.

"What in the hell is it with you and coats? You know, Lionel, some people are just hot. All those layers can be suffocating and confining."

I stop my truck in front of the door, and she pushes her's open.

"You should try wrangling two kids with a big ass puffy coat. It's like being a marshmallow over a fire. You expand with heat until you melt into a big gooey mess." She huffs, gathering her things.

"Sarah."

She stops with one leg hanging out.

"Have a really nice day."

Her eyes flick between mine before her eyelids drop just the slightest bit lower. "You are the biggest shit, you know that?"

She tries really hard not to smile, and it tugs on the place in my belly that hasn't sensed feeling in so long that it takes me a moment to recognize.

Shit.

She steps out and slings her purse across her body, then grabs her lunch bag.

"Your car will be ready in the next couple of days."

"Really?" I hear the excitement in her voice, but that means no more mornings like this, which is for the best.

"Yeah."

"Great."

"You have a ride home?"

Her head falls to the side. She sticks her thumb out, bending and flexing it. "Sure do. This and hiking my skirt up a little higher . . ." She widens her bold eyes. "Works like a gem. It's free, too."

I clench my jaw, and she smiles that smile that pinches something deep inside. I avert my gaze back to the windshield, needing to focus on what's ahead.

She pushes the door closed, but just before I hear it latch, she yanks it back open.

"Hey, Slade." She leans into the truck, and I meet her stare. "Be careful. You keep playing like that, and people might think there's a fun personality trying to escape that big body."

A smirk appears on that pretty face as she closes the door.

I push out a breath, making sure she enters the building before putting my truck in drive. I want to press the accelerator and peel out, running far and fast. This woman poses a threat to my long-held plan and resolve. The one where I've been happily committed to a simple, mundane life. Alone.

I pull out of the parking lot toward the garage, my mouth curling into a smile, and all I can think is . . .

Fuck.

I grab the key fob from the board and hit the button. The garage door rolls open to the dark parking lot.

"What are you doing?" Carson asks from the workbench, cleaning up for the night.

"The wheel bearing is in for Sarah's car." I head to the lot to pull her car in.

"You're putting that on tonight?"

The cold air fills the garage. "She needs her car. If I put the bearing on tonight, we should be able to squeeze in the brakes tomorrow, and then Trig can install the tires."

I unlock it and climb in, wanting to ignore that it smells like her. Light, sunny, and fresh. I hold my breath as I pull it into the garage.

Carson puts the door down behind me. "Seriously, you're working tonight?"

"The schedule is completely full." I toss the keys to him, and he returns them to the hook.

"You want some help?" He strolls over.

"What's it going to cost me?"

He ignores my question and rolls the jack over. "I'm not sure we've ever worked nights before."

I grab the jack stands, hearing the amusement in his tone. "Your ass can go to the gym if you're going to read into this."

He places the jack behind the front passenger tire. "I was just thinking you need to hire another mechanic if we're working nights.

But now that you bring it up, it does seem like this particular job might be getting special treatment."

I kick a stand in his direction. "I'm thinking about hiring someone."

He pumps the jack while I set the other stands by each wheel. "So, us being here and your more-than-usual shitty attitude today has nothing to do with the beautiful woman you've been escorting to work, grocery shopping with, and then delivering cookies to in the morning?"

I already want to ram my head into the side panel. "Do you all have anything else to do besides message each other about what I'm doing?"

He shrugs. "No, man. We don't. You know that."

I should have told him to go to the gym. I need silence where I cannot think and just get this done. All sorts of feelings are starting to emerge, and I'm not sure what to make of any of them. All I know is I don't want to talk about it.

"Did Krissy ask you to go through the townhouse and apartment she's deciding between?" I'm turning this nosey shit off.

He moves the jack in front of the rear wheel. "No."

"I told her to ask you to go with her to get your thoughts."

Carson's family owns a home construction business, and he knows as much about building houses as he does about fixing automobiles, maybe more.

He places the stand under the pinch weld. "I haven't heard from her."

I turn the tables, shoving a little of my discomfort in his direction. "Are you taking time off for Thanksgiving to go home?"

"No."

Funny, all amusement has evaporated from his tone.

We work silently, removing the broken bearing and installing the new one.

"Let's leave it up, and I'll have Wind put the new brakes and rotors on first thing," I say, putting my tools back in my chest.

Carson wipes his hands on a shop rag. "Is finishing this job going to make you less temperamental?"

I groan.

"Don't get me wrong. You're kind of an asshole all the time, but a moderately pretty one with a good heart."

If Carson thinks we're going to get deep and sentimental, he's got another thing coming.

"You know, just because you return her car doesn't mean you can't see her anymore. You could man up and ask her out." He just keeps pushing, so I push back.

"When was the last time you've been on a date?"

"I don't date. It's a waste of fucking time." He pulls his work gloves from his back pocket and tosses them in his tool chest. "I know what I want. Until then, I'm keeping things simple."

I roll the jack to the wall and turn toward him. "Sounds like we have the same philosophy."

He unzips his coveralls. "Nah. See, that's where you're wrong." He points at me. "You pretend you don't want a life outside of this. Someone to go home to and love. A family." He pulls his arms out of the sleeves and stops. "I want all of that. I'm just waiting for her."

I glare at him and his bravery in pointing out what might possibly be true.

He steps out of his coveralls. "You do a good job of pushing people away. Maybe it'd be ok not to push away someone you actually want to stick around."

He smiles that pretty boy smile, and I want to punch it off his face.

"I'm not pushing anyone away. I'm just running my business."

He hangs them on a hook. "I don't know. Seems like this might be a tad bit more than a job."

I replace my tools while Carson locks the garage doors.

He passes me and slaps me on the shoulder. "Let's go to Crusins. You owe me dinner and beer."

"I don't owe you shit."

He laughs. "I beg to differ." He waits by the door, crossing his arms over his chest. "You'll think about this and realize I'm right. On top of that, I don't think you've stopped to consider that maybe Sarah might need somebody, too. Not somebody to take care of her. A friend. A partner. Someone she can actually trust and rely on."

I look at him, and he only stares back. I need to fire his ass. He's too damn insightful to be here.

From what I've seen, it's very likely Sarah needs someone, but I'm not sure if that person should be me. I don't know her story or what brought her here, and I'm not interested in entering a situation where I can't see what's coming.

I did that once, and I was blindsided by my own immaturity and stupidity.

I hit the light switches, turning off the big overhead lights. "If you're so damn smart and know what you want, what in the hell are you still doing here? Why aren't you out there doing it? You don't belong in this garage, and you know it."

He leans against the counter, his gaze shifting into something harder.

I hit a nerve. He's been throwing jabs all night at my weak spots.

Take that shithead.

"It's called strategy. I'm biding my time and figuring out how and when to make my move." One side of his mouth curls upward. "So, for now, you're stuck with me."

I roll my eyes and pull my cap lower. "Shit. You're more like me than you'll ever admit."

He pulls the door open. "Nah. The difference between you and me is that I have hope. Hope that someday, I'm going to get exactly what I want."

There was a time when I wanted everything he described and thought I'd have it. But that blew all to hell, and I've been unwilling to even think about trying it again ever since.

That is, until the stubborn girl next door strolled in, never once giving a single shit about barriers and all the layers I've honed into place to lock it all out.

But now, it's possible I'm seeing glimmers of what I thought I was done wanting long ago.

The problem is, once you have feelings like that—or hope, as Carson calls it—they can vanish just as quickly as you let them rise.

CHAPTER 12

SARAH

I stare at my phone, my heel clicking against the clear, plastic mat. I've been sweating this for three days, but it's time to bite the bullet.

ME: Are you moving to a new network?

I sit, waiting for the three little dots to appear. Nothing.

I jump at a knock on my office door.

"Sorry." Griffin stands in the doorway, minus his suit coat. "I'm checking to see if you're interested in sitting in on the Connor case. Since you compiled and provided a valuation for all the assets, I thought you might like to see how things are settled. Unless you have a deadline to meet for Kat."

"No. I'd love to attend," I say, snatching up the opportunity.

He checks his watch. "Ok. Great. I'll meet you out front in fifteen."

"Sure."

He turns to leave, but I stop him. "Oh, wait. I don't have my car."

"If you're ok with it, we can ride together, and I'll drop you off at home after."

I quickly contemplate it, and even though I'm not excited about him taking me home, this is too good an opportunity to refuse. "Sure. Thank you."

He nods once and disappears.

I tap on my phone screen. Nothing. I drop it in my purse, finish an email, and shut down my computer. I grab my things and step into the hallway, jolting to a stop.

"Hey. Where are you heading so fast?"

A man holds up his hands. He's wearing jeans, a sweater, and a wool coat. The slick smile creeping across his mouth makes my eyeballs want to take a trip to the inside of my head. It's boyish and charming. The very kind of smile that led me exactly here.

I slide the strap of my purse higher across my body and meet his bold stare.

"I've heard about the girl with two different color eyes. Now, I get to see for myself."

I drape my coat over my arm. "I wasn't aware they were such a spectacle. Maybe I should join the circus."

I know people talk about my eyes, but you'd think adults would have more tact than to treat them like some kind of deformity to be gawked at.

His smile grows a little wider. "Tell me. Are they real?"

If I had a dollar for every time I was asked that question, I'd be playing in the sand with Ollie and Frankie somewhere warm with the ocean as our backyard.

"No. I can pop the glass one out anytime I want." I widen my eyes a little.

His gaze flicks between mine, trying to decide if it's true, but then his smile returns. "You're a sassy one. I like it."

I want to vomit on his loafers, but I refrain.

"Junior." Griffin appears behind me, just outside his office door. "I've only got five minutes."

Junior, as I now know him, steps to the side to let me through, but drops his shoulder just before I pass. "You'll fit in here nicely, but stay away from Kat. She bites."

I glance at him, wondering if he's ever been kneed in the balls. I ponder asking, but decide it wouldn't be professional.

I smile, the fake kind. "Don't worry. I bite back." I leave him and his suffocating arrogance to wait for Griffin.

Marcie and Robyn peek around me and down the hall, whispering as they track Junior.

"You met Junior," Marcie says as if I were blessed with a gift.

"I sure did." I cross my arms over my torso, holding my coat.

"We heard him ask about your eyes. He's such a flirt."

I want to gag. The only thing he was stroking was his own ego.

"It's nice that he and Seth have become friends, especially after Seth called off his engagement," Marcie says, and it's filled with pity.

I dig for my phone, choosing not to participate in gossip. It's been clear from my first day that Marcie has a crush on Seth. She follows him around like a lost puppy, and he's either oblivious or ignores it.

"It was for the best," Marcie says as if I asked for details. "She wasn't right for him. She worked at that garage a few blocks away."

My ears snag on that tidbit as I tap my phone to check for messages again. I didn't know a woman worked at Slade's garage. I file the information away for later.

"She never spoke. It was like pulling teeth to get her to say anything. Can you even imagine?"

I hear the distaste in her tone and would bet a hundred dollars if I had it that she thinks she's right for him.

My phone buzzes in my hand, and my heart rate spikes, anticipating Mile's dropping the foreseen gavel with unpredictable consequences.

SLADE: Your car is all set.

My muscles relax when I see Slade's name instead.

ME: Can I pick it up after work?

SLADE: Yes

I hear voices as Seth and Junior come down the hall. Both Marcie and Robyn go quiet. Marcie shuffles papers while Robyn studies her inch-long, brightly painted nails.

Seth is a tall, lean, good-looking guy with a nice smile. He's always pleasant with clients and keeps more typical office hours.

"I'll be back in an hour," he tells Marcie. "If Clinton calls, tell him we need the document notarized."

"Will do," Marcie beams, her long black lashes fluttering.

"Just hold all my calls," Junior says, and they giggle.

"Hey, Sarah," Seth says, pushing out the door, but Junior stops.

"We should grab drinks sometime. I want to hear more about this biting problem."

If this weren't my place of employment, I'd inform him that spending just five minutes with him would require a level of intoxication that mimicked a coma.

"Yeah, no," I say simply, and I can feel Marcie and Robyn's jaws fall open.

"Let's go, Macavoy," Seth hollers from the other side of the glass door. Junior only grins, the kind that tells me this isn't the end.

Griffin enters with his briefcase and pulls on a long wool coat. "I'll be at the courthouse the rest of the afternoon," he tells Robyn as Marcie stares out the window, watching the men climb into Junior's sports car.

"Don't forget you're meeting with Carla Danvers first thing in the morning." Robyn's tone has returned to complete professionalism.

He nods, and I slip on my coat and follow him out the door to his black Lincoln SUV.

We make small talk on the way to the courthouse about my kids and settling into a new city, keeping everything light and away from anything deeply personal.

Inside the courthouse, he introduces me to Arlene Connor. She's a pretty woman in her late forties. I've only spoken with her on the phone while collecting information about the contested assets, but she appears sophisticated and poised.

Steve Connor, her ex, started a real estate company prior to their marriage. His attorney is arguing that all business investments and retirement assets should remain in his name. After twenty years together, this would leave Arlene, who supported his business ventures and stayed home to raise their kids, with nothing.

My stomach squeezes tight, reliving losing every financial resource while my dignity was stripped from me right before my eyes.

But it's why I'm here. I want to help those who are taken advantage of. Those who spend their days in the background, supporting their spouse as they achieve their professional dreams, only to find out it was a mistake to trust and rely on a life built entirely around them.

Court proceedings begin, and I listen intently as Griffin argues that the assets acquired during the marriage and their increase in value should be divided equally between the parties. It's supported by outlining Arlene's involvement in the business, which has been instrumental in the growth achieved over the years.

Griffin summarizes the assets and their value, explicitly pointing out the rental properties I discovered were recently purchased by Mr. Connor in conjunction with his brother, with Mr. Connor listed as the primary owner. I watch as the surprise hits the opposing attorney and his client. I want to smile, but I hold it back. It doesn't pay off to try to be sneaky.

The afternoon wraps up with the judge dismissing us, directing that he'll review all the information presented and make a ruling. Arlene smiles in relief as she shakes Griffin's hand and then mine.

As Mr. Connor exits the courtroom, he stops beside Arlene. "Sleeping with my best friend wasn't enough. Now, you want half of everything I built." He huffs a defeated laugh, shaking his head as he turns and walks away.

Arlene inhales sharply, but I watch the man dragging behind his attorney, shoulders slumped under the weight of the blow.

My eyes fall to the floor, searching for sense in what just happened. My gut coils with the shock of injustice—the one I assisted with.

A pit forms in my belly as we exit the courthouse. I don't know the details of this couple's marriage or what caused the destruction, but I can't help feeling blindsided by the realization that fighting for what is right might not be as clear-cut as I want it to be.

"My office will be in touch once I receive the ruling," Griffin states, and we part ways with Arlene in the parking deck and climb into his SUV.

"You did good finding those hidden rental properties. She'll be able to afford health insurance and retire comfortably."

Did I. . .do good? I'm not naive enough to think everything is as it appears. I know first-hand that things can vary drastically from a one-dimensional perspective. I've lived it many times over, and I'm currently hiding the true state of my situation.

In this case, I'm questioning the definition of doing good when it's clear there's so much more to be considered to determine if that's true.

My mind swirls, and I'm ready to go home. "Could you drop me off at the mechanic shop? It's about three blocks from the firm. My car is ready."

Griffin glances at me. "Cal's?" There's a slight intonation in his question that sounds skeptical or surprised, maybe.

I toss it aside. My brain is unable to dissect anything else at the moment. "Yes."

"Sure." He exits the parking deck. "So, it was your first day in court. What did you think?"

I stare out the windshield and ask the question floating on the surface. "Did you know Arlene had an affair?"

Griffin peeks at me, his brow furrowed. "I did. She told me when we had our first consultation."

I don't say anything, letting that roll around.

"Sarah, one of the things I've learned over the last thirty years is that there's no such thing as innocent and fair when it comes to divorce and settlement. As with most legal matters, it's often who can make the best argument."

He makes a right turn. "In this case, I think we proved Arlene was due those assets. It doesn't matter what happened personally between them. It's just sorting out how to divide what was once shared."

I tuck my arms in my lap, processing his words and wondering if it's callousness or factual—that right and fairness never really come into play at all.

It hits like a ton of bricks. "Do you ever feel like you helped the wrong team?" I ask bluntly, really wanting to know.

He laughs. "There is no good or bad, just people with something to lose. It's our job to help win back whatever we can."

Win. I wonder if there's ever truly winning in this. I think about Ollie and Frankie. No matter what happens, there's no winning for them.

But he's right. Sometimes, people really do have everything to lose. It's just. . .what if you're the one who helps take it all away?

I check my phone—still no message from Miles. My stomach sinks even further.

Griffin pulls into the garage lot, and I see my car parked in a spot at the far end. I gather my things, pushing the door open. He puts the car in park and hits the button, turning it off.

I glance at him.

"I'll be sure everything is set before I take off."

I tug the shop door open, and Griffin holds it, following me inside. The air smells like metal and oil, and the noise is piercing. Krissy sits on a stool, her shoes propped on the counter, with her phone in her hand.

The door bangs closed, and her eyes pop up to us. She smiles, but it falters slightly as she zeros in on the man behind me.

The sound dies off except for a radio, and the room suddenly stills.

"Hi," I say, glancing around the space for Slade but only seeing three other men staring back at me. "Uh, Slade said my car was done."

Krissy removes her feet from the counter and sits forward, her eyes moving back to me.

"It's ready," a deep voice strikes the stillness.

My gaze snaps to the big man standing just outside a dark hallway. His flannel shirt is rolled up to his elbows, revealing the intricate inkwork that covers his arms.

With his hat backward, I see the intense scowl pointed in my direction. Usually, I'd give him shit and watch him struggle to maintain that glower, but my emotional energy is depleted, and my sarcasm has run dry.

"Great," I say, wanting to make this quick so I can go home and snuggle my kids.

"Why are you here?" Slade asks in a low, demanding tone, but it's directed at my boss.

Griffin shifts next to me. "I'm just making sure Sarah's all set before I take off," he says matter-of-factly.

"Sarah will be fine. You can go now," Slade states in a direct order.

My eyes flick between them as they stare at each other in some kind of standoff. The weight of the entire room settles on me, and my body heats to a thousand degrees. Feeling warm and confined, I want to peel my coat off and maybe a layer of skin.

What in the ever-loving hell?

Griffin only nods, his attention moving to me. "I'll see you at the office. Thanks for your help today."

I force a small smile. "Thank you for the ride."

The door bangs closed, and the noise resumes. Krissy hops off the stool to help roll a set of tires to a vehicle.

I drop my bag and shed my coat before the hot flash sends me into an overstimulated rage.

"Everything ok?"

Free from my personal fabric-holding cell, I drag my eyes up to Slade's. Those green irises no longer hold a death wish.

"Yes." I shove my coat under my arm, contemplating asking what that little showdown was all about, but I've had enough today. "I'd really like to go home."

His eyes roam over my face. "You all right?"

I don't have any idea anymore, but I won't be getting into that here, so I nod.

His gaze lingers on my face as if he's thinking about calling my bluff, but then he reaches for my keys hanging on the pegboard.

I pull my wallet from my purse. "Do you have the invoice?"

He slides the paperwork from a slotted holder and hands it to me. I run through the charges for the oil change, wheel bearing replacement, and labor. The total amount is a fist to my already queasy stomach.

I hand him my credit card, and Krissy returns to the counter.

"How are those babies?" She leans, resting her chin in her hand.

"They're good. Ollie is working on his piloting skills, and Frankie is on the verge of climbing into the refrigerator." I try to smile, but it's weak.

"They're such cuties. I'm serious. If you ever need a sitter, I'd love to watch them. I'll give you my number." She pulls a Post-it from the pad and scribbles her information on it. "I'd rather play with kids than listen to these idiots." She waves her pen around the room.

"Thank you. I'll keep that in mind." I put the note in my purse.

"Also, I don't know if you're into sports, but we watch football on the weekends. If you're free, you should bring the kids over. It'll help limit the burping contests and unclaimed farting." She smiles.

Slade groans.

I laugh, and it feels good, like a reminder that hope still exists.

"I used to have Alex to hang out with, but she's off living the fairytale. So, please save me from having to deal with these numbnuts on my own. It'd be fun."

"You should get back to work," Slade grumbles.

Krissy rolls her eyes but pushes away from the counter. "Watch it, Stone Cold. You're lucky I'm here."

"Am I?" he retorts.

"Yep. If I weren't, you would've sunk your ship twice already." She skips to the raised car, and I hear snickers in the background.

Slade's shoulders slump as he hands me my card. "You should be good to go."

He holds out my key ring, pinched between his thumb and forefinger.

I extend my hand, and his eyes scan over the thin scab across my palm before he lets the fob fall into it.

"Thank you," I say. "Hopefully, no more issues." I really need that prayer to come true.

His eyes flick between mine. "You sure you're ok?" The gentleness in his tone presses against my vocal cords.

Not even a little bit.

I only nod because saying it out loud would lead to the kind of meltdown I'm not sure either of us is game for.

He holds my gaze like he wants to be sure, but if I've gotten to know this man at all over the past few weeks, he won't pry.

"I guess. . .I'll see you around, neighbor." I step away from the counter, feeling a bit strange that I won't see him in the morning.

The room feels quiet again as I turn, but I stop at the door. "Thanks again." I wave my key, and it's possible I see the slightest indentation of a dimple lying underneath that short, dark beard.

I push out the door into the cold evening air, hoping it will cool my skin and temporarily numb my mind.

I climb into my car, so happy to have my freedom back. I dig in my purse to call Roxie, needing her sass and humor to take away this shitty day before I go home. I tap my phone and stop.

> MILES: Sunday morning anchor on The Morning Show to start.
> MILES: I'll be flying out in a few weeks and will stop by on my return. This is a big move, Sarah. I suggest you reconsider things. You decide how this goes.

I breathe in and out, my stomach rolling into my throat. I rest my head on the steering wheel and close my eyes. Even though I knew this was coming, it's not what I needed today or ever.

I hear the threat in his words. He's right. I will have to decide how this goes.

I exhale slowly. It feels like every single thing is shifting rapidly around me. I don't know when the next collision will occur or what the aftermath will be. The unpredictability and uncertainty are terrifying, and I have no idea what I'm supposed to do about any of it.

I start my car and pull out of the lot. The only thing I know is that I need to get it together so that my kids aren't the ones who lose again.

CHAPTER 13

SLADE

"Do you have your own tools?"

His leg bounces, continuing to avoid all direct eye contact.

"Nah, man. Aren't those provided?"

I rest back in my chair. "How would you go about changing a timing belt?"

The kid's eyes flick to mine and then dart away as he twitches. There's silence except for the sound of the compressor.

I cross my arms over my chest. "You able to pass a drug test?"

That has him popping out of the chair. "I don't need this." He charges out of my office door.

I stand, following him out. He swipes an arm across the counter, sending the cup of pens flying. He rips the door open, and it slams shut.

"Another one bites the dust," Trig sings, taking a drink from his water bottle.

"What'd you say to piss this one off?" Carson pulls the air hose around the front of a van.

I pick up the pens scattered over the floor, ignoring their comments.

"All right. That's it." It's Wind's voice this time, but in a dry-ass tone I'm not sure I've heard before.

I set the pens back on the counter, and Wind approaches with his hands on his hips.

"It's been a week. One whole week of this. Any more of your passive aggressiveness, and I'm calling Alex."

I lean against the counter, crossing one ankle over the other. If he thinks that's a threat, he needs to think again. I wish Alex were here. We understand each other. There's no need for talking when we want to keep it all locked up inside until we're ready to face whatever it is. Plus, she'd have these cars moving in and out twice as fast.

"We can't handle much more of this kind of environment. It's hostile and unfit for constructive work. It's mentally unhealthy conditions."

I cock my head to the side. "Hostile?"

Trig screws the cap on his water bottle. "It's worse than usual. I mean, we're used to you barking orders and making demands, but this . . ." He swirls his bottle in a circle. "Mopey, calm, only moderately irritated state is alarming. We don't know how to work like this."

"It's depressing to watch." Wind scratches his neck. "Millie says you're emotionally detaching."

I hold very still, keeping the explosion of laughter that wants to tumble out along with a long string of foul words.

It's been a week since I've seen Sarah, and, dammit, I can't quit thinking about her. I miss our morning rides together, and I hate that. I want my mornings to go back to being routine and simple, where the only person I worry about is myself.

I might be a little quieter than usual. But I'm just keeping to myself and trying to figure out what to do about Sarah. Or really, the thoughts and feelings she's stirring that I haven't experienced in a very long time. Maybe ever. It's itchy and uncomfortable, and I'm trying to block it all out because I know these morons will read into it and want to dissect every last detail. I'm not doing that. So, I've kept my mouth shut and worked, needing to drown it out.

Carson checks the pressure on a tire and stands. "It's enough, man. We're calling an intervention."

"You are?" I scoff.

They stare at me.

"Yeah," Carson confirms. "We're finishing up here and going for beers. Any more of you like this," he points the nozzle at me, "and we'll be running for the door like that kid. It's weird, and this shit has got to stop."

Wind claps his hands together. "Let's go. Wrap this up, so we can get Slade's head out of his ass to see the sun is peeking out after years of darkness and shining too brightly for him to handle."

"What the hell? I'm not a groundhog."

Wind's eyebrows shoot up, and his eyes widen as he turns away.

They work while I figure out how to avoid discussing anything with them.

An hour later, I climb out of my truck in Crusin's parking lot because if I don't, these ladies will show up at my house, which would be worse. Krissy would get involved, and Brandon would have his glass to the wall, listening to the absolute bullshit this little show-and-share will entail.

I just need to get in, drink my beer while I appease these dickheads, and get out. I don't want to talk about feelings or depression or avoidance or any of the other big-ass words Millie is feeding Wind. I want to go home to my quiet house, where I don't have to listen or think about anything. Mostly, the woman across the street who somehow wiggled her way right underneath my decorated skin.

I tug open the door, and the bar is quiet for a Friday night. I spot the table where my friends sit, already laughing and sipping from their bottles.

"Glad you showed. You knew if you didn't, we'd find you." Carson tips his bottle back, hiding a grin like he knows this is taking every bit of my limited patience.

I pull a stool out, and Wind hands me a beer from the bucket. "Here. This will help."

I want to ask why he didn't invite Millie to moderate story hour, but I don't for fear he might actually say she's coming. I like Millie. She's nice and sweet, but I don't need her nose in whatever will go down here tonight.

I rest my arms on the table and sip my beer. If these fools think I have anything to say, they're wrong.

Carson sets his beer on the table. "Pull your phone out."

My eyes meet his, wondering if that bold tone is directed at me.

"Come on. Pull it out." He waves his fingers at me.

Trig and Wind stare me down as if they think I'm actually doing anything they say.

"If you don't, we'll text Krissy and call Alex. She said she was free tonight."

"Have you all lost your damn minds? What do you need my phone for?"

"It's time to grow a pair and message her." Trig leans forward, resting his forearm on the table. "Come on. We'll hold your hand."

"Who?" I play dumb. They are trying to call me out, but I'm not budging.

"Shit." Wind throws his arms in the air, his hands landing on the table, rattling our bottles. "See, we should have just shown up at his house. Then, we could have made him walk across the street and knock on her door."

I lean back, crossing my arms over my chest. "You can't make me do anything. I don't know what in the hell this is all about, but I'm two seconds from being done here."

"Fine. Have it your way." Carson pulls out his phone and taps the screen.

The ring blares from the speaker, and my gaze skirts the surrounding area to make sure everyone is far enough away not to be disturbed by their shenanigans.

"Hey, guys." Alex's voice comes through the speaker. "How's it going?"

"Not good," Wind says.

Lex laughs. "Is he there?"

"Yeah, he's here." Trig's dumbass smirk creeps across his mouth.

"Give him the phone," Alex demands, and Carson extends his phone to me.

I glare at him and take it, leaving my stool and heading outside where I can talk without the gossip girls eavesdropping.

"Hey," I say, putting the phone to my ear and pushing out the door into the peace and quiet.

"It sounds like you're having fun." Her underlying amusement makes me want to groan.

This is just what I need—five minutes outside, not talking to Alex about anything in particular, so I can go back in and tell these assholes goodnight.

"I've been meaning to call and see what you've been working on."

"Not much. Mark's schedule is insane, and with the girls, it's difficult to get any time in the garage."

"How are the girls?"

"Peyton and Ellie are happy being two and getting into everything. Bree is starting to talk about boys and makeup, and Mark is about to lose his shit over it."

I chuckle. "Tell him good luck when the boys begin texting and calling."

She pushes out a breath. "I'll have him call you. You know I'm no good at this girly stuff."

"Well, settle in. It never ends."

There are a few beats of silence, and I know what's coming. I exhale slowly, waiting.

"So, you want to tell me what's going on with you, or is this something we're not talking about because it's a big deal and lots of feelings are involved?"

"Nothing is going on."

She laughs. "Ok. Sooooo, your withdrawn and less-surly mood is a sudden behavioral shift that has nothing to do with the beautiful woman across the street to whom you secretly gifted new tires and brakes?"

Those narks.

I run a hand over my face. "No. And the tires weren't new. She's too smart for that. They're ten percent worn."

Silence. I check to be sure we're still connected.

My shoulders ease down, and I glance up at the sky. "She. . . I think money is tight. She has two kids, and her tires were down to the wear bar."

"Grandpa Cal would be proud of your ingenuity and generosity." I hear the smirk attached to that comment.

I learned from the best. Cal would have done the same damn thing.

"I seem to recall you asking me not all that long ago when enough is enough. I also believe it was you who told me it was time to quit running and hiding and finally go after what I want."

I huff out a laugh. "This is in no way the same thing. You'd been pining after Mark for years."

"But I was scared, and so are you." She drops that there and lets it dangle as if I might bite. Not happening.

She continues. "A lot is changing. Krissy is moving out, the garage is exploding with business, and there's a beautiful woman who might have finally cracked your hardass I-don't-need-or-want-anyone state."

My jaw clenches. "She hasn't cracked anything. I gave her a ride to work and helped her out a few times. It's nothing."

I pause because she knows this nothing feels like something, and I don't want it to. She sits tight, waiting for me to admit it.

I surrender to the one person who will get it. "She's . . .different."

"You know, it's ok if you liked doing those things for her or if you even *miss* doing them."

I roll my eyes, my breath creating a cloud in the cold air. "I don't miss shit. I'm getting back to my regular schedule."

"All right," I hear the annoyance roll through the phone. "Listen, you can deny this all you want. Hell, I denied needing and wanting Mark for eight years. There's a reason this chick has you moping around. It tells me she's different in the best way because there hasn't been a woman who's made you do a double-take in. . .well, ever. So, you need to quit being afraid and pull yourself from your sullen, depressed state and see what could be. You are too good a man, Slade, to reduce yourself to a life of self-imposed isolated loneliness."

She takes a breath. Alex is a woman of few words until she's not. "It's been long enough. Krissy is a grown woman, and it's time, man, for you to get a life. The one we both know you really want." She calls me on my shit and then lowers her voice. "Take it from me. What's on the other side of fear is *so* worth the risk."

My stomach squeezes tight, pushing my beer upward at just the thought of seeing what could be and losing everything I want to call mine.

I hear one of the girls begin to cry.

"I've got to go. Hang in there. Be patient with the guys. They love you."

I grunt.

"Oh, and Slade, just ask her out. I have a feeling it'll be ok."

She hangs up before I can shoot her confidence down.

I watch my breath billow in the air for a few long seconds before heading inside to the blabbermouths.

Alex isn't wrong. I closed myself off from the possibility of a relationship long ago. If I'm honest, it's not because I don't want one. It's just that you can give your entire self to someone, make plans, see the future, and then have it all ripped right out from under you as if none of it mattered at all.

I am afraid. I've been there and have absolutely no intention of ever being that fool again.

Inside, I slide back on my stool, and all laughter and conversation instantly die as three pairs of eyes settle on me.

I hand Carson his phone.

"So?" he asks as if I'll give him even the tiniest nugget of information about what Alex and I talked about.

"The girls are doing great."

Their heads fall back toward the ceiling with simultaneous groans, and I want to smile, but I hold it back.

"Are we ordering food or what?" Their gazes land back on me. "If not, I'm going home. I have *things* to consider." It's all they're getting.

One side of Trig's mouth lifts as Carson's arms cross over his chest.

"I knew it! I knew she'd get through that thick skull," Carson says as if he just won a bet.

"She didn't do shit." I adjust my hat and grab a menu.

"Ha." Wind claps Trig and Carson on the back. "He's back, boys. Now, we can help you adjust to life outside the cave."

"I'm not adjusting to anything. Nothing changes."

Carson's eyes peek at me out of the corner. "Yeah, right. You can be as sweet as you want to the girl next door, but to us, you'd better be the asshole you've always been."

"That won't be hard."

Carson throws his arms out to the side. "Man, it's about time. You've got to make room for the things you want. If you keep shutting everything and everyone out, you're going to push all the good out with the bad."

"I'm not making room for anything."

They all grin. "Hell yeah, you are. It might take time, but we've got you, man." Trig smacks my back.

"It's like a garden, bro," Wind says. "You've got to plant the seeds. Give it time and room for love to bloom."

The three of us look at Dr. Love.

"What in the hell?" Trig says, a beer halfway to his lips. "Are you snorting rose petals and packing a bow and arrow?"

The top of Wind's cheeks turn red above his beard, but he shrugs it off. "Millie has all these books about love languages and shit. There's good stuff in there. From what I can tell, these doctors know what they're talking about."

We all laugh as the waitress takes our order. I relay mine, and Carson lifts his chin at me.

"I'm proud of you."

"You all have lost your damn minds if you think anything is changing."

They glance at each other and then back at me.

I exhale. “I’m only thinking about it.”

They cheer, raising their beers before taking a drink.

Alex is right. It’s been a long time, and I’m scared. I’m scared to even think about spending time with Sarah or anyone. So, I’ll give it time and just see what happens.

CHAPTER 14

SARAH

"Mama, higher."

I push Ollie with one hand and Frankie with the other, alternating back and forth. The cool, fall air swooshes against my face and smells of rotting leaves and dirt. I shiver, but the sun is warm against my black leggings.

"Dat t-t-tickles my tummy," Ollie laughs and raises his arms like he's flying.

Frankie smiles and squeals as I pretend like I'm going to get her as she swings toward me.

"Do you want to go down the slide a few more times before we go home for lunch?"

"I don't want to g-go," Ollie whines as I let his swing slow.

"Bud, Frankie needs a nap, and if we stay too much longer, my fingers might fall off." I rub them together, missing my gloves, which are likely still on the counter.

"They won't fall off." Ollie scoots off the swing and drops to the ground.

"They might." I grab him and find his ribs through his coat with my numb fingertips. "And then the tickle monster will have to tickle you with toes instead."

He squeals, and I release him. He takes off, running toward the slide, and I pull Frankie from the swing.

"What about you, Love Bug? I bet you're getting hungry."

She claps her hands, and I put her on my hip to follow Ollie.

He climbs the stairs and goes down the short slide.

I've missed this. The freedom to take the kids to the library and the park whenever I want. It was only a couple of weeks without my car, but it felt like an eternity. It's funny how something as simple as transportation can make you realize how fortunate you are, even when it feels like so much is against you.

I set Frankie on the steps and let her crawl up. Ollie zooms past and up the swirly ladder. "One more time, and then we have to go."

Frankie makes it to the top and crawls toward the bridge. I scoop her up as Ollie zips down the slide.

"All right, you two. Let's go."

"Aw." Ollie stomps his foot. "Can we come back t-t-tomorrow?"

"We'll see, ok? Maybe we can rake the leaves while Frankie naps."

"Can I jump in them?" He takes my hand as we walk to the car.

"I don't know. There are so many; I might lose you in the pile."

He grins up at me. "Grover will f-find me."

At home, I throw chicken nuggets in the oven while Ollie and Frankie sing the alphabet along with the Muppets.

My phone buzzes on the counter, and I swipe to answer. "You're up already?"

Roxie groans. "Yeesss. My dad is stopping by to discuss an opportunity."

"Really?" I fill two sippy cups with water. "Sounds intriguing."

She moans. "Is there the stench of desperation in the air? It smells like another lame-ass attempt to pull me into the fold where I can be controlled and manipulated."

Roxie's family comes from a long line of wealth and superiority. They are the kind of people who will never understand that life can't always be wrapped up in neat, pretty bows. They live by formality and structure, expecting everyone to do the same and bend to their whims.

Roxie doesn't play by their rules and is determined to break the mold in every way possible. She made that loud and clear, starting with giving up a full ride to a prestigious college to manage the local bar.

"Do you have any idea what it's about?" I ask.

"No, but I'm sure it'll make me want to call the newspaper before running through the streets naked as payback." She yawns. "Tell me something good so I can focus on that while he's piling on the thick layers of family duty and disappointment."

"I got my car back," I say, living on that high for as long as possible.

"You're a free woman again! How does it feel to be released from buses and other people's cars?"

"A-mazing!!" I sing. "Except for the whole, I have to pay for the repairs thing."

"Yeah. That part really sucks, but let's not let it rain on our parade."

"Oh, for real. After this past week, I almost kissed my car when I saw it."

I hear her microwave beep. "What happened?"

"I told you about grocery shopping with Slade." My stomach stirs, reliving it.

"Sarah, people understand money can be tight, especially when you're working and attending school while being the best mom ever. It's a lot. You should be so damn proud of yourself."

I open the oven door to peek at the nuggets, thinking about reminding her that she's never known what it's like to hide your lunch at school because there's hardly anything in it, or had to choose between seeing the dentist and buying groceries. Some things others will never understand, and I'm glad for that.

"I had to ride with my boss to the courthouse."

"You got to go to court?" she asks with her mouth full. "How was it?"

I peek around the doorway at the kids. Ollie lies on his stomach, surrounded by airplanes, and Frankie is standing at the couch, bobbing up and down to the music. I smile.

"It was. . .ok."

"That doesn't sound very enthusiastic."

"I helped gather information on our client's assets, and I imagine she'll be awarded half of everything, including her ex's business investments and equity."

"Look at you already kicking ass and taking names."

"But then I found out she cheated with his best friend."

"It's like daytime drama. Tell me more."

"That's it really. It was eye-opening. Helped me see that maybe this lawyer stuff isn't always about justice or equality, but more. . .who's better prepared and makes a stronger argument."

I'm still sorting through that revelation and what it means.

"Then Griffin dropped me off to get my car, and it was the strangest thing. I think he and Slade have some kind of issue with each other."

"Sounds like two egos having trouble fitting into the same room. We should have thrown my dad in there to see who'd suffocate first."

The oven timer goes off, and I hit the button, grabbing a mitt. "I don't know. Slade is really blunt and. . .guarded, but not arrogant."

"Maybe your boss screwed him over or something."

I pull the nuggets out. "Maybe. All I know is, I'm happy to come and go of my own free will now."

"Have you heard from Miles?" Her water runs and shuts off.

It's the dreaded question.

"He's moving to New York and told me it's up to me how this goes."

"That narcissistic dick." The accuracy of her words makes me smile. "What do you think that means?"

I put three nuggets on Ollie's plate and two on Frankie's, cutting hers into little pieces.

"It means what it always means with him. It's a tactic to get me to *reconsider things*." I set the plates on the table. "He'll continue to withhold child support and issue some crazy demand I'll have to meet in order for him to actually pay it." I fill my cheeks with air and blow it out. "He said he's visiting in a few weeks. I guess I'll find out then."

"Ugh. Can I be there? I'll punch him in the throat and then take a sickle to his lying, cheating balls. I want to see him go on air after that."

"At this point, I don't want anything from him. We're getting by, but I have to know what this move means for Ollie and Frankie. I owe it to them."

"Maybe his moving is for the best." I hear the tentativeness in her statement and can't say that I haven't thought the same thing.

"Yeah."

"Sarah, this might be your chance to really move on. You need to be free from him and his manipulation. All he does is use Ollie and Frankie as pawns in his game. You're a really good mom. You'll do whatever is best."

My throat tingles a little. "Thanks, Rox."

The doorbell rings. "I gotta go. I'll be down for Thanksgiving but can only stay the night. Squeeze those kiddos for me."

We hang up, and I call Ollie for lunch. Grover is the first in the kitchen, ready to mop up whatever hits the floor. Frankie drops to her knees, her arms and legs moving as fast as they can. I scoop her up and kiss her cheek, knowing I'd do absolutely anything for them.

"Lunch and then naptime, Love Bug." I strap her into her seat.

"Can we go outside?" Ollie asks, biting a nugget in half and dunking it in ketchup.

Grover's ears perk at the O-word.

"After I get Frankie down, ok?" I watch her squish the banana between her fingers as she chews a small piece of chicken.

Ollie dances, sitting on his knees, and a giant glob of ketchup lands on his chest. "Ah, nuts."

I swipe the glob with a washcloth and toss it in the sink. "Here. I have to start the laundry." I hold one sleeve, and he pulls his arm out, tugging it over his head as he shoves an overflowing spoon of applesauce in his mouth.

I get the basketful of dirty clothes from my room and place it on my hip to carry it to the basement.

When I open the door, I immediately smell—

"Shit!"

"Mama, you can't say dat!" Ollie hollers.

I switch the light on and stare at the glistening water spread over the concrete floor below, resting against the bottom step. Oh. My . . .

I drop the basket and descend the stairs, stopping on the second-to-last step. I glance around the unfinished space. Thankfully, I cleaned out all of the junk when I moved in. A few small boxes float on the six inches of water, but the bottom of the washer and dryer are submerged.

No, no, no no, no!

I run up the stairs, hoping Google can tell me what in the hell I'm supposed to do. I find numbers for local plumbers and dial the first one. We have a brief conversation involving lots of questions and a warning not to step into the water. It ends with astronomical emergency rates and an iffy promise to call me when he's finished with his current job.

I want to scream.

"Mama, I'm done."

I turn, and Ollie sits shirtless with ketchup smeared over the corners of his mouth.

I stare at him. *What do I do?*

"Go get a shirt on, buddy." I kick the basket of clothes out of the way and close the basement door to be sure Grover doesn't go down.

"Hurry, Ollie." I push him toward his room.

Frankie drinks the last of her applesauce, and I grab a washcloth to wipe up the mess.

"Mama, can we go outside now?" Ollie's shirt is on backward, but it'll do.

"Get your shoes and coat on." I pull Frankie from her booster, leaving the food on the table.

I slip on my shoes, realizing I have no socks, but whatever.

I tug Frankie's coat on, and Ollie pops up off the floor with his shoes actually on the right foot.

"Come on." I fling the door open, really needing him to be home.

CHAPTER 15

SLADE

"Aw, come on!"

I down the last of my beer as the college quarterback peels himself off the ground.

"This is embarrassing." Trig stands from the couch and marches into the kitchen. "Who needs another beer? I'll put a pizza in the oven."

"Can you make pepperoni this time?" Krissy hollers from her spot on the floor where she's painting her nails.

"I thought you had a date or something?" Trig hollers back.

She tips the bottle of remover upside down on a cotton ball. "I do, later, but I'm hungry now."

"How about you put that shit away? The fumes are damaging my lungs." Wind waves his hand through the air from one end of the sectional. "I think we could light the air on fire."

"Oh, quiet. I'll be done in a minute." She tosses a cotton ball to the side. "Where's Millie? You wouldn't talk like that if she were here." Krissy eyes him.

"She's at a bridal shower but wants to know when you're moving into the townhouse."

"You signed a lease?" Carson asks from his spot on the couch behind her.

She twists to glance at him. "Yeah. I can move in on the first of December." She returns to her nails, and Carson takes a pull of his beer.

"Why didn't you have Carson walk through with you?" I mentioned it to her at least twice.

She shrugs one shoulder. "You guys have been super busy." She screws the cap on her polish and climbs to her feet. "Besides, I'm certain Carson has better things to do than inspect rentals." She glances at him before heading into the kitchen.

A commercial blares, and I push out of the recliner, following her to toss my bottle in the trash and grab another.

There's a knock on the door.

"Who's that?" Krissy asks as I step out of the kitchen to find out.

I open the door, and Sarah stands there, holding Frankie as Oliver hops up and down the cement steps.

"Hey." I pull the door open wider.

"Thank God you're here." She blows a long strand of hair out of her face, her cropped sweatshirt bunching at the waist of her leggings. "I don't know what to do."

I frown. "You ok?"

She huffs out a laugh. "I have about six inches of water in my basement."

"What?"

Her shoulders drop. "My basement is flooded, and I don't know what to do."

Oliver's hopping halts, and he stares up at me.

"Oh, that's not good," Wind says over my shoulder.

"Let me grab my boots." I leave her with Wind for the moment.

"Well, aren't you a little cutie," I hear him say, and assume he's talking to the baby.

"Want some help?" Carson stands in the doorway of the kitchen.

"Yeah."

We both slip on our boots, and Wind and Trig follow suit.

"I can come over and watch the kids for a bit," Krissy tells Sarah.

I meet her in the front yard, pacing. "Do you know where it might be coming from?"

Those eyes tell me if she knew, she'd be doing something about it. "I don't think it's a pipe. Could be a problem with the mainline or a backup."

We start toward her house. "What'd you do? Google it?"

Her head whips in my direction, and she stops, her hand moving to her hip. "Are you teasing me right now?" There's that twinkle in her blue eye. "*This* is the time you choose to actually have a sense of humor?"

I'm not sure if she really expects me to answer that, so I stay quiet as Carson and Trig talk to Oliver about cars.

Her chin lifts a little. "For your information, I did. Then, I called a plumber who was only moderately helpful and told me to 'sit tight' while he dug himself out of a literal pile of crap."

"Who did you call?"

Krissy sweeps by and holds out her hands to take Frankie. The little girl leans toward her, and she lifts her in the air.

Sarah's arms cross over her chest, her head falling to the side. "Samsons."

Carson and Wind groan behind me, and her eyes skirt to them.

"Did you give him your address?" It comes out rougher than I intend, and her shoulders roll back. "Call him back and tell him you've found someone else. He's not coming here."

Her brow scrunches, not caring for my direct order.

"Everything ok over there?"

Our gazes shift to my neighbor, standing on the other side of the fence, stroking his rat.

"Take your wiener inside, Brandon!" Trig hollers. "This doesn't involve you!"

Ollie giggles. "He has a wiener."

Sarah runs a hand over her face, giving it her all not to smile, and something in my chest flutters like a damn butterfly.

I watch her shoulders slump with the weight of every shitty thing, even if I don't know what they are.

"I have to have a dry house and running water," she says quietly.

My eyes trace over her face, hearing the exhaustion in her tone. "That might be a while."

She huffs out a laugh. "I know. That's why I need a plumber—"

"He's not coming here."

Her shoulders rise to the occasion as her spine lengthens.

"He's a prick and a—"

"Great." She throws her hands in the air. "I'm used to that. If he can get the water out of my basement and fix whatever the hell is leaking so I can feed and bathe my kids, then I can deal with one more asshole."

Something about Sarah coming a little unraveled sends waves of warmth to my cold-blooded insides. I try my damnedest not to smile, but I can't.

"Oh, for real." Her head falls back as if begging the sky for patience, and the hair falling out of her ponytail catches in the light breeze.

"Carson, you and Trig run and get a pump and hoses from the shop," I order, still watching Sarah. "Wind, see how many fans you can scrounge up."

The three men head to their trucks.

Sarah's attention falls back on me.

"Call Samson and tell him not to bother."

"Listen, I can't—"

"We'll turn off the main supply and get the water out to see what's going on, but you'll have to find somewhere else to stay until the problem is fixed."

I step around her to pull my toolbox from the bed of my truck.

"Uh. . .what now?"

There's a level of panicked sarcasm in her tone that tugs at my gut, so I keep on marching to my truck and focusing on a problem I can solve.

I start toward her house but stumble, almost falling flat on my face, when I hear Krissy's voice.

"It's ok. You can stay with us."

"No," Sarah and I say in unison.

I have avoided this conversation for the last two hours, hoping the idea would disappear as if it had never been mentioned. But I should know better with Krissy.

She grabs my arm with some kind of superhuman strength and hauls me to the living room. The dog follows, sitting at our feet.

"They cannot stay with us," I growl-whisper.

"Why not?" Krissy hisses back.

"Because."

"Because why?" There's an amused dare in her tone that makes my head want to explode.

The little instigator knows why, and she's intent on making me say it.

She backs off, a smartass smirk appearing.

I cannot have this woman in my space. My actual sacred personal space where I'm still trying to figure shit out. Shit, that might actually have to do with her!

"You need this," Krissy says calmly and quietly as if she's suddenly a therapist.

The guys and I have spent the last two hours pumping water out of the basement to find that the water main running in from the street is either clogged or damaged by a tree root.

After a phone call to the city, it could be Monday before someone is available to inspect it. Until then, the water is off, and the basement will be drying out to prevent mold from growing.

What I need is a cold shower and to forget the sound of Sarah's panicked tone, as well as the tight-ass leggings she's wearing and the sliver of skin that keeps peeking out from under her short shirt.

I run a hand over my face to gather my defenses.

"They cannot stay with us. We are neighbors, not BFFs."

She cocks her hip, her hand landing on top as if she's loading a weapon. I do not need whatever is coming.

She leans into me. "Look around," she whispers forcefully as if she's hit her limit.

I glance around the sparse space with a couch and a rocking recliner. A small collection of toys is scattered about the floor, and a stack of books sits on the corner of the fireplace.

"She was riding the bus. She clearly doesn't have any family locally. You're really gonna make those two kids live out of a hotel for however long it takes for the city to get someone out here?"

She stares at me, reaching down to pet Grover with one hand while she waits for an answer. I remain silent, not giving her the satisfaction of her guilt trip.

"That's what I thought." She points at me. "Now, put your Polly Pissy attitude away and get ready to have some fun. It's been way too long, Stone Cold. Whether you will ever admit it or not, you need this. You have to see that there's life outside the black hole you've been living in. It's time to step into the sun and see that good things can happen, even to a crusty old crab like you."

She spins as if this is the end of the conversation, but stops and turns back. "And don't think for one second you're going to just live at the garage these next few days. You will be a present and a hospitable host." She grins. "Looks like we'll finally have a dog."

She turns for the kitchen while I inhale deeply and let it out. Grover stares up at me, his ears perked.

"If you shit in my house . . ."

His butt pops off the floor, nudging his nose at my hand, his tail wagging.

"Who wants to have a sleepover?" Krissy asks in the kitchen.

"Me!" Oliver yells.

I join the crowd in the kitchen. All three guys are huddled near the back door, avoiding direct eye contact, but the fatass smirks on their faces tells me they think this is fucking hilarious.

Carson risks it and points at himself, makes a heart shape with his hands over his chest, and then points at me.

I glare at him, making it very clear that the next time we are out of the presence of women and children, I will knock that grin right off his pretty boy face.

They snicker, and Krissy sits to make grand plans with Oliver and Frankie.

Sarah leans against the counter, her face down, scrolling on her phone.

I take a deep breath, feeling a little dizzy and like I've lost my damn mind. "You should gather whatever you'll need for the next few days." It comes out low and weak. "We'll help you carry it over."

Sarah's head pops up, her eyes wide. "Uh . . . Um . . . I . . ."

I'm glad I'm not the only one having trouble with this.

"M-m-mama, can we s-stay with Swade and Kissy?" Oliver stands on his chair.

Sarah's eyes flick to mine again as if she's asking if I'm for real.

My gut squeezes tight, and I clear my throat. "What do you think about heading over and watching some football?"

Krissy grins, and I'd really like to flip her off.

"I d-d-don't know how to p-play football?" Oliver's chin dips.

"That's all right, little man," Carson says. "Get your shoes on. We'll eat pizza and teach you."

Oliver looks at Sarah, and she offers him a small smile. He jumps off the chair, and Krissy unhooks Frankie from her seat.

"We can take the kids over while you pack," Krissy says as if this is one big slumber party.

Sarah inhales and lets it out as if she, too, is surrendering. Her eyes meet mine again.

Krissy said I need this. What I need is baby steps. Not this woman moving into my house, where our lives fully intertwine.

The door clicks closed, and Sarah and I are left in silence.

Her gaze drifts up to mine. "You sure about this?" The hesitation in her question rubs against every one of my nerves, standing on edge.

I nod once, and she laughs as if she knows it's a complete lie. It is because the only thing I'm one hundred percent sure of is that I'm very afraid. I'm scared of a lot of things, but the fear that hits the hardest is what if, once they are in my house, I don't want them to leave?

CHAPTER 16

SARAH

It's fine. Everything will be fine.

My brain laughs while my stomach hits the dying grass as I haul my life across the street in a duffel bag, backpack, and laundry basket. The big guy next to me is carrying an equal load, while Grover trots beside him, excited for the adventure.

He barks at Brandon, loitering in his driveway and pretending to walk his tiny dog, but watching the reality show taking place on the other side of his fence.

Breathe. Just breathe because what else am I supposed to do?

I have no money and nowhere else to go. The only thing I have is an emergency credit card, which I cannot afford to load up with thousands of dollars' worth of hotel charges that will take me the next decade to pay off.

I grip the basket tighter, trying to strangle my anxiety and calm my desperate mind so I can think.

Smart. I'm smart and resourceful. Just think, Sarah.

But that's what I've been doing for the past thirty minutes while grabbing the necessities. Nothing. I've got nothing.

"If you need anything else, we can run over later." Slade pushes his front door open, and Grover rushes in to inspect.

I step inside, and Trigger, as I now know him, stands to grab the clothes basket from under my arm. Ollie sits beside Carson, almost on top of him, with a plate of potato chips on his lap.

"Mama, they gots ch-chips." He smiles, nibbling the edge of one.

Krissy smiles, rocking in the recliner with Frankie passed out on her chest. "She didn't last long." She runs a hand up and down Frankie's back.

I survey the clean, tidy space.

What in the hell am I doing?

I force out a slow breath, adjusting the backpack strap on my shoulder.

"Where do you want this?" Trigger asks.

"Upstairs. The room on the right," Slade says, bending to unlace his boots.

I kick off my shoes as he picks up the diaper bag and the Pack 'n Play. I follow him up the stairs to a room with a queen bed.

The room is plain, with gray walls and white trim. The only decor is the three framed sketches of classic cars on the wall. Trig sets the basket on the floor and returns downstairs.

"Do you need help with this?" Slade's hand rests on the travel crib.

I shake my head. "No, I got it. Thanks. I'll get it set up so Krissy can put Frankie down."

He nods and turns for the door. I drop onto the edge of the bed and close my eyes.

How did I get to where my kids and I are staying in a stranger's house? Well, maybe he's not a complete stranger, and Krissy lives here, so—

"Sarah."

My eyes pop open, and he stands in the doorway looking at me like . . .

"You ok?" Slade's low voice snaps me out of my momentary silent meltdown.

I don't think so. "Yeah."

His lips press together, seeing straight through me. "Have you eaten today?"

I push my lips to the side, trying to remember if and when I ate.

"Get that set up and then come down. The guys brought food, and Wind is making pizza." The bossy man doesn't move, his gaze holding mine. "Everything is ok."

I pull in air, feeling my lungs relax at his words as if they believe him.

He leaves, and I take another deep breath, my eyes and throat burning, so sick and tired of just trying to survive.

Everything is ok.

Maybe if I keep hearing his words, it will somehow be true.

I set up the crib, and Krissy carefully lays Frankie in it. I place her Lambie beside her.

"I'm glad you're here," Krissy whispers, her gaze on Frankie. There's something in her soft tone I can't identify. "He's growly but harmless." She pauses, running her fingertips over the edge of the crib. "He raised me after our mom died. I give him a hard time, but he didn't have to, you know?"

I'm shocked still as she walks to the door.

"I have to get ready for a date, but I'll be home later tonight. Help yourself to anything in the bathroom. Towels, soap, tampons . . . It's in the closet just outside or under the sink."

I stare down at Frankie for a moment, thinking about Slade raising Krissy. She's right. He didn't have to take that on, but he did. It makes me wonder what else is hiding underneath all that protective gruffness.

I close the door and head downstairs to figure out what this will be like. I stop at the bottom. Carson and Trig are on the couch with Grover sprawled out between them. Slade is now in the recliner with Ollie sitting on his leg, lining up his airplanes on the armrest, and telling him about each one.

"The pizza is done." Wind peeks his head out of the kitchen, flour dusting his shirt. "Ol said he likes cheese. Is that ok with you?" he asks me.

I nod. "That's great. Thank you."

Slade lifts him to the floor. "Come on, partner. Let's get some pizza."

Ollie's plane takes off from the arm of the recliner and zooms through the air. Slade crosses to the kitchen, and I follow him.

I detest accepting handouts or receiving help I cannot afford to repay. "I should go get snacks and—"

He opens the refrigerator and reaches in. "We have plenty. What do you like?" He turns around with a bottle of water in one hand and a beer in the other.

I take the water. "I'm not picky."

His eyes flick between mine, searching for the truth. "Help yourself to anything."

Wind runs the cutter through the pizza, and Slade grabs a plate, handing it to me.

"Swade, watch dis." Ollie's plane lands on the table, skidding to a halt before running off the edge.

"All right, Maverick. You asked for cheese." Wind places a plate with a small slice of pizza on the table.

"I'm not M-Mavwick. I'm Owiver." Ollie slides onto a chair. "Swade, sit next to me and show me dat trick again."

Slade fills his plate with pizza and sits beside Ollie, but those dark eyebrows raise under the rim of his hat, waiting for me to get food.

I let my head drop to the side but take my plate to the counter lined with bags of chips, dip, veggies, a crockpot with meatballs, and Wind's pizza.

I put some veggies and a couple of meatballs on my plate.

"Wind, we need jalapeno poppers," one of the guys hollers from the living room. "This game requires more bacon."

"Do you always spoil these guys?" I slide a piece of pizza onto my plate.

"We take turns. Slade is grilling next week, but cooking is my therapy. It's the only way I can put up with these assssss-dudes."

Slade snorts behind me. "Maybe Sarah can make cookies."

I slowly rotate to look at him, but he's only shoving a piece of pizza in his mouth. Those green eyes avoid mine, and I feel the tension in my body fade.

"I love to bake, too," Wind says, sprinkling cheese on another pizza.

I carry my plate to the table and sit across from Slade and Ollie. "You know, I can actually bake."

"Mama makes the b-best cookies," Ollie says, and I smile in satisfaction.

"Really. Is that because they look like—" I kick his leg under the table, and the man smiles.

He freaking smiles, and it's so unexpected it chases all my nerves right out the door. I stare at him and the dimple I've now confirmed exists.

"Who's making cookies? I need one." Krissy steps into the kitchen, and I have to force my gaze away from Slade's unforeseen playfulness.

She's wearing a long-sleeved top, short skirt, tights, and riding boots. She's beautiful, and I'm reminded of the days when I used to look cute.

"What, your boyfriend won't splurge for dessert?" Carson asks, sliding by her to get to the snacks.

"He would. But I'll never pass up a bonus cookie," Krissy says, grabbing her coat from the hook by the back door.

"You look beautiful," I say.

"Thanks." She smiles, her bright lips setting off her short, dark bob. "Don't wait up, party people."

"Be careful, Kissy," Ollie says, wiggling in his seat.

"Yeah, be careful," Carson says, passing her on his way back to the living room.

There's something in his tone, and her eyes track him all the way into the other room as she settles her purse across her body.

Huh.

She winks at Ollie. "I will, buddy. I'll see you tomorrow. Ok?"

He nods, and she leaves.

The guys groan from the living room, and Wind joins them to watch the replay.

I pop a carrot in my mouth just as I hear Frankie's cry.

I leave Ollie to tell Slade about his Hot Wheels collection. After changing Frankie's diaper, I return to find my plate of food still waiting for me.

Wind cuts a piece of pizza for Frankie into extra-small pieces, and Grover joins us, anticipating the remnants.

When we're finished, I spread a few toys on the floor and sit with her as Ollie bounces between the guys, talking about airplanes and football. Frankie sits in the middle of the floor, her bright eyes bouncing around the room, trying to decide how she feels about it all.

Me too, baby girl. Me too.

The silence is calming, but the space is unfamiliar. I kiss Ollie and run a hand over Frankie, then tiptoe down the stairs, peeking around the corner toward Slade's room at the back of the house. All is dark and quiet.

I switch on the kitchen light, setting my textbook and computer on the table. At home, I'd make a cup of tea and turn on some soft music, but here, I'll stick with water and silence, hoping not to wake Slade.

Grover trots down the stairs, his nails clicking against the vinyl floor. He stops in the doorway, inspecting, and then plops at my feet. I reach down and pet his head, knowing he's as aware of the strange environment as I am.

The guys hung around most of the evening. Wind was the first to leave when his girlfriend called. When I told Ollie it was time for a bath, he refused until Trig and Carson left. They were sympathetic and took off not long after.

I heard the TV while I read to the kids and sat with them until they fell asleep, but now the house is still, and I wonder if Slade is sleeping or if he's hiding now that we're here alone.

I'd be happy to do the same, except I need a few hours and some light, if I even have a chance at still passing my courses.

I open my textbook and then my computer, hoping to get through a couple of chapters and the assignments due.

I make it through a few pages when I hear a car, and then the back door squeaks open. Krissy removes her coat and boots.

"Hey," she whispers. "What are you doing?"

She opens the refrigerator and scans the shelves, pulling out a slice of leftover pizza and placing it on a paper towel. She joins me at the table, not bothering to warm it up.

"Studying."

She frowns, taking a bite. "For what?"

"I'm inching my way toward a bachelor's degree."

She pulls back, covering her mouth with her hand as she chews. "What? Aren't you a lawyer?"

I smile. "Not yet. I'm a paralegal."

"Seriously? I thought . . ." She doesn't finish her statement, picking the onion off the top of the pizza.

I rest my hands on my book. "I've always wanted to be, but sometimes life has different plans." Her gaze lifts to mine. "How was your date?"

She weighs her head from side to side. "Ok. I spent most of the night with friends." She pauses. "He's a doctor and is on call. We had dinner, but he got called in during the middle of it. He's . . . I don't know. He's smart, really good-looking, but also kind of stuck up." She laughs. "He thinks it's ridiculous I still live with my brother."

"What do you think?"

"He's scared of him." She smiles, but I wait for the real answer, if she's willing to share it.

Krissy is beautiful and funny. Watching her with the kids, I know she's kind and sweet. Being only twenty-four, she was young enough when she lost her mom that it left a large, gaping hole. One that no matter how much a big brother might love her, he could never fill.

She shrugs. "I want to find someone who cares about me and not where I live or who I live with. Someone willing to stand up to my brother because he doesn't give a shit if Slade has an issue with it. A guy that would do anything for me."

"You're smart to want those things and not to settle for anything less."

Her gaze lands on mine. "What about you? You said you've always wanted to be a lawyer. What happened?"

I take a second to sort out how to answer that question while she takes another bite. "I fell for a guy who gave a lot of shits about everything *but* me."

"Sounds like a real winner," she says through a mouthful.

I laugh. "I was young and had worked hard to get where I was going, but I deviated from my plan when a guy promised me the things I longed to hear. It took way too long for me to realize those promises were more about him than they ever were about me or us."

Her shoulders fall. "I'm sorry."

I shake my head, offering a small smile. "I got the best things I'll ever do out of the deal, so . . ."

"What now?" She chews her pizza.

I inhale and let it out. "Now, I work my ass off to get my life back or at least one that resembles something I'm proud of."

Her lips push to the side in sympathy. "I'm scared of never finding someone who will actually love me the way I want them to." Her words are soft, as if she's never admitted that out loud. "At least, the one I want to love me that way."

I watch her and see so much of my younger self. Hardworking, determined, smart, and independent. She has her whole life ahead of her, but I understand the desperate need to feel loved, wholly and completely, forsaking all others.

"You know, I think if we're patient and take our time, the right person will come at the right time."

She wipes her mouth with the paper towel, thinking.

I shrug. "Or maybe they've been there all along and are just waiting for the timing or circumstances to be right."

She rests her chin in her hand. "You still believe that?"

I think about it. "I do. I want that kind of love for my kids, so I have to believe that."

"What about for you?"

I fill my cheeks with air and blow it out. "I don't know. I'd like to think so. This single parenting shit is hard."

She laughs.

I tell her what I really still believe. "I think it's all about paying attention and not making excuses for someone who doesn't treat us the way they should or when things start to shift in a direction that doesn't feel right."

I pull at the edges of my textbook, curling the pages back with my fingertips. "It's not something that can be rushed. It's finding someone you know so well, all of their flaws and annoying habits, their bad moods and silly obsessions, that even on days when they make you so mad you can't stand to look at them, you still want to lie in bed with them at night because tomorrow is a new day and they're your partner. The person who sees you at your absolute worst and is still there, choosing you despite it."

She stares at her pretty nails, taking them in. "I wish that for you."

"I wish that for you more," I say, meaning it with everything I am.

She leans across the table and hugs me. "Whoever that dickface was really didn't deserve you."

I laugh.

"I'm really glad you're here." She releases me and tosses her crumpled paper towel in the trash. "I'll let you get back to it. I've got to work tomorrow night, so I'm going to bed."

We say good night, and I get back to reading, but my head swirls with the memories that led me to exactly here.

I don't know what I see for my future. It's difficult to see anything other than the next five minutes because each one seems so damn hard. I'm treading water, barely able to keep from drowning.

Maybe it shouldn't be this hard. Perhaps I've made all the wrong decisions and keep making them. This is my punishment.

I run a hand over my face. I can't think about the future when my house currently has no running water, Miles is moving and up to something, and I have two courses I'm about to fail. That doesn't include my bank account being down to triple digits and trying to anticipate where the next blow will come from.

I pick up my highlighter and jump back in, but my mind is stuck on everything but statistics.

I used to be like Krissy—ready to take the world on and rise above my circumstances. Now, I don't even recognize the woman in the mirror who stares back at me. I'm not sure who she's supposed to be.

I'd made a plan to never be in this position. I was working my way to everything I dreamed of and kicking ass while doing it.

I want that again. I want to know I can do it—stand on my own two feet and take care of my children.

I rest my head in my hands and close my eyes. I did that once. I just need to find that girl again. The girl who was determined and capable and didn't back down, even when no one else believed.

The only problem is that my dreams are a bit fuzzy, and the one who's in doubt. . .is me.

My stomach folds into a knot, and I rest my head on my book. I'm really scared that what I'm chasing so hard shouldn't be the same things anymore.

CHAPTER 17

SLADE

I roll over on my back and punch the pillow a few times, trying to get comfortable. I stare at the ceiling, listening to the soft, muffled voices filter in from the other side of the house.

I could be watching a movie or the sports recap. Instead, I'm lying in the dark, listening to make sure Krissy gets home and wondering what tomorrow will be like with Sarah and the kids.

Maybe I'll go to the shop and get a head start on the week.

As Sarah packed up her things, she asked me four times if I was sure about her staying here, as if she was expecting me to change my mind. Or maybe she wanted me to.

I didn't like it—that she was worried about staying here.

When I told her everything was fine, I wanted her to know it—to believe me.

This evening was fine. It was more than fine. Ollie sat with me, watching the game, and I told him everything I knew about planes. Sarah sat with Frankie, reading books and stacking colorful blocks so that she could knock them over. Her giggles filled the space when Sarah made exaggerated crashing sounds. Then, of course, Trig and Carson joined in.

But now, I wonder what she's thinking. Is she sitting in the kitchen, telling Krissy she couldn't sleep, and this was a huge mistake?

I slap a hand over my face. *What the hell am I becoming?*

This is a neighborly gesture. She's staying for two, three days tops. That's all this is, and then I can get back to focusing on Krissy moving out and hiring another mechanic.

The voices die down, and I hear the stairs creak as they ascend. The silence is worse as I try to calm my mind and relax my body. After another wasted thirty minutes, I throw the sheet off and sit on the side of the bed.

I go to the bathroom and decide that if I can't sleep, I might as well review inventory logs or start on payroll. I walk down the dark hall and find the kitchen light on.

I stop in the doorway, Grover's head rises quickly from the floor, and he stares at me from Sarah's feet. Her head rests on her arm on top of her open textbook with a highlighter still in her hand.

She looks peaceful. Beautiful.

I step into the kitchen and stand over her. Her long hair is a messy pile on top of her head, but loose strands fan across her cheek. I carefully brush the hair out of her open mouth, watching my fingers glide along her soft skin.

She pops out of the chair, almost knocking it over, and I grab her by the waist to keep her from falling with it. Grover lets out one quick bark and then settles with his tail wagging as if this is a new game.

"Holy shit," she huffs, her eyes wide in alarm.

I maintain hold of her as she glances around the kitchen, her chest moving in and out quickly, and then her gaze meets mine. She pushes out a breath, wipes the corner of her mouth with her sleeve, then . . .

She tips forward, her forehead falling gently against my chest, her hands fisting my T-shirt. I. Don't. Move. I inhale the scent of sunshine and ocean, feeling the warmth of her skin through the thin layer of cotton.

"You scared the absolute shit out of me. What are you doing?" Her hands tug on my shirt.

"I was. . .getting something to drink and gonna work for a while."

Her head falls back to look at me. "Now?"

I try not to smile, but it's difficult. "You need to go to bed and get some sleep."

Her hands release my shirt, and I drop mine from her waist. "You're bossy even in the middle of the night."

I think about asking her if her sassy mouth ever stops running, but I decide that might lead me to do something I'm still fully contemplating.

Her sleepy eyes stare into mine as if she's waiting for me to agree.

One side of her mouth curls up. "I have a feeling underneath that strict, commanding regime is a reckless rebel just itching to throw all caution to the wind."

Those tantalizing eyes crease in the corners as they study mine. She has no idea the battle beginning to wage within me.

She reaches up and pats me in the center of the chest. "It's ok, Wildcat. Your secret is safe with me." She grins.

My hands ache to pull her right back to me and find out what her mouth feels like against mine. I exhale slowly, not having any idea what I'm doing.

She twists and closes her book and computer, wrapping them against her chest.

I haven't moved. I'm still locked in whatever the hell this woman is doing to me.

Her eyes fall to my bare arm and the ink that covers it. Her head cocks to the side as if she's observing a rare painting.

I cross my arms over my chest. "I charge viewing fees. Extra for them to be ogled." There we go. This is my house, and I'm coming back. She has not won.

She makes a snorting noise. "I was just considering if a tattoo would help me pass statistics."

Her eyes fall to my tattoo of Newton's third law again.

Her lips move to the side, hiding a smile as she steps around me. "I'll remember the fee and who to come to if I have to take physics. You can text me a quote for borrowing your arm." She and that sassy smile disappear around the doorway.

My eyes roll to the ceiling as my fists uncurl, and my body stands down from everything it was tempting me to do.

I run a hand through my hair.

"Slade," she whispers.

I twist and see her head peeking around the trim. "Good night. Don't let the bugs bite."

This was a fucking terrible idea.

I pull a bottle of water from the refrigerator and guzzle it, knowing that if I'm going to maintain any semblance of my simple life and the comfort it provides, I need to get to the shop early in the morning and stay there.

I scoop coffee grounds into the filter and press the button. The sky beyond the small kitchen window is beginning to brighten.

If I hurry through the shower, I can hopefully make it out the door before Sarah wakes up. I need space to think and process, and that cannot happen when I'm in close proximity to the blue-brown-eyed woman upstairs. She takes all of the strict rules I've lived by and shreds them to freaking pieces with one smartass remark after another. It wouldn't matter, except she pinpoints my weak spots and drills right through—all of the fractures no one else seems to see.

The coffee pot spurts and hisses, and I turn—

Oliver stands in the doorway, rubbing one eye with his fist. "I'm thirsty."

Grover quickly follows behind him, barging into the kitchen.

I run my hand through my hair, pushing it away from my face.

Well, shit. So much for my plan.

I exhale, resting my hands on my hips. "Ok. Do you want some water?" He shakes his head. "What does your mom usually give you?"

He shrugs his shoulders.

"Coffee?"

A sleepy grin curls at his lips. "No, Mama d-d-doesn't let me have coffee."

It's clear Oliver has a speech impediment. I really noticed the day in the grocery store when he was upset about Sarah not letting him have a balloon, but I can tell it's worse when he's excited or tired.

I grab one of the two sippy cups on the towel beside the sink. "If I give you orange juice, will that get me in trouble?"

He shakes his head, but the mischievous look in his eyes tells me it might. I take a gamble and pull the bottle from the fridge, pouring him some.

He tips the cup to his mouth and drinks, the pressure releasing when he pulls it away. "D-d-do you have *Bluey*?"

"What's that?"

"The sh-show with Bandit, Bingo, B-bluey."

"I don't know. Want to go see?"

He nods, running past the couch to the recliner. I search for a cartoon called *Bluey*. "Is this it?"

He nods and smiles. "It's so funny, Swade."

I select an episode and then set the remote on the couch. "I'm going to let Grover outside, ok?"

He doesn't respond, already fully zoned in on the screen, but Grover, having heard the magic word, is at my feet, ready to go.

I quietly open the back door, and he runs into the yard. I watch, calling him when he's done.

I pour a cup of coffee and return to the living room with Ollie.

"Swade, watch." Ollie pats the spot beside him in the recliner.

I sit, and he climbs onto my lap, giggling at the big dog, pretending to toast the two little dogs inside a trampoline.

We watch the full episode of the dogs playing ridiculous games, and Ollie holds my face to be sure I'm catching the best parts.

When the credits roll, he twists. "I'm hungry."

"What do you usually eat for breakfast?"

Another shrug.

He takes another swig of his orange juice, and I surrender. My plan for this morning is obliterated.

"Do you like pancakes?"

His blue eyes, except for that one brown slice, grow wide, and he nods.

"Bacon?"

He nods again.

"Want to help me make breakfast?"

He hops off my lap. "Can I wick the spatula?"

I set him on the counter, and he mixes the pancake batter as the griddle heats. I drop the strips of bacon onto the pan, and it sizzles. He helps me scoop the first round of pancakes onto the flat surface.

"Oliver Tate, you weren't supposed to leave the room without waking me."

Our attention snaps to the doorway and that tone. The one that sounds like we are deep shit.

Sarah holds Frankie against her chest, with a floppy stuffed lamb tucked under her arm, and her face hidden in Sarah's neck.

"Mama! We're making you p-pancakes!"

This kid is smooth. I want to fist-bump him, but I'll save it for later.

"I see that, but you know you weren't supposed to come down without me."

"Sorry." He slumps, and I flip the pancakes and bacon.

I peek over my shoulder, and she's still standing there, in those short shorts and oversized T-shirt. . .staring. I ignore her and how good she looks, still a bit dazed from sleep.

I drop more batter onto the griddle, but I can't take it.

"What?" I ask.

"Nothing."

Now, it's that other tone. The one that lights a fire in my belly. *This* is exactly what I didn't need today.

I turn, crossing my arms over my chest. "What?" I ask again with more patience than I expected.

"I just. . . I've never seen you without a hat. It's like. . .you're Green Lantern instead of Batman."

Ollie giggles, covering his mouth with his hand.

"What?"

She waves a hand. "Nothing." Her lips twitch. "I thought. . .you were probably balding and had one of those spots you were covering."

I rub my beard, trying to understand what I'm supposed to do with this woman. "I didn't have a hat on last night."

Her eyes move back and forth like she's trying to recall. "Truuue, but when you scare the crap out of someone . . . Yeah, I really wasn't thinking about your hair loss insecurities." She steps into the kitchen. "Premature balding is nothing to be ashamed of."

I have to visit the barber every three weeks. I'm not even close to balding, and I suspect she's fully aware of that.

She peeks around me to inspect the food on the stove. "I'm sorry. I hope Ollie didn't wake you."

"I was up. We had a couple of beers and talked about the weather."

She leans against the counter and yawns, running her hand up and down Frankie's back, whose head pops up to stare at me. "Shocking, isn't it, Love Bug?"

I groan, tucking my hair behind my ears, and Sarah laughs.

"The coffee is still hot, and the mugs are in the cabinet behind you."

She sets Frankie on the floor beside Grover and reaches for a mug, pouring a cup.

"Mmm," she hums, wrapping her hands around the mug and holding it to her chest like she's hugging it. "You make good coffee."

I try not to stare at how incredibly beautiful she is, messy and wrinkled as she savors it.

I shake myself from it, and we divide up the pancakes and bacon.

Sarah tears off pieces of pancake and sets them in front of Frankie.

Ollie twists toward me. "Can we g-go to the park today?"

Sarah runs a hand over his head. "Bud, Slade might have things he needs to do."

Ollie's lips push out like a duck.

"I bet I can fit that in," I say. "As long as you help me clean the leaves out of the downspouts later."

"Down s-spouts," Ollie repeats, but Sarah's eyes meet mine.

"You really don't have—"

"It's fine." I don't know where this kid's dad is, but I know what it's like to not have one and what it would have meant to me to have someone take me to the park.

She bites the end off a piece of bacon. "Since you made breakfast, how about I make dinner?"

I raise my eyebrows. "Do you cook like you bake cookies?"

"Oh, good grief." She tosses a piece of dry pancake at me, and it bounces off my chest. "I guess you just have to wait and see."

It sounds a bit like a challenge. I'm beginning to think I'll just have to wait and see about a whole lot of things.

CHAPTER 18

SARAH

I watch Slade help Ollie up the rock wall as I push Frankie in the swing. The air has a bite to it, and the ends of my fingers ache.

"Put your foot here." Slade guides his foot to a plastic rock, standing behind him in case he falls. "Now, reach for the next one. You got it, partner."

Ollie reaches and pulls himself up and over the side.

He grins from the top. "C-can we do it again?"

Slade nods, and Ollie runs, shoots down the slide, and comes back around.

I smile at Frankie's chubby face sticking out from underneath her fuzzy hat, but my heart aches. This is what Ollie craves and what I'm deeply afraid he will never have.

Slade spent yesterday evening explaining to Ollie how planes work. And when I found them in the kitchen this morning, I heard the two of them talking and pouring pancakes. Slade is so gentle with him and patient when it takes Ollie time to get his words out.

This is what I wish for my son. A male figure to laugh with and learn from. Not one who is only around when it's convenient or uses them as a bargaining chip.

I push Frankie a little higher, and she giggles. "Does that tickle your tummy?"

She grins, showing off her tiny teeth.

Slade glances over, his eyes meeting mine, and I smile. He doesn't. He just. . .stares back. That scowly gaze makes my smile grow wider.

I have no idea what to think of this man. One minute, he's stiff and hard, completely closed off, and then the next, he's soft and gentle and says something that makes me know he runs deep.

The way he looks at me sometimes makes me fidgety. It's like he sees all the messy pieces of me I want to hide while I'm trying to sort out who I am now. So, my mouth takes over to defuse the uncomfortableness of him actually seeing too much.

When he woke me last night, I wanted to kill him for scaring me, but also hug him tight because it was just him, and somehow, I know he's safe. I shouldn't. My track record should strip all rights to judge a person's character, but it was Slade—the guy who's still here, telling me it will be ok.

I fell into him, and oh man, it shouldn't have felt as nice as it did. Those seconds with his strong hands and muscular arms holding me steady were the safest I've felt in a really long time. Maybe ever. I thought if I could stay there and hold on tight, maybe everything closing in on me would get tired and disappear.

But I couldn't, so I did what I do. I gave him shit. And he did what he does. Find me entirely unamusing. All six-foot-five-ish inches of him just stood there wholly unaffected. That was until I dared to take a gander at his arms.

The muscled man stood in front of me in a tight white T-shirt, sweats hanging low on his hips, with all that black ink on display. I've been curious about those tattoos since the day he climbed into my car because it's not just one. It's one woven into another and another as if it's a tapestry. A story unfolding. Maybe his story and my mind craves every single detail.

I may have also wanted to know how far they extend. Over his shoulders and chest, or just the sleeves? But after he accused me of ogling, I didn't feel it was appropriate to ask. I also have absolutely no business wondering what lies underneath my neighbor's shirt.

"Do I, Love Bug?" I lean down and pull the swing to my chest to kiss her.

"Do you what?" Slade strolls toward me through the mulch.

"Oh, nothing. Just a little girl talk and figuring out what to make for dinner."

He pushes a swing out of the way and stops beside me, but those green eyes fall to me, knowing I'm full of it. His gaze shifts to watch Ollie.

Frankie babbles from the bucket seat, swinging back and forth.

"Thank you," I say softly.

"He's a good kid."

"No. I mean. . .yes." I wave a hand. "Thank you for coming with us and being so good to him. Just know he'll be obsessed with you now. I hope you're prepared." I pause, trying to say what I want to say. "I haven't said it, but thank you for. . .everything. You didn't have to do any of this."

"You're welcome," is all he offers as we watch Ollie climb up the slide backward.

"Swade, wook!" Ollie throws his arms in the air from the top.

"It must be difficult to do this all by yourself." He adjusts his hat.

I blow out a breath. "I wonder every second how many ways I'm screwing this up. They'll probably spend their entire adulthood in therapy reliving every mistake and bad decision I ever made."

"You don't have any help?" His question is curious and gentle.

I know what he's asking. He's asking about Miles, but things with Miles are complicated. He and I are over. Period. They were over long before I could admit it. There's a time to try to do what's best for your children, and then there is a time to accept that sticking it out would do far more damage than life apart.

I'm still trying to understand what kind of involvement Miles will have or if he even wants to be a part of their lives. So far, he doesn't seem to care in the least, and that's not new. For their sake, I don't want to lose hope that someday, he'll be the kind of man I thought he was when I married him.

"Not currently. My mom lives up north near the border, and. . .their dad is about as helpful as a shiny rock."

Slade grunts.

"He has priorities, and Frankie and Ollie have never been one of them."

I think about telling him about Miles's career and that he'll be moving further away, but at this point, it really doesn't matter. I have to wait and see if Miles has any plans to consider them in this move. My guess is that it's only if it benefits him in some way.

"It looks like you're doing great to me. My mom was a single mom. She didn't always make the best decisions, but she loved Krissy and me fiercely. She sacrificed every day for us and was one of the strongest women I'll ever know. They'll remember that over the mistakes and bad decisions."

I look at my kids, and my throat tingles, hoping he's right. "I've always wanted for them what I never had, you know?" I blink quickly, knowing there is no room for tears in this.

Ollie zooms over the rickety bridge with his arms out the side, swaying like a plane.

"All you can do is try your best to protect them from the things that hurt in this life. But sometimes, I think maybe we can try too hard."

I glance up at him as he watches Ollie, taking in his words and wondering if part of them is a reflection. He's given me tidbits in these last few moments that only confirm the depth inside his big body.

"Sounds like you know a little something about this." I give Frankie another push. "Krissy told me you raised her after your mom passed."

He chuckles. "At nineteen, I had no idea what I was getting into, raising a teenage girl."

"I think you did just fine. Krissy is amazing."

"She's. . .something."

"She's strong, independent, smart. She didn't grow into that all on her own, sir."

He runs a hand over his beard. "Yeah, but I wonder if I focused so hard on trying not to screw up that I forgot to keep living at the same time."

"Swade, c-c-an you help me?" Ollie stands at the edge of the platform, eyeing the monkey bars.

"Hold on," he says, leaving me pushing Frankie, whose eyes are beginning to droop.

My mind explodes with a thousand questions from the little bomb of personal insight he just dropped.

I stare at his broad back as he walks toward Ollie, wondering if he realizes what he just gave away. It feels like a giant bone I'm going to gnaw on for a while, because maybe this man feels a little lost like I do.

I find an open bottle of red wine in the refrigerator and pour a splash into the pot. I stir the chicken and sauce and place the lid on top.

My phone vibrates on the counter, and I swipe to answer.

"Hey, Mom."

"Hi, honey. I saw you called the other evening. Russ and I were at a concert in the city."

I hear the road noise and know she's in the car. I peek out the window. Slade crouches beside Ollie, watching the excavator dig a giant hole in my front yard to uncover the water main.

When we got back from the park, I ran over to grab the ingredients for dinner. We had lunch, and I put Frankie down for a nap while Slade took Ollie and Grover outside to rake and clean the downspouts.

With my entire front yard being excavated, I no longer have to worry about the mounds of rotting leaves.

"It's ok. How was the concert?"

"It was so good." She breaks into song but trails off. "How are you doing?" Her peppy tone is bright as usual.

"I'm ok. The water main cracked or something, and the basement flooded."

"Well, that's crap in an overflowing toilet."

I smile cause she's not wrong.

"Did you get the water out?"

"Yeah, a neighbor and some friends helped."

I have purposely not told my mom about Slade. She would make it into something it's absolutely not, and I don't even want to try to explain it.

"That was nice of them. So, you're making friends?"

I feel ten again, reassuring her I know how to be social. It wasn't easy being the girl with two different colored eyes in a small town. Children are innately egocentric and use abnormalities as a means of exclusion, so I was often forced to the outside. My mom hasn't forgotten the struggle.

Are Slade and I friends? I'm finding I really hope so.

"Yes. Are you heading home?" I attempt to avoid more questions.

"I'm meeting Russ at the pub later. I have a box of things to send with Roxie. I found a killer dress that will look amazing on you. You have to try it on and send me a picture."

Of course there is, like I have use for a cute dress.

"I miss you and the kids. I wish you were coming home. I need to squeeze those babies. If you can't come for Christmas, maybe Cynthia can cover me for a day or two after the holiday rush. She owes me for having to listen to her yak about her family drama."

My mom lives for drama. The trailer park could be its own reality show.

"That would be fun, Mom."

There's a pause that's far too long for my mom, and my skin prickles.

"So, I was in the Gas Stop this morning and ran into Rayanne. She said she heard on The Morning Show that Miles is the new Sunday anchor."

It's official. I should be paying attention to his social activity, but my anxiety soars just thinking about it.

"Yeah. He finally messaged me and told me he's moving."

Out the window, Ollie helps Slade gather a small pile of leaves while Grover barks and tries to bite the end of the rake.

"What will you do?" my mom asks as if I have options.

"What do you mean?"

"He told you if you moved back, he would pay support. Do you think he's trying to pull that again?"

I rest a hand on the counter, needing to get a grip on my awakening nerves as my body tenses. "I don't know. He's aware I can barely make ends meet. I think that's been his goal all along. Seeing how long I'll last without him. But he hasn't once asked about the kids. He has no concern for them or their well-being."

My belly squeezes tight. "I have to be careful and evaluate the consequences of any kind of involvement with him. Ollie is old enough to know if Miles doesn't keep his promises, and I won't let him be hurt and disappointed. Frankie doesn't even know him."

My mom huffs. "Well, he can't take off to the bright lights and extra-large news desk without paying you. His ass needs to take responsibility."

My spine stiffens at her bold insistence. I wish it were as simple as just telling him to be responsible.

"Mom, he's never had any intention of paying child support. There are always threats or conditions attached, but even if I met his demands, he still wouldn't pay. This is what he does. It's all about control. Thinking I can rely on him for anything would be making the same mistake all over again. I trusted him. He did nothing but use it against me."

"Sarah, he'll make millions while you struggle for every penny. That's not fair."

I hear her frustration as the harsh reality of unfairness slams into me again. It's not fair, but sometimes the price of freedom is worth the injustice. It's a reality that's becoming more apparent every day.

"Mom, you know how careful I have to be. He'll do anything to get his way, and I can't go through another public beatdown. I can't afford to fight him and lose everything again." Even with as little as I have, I've got the two most important things. Ollie and Frankie are the only things that matter.

It would be amazing to attack and go after what he owes me, but that requires resources and an affinity for gambling. At this point, there's too much uncalculated risk and too little information about what his angle is. I made rash decisions before, and look where that's gotten me.

I take a slow, deep breath. I've avoided trying to predict what he might do, but that won't help me. "With this new job, I'm sure he's on a power trip again, and I can't anticipate what comes next. I'm. . .just trying to wait it out and see what happens before I make any move or decide if I even want to."

It's absolute shit just sitting and waiting to see what Miles is up to. But I learned my lesson when he took everything I'd worked so hard for and lit my world on fire. My job is to care for and protect Ollie and Frankie, so that's what I'll do.

"I'm sorry, honey. I just wish things with him were different."

There's a long moment of silence for the depressing state of what I once thought was beautiful and flourishing. But underneath, it was only a bed of lies.

I wonder how my mom will turn this sad song around.

"I hate seeing you struggle if you don't have to."

Her solemn tone eases my frustration, and I quickly swallow the swell in my throat that rises in its place.

"I tried, Mom. You know I did. Even when I shouldn't have, I gave him so many chances. I don't want his help if it comes with conditions or if it will hurt the kids. And it always does. He can't see anything but himself."

"You were always my brave girl." Her uncharacteristically gentle tone causes the burn in my throat to reemerge. "Standing on that stage, no matter what anyone said."

I'd like to feel brave now instead of like some knockoff.

"I wish I could help more, but I'm proud of you. You're taking your life back. It's proof he didn't steal everything."

Ok. Here we go. My mom is turning the desperate frown upside down.

I let my head fall into my hands as the emotional ride pulls back into the station.

"Don't think there won't be a show if I run into him. He'll understand a whole other side of the spotlight when I'm finished."

I laugh. My mom is successful yet again.

I hear Frankie cry. "Mom, I gotta go. Frankie is up from her nap."

"Hug those babies and keep making friends."

I hang up and climb the stairs.

"Hi, Love Bug." I hold her close, and she snuggles in before I change her diaper. I carry her downstairs to stir dinner, thinking about everything my mom said.

I kiss Frankie's head, watching Ollie throw his hands in the air when the excavator dumps a heaping pile of dirt.

Things are really tight financially, and it seems like every time I turn around, something else is breaking down or a new disaster is occurring. But I'm doing it. I'm standing on my own two feet without Miles.

Maybe if I keep going and doing what I'm doing, I'll eventually find a version of myself I recognize.

CHAPTER 19

SLADE

"Mama! Wook what Swade found."

Ollie busts through the back door, and I follow, the scent of spices and tomato floating in the air.

He uncurls his fingers to show Sarah the fuzzy brown and black striped caterpillar we found in the leaves.

She bends to look at it as it crawls around his palm, and he stops it from falling with his other hand.

"Swade said we're g-going to get lots of s-snow this winter."

She runs her finger over the crawling fuzz. "He's cute. Did you name him?"

"No. Swade said we have to put him back."

Sarah glances at me as Frankie climbs up her leg to see. "That's a smart idea. Then it can build a cocoon. I bet he's a vveerry hungry caterpillar." Sarah tickles him, and he giggles.

"Let's go put it back in the leaves," I say.

"Aw. Not yet," he whines.

"You only have a few minutes. Dinner will be ready soon." Sarah runs a hand over his head.

The stove holds two pots, and one of them is boiling.

I lean to see what's cooking. "What is it? It smells good."

Her hands move to her hips. "Don't sound so surprised, you big lug. It is good." She grabs the wooden spoon and stirs whatever is in the pot.

I feel something at my feet and peer down at Frankie, pulling on the laces of my boots. Her blue eyes stare up at me as if she is testing the waters. I reach down and pick her up. Her eyes widen, and she studies me closely, completely unsure.

"We're having what I like to call Awesome Chicken and—"

Sarah stops mid-sentence, and now both she and Frankie are staring at me.

Frankie uses her pointer finger and hesitantly pokes my beard. Sarah watches her explore my face, her little finger moving to my lips.

I fake-bite it, and she bursts out in giggles. She does it again, and I snap my teeth at her finger. Ollie laughs this time.

Sarah's mouth turns upward into a soft smile, her head falling to the side.

I do it a third time, then let Frankie catch her breath, and her head drops to my shoulder.

I squint my eyes at Sarah. "Don't look so surprised. I have held a baby before."

Her smile turns into the real deal, stretching so far it reaches into my chest and tugs something loose, making it just a little difficult to take a full breath.

When Frankie puts that little chubby finger in front of my mouth, I snap one last time, making Sarah laugh, too. I like the sounds rolling through my kitchen way more than I should, and I don't want it to stop.

"Hey. What's with all the giggling?" Krissy enters the kitchen in scrubs, saving me from letting a desire resurface that I let die long ago.

She runs a hand over Frankie's back before moving past me to inspect what's cooking on the stove. "This smells amazing." She lifts the top of the pot and inhales.

"Do you have time to eat with us?" Sarah asks, pulling plates from the cabinet.

"Uh, yes. Can you stay forever?" Krissy's simple question blasts into that dislodged longing when I need it to settle back down.

"They said the main should be fixed tomorrow, but you're welcome to come over for dinner any time."

"I am not a good cook, and this guy is eh, so . . ."

I roll my eyes at her lies. "You weren't complaining when you had food to eat," I grumble.

Sarah lifts her chin. "I'd invite you, too, but I'm holding off until I prove your skeptical A-double-S wrong with the best chicken you've ever tasted."

I match her stare. The only thing I'm skeptical of is what I'm feeling.

"Look, Kissy." Ollie holds out his hand to show her the caterpillar.

She squats in front of him. "I used to collect these little guys when I was young, and Slade always tried to run them over with his bike."

Ollie looks up at me.

Nice, Kris. I glare at her. "I always dodged at the last minute."

I hear Grover growl and bark on the other side of the door. "Come on, partner. Let's put the little guy back outside and make sure Grover doesn't eat the rat next door."

Krissy holds out her hands for Frankie, who dives for her.

"You think Stone Cold is funny, huh? You'd be in the minority, sweet pea," Krissy says, taking her.

"I'm funny," I say, following Ollie outside. "Your sense of humor just sucks."

I hear her and Sarah snicker as I close the door.

I'm funny as hell. I just don't give that shit away to anyone.

Ollie runs into the backyard, where Grover is pacing the fence, tracking the taunting wiener on the other side.

I call the dog, and he comes, shoving his head under my hand. I inhale the fall evening air, needing it to clear my brain from the fog of a really good day. The kind of day I want to hold onto. But that's the problem. Tomorrow, things will go back to normal.

I exhale through my nose. I need everything to return to the way it was before the broken wheel bearing and water main, so I can focus on running my business and helping Krissy move out. Then maybe, at some point, I'll sort out if I want to do anything about these feelings I thought I had become immune to long ago.

Ollie squats next to a tree. "Do you th-think he will like it here?"

I drop down beside him. "I think so. He can either climb up if he wants or stay in the grass."

He rests his hand against the base of the tree. "Here you go. I hope you find your f-family."

Grover's nose starts inspecting, but Ollie pushes him away. "No, Grover."

"Come here, boy." I grab the massive furball's collar, realizing I'll miss him terrorizing Brandon's mini wiener.

I chuckle to myself. *See, I'm funny.*

I stand. "You ready for dinner?"

"Yeah." He sounds sad. "I hope he f-finds his mama."

I put my hand around his shoulder. "You know what I think?"

He shakes his head, still staring at the ground.

"Moms are really smart. If he can't find her, she'll find him."

He peers up at me. "My mom's really s-smart. She's also a p-p-princess." He takes off toward the door. "She even gots a crown."

She's too smart. She seems to know every single button I have and is intent on pushing each one of them. All at the same time.

Grover and I trail Ollie into the kitchen. Sarah holds him up to the sink to wash his hands. I hang my coat on the hook along with my hat.

"Mmm. Sarah, this is so good," Krissy hums with Frankie on her lap, a long, fat noodle sticking between her tiny fingers.

I want to roll my eyes at Krissy's exaggeration like she's never had a decent meal before.

"You are definitely coming for Thanksgiving. Bring any dish you want," Krissy says, twirling more noodles around her fork.

Sarah hands Ollie the towel, but he runs his hands down his shirt and then slides onto a chair. "I don't know. My best friend is visiting, and you guys have your own—"

Krissy holds up her fork. "It's a Friendsgiving. It's so chill. Everybody brings something. Wind cooks a turkey, and we watch the game. You guys have to come."

Sarah's eyes flick to mine, still unsure.

"You should come," I confirm.

I can feel Krissy's wide-ass grin without seeing it.

Sarah nods once and grabs a plate, filling it with noodles.

"I don't want that," Ollie says, pointing to the chicken and tomato mixture Krissy is moaning over.

"I have butter noodles for you, but you have to eat your fruit and broccoli." Sarah pulls a sheet from the oven layered with green stuff.

I take my turn at the sink, but not before I see his face scrunch, and I don't blame him.

She scoops some on a plate filled with noodles and blueberries and then hands me a plate.

I take it, inspecting the pot of noodles, the chicken mixture, rolls, and the broccoli, which I won't be touching.

I gesture for her to go first, and a slight smirk appears that makes me think things I shouldn't.

Just one more night, and everything will be back to normal.

She fills her plate, and I follow, sitting beside Krissy.

She pops up. "I've gotta go."

Sarah reaches for Frankie and moves her messy mixture within reach.

"This was . . ." Krissy kisses the tips of her fingers. "I'll think about it all night while I'm orienting and watching babies be born."

"You're no longer in the ER?" Sarah asks.

Krissy grabs her coat and keys. "Nope. I got a position in Labor and Delivery, and I'm loving it."

Frankie's messy little hand opens and closes, and then she slaps her mouth, blowing a kiss.

"Aw. Bye-bye," Krissy whines, blowing a kiss in return.

"Bye, Kissy," Ollie says with a mouthful of noodles.

The kitchen falls quiet as the door closes, except for Ollie's humming.

Sarah taps her fork in the broccoli-infested area on his plate. "Don't fill up on noodles before you eat these."

"Swade doesn't have broccoli." He wiggles in his seat.

Sarah eyes my food and then me. I don't care what she says or does. I am not eating it. It doesn't matter how much I like this kid. He's on his own.

"You don't like broccoli?" Sarah asks quietly.

I shake my head.

"Have you had it roasted?"

I shake my head again, silently pleading the fifth.

Her head falls to the side. "You should try it. You might like it."

I take another bite of noodles and chicken and try not to make a noise as it melts in my mouth. It's so freaking good. This woman may make cookies that look like boobs, but she can cook.

I glance up, and she's staring at me, waiting for an answer. "No."

She smiles. "Just. . .no. That's not very brave or adventurous."

I'm not into adventure. I like well-known outcomes. Although messing with her sly, calm challenge seems like a gamble I'd be willing to take.

Tomorrow, everything needs to go back to normal.

"No. I'm with Ollie. It's the worst vegetable. Right up there with eggplant and turnips." I take another bite of noodles and chicken to keep from gagging just thinking about it.

"Seriously, not even a little bite."

My fork stabs my plate. "No. There's nothing you can say or do to make me try it."

Ollie snorts, slurping a noodle between his lips.

Sarah's eyes narrow, telling me she doubts that to be true.

I hold completely still, waiting for her to dare me. Those lips move to the side in deep contemplation.

I want her to try me. But then again, there might be a few things—

Fuck. What is happening?

Her gaze drops from mine, and I might be mistaken, but are her cheeks just a little flushed?

I shove another bite into my mouth, needing the distraction.

"Well, sorry, Ollie, you have to eat it. It's good for your muscles."

"Swade has huuuggee muscles," he expands his hands, "and he d-doesn't eat it. It's gross."

This kid should be the lawyer.

Sarah's eyes trace over me, stopping at my biceps. I think about flexing to help Ollie, but I refrain.

Her eyes jump to mine, and I let one side of my mouth curl up.

She rolls her eyes and tosses a balled-up paper towel at me. "Careful, don't eat too fast. You might choke." She grins. "If you have dinner at my house, the rules are you have to eat your vegetables."

I'm tempted to ask her what other rules she has, but I shove a forkful into my mouth instead.

Ollie groans. "C-can we just stay here?"

Frankie drops a handful of noodles on the floor for Grover, but Ollie's question has my stomach joining them.

"The water should be back on tomorrow, so it's time for us to go home."

"Aww." Ollie whines. "Can S-swade read to me tonight?"

Sarah's attention turns back to me. "I don't know. *Grumpy Monkey* might be triggering for this guy."

I rest back in my chair as she rolls her lips together.

"He's J-j-jim Panzee," Ollie laughs. "He doesn't know why he's grumpy. Can you read it?" His eyes beg.

"Sure," I say, glaring at Sarah and her pure amusement.

Her eyebrow hitches upward. "You've got to make all the voices."

Well shit. Absolutely nothing will return to normal. I am totally fucked.

CHAPTER 20

SARAH

MILES: I have a meeting in NY the week after Thanksgiving. I'll fly in on my way back. I only have the afternoon.

Garlic. Sour, old garlic mixed with death. It's all I smell, and it's so strong I want to reach for my purse and shove tampons up my nose.

"Why is that in there?" Cory breathes, and I lean away as he scrutinizes the Louis agreement. "Custody has not been resolved."

With that tone and the stench that might infect my brain, I want to ram my chair backward, hopefully catching his toes.

From what Kat has told me, this couple has been fighting over the cat for the last six months. One using it as leverage over the other. Only this week, Mrs. Louis finally agreed to rescind her rights to the eighteen-year-old feline in exchange for the vacation home in Florida.

"Mrs. Louis has turned over custody of the cat," I state, then hold my breath.

Cory makes some kind of throat-clearing noise. I might gag. I want to give him a bottle of peroxide and have him swish for an hour.

"Do you have correspondence of that agreement?"

This joker and his Dracula breath are about to find out what a three-inch heel feels like shoved up his micromanaging ass.

After Miles's inconsiderate message this morning, I'm in no mood to deal with Cory's patronizing attitude.

I twist in my chair, causing him to back up. "Listen, I know I'm relatively new here, and I have a lot to learn. But my ears work perfectly fine, and I can read. I will pull the correspondence Kat emailed me, but this will be the last time you hover over me and question my competence."

His jaw flexes, but at least his mouth is now closed.

"I've been patient with your condescending tone and complete lack of respect for my ability to do this job. If I make a mistake, I will own it. You did not hire me, and nowhere in my job description does it say I am to report to you." I lean forward in my chair a little. "So, from now on, if you come into my office, it better be because you actually *need* something."

I hear snickering in the hallway as I watch his neck and face flush.

"Would you still like to see the email?" I ask, turning back to my computer and not giving his skinny, arrogant ass one second more of my attention.

I hear him exhale. Ugh. I'll have to borrow the can of air freshener from the bathroom to extinguish the smell.

Without a word, he turns and leaves.

Two seconds later, Marcie appears in my doorway, her hand hiding her grin.

Her shoulders scrunch as she enters. "You sounded like Kat. He's terrified of her."

"Does he talk to you and Robyn like that?"

Robyn and Marcie's priorities may consist of nail care and the latest social media buzz, but they do a great job of ensuring they are on top of their duties, with the occasional inappropriate or TMI comment.

She shrugs. "I don't think he has any friends," she whispers. "Like, he has a guinea pig named . . ." She covers her mouth again, hunching down and trying not to laugh.

"Harry Pooter," Robyn spits from around the doorway.

I raise my eyebrows. "What?!"

Both of them squeeze into my office, trying to hide their laughter.

"It was supposed to be Potter because apparently Cory is obsessed. I heard him on the phone with the vet one day. They had it listed as . . ." Marcie starts laughing again.

"Pooter," Robyn wheezes.

I laugh. "Seriously?"

They nod in unison, tears in their eyes.

"He has a guinea pig named Harry Pooter?" I have to cover my mouth now to keep from bursting out laughing.

"He is nutso over the thing," Robyn says. "I wouldn't be surprised if it sleeps with him."

"When he's especially rude and treats us like we're stupid, we ask him questions about The Poots." Marcie's shoulders rise, and her eyes grow wide as she grins. "He hates it."

I think about Brandon and his tiny, snarling wiener dog. "I have a neighbor who has a mini wiener . . ." I don't even get to the last word, and they are bent over wheezing.

I laugh, too, and it feels really good. Who knew Cory had a heart in there for rodents? Then again, it kind of fits.

"I need a good dose of joy. What's so funny?" Kat slides around them and plops into the chair. "Uh. What did you eat for lunch? Onions on a bed of cabbage?" Her nose wrinkles, and she waves a hand in the air, her beautifully bright-painted nails glimmering in the light.

Marcie holds up a finger. "I'll be right back."

"Cory was just here hassling Sarah again," Robyn says, wiping under her eyes to ensure her eye makeup is intact.

"That shit. I'll talk to Griffin and—"

I hold out my hand. "It's fine. I finally told him to knock it off. If he doesn't, I'll say something to Griffin."

Kat's sly smirk appears in approval.

Marcie returns, squirting small puffs of perfume from a miniature travel-size bottle into the air. "It's Dior. You deserve the good stuff."

"This is great." Robyn clasps her hands together. "Since you're both here, Marcie and I were trying to organize a birthday happy hour for Seth."

I watch Kat to see how she responds, wondering if she's aware of Marcie's crush on Seth.

Kat's head falls to the side, her eyes lifting to Marcie. I should never underestimate her.

She presses her fuchsia lips together. "Ok, little pigeon. We've been over this."

Marcie bites the corner of her lip, avoiding eye contact.

"Seth is a great guy, but he's happy being a bachelor. When we were in law school, he didn't even date, worried his mom would shove him down the aisle. After Alex called off the wedding, you can be sure he's not looking to end up there again anytime soon."

"It was clear as day he and Alex weren't right for each other," Robyn says.

Kat squints one eye and taps her temple. "Now, why would a guy be with someone so incredibly not right for him?"

The room falls quiet as Kat waits for an answer. Marcie's eyes dart to Robyn.

"Self-sabotage," I pipe in.

One side of Kat's mouth lifts. "Ladies, I've known him a long time. He's not looking for a committed relationship. I mean, he's hanging with Junior."

"But Junior is such a flirt," Robyn says.

Kat scoffs. "Yep, and that's all it is. For him, it's the challenge. He's had everything he's ever wanted handed to him. He wants what he can't have, and once he has it, he doesn't want it anymore."

It's so familiar it stings.

She points at them. "Let that be a lesson to you. That man leaves broken hearts in his wake. Seth isn't like that, but he's happy where he's at. Single."

"Well," Marcie starts, moving things along. "Can we still have a happy hour? It'll be fun. We never do it, and it'll be close to the holidays, so it can be like a Christmas party."

"Only if there's tons of balloons to piss Seth off," Kat demands. "He hates his birthday."

Marcie grins. "And a big cake. We'll go to Crusins."

"If we go on a Friday, they have the best music," Robyn adds.

"You girls plan it, and we'll be there." Kat slumps down in the chair.

"Great!" They clap as if party planning is what they were born to do. "We'll work on reserving a space."

"Wait." I stop them before they scurry off to start planning. "I won't be able to make it."

They turn back.

"Oh, yes you are." Kat slides up in her chair. "This one time, you're coming. If there are balloons, cake, and an irritated Seth, you have to come. He won't be mad at you."

"Oh, wonderful," I say. "I'll be the buffer because I'm the new girl."

Kat smiles at me. "See if your nanny can stay late just this once."

"You have to come," Robyn says, pressing her hands together in plea. "It'll be so fun, and we never do this all together."

I succumb to the pressure. "Fine. Once you have a date, I'll see if Helen can stay a little later."

"We'll look at calendars and then email a poll to see which Friday is best." Marcie grips Robyn's hand, and they rush out the door.

"I wish I still had their energy and enthusiasm," Kat groans, running a hand over her face.

"You ok?" I rest back in my chair, twisting toward her as she slumps down again.

"I negotiated custody of frozen embryos all morning. I'm tired and a little burnt out. I was up late the last few nights researching and preparing. I think I need a vacation." She slides her hands behind her neck and pulls her long black hair up over her head. She lets out a breath. "People don't warn you of the emotional toll this job takes."

She looks worn out, and I recall my conversation about no-win situations with Griffin.

"How do you do it? Be a mom, have a full-time job, and go to school all on your own?" There's a gentleness in her tone I'm not sure I've heard before.

I push out a breath. "Not very well most days." I laugh. "I don't have a choice. I'd do anything for my kids, so I work hard and do my very best, but school takes a back seat. That's not turning out so well academically."

She offers a small smile. "In college, I kept thinking, I'll get through school, then get married and have kids. But I got through school and began working . . . This job takes every second of my time."

"But you're helping people," I say, wanting to encourage her and selfishly remind myself of why I'm pursuing this career.

"Am I?" She shakes her head again. "Lately, I'm not so sure."

I think about Slade being Krissy's guardian, and I know Kat helped ensure she stayed with him.

She lets go of her hair and sits up as the long waves cascade around her again. "Ugh. Enough of my whining. So, you found a cesspool in your basement over the weekend. What'd you do?"

"Well, I called a plumber who was completely unhelpful, so I ran over to the neighbor who just so happens to be Slade."

Her eyebrows raise. "Really?"

I nod slowly. "Turns out the main broke."

"Is it fixed?"

"Yeah. But the water was off all weekend."

Her face scrunches. "What did you do? I mean, you have the kids, and your ex doesn't live here, right?"

I've not shared anything about Miles. Would anyone in Cincinnati know who he is? Not likely, but that's all about to change when he hits New York and The Morning Show. I need our marriage and the disparagement that followed to be left behind in Chicago.

Would Kat believe me? Maybe. She's smart and has seen the worst of relationships end in war. Am I willing to take a chance? No. This is my job.

"He doesn't. We stayed with Slade and Krissy."

A slight smirk replaces her surprise. "How was that?"

Slade helped me carry everything across the street this morning before I dropped the kids off at the retirement community with Helen.

I thought I'd lost my cookies agreeing to stay with him and Krissy, but when Slade told me everything was ok, he must have meant it because it was. There were parts of it that were even nice. Better than nice.

It was fun going to the park and watching Slade lift Ollie onto his shoulders when he was too tired to walk to the car. But when I turned and saw Frankie wrapped in his giant arms, giggling her squishy face off, I couldn't look away. I wanted to absorb every second. It was a moment Frankie hasn't had and one I'll never stop wishing for her—the safety and security of a man's arms.

My chest warms at the memory. "It was actually really great. Ollie had the best time."

We had fun, and that's something we haven't done in quite some time.

Her eyelids fall, and her mouth slides sideways even further. "You know, he's tall, ruggedly handsome, and there's this soft, sensitive side he seems to keep locked away under that forthright personality."

Slade is nothing if not straightforward, but I sensed a whole lot not being said this weekend. I could almost feel his mind working, and I wanted to know what was happening behind those long pauses and green-eyed stares.

It all stirred feelings I thought were withered by misplaced trust and betrayal—thoughts and feelings that generate joy, excitement, and anticipation. Annnndd a few sexy thoughts I have no business thinking.

But I don't have room for *those* kinds of feelings. I have to keep my head down, focused, and never get distracted again.

"You're right," I admit. "But we're just neighbors, and I think it's possible the big grump might even say we're friends."

She laughs. "Boy, do we need those." She fills her cheeks with air and blows it out. She stands. "If you have time, I'm reviewing a new case. Now that you're an expert, I could use some help sorting through assets."

"Sure. Send it my way."

She stops in the doorway. "You know, it doesn't hurt to flirt a little with a big hunk of a man." She winks and disappears.

I roll my eyes for no one to see. The absolute last thing that will be happening is flirting. My mouth has a mind of its own, and I can't help the involuntary sarcasm that spills out. It's what helped me survive my childhood and my mother's constant obnoxious dramatics. I'm about as good at flirting as I am at answering a rogue question on social issues.

My phone buzzes, and I flip it over.

SLADE: Did you hear from the city? Is the water on?

ME: Hi! How's your day?

SLADE: Fine.

ME: I can tell there's a smile under that 'fine.' I bet the guys have to wear sunglasses to handle all that sunshine.

SLADE: When you get home, you'll have to turn on the shut-off valve.

ME: Aye, Aye, Captain. If the flood waters rise, I'll Mayday.

I smile. I just can't help messing with him. He's like a giant geode I want to crack open to see what lies inside.

I got one smile that showed off his hidden dimple and a couple of chuckles. They were deep and warm and soothed my wary insides like rain after a long, dry spell. I want to hear that low rumble again and know I made it happen.

I rest my elbow on the desk and drop my head into my hand. I *will not* want to hear that subtle, deep laugh again. I have absolutely no right to wish for it.

But it's a really nice laugh. The kind that makes your belly leap with joy, then charges up and bursts into a smile.

I groan. I'm on Operation Get My Life Back. *That* is what I'm doing. I won't be thinking about my neighbor's rare smiles, his tattooed muscles, how warm and safe he feels, or the fact that my kids seem to love him.

No. No. No. Nooooo. No. No. No.

Shit! Shit! Shit!

I slump in my chair.

I was sidetracked by one man, and that won't happen again. Ever.

CHAPTER 21

SLADE

"Yes, sir. I've worked on all types of machines. Mostly farm equipment, but I helped my brother rebuild a Chevy."

The young man lifts his cap and places it on his knee. He can't be more than nineteen or twenty. He's tall and lanky and looks like a farm boy fresh out of the fields.

"Do you own any tools?"

He shakes his head. "No, sir, but I'll work to purchase them."

I cross my arms over my chest. "Are you in school?"

He shakes his head. "No, sir."

"You can drop the sir. The only thing those guys out there call me is asshole."

He smiles.

"Where are you from?" This kid seems bright, and I want to know why he's not in college or still working the land he clearly came from.

"I'm from a small town in Illinois. I know how to work hard and learn fast."

I try again, knowing he's either escaping or running, and I want to know which. "What are you doing in Cincinnati?"

His shoulders rise with a deep breath, and his eyes meet mine. "Truth?"

I nod.

"I followed a girl. She was accepted into the university with a scholarship, but I wasn't. My parents wanted me to stay and help with the farm. Go to a local school. They told me if I left, not to come back." His shoulders droop, his eyes dropping to his clasped hands. "She broke up with me last week. Apparently, four months of college showed her we don't fit anymore."

I stare at him, knowing what it feels like to need a chance. "Why don't you go home and run the farm. It could be a good life."

"Sir, I won't be crawling back home with nothing to show for it."

"I respect that," I say, and his eyes brighten with hope. "You'll have to prove you can pull your weight."

"Yes, sir."

"When can you start?"

"Uh, I have to give the grocery store two weeks, but if they let me go before, I can start that day."

"You'll begin with oil changes and tires."

He nods. "Yes, sir."

I stand. "I'll email you the paperwork."

He pushes out of the chair, placing his hat on his head, and extends his hand.

I shake it. "And if you call me sir one more time, your ass is fired."

He laughs. "Yes, s—"

I eye him, and he catches himself.

I lead him out of my office, and he follows me into the shop.

He shakes my hand again, and I let him know I'll be in touch with the paperwork.

When the door bangs closed, I realize the garage is quiet. I turn to see all eyes on me.

Wind's lunch box is open on the workbench, and Trig takes a bite of a burger.

"He didn't run out of here like you threatened to call the cops, so we have to be trending in a better direction." Carson tosses an apple in the air.

"I hired him." I step behind the counter to pull up the schedule.

I hear the crinkle of the chip bag and the crack of Wind's daily Dr. Pepper.

I scroll through the afternoon schedule, knowing the overflow will have to wait until the morning.

"You hired him? Is he still in diapers?" Trig asks.

"Cal hired you when you weren't much older."

His eyes drop back to his sandwich.

"He might be young, but you can finally do something productive and teach him a thing or two." I point a pen at him.

They groan.

"You're supposed to hire someone to help us turn vehicles over faster. Not someone who needs their hand held and snack time," Trig says through a mouthful.

"Does he have his own tools?" Carson asks.

I don't answer, and they groan again.

"If he jacks up my impact wrench, that's on you." Trig points at me this time.

I cross my arms and widen my stance. "Listen. He needs this job and the confidence that will come with it. He's looking to prove himself, and you all know exactly what that's like. So, you will help him get acclimated and teach him because, underneath all of that loud ass groaning, you're decent men."

I return to the computer to check my email while they throw tantrums.

Trig shoots his crumpled paper sack into the trash can with a swoosh, then rests his arms on the counter beside me. "Soooo, are you going to finally tell us how the rest of the weekend went, or do we have to piss you off enough that you'll reveal things in spurts of rage?"

"We just want to know how this afternoon should go! We want to help!" Wind hollers across the space.

It's been five days since Sarah and the kids went home. She texted me on Monday evening to tell me the water was running and the basement was still dry. I haven't heard anything since.

I've been working late and spending extra time at the gym, realizing I no longer want to go home to a quiet house. It's been a great attempt to ignore all the feelings associated with that, or the fact that I could do something about it.

I've held my phone at least a dozen times, thinking about texting Sarah to see if Ollie and Grover wanted to play fetch or to offer to order pizza. Each time, I couldn't do it. Memories of wanting what would never be mine drowned the urge to send the message.

Instead, I set up interviews, inventoried the parts room, and worked out until my muscles vibrated with fatigue.

"It was fine." If these jokers think I'll provide a play-by-play, they've got another thing coming.

Carson scoffs. "Fine, my ass. A beautiful woman and two amazing kids stayed in your house, and all you have to say is that it was fine."

I click on an email and hit reply to inform another interviewee that I've hired someone. "Yep." I start typing.

Trig sniffs. "We've been patient. Now, you're going to make us do this the hard way?"

I stop typing, lifting my eyes to his. "We aren't doing this any way. You all need to mind your own damn business. She stayed with us since she didn't have water. That's it."

Trig twists, leaning his hip against the counter and facing the other guys, his arms crossing over his chest.

I click send and log off, deciding to finish in my office.

"Where the hell do you think you're going?" Carson asks.

"My office. I've got work to do. You'd be smart to get back to it." I almost clear the hallway when—

"You're scared shitless. Just admit it." It's that tone that makes me want to punch him in the face.

I stop, taking a second before I face him and his prattling cronies. When I do, Carson's face dares me to say otherwise.

I squeeze my fists tight. "I'm not scared. There's nothing to this. She's my neighbor, and I was helping her out. That's it."

His chin lifts, testing me. "Bullshit."

There's nothing but the sound of my climbing pulse.

"Krissy said you all went to the park and had dinner together," Wind says, crunching a carrot. "She said the food was—"

"Oh, for fuck's sake." I run a hand over my face. "Do any of you ever just mind your own business?"

"Nope," Trig says with a smile.

"Just spill it, man," Carson demands. "It's time to finally go after what you've always wanted but are too freaking scared to admit."

I pull in air and let it out. "Nothing is going on. They stayed. Ollie wanted to go to the park, we had dinner, and they went home. That. Is. It."

"Heard you made breakfast." Wind drops his can in the trash, and he has no idea how close I am to dropping his ass to the floor. "You left that out."

Carson crosses his arms. "So, you're honestly trying to tell us that Sarah and those kids, the time y'all spent together, didn't make you want more of that?"

I want to say no and laugh in his cocky face. But I can't, and this jackass knows it.

"When's the last time you've been with a woman?" Trig asks.

I glare at him. I am not answering that.

He points at me. "If you have to think about it, it's been too damn long. You cannot tell me that did not cross your mind once this weekend.

They are pinching my very last nerve. That's just it. I did think about it. I would've never acted on it, but I did think about it.

Carson's sarcastic laugh hits my ears, making my blood boil. "Boys, it's been so long he's forgotten how to do this." He grins. "It's all right. We got you, bro." He rubs his hands together.

Smiles break out across the garage, except I feel like my head might actually explode. These Nosy Nancys need to stay the hell out of my business.

"And I'm supposed to take advice from you, Mr. Celibate-Cause-I've-Got-A-Plan?"

Shit. I just admitted they might be right.

He holds his arms out. "Hey, it's not because I'm afraid. The time just isn't right. I'm a patient man."

I laugh this time, and it's filled with sarcastic rage. I want to fire all of them and their satisfied faces.

"Text her," Trig says, and it's possible I growl. "Go on. Pull your phone out and send her a little something." He waves his finger in front of me, and I have the urge to break it in two.

I glare at him as they all stare me down.

"It's been five days. You're behind. You've gotta break the ice," Wind says, strolling closer.

"What are you doing? Keeping a schedule?" These idiots are ridiculous. "I'm not texting anyone."

"Oh yes you are," Carson says, sliding up next to me. "Because even if Sarah isn't interested the slightest bit in your grouchy ass, this is practice. You need to get some game, bro. All this deadpan and sharp attitude won't get you where you're looking to go."

"I'm not looking to go anywhere," I grit through my teeth.

Wind snorts. "Slade." He rests his hand on my shoulder, and I flick it off. His tone turns soft. "We saw you with that little boy. That's the only direction to go. He needs you as much as you need them."

That little observation hits a tender spot I'm desperate to ignore, slamming right into my pride of wanting to work this out on my own. My spine relaxes, succumbing to these morons and their wisdom.

"We talked about this. It's time, man. We're here to help," Carson says.

"Just pull out your phone and message her." Trig makes it sound so simple. "What can it hurt?"

My entire heart. It can hurt the whole damn thing. Permanently.

"There's a time for fear, and there's a time to grab it by the balls and choke that shit out. You don't really want to be a lonely, miserable son of a bitch forever." Carson nods. "Come on. Make a move."

I inhale and let it out, thinking of all the times over the past few days when I almost did but didn't. My mind flashes to Sarah's head on my chest, holding her close. I want more of that. More moments around the dinner table. I want to hear Frankie giggle and chase after Ollie at the park. I want noise and laughter and fun. At least I want a chance of having something like it.

"And say what?" I grunt.

There's silence as these dickheads think about it.

My shoulders fall, and I roll my eyes, turning for my office.

"Wait!" Carson stops me.

"Are they coming for Thanksgiving?" Wind scratches his beard. "I need to know what size turkey to buy."

I turn, walking toward my office again, not wasting another second.

"Hold on." Carson stops me. "That's actually not a bad idea."

Wind's hands move to his hips as he smiles.

"It's checking in with her without being overly eager or obvious. It lets her know you want her there and ensures she's still coming," Carson grins.

Trig runs a hand over his scruff. "Yeah, Carson's right. You can't go from borderline jerk to smooth operator overnight. We've got to ease into this."

At least they understand I need baby steps. I need to tiptoe into whatever this might be until I figure out what I want it to be.

There are so many things I don't know about Sarah, and that makes me nervous. But that's what this is about—getting to know someone.

"She's my neighbor. What if this goes bad?" It's a thought I've had.

"You move." Trig's casual answers show his immaturity.

"It'll be ok. We're not going crazy here. Just message her and remind her that she's still welcome. That's step one." Carson grips my shoulder, and I want to brush it off.

"What's step two?"

"Let's not get ahead of ourselves." Wind rocks back. "We have to see how the holiday goes first."

I retreat to my office.

"Where are you going?" Carson asks, but I don't stop this time.

"To my office. I'm not messaging her with you all looking over my shoulder."

"You better do it," Trig hollers. "Or we'll find out."

I slip my phone from my pocket and pull out my chair. On the worn fabric lies a book with a yellow Post-It.

Don't trash this. It's Millie's. There's good stuff in here. Read it.

I roll my eyes at the book title: *Let Your Heart Beat Again.*

I toss it on my desk rather than the trash and fall into my chair. I stare at my phone.

It's just asking about Thanksgiving. I'm not committing to anything.

I tap out a message. Delete. Type. Delete. Type.

ME: Are you still able to come for Thanksgiving? Wind needs to know what size turkey to buy.

SARAH: Hi, Roary Pants.

My lips curl upward spontaneously—this woman and her need to set me off guard. I don't respond, and after a minute, I see three dots.

SARAH: My best friend will be visiting. I don't want to impose.

ME: You won't.

Shit.

ME: I'll count you all in.

SARAH: I take it back. I should've said, "Hi, Bossy Pants."
SARAH: Do you ever not tell people what to do?

ME: No.

SARAH: Maybe you should try it.
SARAH: Think of it as an experiment.

I laugh, then hear a gasp. All three guys are peering in my doorway, but they run, letting out a whoop and a whistle.

"Get your asses to work, or you all are seriously fired."

"Nah. You need us now more than ever."

I rest back in my chair. I don't know what in the hell I'm doing, so they're not wrong.

I just really need this not to ruin me like the last time I trusted someone enough to let them into my world. I more than let her into my world. I was building a life around her. That is, until she told me I shouldn't bother.

CHAPTER 22

SARAH

"I've missed you so much." I hug Roxie tight as Ollie squeezes between us, looping his arms around her legs.

"Auntie Rox, c-c-come see my planes!" He grabs her hand and tugs her away from me.

"Just a second, little man." Roxie ties her long blonde waves back, twisting her hair into a bun. "I need to see this little dame. She's grown so much." She takes Frankie from my arms, holding her in the air, and then brings her close to kiss her cheek.

"You go play. I'll let Grover out and grab your things from the car."

"Sounds good, Mama." Rox sits on the floor next to Ollie with Frankie in her lap.

Grover trots to the back door. I open it, slipping on my shoes.

While Grover roams the backyard searching for the perfect spot, I throw Roxie's bag over my shoulder and lift the box full of clothes and accessories my mom sent with her.

I push the door closed with my hip and movement across the street catches my eye. Slade's garage door lifts slowly, and I watch as he rounds his truck but stops.

I lift my hand and wave. He gives a slight nod in return before climbing in.

We haven't seen each other since we spent the weekend at his house, but we've texted a few times. I was surprised when he messaged me about Thanksgiving. I thought maybe he and Krissy would forget, but in typical Slade form, he told me we were coming.

I hear the rumble of his truck as I head inside.

"Hey."

I twist at that low voice. Slade's truck sits in the street at the end of my driveway with his window down.

"I'll see you tomorrow around noon."

I laugh and salute. "I'm bringing a pie."

"You sure that's a good idea?"

I glare at him. "Listen, it was one cookie snafu. You need to let that go."

Those eyes linger from underneath the rim of his hat for only a moment, and it's possible I see a hint of a smile. Then he nods once, rolls up his window, and drives off.

I smile, knowing my mom would be proud. It feels really nice to be making friends. Besides Rox, it's been a long time, but I think that might be what's happening—Slade and I are friends. After tomorrow, maybe I'll have a few more.

I pull the door open, kicking off my shoes to the sound of giggles.

I set Roxie's things in the hallway, and she's lying on the floor with Frankie on top of her shins. She holds her little arms out and lifts her legs, as if Frankie is an airplane. She squeals, and a line of drool drips from her mouth onto Roxie's shirt.

"Ok, that might be enough of that," Roxie says, rolling up and sitting her on the floor.

"Rox, wook," Ollie runs back into the room with his arms full of Hot Wheels. He drops them on the floor and spreads them out.

I join their little circle as he tells Roxie about each one, relaying the information Slade told him about the different cars and their "features."

"D-dis one is a s-s-supercharger. It's super f-fast." Ollie pulls it back and pushes it across the floor.

We play and laugh through the afternoon, then bundle up to take the kids for a walk before throwing frozen pizzas into the oven for dinner.

While Roxie gives the kids a bath, I open my computer to finish up an assignment and email it to my instructor. With only a few weeks left of the semester, I've been staying up extra late to study for finals.

When the kids are in bed and sound asleep, we open a bottle of wine.

"Soooo, you never told me what happened with Declan or what your dad wanted." I lift my glass and take a sip, savoring the treat Roxie brought as a housewarming gift.

She flops back on the bed with a groan and slaps a hand over her face. "Why does he still have to have *that* effect on me?"

"What effect?" I know exactly what she's talking about, but I will make her say it.

She glowers at me. "The one that makes me want to pull him into a dark closet like we're seventeen again. Only this time, I'm afraid I wouldn't care about the consequences."

I raise my eyebrows.

She sits up, careful not to spill her wine. She crosses her legs in the middle of my bed, facing me. "He's still dangerous. He's every mistake I want to make over and over again."

I take another sip. "What if it wasn't a mistake?"

She looks at me from under her eyelashes.

"I mean, he's military. He's clearly dedicated and has to have some level of maturity. He's not the kid who ran around causing a ruckus just to see how many people he could piss off. Is he dating anyone?"

She shrugs. "I don't know. I poured him a beer. We caught up for a few minutes. He smiled that devilishly handsome smile, and then I forced Micah to tend to the bar so I could wait tables."

I've known Roxie almost my whole life, and I know she didn't just run and hide. There's more.

I squint my eyes at her. "That's it. That's all that happened. No exchange of phone numbers or keeping in touch. Nothing."

There's silence, so I sip my wine until she's ready to give up the goods.

Her lips push to the side, avoiding eye contact.

"Rooooox," I say, definitely knowing this will be good.

She cups her glass with her hands. "He waited until closing and walked me to my car." Her eyes flick to mine.

"Annnndddd."

"He hugged me. And good Lord, he smelled amazing. His arms came around me, strong and firm. We stayed like that for too long, like we were lost in a moment of the past." She rubs her forehead.

A quick flash of Slade's intoxicating spicy scent and the feel of his arms around me sends a shiver up my spine. I shake it off, forcing my attention back to Rox.

"When I realized I couldn't hold onto him, I pulled away. He pushed my hair behind my ear and just. . .kissed me." She squeezes her eyes shut tight, her face scrunching. "And I kissed him back." It comes out in a rush.

I smile.

"And it was so much better than I remember. That man can kiss like there's no tomorrow."

"So, you made out in the parking lot?"

She grins. "Yep, and it was fantastic. But." She holds one finger up. "I was smart enough not to take him home because I knew there would be no going back from that. I'd for sure be sentencing my heart to Declan jail forever."

She chugs her wine and stares into her glass. "He's always seen me for me, you know. Not the rich girl, or Eve and Reggie's daughter, or the wild screw-up who won't get her life together."

"You're not a screw-up," I say, knowing Roxie is like the rest of us. She's looking for someone to love her in a way she never has been. Someone she can be her whole self with. "So, what happened?"

She shrugs. "I told him it was nice to see him, then climbed in my car."

"That's it?!"

She nods. "Yep. I got the hell out of there as fast as I could. One more second of that, and I would've made choices that wouldn't have been good for either of us."

"So, that's really it?"

She smiles. "Yes, and now I have to let that man go. That kiss had to be sayonara for good."

She has been in love with him since she was sixteen.

I let my head fall to the side. "Just like that. After all these years, you're just shutting it off."

"Yep," she says, popping the P.

"And how are you going to do that?"

"Funny, you should ask?" She sits up a little taller. "I'm getting married."

My mouth falls open as I stare at her. "Uh. . .what now?"

"That's what my dad wanted to talk about. Apparently, he's sick and will be retiring. He's getting things in order, and if I want any part of the family name and assets, I have to demonstrate that I will take managing them seriously. I've been informed I can begin to prove that by getting married."

I frown. "I don't understand. What does getting married have to do with anything?"

She picks at her nail. "I cannot be trusted to make good decisions." She lowers her voice. "They need proof I understand the obligation and duty I have to my family before they will entrust any portion of the Steinbeck legacy into my care. "

"Rox." It's my turn to guzzle my wine. "And who exactly are you marrying?"

She extends her glass, and I grab the bottle from my nightstand to refill it. "Do you remember Leo?"

I meet her gaze. "Leonard, your brother's best friend?"

Leonard Roland had a massive crush on Roxie when they were kids. He's been her brother RJ's assigned best friend since birth. Their parents are cut from the same couture cloth. Although Leonard was the quietest nerdle out there. He was short and scrawny, with wire-rimmed glasses, but the brains of a mathematician.

When she started dating Declan, he transferred to a private high school out of state. Was it a coincidence? Maybe. After, he attended Yale with RJ. Last I heard, the whiz kid was climbing Wall Street and spending his summers in the Hamptons.

"Have you lost your mind?" I'm pretty sure I'm dreaming, or this wine has made me delusional.

"Nope. We both know it's only been a matter of time before I was sucked into their plans for me." She sips as if this is resolute.

"Rox, you can't marry Leonard. You don't. . .love him. You don't even know him. When was the last time you even saw him?"

Her eyes roll to the ceiling, thinking.

"See. If you have to think about it . . ."

She shrugs. "It could be worse. He was at least a decent guy. Sometimes, even kind of. . .sweet in an innocent, fragile bird-like kind of way."

"Oh, somebody help me." I run a hand over my face. "Was, Roxie. He *was* a decent guy. Who knows what he's like now? Roxie, you cannot marry him."

"Ooooohh, but I can. I emailed him and explained my situation. After a few rounds of questions, he said yes. Turns out he's been contemplating returning to take over his family's investment firm."

I stare at her. "You're serious about this?"

She waves a hand. "It'll be a long engagement to give me time to warm up to the idea of life with Leo."

"What about love and happiness? Don't you want to spend your life with someone like Declan. Someone who kisses you breathless and drives you crazy in all the best ways? What about kids and family?"

"Declan and I could never be. Not for real." Her voice drops in defeat. "His life is soldiering, and my life will be in a big house, hosting parties and chairing committee meetings. It's been the design since the beginning, and I've avoided it long enough." She shrugs. "It could be worse. I could be forced to marry someone like Miles." Her face scrunches. "Sorry."

That pinches a little, but the truth is, we don't know that Leo's not like Miles. I keep that thought to myself. For now.

My heart aches for her. "Are you sure you have to do this? There are single businesswomen all over the world who've proven marital status has nothing to do with success."

"That may be true, but that's not how my parents think. Despite their ridiculous, strict, traditional values, I can't see everything my grandparents and the generations before worked so hard for to go to RJ. That means nothing will ever change. Besides, the land is beautiful, and despite their haughtiness and snobbery, it means something." She smiles, but it's weak.

She inhales and lets it out. "All right, what's the latest on that man who can't keep his pants zipped and his mouth from spewing anything but complete bullshit?"

I rest back against my pillows. "Well, he's moving to New York and hopes I've been thinking."

"What the hell does that mean? Have you warned him that if he doesn't start paying child support, you'll run his ass into the ground? That won't look so good for his new gig when people finally see the lying, cheating, deadbeat he is."

I roll my neck. "I'm not sure, but I bet I'll find out. He's graciously flying in next weekend and allowing us an afternoon."

She snorts. "An afternoon? He hasn't seen Ollie and Frankie for more than an hour since he kicked you out. Hell, he can't even call you back. Once he's in New York, he'll be too busy touring with his ding-a-ling to do anything but ring his own bell."

I pull air in through my nose and push it out, knowing she's not wrong. "You know, I've been thinking maybe his moving to New York is for the best. He hasn't even mentioned Ollie or Frankie. I should've expected as much. He didn't care what it did to them when he locked us out and left us with nothing, or when he dragged me through the mud to save face. I just want to move on and not allow him the power to hold anything over me again."

"But you let him. You didn't even fight it."

"What good would it have done? All it took was a few anonymous posts, and people made up their minds. I wanted to protect Ollie and Frankie. That's my job. Clapping back or defending myself would have done nothing but add more fuel to a fire I needed to put out."

She sits taller. "But, Sarah, when is it enough? You can't just let him continue to manipulate you? You and I both know that's what this *afternoon* is about. He stole everything you worked so hard for. He carefully confiscated your identity."

It's a swift jab in the stomach. I breathe until the pain lessens. "That's what this move was for me. I got myself outside of his circle, and now I have to figure out what *I* want again. If Ollie and Frankie truly don't matter to him, and he's made it pretty clear that they don't, then I want him to go to New York and leave me the hell alone. I don't want *anything* from him. I will take care of Ollie and Frankie just like I have been."

Her body slumps, and her voice softens. "But you want to be a lawyer and make a difference. I mean, it's why you worked so hard to get your voice heard. You climbed your way out of our small town and made it happen." She pauses. "Sarah, you can't keep going like this. You can't do all of this by yourself. At some point, you're going to hit a wall."

Rox is right. It was always my dream to be a lawyer. It's what I've wanted and why I chose the path I did, but motherhood changes you. Lately, I've wondered if maybe those dreams sailed away long ago with what once was my reputation.

"I'm taking it one day at a time and figuring things out as I go. I'll see what Miles has to say. I owe Ollie and Frankie at least that much, but. . .I need him to either be involved in their life or go to New York and move on. Not continue to hold it over my head and use it as leverage, thinking I'll come crawling back."

She crawls up to rest back next to me. "You've always been so strong. You kick ass, you know that?"

I laugh. "I think it's my ass that's been getting kicked."

She grabs my hand. "Maybe, but it's time for you to fight. And maybe that's finally telling Miles to piss off for good. You don't need him. You never have."

I rest my head on her shoulder.

She squeezes my palm. "I want you to be happy again. If anyone deserves it, it's you."

My throat tickles. "I want you to be happy, too."

"You're a really good mom. It doesn't matter what the dickhead says or does. He lost so big the second he even looked in another direction. It all really, really sucked, but Sarah, you're so much better off. No matter what you do, you're going to have a beautiful life. I can feel it."

I want to believe her, but right now, I can't quite see it. I'm swimming in murky water, and I don't know which way is up or if, when I get there, it will look anything like I imagined.

CHAPTER 23

SLADE

Voice message from Alex: Hey, Happy Thanksgiving. I miss you and wish I were there. Mark has a game in town in a few weeks, so the girls and I will be staying with Grandpa. Round up the guys for a beer. I want to know everything you've been working on. Tell them all hi and to give you extra shit for me. K. Love you. Bye.

"You've got to actually talk to her," Carson whispers.

Trig pulls a beer bottle from the bucket and points the neck at me. "You haven't said a single word to her since she got here."

"It's been two minutes," I grind through my teeth. "And I don't need your help with this."

They literally just got here. I opened the door, and Krissy rushed the kids while Millie pulled Sarah and her friend Roxie into hugs as if they were long-lost friends. So, I took the pie from Sarah and stepped aside.

I set it on the counter and crack open my beer. "Just mind your own damn business or go home." I lean back against the counter and take a cool, fizzy swig. "I will handle this my way so you two busybodies can go practice your elite social skills rather than pester me."

They glance at each other. "If you blow the opportunity we set before you, we aren't helping you anymore."

"Is that a promise?"

They groan and leave my kitchen, allowing me the moment of peace I need. I'm not nervous. I'm just anxious with all these people in my space and those buffoons making eyes at me every two seconds like they're some kind of matchmaking queens.

I don't want to be watched or forced. I want to get to know Sarah and have this unfold if and when it's supposed to. Slowly.

I will never tell these assholes, but I may have peeked at the book Wind left in my chair. It drones on about the grieving process. I might have gotten stuck in stage two some time ago, but they don't need to know that either. I'm working on it.

The book says these things take time, and that's what I'm doing, taking my slow ass time.

Krissy's head pops through the doorway. "Quit hiding in here. You're being rude to our guests," she whispers.

I take another long swig of my beer and push out a breath. *Maybe I can convince Ollie to go outside.*

I leave the comfort of my kitchen and join the crowd in the living room. Carson and Trig stand along the far wall, each holding a beer. Trig elbows Carson. When their gazes land on me, their lips slide into smirks, and my middle finger covertly waves in their direction.

They laugh, and I want to grab them by their necks and drag them to the front yard.

"It's wonderful to meet you. I've heard so much about you and these sweet kiddos," Millie says as Wind throws his arm around her shoulders on one end of the sectional. Next to Wind, her small frame looks even smaller.

Sarah sits on the other end, her hands around Frankie, who's standing against the back of the couch, inching her way to Krissy's outstretched arms.

Her friend, Roxie, is beside her with Ollie in her lap, his plane doing aerials through the air.

"Your eyes are absolutely mesmerizing," Mille says as if she's unable to look away.

"Have they always been like that? Two different colors?" Wind asks, and I want to reach across the room and smack him upside the head.

Sarah laughs. "Yes."

"Kids at school used to call her a mutt," Roxie says.

Sarah's eyes lift to mine but drop away.

My hands ball into fists, thinking about anyone saying things like that to her, but I have no doubt she's heard her fair share of cruel comments.

"They all ate their ugly words when she grew into a bombshell."

"Rox," Sarah warns.

"What? Seriously, look at you, and when you won—"

"Rox." Sarah widens her eyes, stopping her from finishing her sentence.

Roxie frowns in return.

I want to know what she was about to say.

Roxie isn't wrong. Sarah is crazy beautiful, but it's clear that she wants to be seen for more than that.

"What's a m-mutt?" Ollie asks, zipping his jet through the air.

The room goes silent as we all stare at Ollie and his innocent question.

"Hey, Ol," I say, catching his attention. "Let me see what you've got."

Roxie releases him, and he hops off her lap. Her eyes run over me before she returns to the conversation that's morphed into Krissy's new townhouse and decorating ideas.

I squat, and Ollie hands me his jet. "This is cool."

"It's s-s-super fast." He pushes it off my palm, and it takes off. "Can we go outside and play?"

This kid and I understand each other. "Uh . . ."

"Put your coat on," Sarah says, and my gaze snaps to hers. I want to ask her where her coat is, just to see her reaction. As if she can tell what I'm thinking, her eyelids drop slightly as she presses her lips together, trying not to smile.

My skin warms, and I need some air. I stand, feeling Ollie's little fingers latch on to mine as we head for the back door.

"We'll come with you."

I glance over my shoulder at Carson and Trig following. I want to laugh my ass off, but I hold it in until we make it into the garage.

"So, would you two like to explain to me again how to make conversation and socialize?"

Trig makes a clicking noise with his mouth. "Man, we didn't have anything to contribute to Krissy's decor choices. We just need to know when we're hauling her shit to the new place."

"That's a bad word," Ollie says, picking up the baseball I scrounged up the weekend they stayed. He tosses it gently in his little hands.

"Sorry, little man," Trig says.

"It's ok. Mama says it s-s-sometimes, too."

Carson turns on the TV over the workbench, and sports news fills the air, along with the smoke filtering into the garage from the smoker.

"Can I see those?" Ollie points to the classic Hot Wheels I collected as a kid that now sit lined up on a shelf.

I lift him, and he runs his fingers over each one as Wind joins us.

"Don't go in there? Krissy's telling labor stories." He shivers, lifting the lid on the smoker to check the turkey.

"What's this one?" Ollie holds the tiny, forest-green car.

"That's a '68 Mustang. My mom gave it to me, and it's my favorite. You know why?"

He shakes his head.

"It's called Bullitt, but see this here?" I point to the slanted back of the car. "It's a fastback. The most high-performance styled Mustang."

He makes it do a burnout and then races across the shelf.

The garage door opens again, and Roxie steps out this time. She glances around the space. "Well, this is quite the man cave, but spare me the burping and farting."

Ollie giggles, picking up another car.

"We'll try, but we make no promises," Carson says.

"Fair enough," she shrugs, stepping further into the garage. "You all skedaddled like a nest of field mice. I didn't catch which one of you called Sarah an a-hole." She crosses her arms.

I know women talk. I spent years listening to Krissy go on and on with 'she said this' and 'she said that.' In all cases, I couldn't give two shits what they were talking about unless it had something to do with hurting Krissy's feelings. But for some reason, I would like to know exactly what Sarah has said about me.

"That was Slade." Wind throws a thumb over his shoulder in my direction as he pulls on a turkey leg. "Don't worry, he calls us that all the time, but it's filled with love."

"I'm sure it is." Her head falls to the side, studying me.

I hear snickers from the corner where Trig and Carson have settled with their beers on the workbench.

She lifts her chin. "So, you live here." Her eyes squint a little, and her lips curve upward ever so slightly.

I'm unsure whether it's a question or a statement, so I remain silent.

"Swade's our n-neighbor," Ollie says.

"Huh." She strolls closer, and I put Ollie down, wondering where this might go.

"Let me see that ball." Trig waves Ollie over.

Ollie tosses it to him and follows.

Roxie squares her stance beside me. "So, you're the one who repaired her car and gave her a ride to work."

I'm unsure whether this woman is questioning me or drawing some sort of conclusion. Either way, I'm not interested in discussing my time with Sarah.

She turns toward me, crossing her arms again. She stares at me long and hard as if she's searching for something.

Her voice softens. "You know, she's new here, doesn't have a lot of friends, and is taking care of these two babies on her own."

Sarah told me she didn't have any help, but the additional confirmation is good to know. I watch Trig show Ollie how to grip the ball and then toss it to Carson.

"She's not one to ask for help even when she's drowning. It's. . .really nice, the things you've done. Thank you for looking out for her." She inhales and lets it out. "But," her chin lifts, her eyes holding mine, "she's had more than her fair share of heartbreak, so if you mess with her in any way, you'll be walking around nutless. And *that* is a promise. Got it?"

I nod once, wanting to know more.

She smiles and pats me on the arm. "Good talk." She takes two steps toward the door but stops. "Oh, you gonna be around next weekend?" She makes a circular motion with her hand.

I frown but nod again. "Yeah."

"Good." She smiles and spins for the door.

All three pairs of eyes land on me as the door closes, and Ollie runs after a rogue ball rolling out of the garage.

Carson and Trig join Wind, who's conveniently done messing with the turkey.

"What the hell is happening next weekend?" Carson asks.

I run a hand over my beard, watching Ollie try to launch the ball across the front yard. "I don't know."

"Why the hell didn't you ask?" Trig crosses his arms over his chest. "We're moving Krissy, aren't we?"

"Since you're so good at listening to other people's conversations, why didn't you ask?" I snap back.

"Both of you hush," Wind says, turning toward us. "You need to get in there and find out. If something is happening with Sarah or the kids, we should know about it. I like her, so your grouchy, sour-ass attitude needs to simmer down." He points at me.

"Yeah, we like her," Carson agrees. "If you screw this up, and she never wants to see your ugly, scowling face again, that's tough shit for you."

"I'm not screwing anything up. Nothing is happening."

All three snort.

"And whose fault is that?" Carson drawls.

My head falls back toward the sky, begging for patience.

"I'm just saying. You can take your slow ass time, or you can get in there and go after what we all know you really want."

"I don't know what I want." That might be a bit of a lie, but I go with it. "I don't know much about Sarah, and you three need to back off."

I march toward Ollie in the front yard, having had enough.

"Hey, that's the wrong way," Trig yells.

I flip them off behind my back, knowing this is the only way. If something is happening with Sarah, she's got to be the one to tell me. If she wants to. The only thing these jackasses are right about is that I have to create the opportunity for her to do that.

CHAPTER 24

SARAH

I stir the mashed potatoes and set the large spoon aside. A cold hand grips my wrist, tugging me away from the counter and through the doorway.

"Hey, what . . ." I follow Roxie, who's clearly on a mission.

She stops when we are safely out of the kitchen and turns toward me. "*That's* Slade?" she whispers, pointing in the direction of the garage where she escaped to rather than helping set food out.

I stare at her, wondering what she's getting at.

She crosses her arms, her head falling to the side in annoyance. "Tall, tattooed, and brawny. Looks like he should grace the cover of *Sexy Uptown Lumberjacks*."

I laugh, and she doesn't break her miffed state.

"*He's* the guy who fixed your car, drove you to work, and that you've been shacking up with?"

I frown, hearing the back door open, and Wind announces the turkey is done. "We are not shacking up together. We stayed here for two nights because I had no *running* water."

She cuts a hand through the air. "Semantics. You did *not* tell me that A: He and Ollie are like this." She crosses her fingers as her eyes bug out. "And B: He's clearly got it bad for you."

Laughter tumbles out of my mouth, and I cup a hand over it, hearing the guys enter the kitchen.

"He does not have it bad for me," I whisper. "We're friends, and that's it. I'm pretty sure he only tolerates me because I remind him of his mom, who struggled to raise two kids on her own."

She rolls her eyes. "Oh, please. Keep telling yourself that, sister." She leans closer as the noise in the kitchen grows louder. "I saw the way he looked at you earlier, and let's just be real, he was *not* thinking about his mother."

My cheeks grow warm, knowing what look she might be referring to, but I don't think it means what she wants it to. Or maybe I'm not sure if I want it to mean that.

I recall his strong hands and the way they gripped my waist. Yep, that doesn't help.

"It's nothing," I say, needing it to be true. "We're just. . .friends."

Her stance and eyes soften. "You know, you can let yourself think about it being more than that if you want it to be, right?"

I glance at the floor. Given my record, I'm not sure it's a permission I should be in charge of.

"It's been a long time, Sarah. Way too long. Everything that happened that wasn't about you. It was about him." She waits for me to meet her gaze, and she grins. "The best revenge is to let yourself be happy."

I roll my eyes and smile, grabbing her hand and pulling her back into the kitchen.

We step into the tight quarters, and Slade stands just inside the door with Frankie in one massive arm. She pulls on the bill of his hat, and he tickles her side.

I get a sharp elbow to the ribs. "Yeah. Good luck sticking to that friend zone," Roxie mumbles, and I elbow her back.

"Come on. Line up and load up." Wind waves people toward the plates.

"Wook, Mama!" Ollie holds out his hand with an old green car. "Dis is Swade's f-favorite. His mama g-gave it to him." He speeds it across the table, making the appropriate noises.

I glance at Slade, but he avoids eye contact, tickling Frankie again.

I fill Ollie's plate and settle him at the table. Slade sits beside him with Frankie on his lap, patting the table and babbling.

I reach for her, but Slade stops me.

"You go first, then you can sit with them."

"You sure?"

He nods.

"Kris, how many loads will it take to get all your sshhh-stuff moved next weekend?" Trig asks from the back of the line.

"Probably a few, and I need help getting a couch from one of my co-workers this week. If you all work hard and keep your groaning to a minimum, I'll buy pizza and beer for dinner."

"I w-wanna come," Ollie says, dropping a strip of turkey in his mouth.

"You guys should come for dinner. I'll give you a tour of my new place," Krissy says, sliding around the table next to Ollie.

"Thank you. That would be fun, but we can't," I say quickly.

"Aw. I wanna go," Ollie whines. "That's n-no fair." He pouts, crossing his arms over his chest and tucking his chin.

"Ol," I say, needing him to knock it off.

"Another time, ok?" Krissy rubs his back.

"Hmph," he grunts.

"Ollie, don't be rude."

"Eat up, folks, and get ready for games," Carson says, rubbing his hands together. "We'll start with charades, Slade's favorite."

"I'm not playing your games," Slade grumbles.

Trig turns from scooping stuffing onto his plate. "You haven't been practicing your miming skills? We warned you last year."

"You're gonna have to be on your own team," Wind says, carrying a heaping plate to the living room. "I've never seen someone so terrible at acting out eating."

Slade groans, and I roll my lips together, trying not to laugh as I set my plate on the table.

"Or driving," Krissy snorts, covering her mouth as she laughs.

"That was unfair, and you all know it," Slade points at her.

"But was it?" Carson asks, and the room erupts with laughter.

I can't hold it in, and his eyes land on me.

"I wouldn't laugh. These jokers cheat," he says, completely serious.

I reach for Frankie. "I'll have to judge that for myself."

He glares underneath his hat as he hands Frankie over.

I take Frankie, helping her with the mashed potatoes while she shoves pieces of roll into her mouth. Voices and laughter fill the house, and I listen, trying to remember a Thanksgiving like this.

Growing up, my mom and I ate in the community building of the trailer park. When I married Miles, he was always working, so I never cooked a meal, and it was just Ollie and me.

But this is nice—the teasing and laughter. Being here is easy and comfortable, and I haven't felt that before.

We eat, and when the kids are done, I hand Frankie off to Roxie, then help Millie and Wind store food and clean the kitchen.

When we're finished, we join the group in the living room. I sit on the floor with Roxie as Frankie walks along the edge of the couch.

As promised, the games begin. Krissy stands in the middle of the floor, drumming and marching, and the whole room starts to shout.

"Marching band," Trig yells, and Krissy circles her finger in the air.

"Parade," Carson guesses, and she throws her hands in the air.

Millie draws next and takes her spot front and center.

Slade sits quietly in the recliner with Ollie, watching the football game. He said he wasn't playing, and he wasn't kidding. I expect nothing less of the man who seems to do exactly what he says.

When Millie's turn is over, Roxie scoots closer. "I have to get going."

I nod. "Ok. Let me get our—"

"No, all my stuff is in the car. You should stay."

She stands and kisses the kids goodbye, thanking everyone. I walk her outside and hug her tight, not wanting her to go.

I hold onto her, forcing out the thing that's been on the tip of my tongue since last night. "You can't marry Leonard, Rox. I know you're trying to do the right thing, and it's important to retain part of your family's legacy, but you can't marry him. It's the rest of your life."

She squeezes me and then pulls away. "I don't have a choice."

"Yes, you do." I inhale the cool, brisk air. "But, you've got to stop running and trying to punish your parents long enough to figure out what you really want. Spontaneously marrying Leonard is just another way to lash out."

She laughs, but there's a tinge of ridicule in it. "Actually, Leo is exactly who they'd want me to marry."

"But it gives you additional ammunition to despise them and lots of opportunity to throw your unhappiness in their face. Is that worth what it will cost you?"

Her eyes flick between mine, and she scoffs.

"Isn't that what you've been doing?" Her tone is like a punch in the gut.

"What?"

"Running and hiding." She gestures toward the house with her chin. "In there. Here." She holds out her arms. "Seems to me you ran, and you're still hiding. First, it was behind Miles and his loud-ass ego, while that man did nothing but take from you. Shit, he still is."

"Rox, that's not fair. I have Ollie and Frankie to think about."

"But now you're here. New home, new job, new life, and you're still hiding. You won't tell Miles to pay up or fuck off. You continue to let him string you along and play into his manipulative hand while he flounces around pretending to be the next bachelor."

I pull in air, not knowing what to say.

"You don't even want those people inside, your new friends, to know who you are. Do they know about Miles? Who he is? What he did? It was clear you didn't want them to know anything about you—who you are and what you accomplished before he stripped it from you. Everything you fought so hard to achieve."

She pauses, and my heart pounds to each beat of silence. "I'm not the only one running, Sarah. You're scared to actually move on and let people in."

My lungs ache, moving in and out quickly, making it difficult to breathe. "It's embarrassing." I squeeze my eyes shut tight, choking it out. "All of it. You think this is what I wanted? Who I want to be?"

I shake my head, my eyes and throat consumed with a raging fire. "I used to know who I was. That brave girl you remember, I made her who she was, but . . ." I swallow, needing to wash it all down before the flood bursts through my only remaining reinforcements. "I lost her, her dreams and ideas, and I don't know if she's ever coming back. I don't know what else to do other than. . .this."

It's the whole truth. The one I've never released out loud, so damn afraid of what it means. That's what happens when you allow yourself to be consumed by someone else. When they use you and your trust. When they lie and cheat over and over again, you no longer love or trust yourself. You become the person you despise. The person you told yourself you'd never be. And it's devastating and humiliating.

She sniffs, and I open my eyes as she swipes her cheek—my best friend. "I guess we both have to quit running and hiding from the things that scare us. Maybe it's time we figure out who we're gonna be now."

She holds my gaze a moment longer before turning and descending the steps. I watch her cross the street and climb into her car. I hold my breath to contain the sob that's on the verge of breaking me.

I swipe my tears away and drop to the top step, needing a minute to ease the burn of her raw words. The ones that only hurt so damn bad because they're likely filled with truth.

Only a best friend can do that—call us out and force us to face ourselves to give us a chance to be free of all that holds us back from being who they know we truly are. It doesn't mean it's less painful. Sometimes, love hurts.

I watch her car disappear down the street, knowing she's absolutely right but not having any idea what to do about it. I'm trying the best I know how. With Miles, I want to do right by Ollie and Frankie, but I also can't let him jerk me around. I can't keep leaving space for him in their life when he hasn't earned it.

I used to be so sure of everything I wanted and what I was working toward. But now, I wonder if I'm trying to shove old dreams into a life that doesn't have room for them. Or maybe I'm hiding behind them because I don't have a clue what life looks like without them giving me direction or purpose. Maybe I'm scared of where I'll end up with nothing guiding me.

The screen door pushes open and closes behind me, and I swipe my cheeks with my sleeve, drying them quickly.

"You ok?"

I squeeze my eyes shut tight at that soft, low tone, guessing he saw our conversation play out from his chair.

Fan-fucking-tastic.

"Yeah." I sniff, clearing my nose. "Just the truth really sucks sometimes."

His boots land on the step below, and he takes a seat beside me. We sit in the silence of the brisk, gentle evening breeze for a few moments.

If I'm going to stop hiding, maybe this occasional, abrasive, blunt grump is the one to test it out on. I'm pretty sure I don't have to fear him sparing my feelings.

I wipe my nose on my sleeve, curled around my fist for comfort. "Do you ever feel like one of those dogs chasing after the fake rabbit? You're running as hard as you can, but you might get to the end of the race and find out you've been punked?" I feel his gaze drift down to me. "Or worse, you realize you put the dummy out there to begin with, so you only have yourself to blame for all the wasted time and energy and the absolute mess you're left with."

"I've chased a stuffed bunny or two." It's all he says.

He sits quietly, and I drop my head onto my bent knees. "I have no idea what I'm doing or what I'm supposed to do. I think instead of a fake rabbit, I might be chasing my own damn tail."

"What do you want, Sarah?" His calm, deep voice asks the million-dollar question.

I pull myself up. "That's just it. I used to know, but now . . ." I stare at the street, needing it to give me direction. "I want to be the woman I used to be." The words bleed from me, and it's agonizing to admit it. "The one who knew exactly what she stood for and what she wanted and didn't give up. I want to be brave and not give a single shit what anyone thinks or if anyone believes I can't make it."

"Who doesn't believe?" His question is soft but skeptical.

"At the moment. . .me." The truth stabs me square in the chest.

I inhale a deep breath and blow it out. "I've always wanted to be a lawyer. I want to help people and make a difference. It was my plan. I did all the right things and was on my way." I glance at him, deciding not to hide this time, at least not from him. "But I got sidetracked by the wrong guy and made a lot of stupid decisions, sacrificing myself in the process."

I wipe the tears that won't quit flowing, "Now, Ollie and Frankie are my life. They're everything, and I'm terrified I'm screwing up more than I already have. I don't know how to do both. Be the kind of mom I want to be, keep up with school, and work the hours it would take me to get there."

He glances at me, and his eyes linger for a second, but I keep my attention on his withered yard. "Is that what you still want?"

I shake my head. "I don't know. I moved here to start over with a job that would help me climb my way back, but. . .I'm not going anywhere. I think I'm stuck in the same damn place. Or what if it was the wrong plan all along, and I just didn't know it?" I let my head fall back. "I'm a mess," I whine.

The silence falls around us. When he doesn't say anything, my temperature spikes along with my desire to melt into a puddle of goo and slide down the steps one by one like a cartoon character.

Finally, he speaks. "Maybe you don't have to figure it out all by yourself." His gentle words halt my panic.

I inhale, letting that thought sink in. I'm not used to having anyone to rely on. Miles is Miles and selfish to the core. As a kid, my mom was busy working, and when she wasn't, she was dating and being the socialite of our small trailer park community.

Even she didn't understand my need to step outside our town and the routine she lived by. It was freaking lonely, but I did it.

I bump his bicep with my shoulder. "Something tells me that doesn't come naturally for you either." I glance at him again. "What about you? Do you know what you want?"

His shoulders rise with an inhale. "The guys and my best friend say I need to get a life now that Krissy is moving out."

That didn't quite answer my question, but I let it slide. "Is that true?" I want to see if this quiet, sealed-off man will give me more.

"I've been on autopilot for a long time, but I'm realizing if I keep that up, I'll be missing out on everything life could be."

I swing back around to the original question this man slyly avoided. "But do you *know* what it could be?"

His green eyes peek at me. "I'm beginning to see flickers."

I take a deep breath and shiver, tucking myself into a ball. One heavy arm drops around me, his long fingers curling around my side. I don't even think about it, leaning into him and resting my head on his shoulder.

We sit like that for a minute, and I close my eyes, wanting to stay where he can block all that waits for me.

"Everything is going to be all right, Sarah."

"You sound so sure of it." I want to believe like he does.

"At some point, you're just going to have to trust me."

I laugh. "You might be underestimating the size of the mess."

His arm falls away before I'm ready for it to.

"Maybe." He climbs to his feet and extends his hand to pull me up. "But anybody who'd underestimate you would be a damn fool."

I look up into those deep green eyes and see he believes what he just said. A burn crawls up my throat with amazing force, and I have to breathe through it.

The only thing I know for sure is that I should *not* be thinking what I'm thinking or feeling what I'm beginning to feel for this man. I need to lock that shit down until I know what I'm doing with my life.

I blow out a breath, take his hand, and he tugs me up. I pull open the screen door.

"If they're still playing those stupid ass games, Ollie and I are taking Grover out."

I raise my eyebrows, turning to look at him. "You know, now that you'll finally have a bachelor pad and are looking to explore what life has to offer, you should consider game nights. They're highly entertaining and create a great low-key opportunity to socialize. It's perfect for you."

His eyelids droop. "I'd rather punch myself in the face."

I laugh, pushing the door open. "Who knew you were so dramatic?"

We step inside to the guys yelling at the game on the TV, with Ollie sitting between them, lining their long legs with planes for a makeshift runway.

"Ma-ma," Frankie's eyes brighten as she twists to see me from her spot on the floor with Krissy. She cuts a beeline for me, and I scoop her up.

Her squishy arms squeeze my neck.

"Mama, w-why does my b-butt have a crack in it?"

The room goes still at Ollie's matter-of-fact question. Then, the snickers break free, and Ol giggles, his small shoulders scrunching to his ears as he grins that mischievous grin.

I smile at him and press Frankie to my chest, kissing her cheek in return. These babies. My everything.

Somehow, I'll figure this out, and it'll be ok. I've got them, and that's all I need. I just have to hope that, eventually, everything else will sort itself out.

CHAPTER 25

SARAH

MILES: My flight arrives at 12:30 p.m. on Saturday. My assistant has reserved a car. Send me your address.

I stare at my phone. I haven't been alone with Miles since I told him I was taking Ollie to stay with my mom. I'd just found out I was pregnant with Frankie, and thankfully, Ollie doesn't seem to remember it.

I could ignore him or tell him he's not welcome, but we need to talk. It's been a long time coming, and I have to know where we go from here. Miles lashes out when things don't go his way, and I don't need any more thrown onto my pile. I need understanding and direction.

"Everything ok?"

I set my phone back in my lap. "Yes, sorry."

Kat flips through the report. "So, this is everything? Have you requested all investment accounts and real estate records over the last five years?"

I nod. "All marital assets are jointly owned, and each has a retirement account. Although they've contributed far more to his than hers."

Kat smiles. "Very nice." She shuffles the papers together and taps them on her desk. "Excellent work. Now, if only I can get these two to sort things out amicably."

"It seems like it should be pretty clear-cut."

She rolls her eyes. "You'd think so. You should sit in if you don't have anything pressing tomorrow morning. Hopefully, you can get a glimpse of what it's like when people know how to be reasonable rather than spiteful."

I smile. "Yes. That would be great."

"If you want, we can ride together and grab lunch afterward."

"Sounds good."

She tips back in her chair. "How was your Thanksgiving?"

"It was good. We went to Slade and Krissy's Friendsgiving. We had a really great time."

It's true, except for my tough conversation with Roxie. It might have been necessary, but I hate how we left things.

"How about you?" I ask, avoiding further questions.

"I flew home and spent time with my nieces and nephews while dodging subtle comments about my age and childbearing years."

I wave a hand. "You have plenty of time."

"Not if this job sucks all of the life and vitality out of me," she laughs.

My phone buzzes, and I flip it over, seeing it's Ollie's school. "I'm sorry. It's the preschool."

She shoos me to answer. "This is Sarah." I dart back to my office.

"Mrs. Atwater, Ollie is in the office. He's not feeling well. You need to come get him."

"Uh." I glance at my watch. It's only ten thirty, and I don't qualify for paid time off. "Ok. I'm on my way."

I shut my computer down and grab my things.

"Where's the fire? It's not even lunchtime."

I spin, and Junior leans against my doorway. "Nope, but I have to go." I tug my coat on and throw my bag across my body.

"I'm too late then. I thought you could join Seth and me. We could get to know each other." He smiles.

I would roll my eyes if I had time. "Sorry, not today. Or really, ever." I charge forth, and he moves out of the way.

"Next time, then." He hollers at my back.

I push into the waiting area and stop at Marcie's desk. Robyn notified us through a group email this morning that she wouldn't be in. Her roommate had a traumatic experience with a spider, and she was comforting her.

"May I put you on hold for a quick sec?" Marcie presses the button and places the phone on her shoulder. "How many ways can you say I'm not entitled to give you that information?" She huffs but then smiles.

"I have to go. Ollie is sick."

Her mouth turns down. "I'll let Griffin know when he gets back. I hope he feels better."

Fifteen minutes later, I find my little guy curled up in a chair in the office. I squat down and run my hand over his warm head.

"Mama."

"Hey, buddy. You ready to go home?"

He nods, and I pick him up.

"Thank you for calling me," I say to the assistant.

"We hope you feel better, Oliver," she says as we exit the office.

I carry him through the building and almost reach the door.

"Mrs. Atwater."

I turn, adjusting Ollie's weight, and his teacher smiles.

"I was hoping to catch you. I provided Helen with information about speech therapy, but I wanted to ensure that you received it as well. Oliver is doing great, but you may consider getting a jump start on those speech issues." Her head weighs from side to side. "Kids are kids, and it won't get easier for him."

I try to smile, but I can't. "Thank you. I'm. . .looking into it."

She nods once, running a hand over Ollie's back. "Feel better, Oliver. We'll see you soon."

I turn, ready to get him home.

Ollie's feverish head rests on my thigh, and I have no doubt a large pool of drool has soaked through my leggings. I peek down and pull a Kleenex from the box, folding it to wipe the line of snot pouring from his nose. I toss it in the makeshift trash and carefully scoot down into the couch a little further.

Frankie is sound asleep on my chest as I watch Bluey and Bingo play a game called Elevator. Helen had offered to stay so I could go back to work, but Ollie cried, and the decision was made.

I rest my head against the couch, closing my eyes.

My phone buzzes, and my eyes pop open. I glance around, trying to remember where I am. It vibrates against my leg, and I shift Frankie to glance at it.

Roxie.

I swipe to answer. "Hang on sec," I whisper, slipping my feet out from under Grover.

I ease Ollie's head off my leg and carry Frankie to her bed, hurrying back for my phone.

"Hey, I'm so glad you called."

"Why were you whispering?"

"Ollie's sick, and Frankie fell asleep on me."

"Oh, that's no good." She pauses while I load the dirty dishes into the dishwasher. "I was going to call yesterday, but I had to go to work early." There's a brief pause. "Sarah, I'm sorry."

I adjust the phone between my ear and shoulder and push Grover away from licking the dishes. "I'm sorry, too. I shouldn't have—"

"No. You're right. At least about wanting to punish my parents and then throwing my unhappiness in their faces. I would definitely do that."

"Well, you weren't totally wrong about me hiding either. I am. I just don't know what to do about it. I don't want people to see what I've become."

"Sarah." The way she says my name sounds painful. "You don't have anything to be ashamed of."

"But you know how people judged even before Miles, and then when he posted all those lies . . ." I rinse a cup. "Everyone believed it without a second thought. I just. . .want to leave all that behind." I whisper the last of it. "I think I want to leave the person I was behind, too."

There's a long moment of silence for the sad truth.

"But she's part of you, and she's amazing. You're incredible, Sarah. Don't let what Miles did make you afraid to love her still and be proud of who she is. It gives his lies way more power than they ever should have had."

I think about that, and she's not wrong. Trying to leave that woman behind might be part of my problem. I might just need her and everything she went through to piece together who I'm supposed to become.

I blow out the heaviness of that revelation, admitting the rest of it. "I'm scared to face Miles." I grip the phone tightly. "I keep hoping he'll show he cares about Ollie and Frankie, but I'm really afraid that won't happen. Then, I'll have to finally accept the kind of man I married. Even worse, no matter how much I wish I didn't, I could use his financial support."

My entire body sags with the weight of the whole truth—every pathetic bit of it.

"But you can't let Miles walk all over you or be a puppeteer." Her voice is so soft. "It won't change him or who he is. Sarah, you have to be able to move on for real and find out what you truly want. For Ollie and Frankie, but also for yourself."

"I know." And I do. I need answers so I know where to start rebuilding from. "He'll be here Saturday and has to decide if he wants to be a part of Ollie and Frankie's life. He'll have to do more than say it. He has to show it."

"Now we're talking." I smile at her encouragement. "While you're laying down the law, knee him in the balls for me."

I laugh, needing it. "How about you? Are you and Leonard still getting hitched?"

I hear her push out a breath. "Yes, but hear me out. I've only been biding my time managing the bar to irritate the shit out of my parents."

"But you love it." I remind her.

"I do, but there are other things I can love. I just have to figure out how to do them my way."

"You're talking about marrying a stranger," I say softly, knowing he's not a complete stranger, but she hasn't seen Leo in years, so he might as well be.

"Would it be nice to marry a guy I was attracted to and in love with? Sure, but it takes a special breed to withstand my family and their expectations and obligations. Despite how much I'd like to, I'm not willing to give it all up. I never have been. It's why I'm still here."

"So, you're marrying Leonard Roland."

"Yep. He agreed anyway. He's in the same boat. He could marry me or worry about marrying someone who's only with him for his money."

"Rox, I want you to be happy. What if he's no longer the nerdy, fragile bird but a socially awkward, arrogant, brilliant ass who can't hold a conversation with regular folk because he thinks we're imbeciles who aren't worth even a second of his time?"

"Whoo! You're starting to sound like me." She laughs. "Well, we'll have a long engagement, and I'll still have time to speed date."

I laugh at the craziness of it all.

"Speaking of dating," she sings. "It's time for you to know what that's like again. And I think there might be a tall, ruggedly gorgeous man across the street who could help with that." I hear her smile.

My cheeks begin to warm just thinking about Slade in the way she might be suggesting, but then I hear it. The sound no person wants to hear—a heavy grunt and then a rush of liquid splatting against the floor.

"M-m-mama," Ollie whines, bent over the mass of puke.

"Rox, I gotta go." I haul Grover to the door by the collar and shove him outside.

"K. Love you. Bye."

I drop my phone on the counter and swipe the paper towels, along with the disinfectant and the trash can.

This. This is my life. I shove down all nerves and fear and get to work cleaning up barf.

Somehow, everything will be ok. I have no choice but to believe it.

CHAPTER 26

SLADE

"I compared it to Mom's medical records, and I don't have the genetic markers." Krissy leans over my desk, pointing to the report that might as well be written in a foreign language.

The impact gun grinds in the background. "That's good, right?"

"Yeah, but I've done some research, and this other stuff doesn't make sense." She slides her finger over the report like I'm supposed to be able to decipher what it means. "Mom didn't have this descent." She stares, waiting for me to connect the dots.

"What?" I rest back in my chair, my eyes lingering over all the information again.

She plops down in the chair across from me. "It means our dad is likely a carrier."

My gaze lifts to hers, and she lets that sit there for a moment.

She fiddles with the hem of her shirt. "I've. . .been thinking about seeing if I can find him."

"Kris, I don't—"

She holds up her hand. "I know you've never wanted to talk about him or know anything, but this is different. We're talking medical history. I don't want anything from him. I just want to know if there's a history that we should be aware of. I mean, stuff like this can be important."

I set the paper on the desk and stare across the space at my sister. I know she wants far more than that, but she'll never get what she's really searching for.

"Kris, there was a reason he wasn't involved or around, and Mom never talked about him. Whatever this test shows, it doesn't really matter, does it?" I need that to be true for her sake.

She shrugs one shoulder, inspecting her nails. "It might." Her eyes lift to mine underneath her long, dark eyelashes, her hands dropping into her lap. "I just . . . Don't you ever want to know what he looks like or what he does? I mean, he might be a drug dealer or addict, or a crime boss. What if he's spending life in prison?" She straightens in her seat. "Some of those things can be hereditary. Wouldn't you want to know if you're in jeopardy of becoming a serial killer?"

I tip back in my chair. "Really?" I stare at her. "Kris, nothing good will come from you digging into something that had nothing to do with us."

She crosses her arms and exhales, then pushes her lips to the side. I can see her frustration and disappointment. "You could do a test. At least we could see if you're also a carrier of some of these things. It might give us a better idea of how prevalent or serious it might be."

"Like developing serial killer tendencies?"

She shrugs both shoulders this time. "You are kind of obsessive about certain things."

I roll my eyes. If a quick spit test keeps her from searching for our father and possibly creating a shit storm we don't need any part of, then it's a no-brainer. "Fine."

She smiles. "Thank you. I'll order one, and it'll be here in a few days, but you have to mail it in." Her smile fades. "Aren't you ever curious who Mom was hiding and why? She was so beautiful and fun and full of life." Her eyes drop to the floor. "There are so many things I wish I could ask her."

Our mom was beautiful and smart and deserved so much better than what she got. But I learned long ago that sometimes we won't ever understand why even the people we love the most do the things they do or make the choices they make.

In her case, she loved someone who never loved her back. She was second choice, a long-time secret, and Kris and I were casualties.

"Truth?" I ask, and she nods. "I got tired of wondering and her non-answers." It felt like she was protecting him, and I never understood that. "It's one of those things we might always wonder, but she loved you. . .so much. That's what matters."

Her lips form a sad smile. "She loved you, too."

The complicated wave of feelings I try to avoid stirs, and I need it to settle back down.

"Order the test, and I'll send it in."

She smiles and pushes out of her chair, folding up the paper and placing it back in the envelope.

I follow her out of my office and into the noisy shop.

"Boy, who showed you how to zip a tire like that? You're gonna give Trigger a run for his money." Carson stands next to Luke, inspecting his quick work.

Luke emailed me over the weekend and told me that he could start on Monday. The farm boy was here before I arrived this morning.

"All right, boys," Krissy hollers. "Saturday morning, bright and early. Bring your muscles, but pissy attitudes and groans will be parked at the curb."

Trig rolls out from underneath a truck and sits up. "Do you want our help or not?"

Krissy sets her hands on her hips. "Yes, but for every smartass comment or complaint, there will be a deduction from the dinner allowance."

"That's not fair. We'll end up paying for it after helping you move," Wind yells from the pit.

Krissy grins.

"I can help." Luke pops up, his bright, young eyes focused on Krissy.

"Are you capable of lifting boxes and moving quickly?" Krissy asks, and he nods. "You're hired." She gives him a thumbs up, crossing to the door. "Pizza and beer are on me if these numbnuts can keep their traps shut."

"Lata losers." She waves duces, and the door bangs closed.

Wind's voice comes from the pit. "Hey, Princess Leia. I know you're trying to be helpful, but just know that's Slade's sister."

"Eyes and hands to yourself, man, and finish that up," Carson points to the remaining tires needing to be installed and walks toward me.

Luke's cheeks turn bright red. "I was just . . ."

"It's all right," Trig says, slapping him on the shoulder. "We gotta lay down the ground rules. It's part of the initiation."

I pull up the afternoon schedule, and Carson leans against the counter.

"Everything ok?"

Krissy walked in with our lunch orders and announced she had received her DNA test results. When she started to dissect them, I pulled her into the office, not wanting to discuss her personal information in front of everyone.

I scroll through the remaining appointments. "Yeah. She wants me to do one of those tests."

He runs a hand over his scruffy face. "But her results are ok?"

His eyes flick between mine, and I frown, wondering if she told him about the test and why she was doing it.

"Yeah. She's not a carrier for the genes our mom had."

He nods slowly. "That's good. She wants you to do a test?" His brows pull together.

"There's some stuff she thinks is strange. She wants to see if my results show the same thing."

"And that'll tell you something?"

I huff. "Hell if I know. If it'll keep her from searching for our dad . . ."

Carson is the only one who knows about our dad, and that's only because we ran into him one night while having a beer after the gym.

"She wanted to?" he asks softly.

"That asshole will only hurt her, and I'll be damned if I see that happen."

He pushes out a breath. "Want to hit the gym tonight?"

I nod. "Sure."

Wind joins us, leaning his elbow on the counter next to me. "So, have you heard anything from Sarah? Re-extended an invitation for Saturday dinner at Krissy's, perhaps?"

Carson stifles a laugh as I turn my head to look at him. "Are you logging a spreadsheet? And why the hell are you talking like that?"

He straightens. "Just being an accountability partner, and Millie's been watching Downton Abbey. The dialect gets stuck in my head."

"Well, stop it. It's weird and uncomfortable, and who the hell says perhaps?"

"So? Have you?" Wind pushes.

I grunt. "She said she was busy, but do you honestly think I'd tell you?"

The answer is no, but I'm not telling him shit. It's only been a few days since I sat with her on my porch, and she revealed things I assume aren't for public consumption.

She told me that truth hurts, and sometimes it really does. These idiots are making me face a fear I've avoided long enough. It's a risk to put myself out there. It's the fear the nineteen-year-old me didn't even consider—just a kid seeking love and comfort amidst heartache and pain. Instead, I watched every single thing slip through my fingers, and I couldn't do a damn thing about it.

But when Sarah told me she wanted to be brave and the kind of person who doesn't give a shit what other people think, it made me realize I've been a coward—sealing myself off and making excuses, terrified to go after what I want. If I'm honest, it's what I've always wanted.

"We saw that sweet moment on the porch. You puttin' your arm around her," Carson drawls. "Smooth move, man. I didn't know you had it in you."

"Listen, she was having a tough time. I did what any of you would have done if it were Krissy." The difference is I didn't want to let her go, and when her sad eyes stared up at me, a wave of need swooped through me with a power I'd not felt before.

I didn't just want to hold her. I wanted to haul her to me and kiss her until she believed everything would be all right. I wanted her to know she doesn't have to figure things out by herself and that I can help. That maybe we could be scared together.

I won't be doing any such thing until I understand more. I want to know about this guy Roxie mentioned. The one I suspect is Ollie and Frankie's father. More than that, I want to get to the bottom of why she doesn't believe in herself and who is responsible.

"It's all buttoned up." Luke strolls over, saving me from this conversation.

"Have you ever changed an oxygen sensor?" I ask.

He shakes his head.

I nod in the direction of a Ford Escape. "Come on. I'll get you started."

Wind returns to the Dodge van with a coolant leak, but points at me. "I'll be in touch, partner."

"This isn't AA."

He laughs. "Sure isn't, but we are in the business of recovering hearts." He holds his hands in the shape of a heart over his chest.

"Who else has a broken heart?" Luke asks, glancing around the room through the mop of hair falling over his forehead.

The garage stills to the sounds of Trig guzzling his water. He burps. "I don't."

Carson snorts. "That's cause you chase tail like it's your day job. Someday that's gonna catch up with you," Carson says, pulling a wrench from his tool chest.

Trig tosses his bottle in the trash. "Nah, man. You're just too much like Slade. So serious all the time. You don't know how to let go and have fun."

I hand Luke a wrench. "Lesson one: Don't listen to these morons."

"What's lesson two?" His earnest, boyish face shines with eagerness.

My hand pauses in front of the firewall. I think of Cal and everything he taught me. He gave me a job and a place to bury the pain. Over time, he showed me what it means to be a man.

I look at him. "Figure out the kind of man you're gonna be."

"Then, what?"

"Shit, kid. This is a one-step-at-a-time program."

"Hell yeah, it is!" Wind hollers.

I roll my eyes. They might be total pains in my ass, but I'd follow these misfits to the front line anytime, anywhere.

And it doesn't totally suck to have them in my corner as I navigate the intimidating unknown, either.

CHAPTER 27

SARAH

He sits, his forearms resting on his knees, his attention solely on his phone.

I glance at Ollie. He wipes his nose on his sleeve and then makes airplane noises as his jet takes off. I rock Frankie, who still has a slight fever and snot pouring from her nose.

I shiver, ready for him to leave so I can lie down.

Ollie coughs, and Miles's eyes flick to him. He leans away, inching back against the couch. "You need to cover your mouth."

My entire body aches, but I roll my eyes despite the effort. Even my hair hurts.

Ollie ignores him. "D-d-do you want to see my c-cars?" He asks tentatively, expecting Miles to say yes. "They're in my room."

"Um. . .how about you get them?"

Ollie heads to his room, and Grover follows close behind.

Miles's gaze turns to me. "He still talks like that? He can't start school that way. They won't even be able to understand him."

If I didn't feel like I was in the process of being run over by a truck and had the energy, I'd punch him.

He pulled up an hour ago, sliding out of his luxury rental, and tiptoed in here, as if this were the low-income housing I grew up in. His eyes lingered over Frankie for only a moment. She tucked herself into a ball against my chest as he sat on the edge of the couch to peruse his phone. Ollie clung to me for the first fifteen minutes but tried to get Miles's attention multiple times to no avail.

His eyes survey the space. "So, this is where your dad grew up?" His nose scrunches slightly.

This is what he wants to talk about.

I rest my head against the back of the recliner, ready for him to go. "You're aware I don't know the answer to that. He was listed as the beneficiary, but since he's dead, I was next of kin."

He twists, still examining the space. "How old is it?"

I exhale. "Miles, why are you here?"

He straightens and huffs; that familiar smug look reminds me I'm an idiot. "You know why? This is ridiculous. You living here." He glances around again, disgust filling his freshly facialed face. "You made your point. Are you done now? I got the job in New York. Sunday mornings are only the beginning. This is it. This is what we always wanted."

I stare at him. "Uh. . .what?"

His leans forward again. "Sarah, I gave you the life you wanted. I got you out of that dump you grew up in, and now I'll take you all the way to the top. If you want to go to school, fine. You can do that in New York. You'll be beside me as we sweep in as Manhattan's new 'it' couple."

My body heats to a thousand degrees as my mind explodes into a million pieces. I stare at him. He's fucking serious.

Ollie slowly walks back into the room, using his shirt as a cradle for a pile of Hot Wheels. He spills them on the couch next to Miles and begins to line them up.

"Dis one is a c-c-cupcake car? Grandma Susie j-just sent it to me." Ollie holds up the tiny, pink cupcake with wheels.

Miles only looks at it.

"And dis one has a turbo engine. It goes s-s-super fast." He races it along the couch and up Miles's leg, then holds it in front of his face.

Miles leans away. "Can you say cup-cake?"

Ollie's eyes move from the car to Miles. "C-c-cupcake."

I've had enough. "Hey, bud, can you go find your blue Charger?" I scoot out of the recliner, careful not to wake Frankie.

I follow Ollie and lie Frankie in her crib, pulling the door closed. I hear Ollie rummaging through his cars and head back to the living room.

Miles is to tapping away on his phone.

"It's time to go."

His gaze shoots to mine.

When he doesn't move, I drag myself to the front door and pull it open, making myself clear.

After a moment, he stands and finally shoves his phone into his pocket. I follow him onto the porch, closing the door behind me.

He turns to face me. "So, how is this going to work?"

I blink, wondering if the fever is making me delusional. I blink again, and his too-smooth face still stares at me with anticipation.

I inhale, needing patience to be in the air. "How is what going to work?"

"Us. New York." His brow creases.

"You're serious?" I really need to know if this joker has somehow developed amnesia. Has he somehow forgotten the past six years and the things he's done?

His eyelids droop. "How long will you keep doing this?" He huffs a little laugh. "You're never going to make it." His eyes run over me. "Look at you. You're a mess. You don't even look like you." His hand flies out to the side. "This house is old and already falling apart." He points to the muddy mess of my front yard. "Oliver can't even talk, and there is absolutely no one here to save you." He pauses, and I wonder how he'd like a fist to the throat. "It's not like you can go back to prancing around a stage using your body to spark a career."

There we go. The lowest blow, but for some reason, the bite doesn't sting quite so bad.

"You're a mom now. Even your eyes can't make up for what that changed."

I cross my arms over my chest. "You done now?"

He crosses his arms, satisfied with his belittlement.

"Miles, it's time for you to go to New York. I hope it holds everything you're looking for."

His hands fall to his waist. "You're seriously going to do this?"

"I'm not doing anything. There's nothing left to discuss."

He huffs and turns, descending the stairs. I follow, needing this to be over once and for all. I have to get my life back.

He stops at the door to his fancy SUV and turns toward me with a smile curling at his lips. "We can do this the easy way, and you can come with me, or you can stay here, and we'll just see how long you last."

I shake my head. "In what world do you think I would even consider following you anywhere. Miles, we are *never* getting back together. We aren't a family. You don't want those two babies. You've made that perfectly clear."

He doesn't move, completely unaffected.

"You don't even want me." I have to hold back a laugh. "You never did."

His shoulders roll back. "I did want you. I still do."

This is pointless. "You don't. You want a crutch to hold your hand as you take on the big city. Someone you can cast your stress and anxiety on until you don't need the bracing anymore."

He only stares at me, apparently unable to deny it.

"I was foolish not to see it before, and once I did, I held on, wanting to be so wrong. We had children together because *we* wanted them. It was just more lies."

"We can be a family in New York."

I laugh. "Have you lost your mind? Miles, you made me out to be a villain. Publicly. We're divorced."

He takes a step closer. "I told them we'd resolved all that. Couples reconcile all the time, especially in the industry."

I close my eyes, trying to breathe, as the kind of anger that's new for me begins to boil. I should be surprised, but I'm not. This man and his narcissism never cease to amaze me.

I inhale and exhale, trying to wrap my head around how I'm supposed to respond. I've known he's a perpetual liar. But this. What the actual fuck?!

It was only ever a show to him. Build something that looks like a family, but never actually be one. He just wanted someone to look and act the part. Now, he wants to use the kids for the same reason.

I sway a little, feeling like I might vomit.

"Sarah." He says my name, and I want to scream. His hands wrap around my elbows to pull me closer, but I'm lost in the abyss of the sickening reality.

"Come with me. It will be just us this time. I promise."

CHAPTER 28

SLADE

"Piece of shit!"

I hear a clang and bang echo from the kitchen.

"Uh . . . Carson says he needs a line wrench to replace the shut-off valve under the sink," Krissy says, dropping another flattened cardboard box onto the pile.

I lift her flat screen onto the makeshift stand, which will have to do for now.

She rests her hands on her hips. "It's looking good. There's still a ton to do, but we've assembled all the big stuff. I should be set to stay tonight."

"Are you sure they switched out the locks from the previous tenant?"

She rolls her eyes. "Stone Cold, you've got to chill. I checked with them twice already."

Luke and Trig come around the corner and drop onto the couch.

"Seriously, how many clothes can one person wear? I'm not hauling any more hangers. They have messed up my hands." Trig inspects his palms and fingers.

"Does Carson need me to run home and get the wrench?"

Wind exits the kitchen, where Carson is battling the plumbing. "Yeah. He looked in his toolbox but didn't have the right one."

I nod. "I'll grab the rest of the boxes and be back."

"Hold on." Krissy disappears into the kitchen and returns, tossing me a mailer envelope. She forced me, first thing this morning, to spit in the tiny tube, and now I'm sure my DNA will be broadcast all over the globe.

"Put that in the mailbox." She smiles sweetly. "Oh, and grab the beer from your fridge. I'll order the pizza."

"Make sure to bring back some Pedialyte for Princess Leia." Trig tips his head at Luke.

"Hey, you'll thank me for not drinking when I have to haul your ass home." Luke has settled in with this group just fine. "Also, Pedialyte is amazing at replenishing electrolytes."

I find my keys and head home.

Pulling into my driveway, I see a black Range Rover parked at Sarah's. Climbing out, I glance across the street, fully aware it's none of my business if she has visitors, but I haven't forgotten Roxie asking me if I'd be around.

I toss the wrench in my truck, then head inside to use the bathroom and carry down the rest of her boxes. With the case of beer in my hand, I hear a rapid knock on my front door.

Apparently, I don't move fast enough, and the quick tapping resumes. I tug open the door, and Brandon stands, cradling his snarling rat.

"What?"

"Um . . ."

"What do you need, Brandon?"

He throws a thumb over his shoulder. "There's. . .something going on over there."

I glance over his head and see Sarah talking to a guy. She motions aggressively with her hands and then drops them.

"He's been there for a while. An hour or so, maybe. They went inside, but when they came out, Sarah didn't look very good. I think they were arguing."

I'd like to ask why in the hell he's spying on them, but I watch as Sarah wraps her arms around herself, and her head falls forward. Then, he grabs her and pulls her to him. She slumps a little and . . .

I shove past Brandon, closing the door, and charge across the street.

I hit the end of her driveway, and Sarah sways a little.

"Get your hands off of her."

The man's head whips in my direction. "Who are you?" His look and tone tell me this guy is a dick.

"Let go of her," I growl, and Sarah pulls out of his grasp and falls against me. I steady her. "You all right?" I ask her as the douchebag stares at me.

"She doesn't need your help. She's fine." He reaches for her, and I slide her away from his grasp.

"I don't give a fuck what you have to say." He can try me.

Sarah's head rolls back, and she doesn't look well.

"You all right?" I ask again, still holding onto her, the sound of my pulse building in my ears.

She finally nods, her gaze returning to the man who's one touch away from losing his veneers. "Miles, you need to go. This is done." Her voice comes out strong, and I release her.

He huffs a laugh. "Are you serious?" His eyes run over me, and I'd like to rip the smug look off his slick face. "*This* is what you've been doing?"

I don't miss his implication.

"Miles, we're divorced, and you lost the right to know anything long before that." She crosses her arms over herself and shivers.

"You don't know what you're doing."

It sounds like a threat, and my fist begs to grab this prick by the throat.

"We are *never* getting back together. You'll have to hire some other fake family to play the part in New York." She steps back and bumps into me.

He huffs and tugs his car door open. "You're making a mistake." He stops before climbing in. "I took everything before but Oliver and Frankie. I guess maybe it's time I fix that."

He slides in and closes the door, turning the engine over.

Sarah's body slumps against me as if the weight of his words blasted right through her. I wrap my arm around her, my fingers grazing the skin at her waist. She's on fire.

"Did. . .he. . .just threaten to take Ollie and Frankie?" Her words come out weak and a bit winded.

"Hey," I turn her toward me. "Are you ok? Breathe."

She stares at my chest, her body a bit limp.

"Sarah." I brush her hair out of her face, and her forehead is sweaty and burning up. "Are you sick?"

Her glossy eyes drag up to mine. "He's going to take my kids."

"Come on. You need to get inside." I lead her up the porch steps and into the house.

Ollie is on the floor, enclosed by a circle of Hot Wheels, and Grover pops up to greet me. "Swade, wook! I gots all my trucks." He points to his organization while I usher Sarah inside.

Frankie's cries filter down the hall, and Sarah snaps to. She disappears into a room while I try to figure out what in the hell to do.

I squat down beside Ollie. "Hey, partner." He begins on a ring of cars. "Is your mom sick?"

He shrugs one shoulder. "I p-p-puked in the kitchen the other night. It was so g-gross."

I pull out my phone and message Krissy, letting her know I might not be back.

Sarah returns with Frankie curled against her, but she looks like she might pass out. "Sorry, you shouldn't—"

"Give me the baby, Sarah."

Her eyes rise to mine. "She's sick and full of snot."

"Give her to me."

She stares at me, looking like she might melt to the floor.

"I'm not afraid of snot or anything else." I hold out my arms. "You need to lie down." I nod toward the couch.

After a moment, her face scrunches. "I think I might be sick." She pulls Frankie from her chest and hands her to me, then drops to the couch, curling into a ball.

I adjust Frankie against me, resting her head on my shoulder. I lean, running the back of my fingers over Sarah's forehead. Her eyes fall closed.

"Have you taken anything?"

She shakes her head.

"Do you have Tylenol?"

"Only for the kids," she mumbles.

I push out a breath, thinking. I carry Frankie to the kitchen and pull the first aid kit from above the refrigerator. Thankfully, it includes Ibuprofen.

I get a glass of water and sit on the end of the couch. Sarah sits up enough to swallow the pills. When I shift, her hand jets out and grabs mine.

"I need you to stay." Her eyes are closed, but her voice is filled with worry.

I sit and run my fingers over her cheek. "I'm not going anywhere." Those words crack open something deep inside me, and warmth cascades over the cold fears of not being needed or enough.

This is where I want to be. I want to help and make just one thing better.

"He'll take my kids," she sniffs, and a tear trickles from the corner of her eye.

"Shhh." I brush the hair away from her face. "It's going to be ok."

She grabs my hand and holds it to her chest as if she might never let it go.

I inhale and let it out, thinking I might be ok with that.

Frankie's face presses into my neck, and her stuffy, rhythmic snores calm my nerves.

"Hey, Ol," I whisper, and he looks up at me, a line of snot dripping onto his lip. "Go grab the Kleenexes."

He runs to the kitchen and returns with a large box.

I wipe his nose, then nod to the arm of the couch. "Do you want to watch *Bluey*?"

He grins and climbs up next to me. I turn on an episode, and I listen to him giggle.

I'm not sure what happened or what's coming next. I peek at Sarah, drooling on the couch, and I realize I don't care. This is where I want to be.

It's been a long time since I've felt needed, and it feels damn good.

CHAPTER 29

SARAH

Rough fingers drag against my temple, then over and through my hair. I keep my eyes closed, hoping it continues. It soothes my aching body and calms my mind, which wants to chase fear—a fear so great it will consume me.

The back of his knuckles run over my cheek and along my jaw.

When he charged over this afternoon, I'd never been so happy to hear that overpowering growl. It was as if he knew I needed him.

And he's still here.

I recognize the low hum of the TV and shift just enough to become aware that my head is not resting against the worn couch but against Slade's muscled thigh.

I pop up, searching for Frankie and Ollie.

"Hey." His fingers grip my hip, keeping me from falling off the couch.

Ollie is sprawled on the floor, sound asleep on a pillow and wrapped in a blanket. Frankie is tucked inside Slade's arm over his chest, her cheek squished against his pec. She looks so peaceful. I can't blame her. I know exactly how safe those massive arms feel.

I lie back down, not even caring how incredibly inappropriate it might be to put my head in his lap. My life was already swirling around the drain, but I was just sucked under.

I stare at the silly Australian cattle dogs discussing moving and what's best for their family. My throat burns with despair and anxiety as they realize home is where they should stay.

I squeeze my eyes shut tight, needing it to squelch the fire. I can't even think about what could be coming.

The raging force is too great, and the truth spills out in a whisper. "Slade, I'm scared." I clench my jaw, withholding the sob that wants to break free. Maybe if I say it out loud, the threat will lose some of its power.

I feel his gaze drop to me, but I can't look at him. His large hand cups my shoulder, his thumb running back and forth.

"I was so young and stupid. I think maybe he knew that. Saw straight through me and how naive I was in a brand new world. I believed everything he told me, even when his actions didn't match up."

My mind swirls with memories. Miles missing dates and making excuses. He wouldn't call or be home when he was supposed to. He didn't put his hand on my pregnant belly or talk to Ollie. When I saw the text messages and caught him in his office with another woman the first time, I believed him when he told me it wouldn't happen again. Or maybe I just wanted to.

"How did you meet him?" Slade's question is soft and calm.

"I was living in Chicago. I went to an event and never saw him coming. It's a tale as old as time." I sniff, trying to clear my stuffy nose. "He was charming, successful, and told me all the things I wanted to hear."

My stomach pulls into a tight knot and twists with reality. "I can't fight him. He's smart and has all the right connections and a platform."

"What do you mean?" It's that low bark, and it almost makes me smile. Almost.

"He's a news anchor in Chicago, but he just got the Sunday slot on The Morning Show in New York."

"Like on KBC?"

I nod against his leg. "I think he spent more time in his office with the pretty young interns than behind the news desk. He's the golden boy of the news hour. People love him." I swipe my nose. "I knew he was cheating on me. How pathetic is that? When I had Ollie, I wanted to believe he had found something more important to do with his time. He'd only gotten better at hiding it." I breathe through the ache. "I didn't want Ol to grow up without a dad, wondering why he was never enough to stick around for."

Slade grunts like maybe he understands that feeling.

"When I found out I was pregnant with Frankie, he was out of town. I called him. He must have hit the speaker or something instead of hanging up. I heard them." I can still hear the giggling and the soft promises. "I was devastated and so angry. I was filled with rage and disgust. Mostly at myself for believing him."

I curl my knees to my chest. "I knew then I could either stay and turn bitter and angry or leave and hopefully show these two what love is supposed to look like. I want so much more for them than to be surrounded by anger and betrayal." Fire consumes my throat. "He doesn't want them." It hurts so damn bad to say it. "He only wants to appear like the family man he's convinced the network bigwigs he is."

I inhale as the nauseating reality rises again.

He brushes the hair off my neck. "He can't do that, can he?"

"What?"

"Get custody of them?" Slade sounds skeptical, but I know better.

"I don't know. It could only be a threat, and once he's there, he'll disappear into the city, doing what he does best." I exhale, my tense body succumbing to exhaustion. "But I don't have the resources or the status to fight him." That's the only truth I know.

Slade's hand spreads across my back. I press my eyes closed, wanting to fall back asleep and wake up to find this only a nightmare.

I listen to *Bluey* and Frankie's soft snores and melt into Slade's safe warmth.

"Just get some rest. Everything will be ok. We'll figure it out."

I hear his soft promise as I drift back to sleep, desperate to believe him.

Strong arms lift me into the air, surrounding me with the spicy scent of pine and cedar. I snuggle into his neck, wanting his gentle comfort to remain, always.

"What are you doing?" I mumble as he takes a few steps.

"You need a good night's sleep."

He twists to carry me down the hall, and I jerk awake.

"Stop." I hold out my hand to grab the wall.

He halts, cradling me in his arms. "You're burning up again. You need more Ibuprofen and to go to bed, Sarah." It's a command.

"Ok," I say, without arguing, hoping he'll put me down, but reeaally not wanting him to. I try to wiggle out, but he doesn't budge.

He takes two more steps toward my room.

"Stop," I say again with more force, and he does.

Even in the dark, I see his brows furrow.

"Put me down. Please," I say softly, knowing this is ridiculous. But also, it's not. Miles's low jab strikes me in the gut all over again.

Slade carefully releases my legs but keeps his arm around me until I'm fully grounded.

I brush my hair out of my face, unable to look at him. "Thank you for staying. I'm sorry, you can't . . ."

"Sarah, I wasn't—"

I hold up my hand. "I know you weren't. I just . . ." I just what? I don't want you in my room because you will judge me before I have a chance to explain.

I shiver, swaying a little, and his arms steady me.

I press my eyes closed, wanting to fall back into him. Maybe he'd just stand here and let me sleep against him like a deeply rooted tree.

My aching body sags. "Thank you for sitting with me and the kids."

His head hangs a little. "Ollie and Frankie are in their beds." When his eyes finally drag up to mine, all I see is confusion and what might be hurt.

It's a spear straight through an already bleeding heart.

His eyes run over my face only a moment longer, and then he turns, moving to the front door. "I let Grover out, so the back door is locked. Make sure you get this one."

I hate myself even more than I did a few hours ago, but I cannot explain one more thing tonight. Something I'm not sure he'll understand. At least, I'm terrified he won't.

I nod.

He pulls the door open, and cool air filters in as he closes it. It's just another blast to my aching body, and I have no doubt my fever is returning with a vengeance.

I take two more Ibuprofen and crawl into bed, curling into a ball. I stare at the ribbons, knowing if I had the energy, I'd take them to the backyard and burn every single one.

At one time, I wore them with pride. They represented success. Now, they're tainted, and it hurts to look at them. Except for Ollie and Frankie, they've brought me nothing but pain and humiliation ever since.

I close my eyes before tears slip out, wishing I were back on the couch with Slade's hand on my back, reminding me I'm not totally and completely alone. But maybe after tonight, I will be all over again.

CHAPTER 30

SLADE

"Man, we're all hiding something, but at this point, she doesn't owe you anything."

I drop the dumbbells and roll up to rest my arms on my knees.

"I came to the gym to work out and relieve stress, not for an unsolicited therapy session." I wipe my face on the hem of my shirt.

Carson grabs a set of dumbbells. "Would you rather discuss this over a candlelit dinner and wine?"

I groan, lying back on the bench and lifting the weights for another set.

He lunges and pushes out a breath. "Even better. I'll call the guys and have them meet us at Crusins. We'll get the whole gang involved."

He has a point. He's kept his freaking mouth shut this time after I told him about Sarah's panic at me entering her room. I don't know what that was all about, but it frustrated me.

I don't like secrets, and even more, I don't want her to feel like she has to hide things from me. That's what stings most of all. But I understand trust has to be earned.

I press the weights into the air and lower them, each time needing the strain to release the confusion that's lingered since that night.

It's been a week since I sat with her while she burned with fever and anxiety. She shed tears of despair, trusting me with what had happened in her marriage and her worries about what her ex would pull next. But she flipped when I was just trying to carry her to bed.

I would have stayed and sat with her all night if she'd asked me, and that is the thought that makes me want to kick my own ass. I'm happy to excuse myself from where I'm not wanted.

Carson drops his weights, catching his breath. "If you're going to throw a tantrum every time you get the least bit scared, she definitely won't be inclined to share personal things with you."

"I'm not throwing a tantrum. I'm just steering clear of a situation that doesn't involve me." I ignore the grenade he dropped about me being scared.

He scoffs. "So, that's it? You're mad she didn't want you in her room, and you're done with her now?"

He makes me sound like a jerk.

I drop the weights, having had enough. "I'm not doing this again. I was building my entire fucking life around someone who liked to keep secrets and hide things." I huff a laugh. "Shit, she was living a double life. *With* someone else."

He drops his hands from his hips. "Slade, she was nineteen. How many dumbass mistakes did you make?"

I can't think about it, but I know Melissa rises to the very top of the list. I choose not to respond.

"Exactly, you've got to let that shit go. I know it was hard, and you were hurting in so many more ways than one, but Sarah is a mom. She's lived a whole lifetime before you, and you need to let her tell you about it. When *she's* ready."

I want to stomp out of here and not listen to any more of this. Especially when he might have a point.

He places his weights back on the rack. "This stuff takes time. You've got to be patient and realize not everyone will disappoint you. Not everyone will break your heart."

He sounds confident, but I'm not so sure. Everyone I should have trusted broke my heart. First, the man who provided sperm and nothing else. Then, my mom for making so many stupid decisions and also leaving me way too soon. And Melissa, when I was only hanging on by a thread, she snipped that line and left me to drown without looking back.

I don't want to be patient. I want to know with certainty I won't end up there again.

He grabs his towel and turns back toward me. "Besides, I'd bet my entire paycheck you haven't told her a thing about you."

I grab another set of weights, not wanting to address that. I lunge. He's right. I haven't told her anything because I don't talk about it. Talking about it makes me feel weak and pathetic. I have to relive watching my mom die and not being able to do a damn thing about it.

"Are you done now?" I switch legs.

"Working out, or trying to knock some sense into your hard-ass head?"

I roll my eyes, pushing out a breath. "Both."

He throws his towel over his shoulder. "I have to get home and call my brother. He's called three times, so something must be up."

I almost grin at the irony, finishing up my set. "What was it you were saying about being scared?"

He points at me. "Don't even. It's not remotely the same."

I set the weights on the rack, breathing hard. It's my turn to place my hands on my hips. "Oh, really. You avoid your family and everything you left behind. That has nothing to do with fear?"

His head lolls to the side. "If you wanted to talk about messed up shit, I'll raise and re-raise you."

I only know a little about what Carson left behind, but I can't say I blame him.

I follow him toward the exit. "So, you have no plans of ever returning to the business your family built?"

Carson's passion is construction. He's meant to be amongst wood and finishings, not grease and broken machines.

He shrugs. "I'm not ready. Not sure if I ever will be."

"Maybe you need to make more than a phone call."

He stops, turning toward me. I want to smile. I push him just like he pushed me. Payback is a bitch.

"I have something to sort out first. Then, maybe I'll think about facing my family and finding out if I want to be a part of it again."

I roll my eyes. Him and his grand plans.

I wish I had a plan. It might be comforting.

I drive home, trying my damndest not to think about everything he said. I stand in my dark living room, staring at the small brick bungalow across the street. A dim light filters through her windows, and I wonder if Sarah is studying.

I could message her and ask, or I could give it time. I debate which is better for my heart.

I'm no good at patience or being smacked with the truth. Carson is right. Sarah doesn't owe me a thing, and I have to be ok with that. More than that, I have to quit being so afraid. Life is about risks, and if I never take one, I'll be stuck here forever—scared and lonely, and having absolutely nothing worthwhile to show for it.

I exhale, letting that realization and every jagged edge of it settle uncomfortably. Recognizing and admitting it is one thing. Actually doing something about it is entirely another.

All I know is I've got to figure out something better than this.

CHAPTER 31

SARAH

"Are you ok?"

I wipe my eyes, breathing and hoping I don't actually hack up a lung. "Yeah," I choke out.

"You still sound awful," Roxie says as I take a sip of water.

I might be feeling better, but the phlegm and cough still sneak attack.

For three whole days, I moved the kids' toys into my room and spent the day in bed, moving as little as possible. They were angels, and since they weren't feeling the best either, we spent lots of time sleeping, cuddled together.

I had to miss work, which will only put me further in the financial hole this month, but what's new?

I pour Goldfish into small bowls. "At least the hacking spasms have kept Cory out of my office."

"Hey, there's my girl, and the bright side," Roxie cheers.

I'm happy she's seeing rays of sunshine. My projected forecast is predicting nothing but doom and gloom.

I hand over snacks and sit on the floor with Ollie and Frankie.

"You still haven't heard anything from Miles?"

There we go. We're back to shitty reality.

"No, I'm praying he becomes so consumed with the new attention and big city life he forgets all about us."

It's the sad, pathetic truth. Ollie rubs his stuffed fish against his face, loving on it, and Frankie climbs into my lap, hitting me in the chin with a board book. *Ouch.*

I never thought I'd be in a place where I lost hope of giving them what I never had, but I'm there. I think my babies will truly be better off without him.

"I won't be contacting him. That's for sure."

"So, what now? What's the plan?" She's back to Roxie the Riveter.

I need her "We can do it!" attitude because I'm seriously doubting my ability to do anything. "I don't know. Just keep going, I guess."

"Just keep swimming," she sings. "You know, that's kind of a suckass attitude."

I laugh. "I think you've been spending too much time with my mom."

"Hey, she's helping me spread the word about my impending engagement in the most unconventional ways, and my parents are having none of it. She's really the best. What about Slade? At least tell me you've finally talked to the gentle giant."

My body sags against the couch. I haven't. I'm the enormous coward who doesn't want to face him or the possibility that I hurt my closest friend here. The man who sat with me and held me while I was sick with both the flu and the consequences of my life choices.

I've been hiding for the past two weeks, hoping to casually run into him when we were outside with Grover or coming and going from work, but nope. It makes me wonder if he's avoiding me, too.

"No, I think maybe he's realized what an absolute s-h-i-t show my life is and has intelligently removed himself."

"Pfft. That sounds like an excuse." She pauses, and I can't even defend it. "I'm going to say something that sucks, so brace yourself."

I think about hanging up. I can't take much more.

"You need him. Someone you can depend on for help and support. Sarah, he took care of you and the kids when you really needed it, without even being asked. Men, don't do that for fun. No offense, but you can't afford to lose that kind of friendship."

It's a bit of a slap in the face, but she's not wrong.

"And you need to quit being ashamed or embarrassed or whatever the hell it is about those damn ribbons and crowns. Miles is a complete dick and will say anything to hurt you. You rocked beautiful ass, and you should be proud."

I debate the accuracy of that last part.

"That hunk of a man was carrying your sick, worn-out body to bed, and you should've let him. You also should've had him crawl in with you. Just sayin'."

A warm rush crawls through me at the thought of snuggling his big, firm body. I inhale through my newly opened nostrils, wanting to conjure up his unique scent. He smells so damn good.

I shut it down immediately. I will not be thinking about how any man smells, especially the broody, blunt grump across the street.

"What do you have to lose? You're already pushing him away."

She can't see my massive eye roll, but it's noteworthy. *A man I'm really beginning to care about, along with my only remaining microscopic specks of trust.*

When I don't respond, she pushes. "What are you afraid of?" Her gentle question slams into the truth.

This, I'm willing to answer out loud. "Uh. . .maybe the truckload of judgment and ridicule that comes when people find out."

I admitted things to Slade that I haven't told anyone. I don't know if it was the fever or his fingers running through my hair that coaxed it out of me. But I told him about Miles, how stupid I was, and the mortifying details of my marriage.

Did I tell him everything? No, but enough. And now, he's avoiding me, which is also probably my fault.

"I know most people don't understand what you accomplished and what it took, but you've got to toss out those trolls, the wenches you called friends, and Miles completely out of the picture. His stupid ass will prance around with his ding-dong leading the way like Rudolph-The-Freaking-Times-Square-Reindeer."

I smile, knowing she's right, but also, she didn't have to face the brunt of the comments and insinuations. People judged, mocked, and liked to make uninformed assumptions about what I actually did. I don't know if I can handle one of those people being Slade.

"You're not giving him enough credit," she says lightly.

I kiss the top of Frankie's head. Maybe I'm not. But it's been over seventy years, and there's still a shitload of misconceptions and false ideas. The truth is, I care what Slade thinks. I really care.

That realization settles like a giant rock in my gut.

There's a knock on the door, and Grover barks, his tail wagging. I see the outline of a figure beyond the frosted glass, and my heart jumps a little at the thought of it possibly being Slade.

"Rox, someone's at the door."

"Ok. Just talk to him. Tell him or don't, but at least talk to him." There's another knock. "K. Love you. Bye."

I carry Frankie with me, using her cute smiley face as a shield against the grumpy scowl that could be present on the other side of the door.

I yank it open.

"Hey. You're home," Krissy says, holding a brown grocery sack. "I've wanted to stop by and see how you all are since Slade said you were sick, but my schedule has been crazy."

I step back, inviting her in while the flickers of anticipation are snuffed out.

She holds up the bag. "I'm super late to the party, but I brought you some soup. It's only a jar from the store, so you can save it for next time."

"Thank you. That's so thoughtful." I step back, inviting her in and she sets the sack on the small bench by the door.

"Kissy!" Ollie jumps up and grabs her hand, tugging her to the floor.

Grover nuzzles her with his wet nose, and she accepts his kisses.

"Pout-Pout is the a-a-aircraft carrier. See." He's lined two jets on top of the flattened fish.

"I see that." She smiles as one jet takes off. "So, you're feeling better?"

I nod. "Yeah, finally. It's taken a few weeks, but we're back at it."

Frankie crawls into Krissy's crossed legs and makes herself at home in her lap. She runs a hand over Frankie's growing mullet.

"I'm glad. Slade said you were pretty sick."

I wonder how much he said about what he walked into. I think about asking how he is to see if I can get a clue about where we stand, but . . . "How's the townhouse?" Roxie bawking like a chicken rings in my ears.

"Really good. It's nice having my own place. Some friends came over, and we had a little housewarming party. I'm slowly decorating and figuring out what I like." She laughs. "I've been hitting up all the thrift stores. I place something somewhere and then move it the next day to see if I like it better. It's so lame, but I'm having fun. Were you able to finish your classes?"

I blow out a breath. "Yeah, by the skin of my teeth, I passed my finals. Now, I have to decide what to take next semester or let my grant drop and sit out until I have more time."

I was certain I failed my statistics exam and teared up when I saw that beautiful C as my final grade. Luckily, my GPA didn't suffer too badly.

"Maybe you should take something fun." She grabs a handful of blocks and stacks them in front of Frankie. "I took a ballet class and made a complete fool of myself, but I had a blast."

"I never took dance. I have no grace." I weigh my head from side to side. "I'm thinking about changing my major."

"Really? You don't want to be a lawyer anymore?" She sounds shocked.

Ollie's jet zooms past our faces in a fly-by.

"I've just seen what it takes, and I have these two boogers. I don't want to miss this." I watch Frankie stack the blocks carefully.

Plus, I may have a custody battle ahead.

"What would you switch it to? I always wanted to be a nurse. I knew the minute I found out my mom was sick. I love working in the labor department. It's kind of the best of both worlds."

I shrug. "I don't know. I'm looking through the course schedule. Maybe something with finance. I seem to be good at it."

"Well, the women's clinic is looking for a bookkeeper if you're ever interested. The board is fantastic, and the pay isn't bad either for being a non-profit."

I tuck that away to think about another day. There are too many uncertainties to consider making any major life decisions, such as switching jobs.

She checks her watch. "I have to get going. My shift starts soon."

I hold out my hands for Frankie, but she stays put. "I have to get these monkeys in the bath and then bed."

"No m-more monkeys j-j-jumping on the bed," Ollie sings, and Frankie bounces, ready to play the bedtime game.

Krissy laughs as Frankie's little diaper butt hits her legs, but she doesn't move to get up. The room quiets, and I wait.

"He's being a jerk," she says, pulling Frankie's fine hair into a tiny ponytail.

I frown, wondering if the doctor is displeased with something else now that she's moved out of Slade's. I might punch him. "Who?"

"Slade." My gut reaction eases. "He's just. . .scared, you know?" she says quietly, like it might be a secret.

He's not the only one.

"When our mom died, he shut down and closed everyone out. He went into protection mode. He focused on making sure I was ok and had everything I needed."

She glances at me. "He couldn't fix it. Bring her back or make it all right. So, he did everything else he could to make it better."

His whispered words float around me. *Everything will be ok.*

She laughs a little. "He tried so hard before she died to show her that we'd be ok. He even . . ." She doesn't finish her statement, and I wish she would.

This paints a clearer picture of the man who seems to want to help everyone else but doesn't tend to himself. He's a growly lion trying to protect his pride.

"I think. . .I hurt his feelings," I admit. "I didn't mean to, but sometimes we make stupid decisions to guard ourselves." And that's exactly what I did. I pushed him and his comfort away, too afraid of what he might think.

"Well, he does that every day." She laughs. "He's pretty forgiving, though. I mean, I push him to the max all the time just to see how long I can get him to pop his head out of the trash can."

"Oscar lives in a trash can," Ollie says, flopping on top of Grover. "But Grover is silly." The fluff ball licks his face.

We laugh.

"He sure is," Krissy says, climbing to her feet. "You guys still need to come check out my place."

"And have pizza!" Ollie throws his arms in the air.

"Yes. Definitely pizza." She grins.

I hug her, and Frankie blows her kisses. I stare across the street, watching her pull out of the driveway. I wave, knowing what I have to do.

There's no room in my life for cowardice, and if I'm going to be brave, I know the first place to start.

I just have to face the big guy and hope he's also willing to lay down his fear enough to meet me halfway.

CHAPTER 32

SLADE

I fit the hose onto the bleeder screw. "You'll pump the air out first to get the fluid flowing. I'll do this one, and then you can do the rest."

Luke nods.

"All right. Hit the brakes," I holler to Wind, and watch the liquid fill the tube.

We finish the first, and Luke moves to the next. I wipe my hands with a shop rag and climb into the driver's seat, waiting for the go-ahead.

Trig rests an arm on the open door. "Do you care if I bring my bike in this weekend? I've got to make some updates and adjustments. I'm putting together a parts list to get a head start on next season."

"You're serious about this?"

He nods. "I need to get the attention of sponsors."

"Hit the brake," Luke hollers, and I depress the pedal and hold.

"It'll take effort just to qualify and gather a team."

He grins. "Are you volunteering?"

"Again," Luke yells.

I shake my head. "I'm not watching you get peeled off the pavement."

He rolls his eyes.

Motorcycle racing in controlled conditions has its risks. But Trig and his buddies ride the streets popping wheelies and doing the kind of stunts that get people killed. Maybe getting serious about racing will help him mature.

I pump the brake again. "No sponsor will put up with your recklessness. It's business. They won't invest in someone who takes unnecessary chances on or off the track. It doesn't matter how good you are."

I've seen him race. The kid has the talent and passion to get him where he wants to go, but he's got to earn it first.

"I've gotta have a bike that performs the way I need it to first." He smirks.

It's my turn to roll my eyes. "Fine, but any mess you leave comes out of your paycheck."

"Yes, sir." He salutes me, and I groan. "I'm breaking for lunch."

"Where are you going?" Carson asks.

"Somewhere cheap. Wanna go?"

"Sure. Just give me five to wrap this up."

"I want in," Wind says. "Millie is at a conference this week, so I'm not packing lunches."

"Absolutely no Taco Bell." Carson cuts his hand through the air. "We cannot do that again. It's a miracle we survived those days after."

Wind waves him off, but his cheeks turn a little pink.

"Wait for me," Luke grunts, getting under the rear wheel well.

"You coming?" Trig asks me.

I shake my head. "We've got two drop-offs coming in."

As the guys head out for lunch, I warm up my leftovers and carry them to my office. I send out a quote and pay a few bills while I eat.

I hear the heavy metal door bang closed. I push out of my chair but stop, recognizing the distinct rhythmic click of heels.

I stay put, my heart beating a little faster, fueled by hope for what's probably too good to be true.

Sarah appears in my doorway. "You're here. I wondered if you'd be out for lunch." Her gaze roams my office.

I stare at her. Part of her long brown hair is pulled back from her face—the silky strands I ran my fingers through over and over again. She's wearing a coat that does not cover her long, bare legs, and I wonder how she doesn't get cold. More than that, it seems incredibly unfair that other people get to see them, but I have no right to feel that way.

I run a hand over my beard. "Hey." It's all I can say. She's beautiful as always, and I have no words.

It's been two weeks since I sat with her while she was sick, and I've had plenty of alone time to think about everything Carson said. She doesn't owe me anything, but I'm so happy she's here. My heart skips a few beats, anticipating what she has to say.

She wouldn't be here just to tell me to get lost because that's exactly what I did—run the minute it felt like she might be hiding something.

She eases into my office and stands on the other side of my desk.

I sit, needing to chill the hell out.

Her shoulders rise with a deep breath. Then she reaches into her massive bag, pulls out a long, thick ivory ribbon with dark stitching, and lays it on my desk. She sets a sparkly crown on top of it.

I stare at them.

"There's a handful more hung in my room."

I drag my eyes up to meet hers. She bites the corner of her bottom lip and crosses her arms over herself.

"*That's* what I didn't want you to see." Her eyes flick between mine, and I hold her gaze, very aware this is taking effort.

"Do you want me to see now?" I ask, only wanting what she's willing to give me, but never by force.

"Are you going to judge me?" She stares at me, waiting for a straight answer to her direct question. "You know, just so I can prepare myself." One side of her mouth lifts, but I see the nerves behind it.

"Do you want me to lie to you, Sarah?"

She shakes her head. "Nope, and that's why I'm here. I need a friend who won't lie to me. And while I'm being honest, not to judge me either."

The word friend pinches a little, and I try to brush it off. I want to be Sarah's friend, but I'm concerned that what I'm beginning to desire might go far beyond friendship.

"I don't lie, and sometimes that can be a problem." I'm giving her exactly what she asked for—the complete and total truth.

Her lips skirt to the side slightly, and moments pass while I let her decide.

"I grew up in a trailer park." She watches me. "In a tiny town, where that one minor thing, along with my eyes, defined who I was. My mom is young, vibrant, beautiful, and often the talk of the town. The woman with big dreams and even larger dramatics who's never seen anything outside her double-wide."

She inhales and lets it out. "All I ever wanted was eyes that matched and a way out. From the whispers and the condescension. From a whole town of people who made up their small minds when they didn't know a damn thing."

She glances at me, but her eyes fall away. "When I was fifteen, I heard girls talking at school about my mom dating one of the teachers. They said mutts carry fleas, and Mr. Brenner would need treatment for disease."

She huffs a little laugh, but it's not humorous. "It was enough that she was dating my teacher, but it was more than that. I knew I'd never be seen as anything else." Her gaze falls, and she shakes her head. "Sometimes, no matter what you do, people won't ever see past your circumstances."

Her head drops to the side, and she exhales again. "So, I made a plan. I was getting the hell out. I got my first job and worked as many hours as possible to save up. I graduated early and entered my first pageant when I was seventeen."

She peeks at me, her eyes locking on mine and waiting for a reaction. I don't give her one.

"I changed everything about myself. Made what was undesirable desirable. I got contacts. Worked out like crazy. Did every beauty treatment I could afford outside of surgery. Eventually, I got a coach, and I won."

Her gaze hits the floor. "I kept winning and climbing. I had sponsors and modeling contracts. Then, I met Miles and quickly succumbed to his world and success. Everything we did was about him and advancing his career."

Her voice softens a little. "I thought we were doing it together, and his achievements were ours. It took me a while, but eventually, I saw things for what they were. I fell for a man who used me for appearances and his benefit."

Her arms drop to her sides, and she adjusts her purse. "When he had nothing left to gain, he used it all against me. He turned what I earned for myself, something I was proud of, into nothing but painful memories. He took everything but Ollie and Frankie. The two things I'm beginning to think have never mattered to him." Her voice cracks, and she blinks quickly, pressing her lips together.

She straightens, pulling herself up and rolling her shoulders back. The woman I've gotten to know is returning. "I have no idea what he'll do or say, but he's never fought fair."

I stare at her, trying to process it, but knowing I don't want her ever to be uneasy with me. "You were really afraid I'd judge you?"

Her shoulders sag again. "I have been my whole life. Even when I started pageants, everyone had an opinion and something to say. Most of it was unkind. People make uninformed assumptions and jump to conclusions that aren't even remotely accurate. I saw how you looked at me the first time I stepped in here. You were Judge Judy slamming her gavel, convicting me as a stuck-up, socially privileged professional who was out to prove you were trying to rip me off. I was scrambling to figure out how I could pay you."

It's like a jab to the gut. "That's what you thought?"

Her shoulders drop. "Slade, you know you were sizing me up and deciding all the ways you could detest me."

She has no idea what I was thinking. I raise one eyebrow. "And you weren't being just a tad judgmental?"

She scoffs. "Absolutely. You were kind of an abrasive asshole, but I married the slick dick with a thousand-watt smile who told me everything I wanted to hear. It was refreshing to have someone shoot me straight for once. No bull shitting or condescension." She pauses. "You were blunt but real. *That* is what I need."

It sort of sounds like she needs me, and my heart does a little leap.

I ignore the items and push out of my chair, moving around my desk to sit on the edge so we are eye to eye. "Sarah, I won't ever lie to you. It doesn't mean you'll always like what I have to say. I will do my very best never to judge you, but intentional or not, we do that shit sometimes. I think it's human nature to analyze and evaluate to figure out where we stand and what we stand for."

She bites her lip again, and I wait, realizing I want her trust more than just about anything.

Her eyes fall away. "I didn't want you to see. Hell, I'm not sure I can stand to look at them." She runs her fingers over her forehead. "I held onto them, needing a reminder of what I can actually do. Motivation. Proof that I can succeed." She shakes her head. "But I'm not that person anymore. I'm not sure I ever really was. I was hiding behind blonde hair, layers of makeup, beautiful clothes, and gowns. Behind a man who appeared to represent all I'd fought so hard for."

Her eyes drift to mine. "It's embarrassing and humiliating that I didn't see it. Any of it! And then all I could do was sit and watch while he took it and lit my whole world on fire. He left nothing but ashes . . ." Her lip quivers. "And I'm really scared that girl, the one who fought and overcame, the one left stripped of her dignity and hanging on to only a shred of hope, burned along with everything else."

Her chest rises and falls as she blinks. I see the fear well in her eyes.

My chest aches as if I can actually feel her heart breaking inside my own.

I fist my hands, the urge so strong to grab her and tell her I see her. I see everything that she is. "But it brought you here." *To me.*

Her eyes lift to mine.

"No matter what, it made you who you are right now. You're still fighting."

Sarah is stronger than she knows.

She swallows it all down, forcing it away, but I wish she wouldn't. She doesn't have to be brave with me.

"It'd be nice if, for a little while, I didn't have to fight so damn hard."

I hear the exhausted vulnerability behind her words.

Her head tilts, a small, sad smile returning. "So. . .will you still be my friend? Will you tell me if I have food in my teeth? I mean, only a true friend will do that. Or a booger in my nose?"

I need her to quit clarifying so much with that platonic-sounding word. "You want me to tell you if you have a bat in the cave?"

She laughs a little, and her smile sends rays of sunlight through me, warming everything that's been frozen for so long. "Yes."

She glances at her shoes, tipping one back onto its heel. "It's gotta go both ways, you know." Her eyes lift to mine, peeking at me from under her long, dark lashes. "I won't be the friend who takes all the time. I hope maybe someday, you'll be willing to let me help you, too."

I want that. I'm just not sure how to do it—be that vulnerable.

Her eyes, one blue and one brown, hold mine almost as if she can see my struggle. The corner of her mouth lifts as if she wants me to know everything is ok. She turns but stops in my doorway.

She pulls that bottom lip between her teeth, and my stomach dips and swoops. "You know, Thunder Cat, at some point, you're just going to have to trust me." I see that smirk before she disappears.

I listen to her heels clicking down the hallway.

I rest my arms on the desk, wanting this woman like I've never wanted another. That is exactly the problem. I'm thinking about trusting her. But I am scared shitless, and she's only looking for a friend.

CHAPTER 33

SARAH

"Come on, girls. We've got to get there before he does." Marcie leans around the doorway. "Robyn and I are picking up the balloons and cake."

"Ok. We'll meet you there," I say, and they disappear around the corner.

Kat slumps down a little further. "I want to go home, take a hot bubble bath, and reconsider my life decisions."

She just returned from two days of court proceedings regarding the rights to frozen embryos.

"This job is not what it once was and has evolved into something I'm not even sure I understand anymore." She sounds defeated. "Are you sure this is the career path you want to take?"

I think she's joking, but her face tells me her question is legit. With my courses wrapping up, I've had time to think. I switched my major to business and enrolled in an accounting class. Since I can only take a course or two each semester, I've surrendered to exploring my interests and options. I need to sort out what I want for myself and what is realistic while raising two kids.

"Sarah, you're incredibly smart, young, and beautiful. This job can make you callous and view the world and people with skepticism and negativity."

I think about telling her that marrying a narcissistic cheater does that, too.

She groans. "It's making me bitter and jaded."

So many things have tempted me to fall into a pit of resentment that churns with a vengeance. One so deep I'd never climb my way out of, but so far, I've been held to the ledge by hope. Hope that someday, things will be different.

"Have you ever considered taking a break or practicing a different type of law?" I ask carefully, knowing she's poured her life into this firm.

She peeks at me from under her long black eyelashes. "I wouldn't know what to do with myself without this." She slumps down in the chair further. "How pathetic is that? I need to get a life that doesn't involve couples trying to separate theirs."

She runs a hand over her face. "On second thought, let's go. I need a drink. We can ride together. That way, I'll have an excuse to leave early." She stands. "If we hurry, we can change and drop your car off at home."

I glance at my dress pants and sweater.

"Oh, please." She waves a hand at me. "If we're going out, we aren't looking like we are locked up in cubicles and courtrooms all day." She nods toward the front. "I have a dress in my car. We'll find something at your house."

She disappears, and I shut down my computer. It's only two weeks until Christmas, so I'll be spending the weekend surfing Facebook Marketplace and getting creative with the kids' gifts, hoping to find something similar to the massive train set Ollie has been asking for. I'm looking at it as an exciting challenge rather than a depressing reality.

Kat follows me home, and I quickly change into the velvety cocktail dress my mom found. The long-sleeved black dress is tight-fitting with a short, flowy skirt. It's a good mix of fun and casual.

"Dang, look at you," Kat says, standing in the living room as beautiful as ever.

"You're one to talk." She's wearing a bright red satin dress.

I kiss the kids, assuring Helen I'll be home before bedtime, and slide into Kat's SUV.

"Are you sure you want to drive me home after?"

She backs out of the driveway. "Yeah. I want to go to bed early and hope to wake up inspired to resume this life tomorrow."

"You should go on one of those cruises that take you around the world."

She glances at me. "What? There's a ship that takes you all the way around the world?"

"Yep." I pull down the visor and apply the lightest layer of lip gloss from a tube that's likely two years old. "I saw a pamphlet at the library. They stop at all these amazing ports. Can you even imagine the things you'd learn and see?"

"A long cruise does sound nice, but we have a growing client list." She blows out a breath. "Maybe I'd actually have time to meet someone if I were on the other side of the world." She laughs.

We enter the pub just in time to see Seth's reaction to the cake and balloons Marcie and Robyn placed around the small room adjacent to the bar.

His eyes wander to Kat with a slight glower, and she pops a few peanuts into her mouth to hide her grin.

"He doesn't like his birthday, or he has a phobia of balloons?" I ask, placing a few nachos on a plate.

"I don't know. In college, he never wanted to celebrate. Seth's not usually grumpy, but he's a real scrooge about this day in particular."

"Hey. Here's a menu. The food is amazing." Robyn slides the laminated list in front of me. "And go get a drink. We gotta get this party started." She sways her hips and lifts her wine in the air.

Kat's eyes roll in my direction. "She doesn't have to tell me twice."

I follow Kat to the bar, but I hear my name. I twist to see Carson, Wind, and Trig with another guy, but no Slade. My heart sinks a little.

When I stopped by the garage the other day, I hoped to make amends for hurting or offending him, but I haven't seen or heard from him since. Not that I necessarily expected to, but I was hopeful after what Krissy said about him being scared. I thought if I were vulnerable and shared some of my past, he'd see that his friendship is important to me.

"Well, hello, boys," Kat says, resting her arms on their high-top table. "Is this the Friday drinking club?"

"If only," Carson says. "Alex is in town, so it's our excuse to drink beer and eat grease."

Kat's shoulders slump forward. "Must be nice to consume all those calories and never suffer the consequences." She pops a homemade chip in her mouth.

Trig turns toward us. "You should join us." He slides off his stool.

"We're here for an office party." I tip my head toward the room Marcie and Robyn reserved.

"Well, we're watching the game at Slade's this weekend," he says, sipping his beer. "You should bring the kids over. We need to work on Ollie's throwing arm."

"And I'm making lasagna," Wind tosses out.

"Thanks. He would love that, but I'll have to see." I smile, knowing it would be fun, but I won't be going without Slade inviting us. "Ollie has a Christmas program at preschool next week if any of you want to watch one teacher try to keep twenty-five little kids in sync and from picking their noses on stage. He'd be so excited to have you there."

"Absolutely," Carson says. "Send us the details."

"We're getting a drink." Kat pushes away from the table. "See you guys later."

"Have fun catching up with your friend," I say, following her.

Kat squeezes between people to make room at the bar. "What are you drinking?"

"Just water." One of her shoulders drops, and I smile. "I have two kids to put to bed tonight." Plus, I cannot afford wine.

Kat stares over my shoulder, waiting for the bartender. "Great. Junior is here. I don't have the mental energy to restrain myself from punching him in the nuts again."

I crane my neck and see him slapping hands with Seth. When I twist back, my gaze snags on a large figure at the other end of the bar. My big, burly neighbor leans, attempting to get the bartender's attention.

Kat chats with the woman beside her about how long she's been waiting, while I contemplate what to do.

I glance at him again, watching the sports news and patiently waiting.

Screw it.

I tap Kat's arm. "Hey, I'll be back."

She nods, continuing her conversation.

I make my way down the bar, dodging people, and slide into the five-inch space beside him. "Funny seeing you here."

He peers down, his brow furrowing a little as his eyes trace over me.

I tip my head in the direction of the other end of the bar. "Office birthday slash Christmas party."

A person elbows me from behind, and Slade shifts, allowing me to inch closer to give them room to carry their drinks away.

"I saw the guys. They said you have a friend in town?"

He nods. His eyes haven't left me, and it's beginning to feel awkward. My skin warms, needing him to say something.

Maybe this was a terrible idea. I left the sash and crown on his desk. What if he Googled and made up his mind about me like everyone else did?

Someone brushes up against my back, and I twist to face Junior's cocky smile. He looks like the Cheshire Cat who just trapped his prey.

"I've been waiting weeks for this opportunity." His eyes linger over my body. "Damn."

I could be home in leggings, my comfiest sweatshirt, and braless, not worrying about what's happening underneath Slade's silence or having to deal with Junior's smugass one more time.

"Looks like it's my lucky night." He tips his head toward the bar, his grin spreading wider. "I get to buy you a drink."

"No." I squeeze back, creating room between us and bumping into Slade.

"Aw. Come on. It's one drink. I'll let you buy every one after to prove you're an independent woman."

If I were a dog, I'd pee on his expensive shoes. Maybe I could settle for regurgitating my lunch. "I'd rather drink toilet water."

His amused eyes run over my face. "You know—"

"She said no." It's that sharp, low bark.

I feel Slade's presence expand behind me.

Junior's eyes flick to him but return to me completely unfazed. "I don't think this one has any trouble speaking for herself."

Slade's hard chest presses against my shoulder. "She already did. You have trouble listening."

Junior straightens, shoving his hands in his pockets. "You know him?" He lifts his chin at Slade.

I turn just enough to glance up at him. That intimidating glare dares Junior to say the wrong thing. I like the protective feel of his massive posture way too much.

I might've totally screwed up this relationship already, so I throw caution to the wind.

"Actually, I was hitting on him."

Junior's unimpressed gaze moves to Slade. "You're hitting on *him*?"

"Yep. We independent women aren't afraid to ask a guy to buy us a drink. We're not really into men who just assume they have a shot." I smile at Slade. "Besides, I like a man who knows how to hold a baby and isn't afraid of bodily fluids."

Slade's mouth twitches.

Junior stares at me as the bartender stops in front of us.

"I need a bucket of beer and . . ." Slade says, as his hand slides around my waist to guide me in front of him and away from Junior.

Well, ok then.

I smile up at him. "Just water. Thank you." I always seem to get myself into a mess, but at least Slade is going along with it.

I turn back to Junior. "You should take notes. Maybe try being a little less," I weigh my head from side to side, "'every woman's gift' and more 'I hope someone will give my arrogant ass a shot.'"

He huffs a laugh, his amusement falling away. He eyes Slade, who he clearly thinks is far beneath him. "I hope this works out for you."

I force a smile. "No, Junior. I hope things work out for you. Merry Christmas."

Junior rolls his shoulders back and returns to the party.

"He's a dick," Slade says, keeping an arm on the bar and around me.

"Yep, but a small one." I smile.

The corner of his mouth curls upward, and it's like the tiniest glimmer of hope. "Do you know him?"

"Not really. He's Griffin Macavoy's son. He's come into the office a few times."

Slade's eyes move over my head, his face falling into a deep scowl.

"So, I. . .just wanted to say Merry Christmas. You know, in case I don't see you."

His eyes remain over my head. "Are you going somewhere?"

I'd like to ask him the same thing, but more like if he's already gone. "My mom is begging for us to come home next weekend."

"You don't want to?"

I inhale and let it out, frustration building with the small talk, as if I've once again trusted someone with something I shouldn't have.

"I miss my mom, but the whole town will be made aware. I'm not sure I have the energy to deal with whispers and stares and questions. I'd had enough of that before I moved." I shrug. "The trailer park community is having a big party, though." I glance at my heels. "They're like my family, so I don't know."

"Your mom still lives there?"

I stare at him, wondering what's with all of the questions. "Yeah. All the neighbors would get together and stream my pageants. The irony, huh?" I laugh. "My mom made sure it was the highlight of the community. Now, it's just The Bachelor and potlucks."

The bartender sets a bucket of beer and my water on the bar. I lift the glass. "Thanks for this."

His eyes finally drop to mine. "Thanks for hitting on me."

I stare at him, wanting to know everything that goes on inside his ruggedly gorgeous head.

"It's not every day I get to buy a drink for Miss USA."

Those lips curl up underneath his trim beard.

I roll my eyes, needing his smile to mean everything is ok between us.

I turn toward the party so I can go home. "Don't feel too special, Tomcat. That is a former title that's long dried up."

I think I hear what might be a soft chuckle as I leave him with his bucket.

I spend an hour talking to Kat as she slowly drinks herself into a positive outlook while we watch Junior's ego inflate with Marcie and Robyn's flirty attention. Cory lurks in the corner, talking with Griffin and his wife, whom I met when they arrived. We spent a few minutes talking about Ollie and Frankie before they headed to the bar for drinks.

That was just about the time I glanced over to see Slade bear-hugging a beautiful blonde, who I believe is his best friend. I wonder if he actually talks to her and tells her all of the things he's thinking and feeling.

I slump on my stool, sipping my water and wishing it had a splash of whatever Kat is drinking. All I want is for him to tell me one thing. Just something about why he's so closed off and guarded. I want to know what he's protecting himself from.

"That's Seth's ex-fiancé," Kat whispers, but it's a bit slurred. "She's really beautiful and s-smart."

I peek in that direction. Slade laughs with the rest of the guys and Krissy at something she said.

Marcie slides up to our table with Robyn right beside her. "Did you see Alex is here?" She says it like it's breaking news.

"*That* will be super awkward if Seth runs into her." Kat stirs her drink with her tiny straw.

Marcie leans closer to me. "She ran off and married an NFL quarterback after breaking it off with Seth." She glances over her shoulder at Seth and Junior. "It's his birthday. We should get him out of here."

"Good idea." Kat lifts her glass. "Tell him I'm drunk and need a ride home."

"Perfect. Ok." Marcie turns, but Kat grabs her arm.

"Tell him if Junior follows us, I will be forced to retaliate."

Marcie laughs.

"Don't worry. I'll distract him." Robyn winks.

They leave on their mission.

I, on the other hand, have to figure out how I'm going to get home.

Marcie relays the information, and Seth's gaze crosses to Kat. He heads over as if he has just received a get-out-of-jail-free card.

"Seth, I'm just a teensy bit drunk." Kat slides off her stool, wobbling a little, and he takes her arm.

"I can see that."

"But I'm saving you, so don't forget it." She pokes him in the chest.

"This feels like old times," he mumbles as she grabs her purse.

"You ok?" he asks me.

"Wait, we rode together," Kat says, leaning on the table.

"It's ok. You should go home."

Her lips turn downward. "Seth can take you home, too."

"No, it's really ok," I say, even though this feels like one more time life is laughing in my face.

"Ok. I've gotta go before I fall asleep and Seth has to carry me out." Kat sways just a little.

"Yeah. Let's go. I'm not doing that again."

She swats him. "It was one time. My boyfriend just broke up with me."

Seth ushers her forward, looking like he's about to run for the door, and I can't blame him. I'd be right behind him.

I glance at my coworkers and know there's no way in hell I'm asking them for a ride or going anywhere with Junior.

I head to the bathroom, pulling up the Uber app I haven't used in ages. What's one more thing on the emergency credit card?

CHAPTER 34

SLADE

"So, that's her, huh?" Alex bumps my elbow.

I haven't been able to take my eyes off Sarah, knowing she's in the same room as Macavoy's kid. What's worse is that I saw the man himself enter a bit ago. I'd really like to pull her out of there and away from all of them. Not only because she's in that dress—the kind of dress that makes a man think crazy things—but because I want her to be here. With me.

"Seriously, man. If you stare over there any harder, the walls might crack." Carson pulls a beer from the bucket.

"Slade likey Sarah," Krissy says.

Wind snorts, and Krissy pulls the neck of her sweatshirt up over her mouth, trying to hide her joy at my suffering.

I scratch my nose with my middle finger, and she laughs.

Her head pops up like a prairie dog out of a hole. "What? I'm just happy someone finally cracked through the frigid, solidified layers surrounding you."

My eyes roll to the ceiling, but she doesn't even know the half of it. Sarah and those kids blasted a giant ass hole that's leading straight to my heart.

"Kris, why the hell are you still here? I thought you were meeting that doctor for dinner."

"Why isn't he coming here?" Carson takes a long pull of his beer.

I want to smile, having unleashed these hounds to nip at her instead.

"Yeah, we want to meet him." Trig rests his elbows on the table.

"Are you afraid we won't like him?" Wind asks in complete offense.

I meet her eyes and lift the corners of my mouth. Take that, you little shit.

Her long eyelashes drop into a glare.

"Even more reason we need to meet him," Carson says.

Krissy swirls her wine. "You guys are too much."

"Hold on." Trig stops from popping a cheese ball into his mouth. "Are you saying you're scared to bring him here?"

I listen for her answer, but my eyes drift through the crowd to Sarah. If Krissy doesn't want to bring him here, it's either because he's not good enough or she doesn't see it going anywhere. I'm curious which it is.

"You guys are a lot," Alex says, defending Krissy. "I don't blame her for keeping him away."

"Damn right, we are." Wind scratches his beard. "If he's going to date you, he needs to understand what's up. It won't just be Carson coming after him this time."

Krissy goes perfectly still, her eyes shifting to Carson.

My eyes meet Wind's, then flick between my best friend and my little sister. "What the hell is he talking about? Who did you go after?" I turn toward Carson.

No one moves except for Wind's eyes, seeking refuge from anyone but me. Carson's gaze tips to Krissy, who still isn't moving.

"Someone better tell me exactly what happened and when?" I wonder how I didn't know about this.

Krissy straightens, her shoulders falling back just like they used to as a teenager when I snagged her ass in a lie. "It wasn't a big deal. It was when I was hanging out with Colton. He was being a jerk, and I'd had a few drinks." Her eyes flick to Carson. "Carson had a few words with him and then gave me a ride."

Carson's gaze finally shifts from Krissy to me. "You were visiting Alex. He was an asshole, and I made sure he stayed far away from her."

"That guy was a complete dick," Alex confirms. "Ok, back to the pressing matter at hand." She turns to me. "Are you gonna blow another chance or make your move?"

I roll my gaze to hers, but she only smiles. "You've been with Mark too long."

"Nah. Forever won't be long enough." She grins, so obnoxiously in love with that guy, it's sickening. "You know, he showed me it's easier to be scared *with* someone than try to fight it alone."

I'd like to clap back and tell her I'm not scared, but I am, and she knows it. "Calm down. She just wants to be friends." I'm beginning to loathe that word.

Sarah made it perfectly clear that friendship is all she sees, but I've spent time thinking about it. I don't know if that's because she's not interested in us being more or if it's because I'm not giving her anything other than closed-off friend vibes.

I'm annoyed at not knowing which it is. But to find out, I have to take a big risk, and I have to decide if I'm ready for that.

I watch Sarah's head fall back in laughter at something Katrina said. My gut squeezes tight. I want to be the one to make her laugh like that, but I stood tongue-tied like a teenage boy when the prettiest girl in school finally noticed me.

After she stopped at the shop this week, I unraveled the pile she left on my desk. Written across the gold-trimmed ribbon were large letters that spelled out Miss USA. Somehow, I wasn't surprised. I can picture Sarah commanding a stage and being the most beautiful one up there, but not because of her amazing body. She has tenacity but also a graceful grit that's captivating. You can't look away. And it's intimidating as hell.

Trig says something, and the table erupts.

"Come on. Just go talk to her, you big lug." Alex bumps me with her shoulder.

"She tried to talk to him at the bar, but he was Stone Colding. Big time." Krissy sips her wine. "She's probably getting tired of his grumpy-standoffish shit. I know I would."

"It's the dress," Trig says. "When a woman wears a dress like that . . ." He whistles, and I want to punch his lights out so he can never look at her again.

Carson takes a swig of his beer. "And then some douche tried to hit on her."

"Did you all take a video, too?" I groan.

"Nooooo, but now that you mention it, we should have," Krissy whines. "Then we could've had a lip reader translate it so we'd really know what was going on."

"It did look kind of intense," Wind says.

Alex leans on the table. "Intense in a good way?"

"Oh, for fuck's sake." I stand, and they laugh, having the time of their life. "I'm going to the bathroom, then heading home."

"I gotta get going, too," Alex says. "The girls need to get to bed if they'll survive game day without meltdowns."

"You could leave them with me," Krissy says.

I leave them to sort out plans.

I think about Sarah telling Macavoy Junior she was hitting on me. My heart grew three sizes. That didn't feel like just being friendly, and I liked it—claiming her, if only pretending for those few minutes. Just the fact that she came over to talk to me, even though I'd once again left her high and dry after she was vulnerable.

But Alex is right. I have to get my head out of my terrified ass if I want a chance at whatever could be with Sarah. And I'd really like to know what could be.

I tug open the bathroom door, and Sarah is tucked in the dim hallway, scrolling her phone.

"Hey."

Her head pops up. "Hey."

"What are you doing?"

"I. . .uh." She glances at her phone, and then her shoulders drop. "Ordering an Uber." Her hands fall to her sides. "I rode with Kat, but she had a bad day and drank a little too much, so Seth took her home. I'm not asking anyone else—"

"I'm taking you home." I step past her. This is an opportunity I will not screw up.

"No." She grabs my arm. "You're here with your friends. I have to get Ollie and Frankie in bed. You should stay."

"Sarah, I'm ready to go. Alex has two little girls. She's leaving, and I see the guys every damn day. I've had enough of them."

Her brow scrunches. "Are you sure? I hate—"

"I have to get my coat." I tip my head in the direction of the busy room. "Let's go."

The bar has only gotten louder and more crowded as the night has gone on, and I have to push through people to get back to the table.

I reach back to be sure Sarah sticks behind me, and I feel her hand slip into mine, gripping tight. This. This is what I've wanted all night. For a hell of a lot longer, if I'm honest.

"Sarah!" The guys erupt as I pull my coat from my stool.

"Looks like your mission was accomplished," she says, gesturing to the empty beer bottles and baskets of food.

Alex hops off her stool. "I'm Alex." She smiles at Sarah. "It's really nice to meet you, but I have to go." She extends her arms and hugs me. "Stop protecting yourself and take a risk," she whispers, eyeing me as she pulls away.

She hugs everyone, and Carson walks her out.

"Sarah needs a ride home, so we're leaving," I announce, knowing the looks I'll get, but I don't give two shits. I glance at Sarah. "Where's your coat?"

She smiles up at me, and it only spreads further when I roll my eyes. I drop my coat over her shoulders and grab her hand. I know she wasn't expecting it. Hell, I wasn't expecting it, but I made the mistake of letting her walk away earlier, and I'm not dumb enough to do it again.

I inhale long and slow. It's time I quit protecting myself. If I want Sarah as a friend and maybe more, then I have to actually do something about it.

"Ready?"

She nods once. "See you guys later."

"Seeeeee ya!" Krissy sings, but I know there is a fat grin attached to it.

I keep her close until I push out into the cold air, and it's a shock to the nerves swirling inside me. Sarah is fearless, but I've been stuck holding onto the repercussions of something that was never meant to be. And I'm sick of it.

I keep a hold of her hand as we walk to my truck, only letting go to press it to the door to stop her from opening it. She twists, and I leave my hand right where it is, caging her in. I need her right here, so I won't chicken out.

She blinks up at me. "Hi. What are you doing?" That hint of sassiness shoots sparks throughout my body, giving me courage.

I lean closer, wanting her to understand. "Trying."

Her brows pull together, those magnificent eyes running over my face.

I exhale, and my breath billows in the cold air, mixing with hers. "I'm gonna need you to go easy on me."

One eyebrow raises, and the corner of her mouth lifts with it. "You'll have to be more specific."

This woman has no idea the power she holds and the grip she has on me.

"I'm not good at being vulnerable or. . .sharing things. I'm working on that."

Her gaze drops from mine, tucking herself into my coat, and I want her to stay there always. My chest tightens a little at the thought.

She lifts her chin. "You're always helping me. But you never let me help you. It feels one-sided. I don't like that."

She told me she always wanted me to tell her the truth. So I do. "You are helping me. All the time. You just can't see it."

She bites the corner of her lip, and I stare at it, wanting to lean just a few inches closer but knowing we're not ready.

"I want to feel it. Somehow." Her soft words melt through me.

I stare into her eyes. "I've been alone a long time." I search for the rest of the truth. "I'm not sure I've ever really let myself need someone."

Her head dips to the side as her eyes fill with sympathy. "That has to be pretty lonely."

It is once you recognize it enough to feel it.

One of her hands peeks out of my coat and tugs on my shirt, her eyes dropping to her hold. "Maybe. . .you could let me help you sometimes. You know, when the house is too quiet or the day is long." She looks at me under her long, dark eyelashes. "Think of it as an experiment." She tucks her bottom lip between her teeth, and my self-control dwindles to absolutely nothing.

I slip my hand inside my coat and around her waist, guiding her closer. She watches me intently.

Her palms fall against my chest, sliding around my back. Her warmth surrounds me, and it doesn't feel scary at all. It feels exhilarating and safe. Her body presses against mine, and I breathe her in as she closes her eyes.

I fist the velvety material of her dress along her lower back, and she inhales. Her fingers dig into my shoulder blades, holding on as my mouth hovers over hers.

"Slade," she whispers my name, and it's so achingly soft.

I brush my lips against—

A car alarm blares, and Sarah jumps. I grip her waist, holding her tight. She collapses against me, my face falling into her neck.

"Shit." I breathe out.

A laugh tumbles from her, making me smile as she burrows into my chest.

I rest my chin on her head, holding onto her and not wanting to let go. Our pounding hearts ease back to a normal rhythm together.

"I'd better get you home." I pull her door open, and she releases me. I help her in, knowing I will relive that moment, hoping to get another like it.

I climb in, and the silence falls around us. I glance at her, the reflection of the street lights moving over her face as I drive. The only thing I know is that when I kiss Sarah, I want her to know me. I want there to be no guessing or wondering. I need to be certain it's real.

"I was seeing someone when my mom died. One of her caretakers." I grip the steering wheel, letting myself float back for just a moment. "I'd just started my second semester of college when she told me she was sick. Once I realized how bad it was, I dropped out and came home. I was young and looking for comfort from someone I thought understood."

Sarah shifts in her seat, tucking her hands in her lap.

"She ended up pregnant. I was so happy. I couldn't save my mom or take away any of her pain or suffering, but I could show her we were going to be ok. Melissa and I with Krissy and the baby. We'd be a family."

I inhale and let it out. "I got the job at the shop, bought a ring, put a nursery together, and then my mom died. She was all Krissy and I ever had. She wasn't perfect, but she would have sacrificed anything for us, you know?"

Sarah nods. "Yeah, I know."

I can see that Sarah would do anything for Ollie and Frankie.

"I had no idea how to make any of it better for Krissy, but we had this baby coming. Something so beautiful to look forward to while everything hurt so damn bad."

My sweaty palms slide against the steering wheel as my chest wall shrinks. "A week after she died, Melissa told me the baby wasn't mine. Apparently, she wasn't mine either."

Sarah's warm fingers wrap around my forearm.

"I didn't even see it coming."

She tugs my arm away from the steering wheel, and her fingers wrap around mine. I know she understands that kind of betrayal and hurt. But I didn't keep going. I shut everything out that could hurt me like that again.

I pull into her driveway, and she unbuckles but grips my hand.

"Slade, that amount of heartbreak would take a long time to heal." Her voice is so soft, and the understanding in her tone reaches in and soothes what still hurts to think about.

She stares at our joined hands. "I keep telling myself that just because I messed up once and trusted someone who never deserved it, it shouldn't mean no one does." She glances up at me. "Giving someone's deception that kind of power allows them way too much control over the rest of our lives."

It seems so clear and simple when she says it like that.

She huffs a laugh. "There are eight billion people in the world. I have hope there are a decent few who are trustworthy and might think I'm enough to want to stick around for."

I stare at her. There would be an entire crowd chasing after her, and she doesn't see it. I want to stick around as long as she'll let me.

Her beautiful face lights up with a small smile. "Feel like helping me wrangle two kids into the bath?" she asks, saving me from going home to my quiet house with all this swirling through me.

I nod, my lungs expanding with air and hope.

She pops the door open. "Good. Do you think you could teach Ollie how not to pee on the wall while you're here?"

I smile, climbing out of the truck to follow her into the house.

"Mama!" Ollie yells, running into the kitchen and looping his arms around her legs. Grover dodges them to sniff my hand. "Swade, can you come play cars with me?" He grabs my hand and tugs.

An older woman appears in the kitchen doorway, holding Frankie. "Hello, dear."

"Hey, Helen." Frankie leans toward Sarah, and she takes her. "Thank you so much for staying."

"It was no issue at all." Her smiling eyes move to me.

"Oh, this is Slade," Sarah gestures to me. "He lives across the street and gave me a lift home."

"Very nice to meet you." She clasps her hands in front of her. "I should scoot and see if I can make the last round of BINGO."

"C-come on, Swade." Ollie tugs harder.

We follow Sarah and Helen into the living room, and I sit on the edge of the couch. Ollie dumps his basket of cars at my feet as Helen pulls on her coat.

"They both ate a good dinner, and this one took a long nap this afternoon." Helen tickles Frankie's side, and she giggles, curling into Sarah.

"Thank you so much," Sarah says, hugging her.

"We had the best day. Oh," Helen stops before opening the door. "This was delivered this afternoon. I had to sign for it." She picks up an envelope from the bench and hands it to Sarah. "I'll see you on Monday. Make a list of anything you'd like me to help get ready to go see your mom."

They say goodnight, and Sarah locks the door but doesn't move.

"Everything ok?" I ask, watching her.

She stares at the unopened envelope. "He's going to take them from me." It comes out in a breathy whoosh.

"Swade, wook at dis one." Ollie places a car in my hand.

"Hold on, partner." I set the car aside and move to her.

"What?"

"He's actually doing it." Her gaze slowly drifts up to mine. "He's suing me for custody. He warned me, but I didn't . . ." She blinks, and I see her swallow.

"How do you know?"

Her gaze drops to Frankie.

"Maybe it's not—"

"You don't understand." It comes out in a rush, and there's an underlying panic in her soft tone.

She steps away to set Frankie down amongst the toys. Ollie digs through his pile and lines his cars and trucks along the edge of the couch.

She turns back to me, her body rigid as if bracing herself for a blow, and her eyes are wide with fear. "He took everything when I left. I had nothing. He changed the locks. Tossed all our clothes and belongings as if he could just throw us away. It was a game. He tried to starve us out." Her eyes press closed, trying so damn hard to suck it all back, but I catch her trembling hands.

I take them in mine and ease her closer. "It's going to be ok."

"Slade, you don't know. He'll do anything." Her body slumps as her glossy eyes tip up to mine. "He . . ." She glances at the kids. "He fabricated stories that made everyone question whether Frankie was even his to cover himself," she whispers, trying to blink the tears away.

"All my sponsors dropped me, and the organizations I worked with asked me to step down. He took everything. My dignity and reputation."

Her bottom lip quivers, and she can't hold it back. "They're all I have left. The only thing that really matters, and he'll win." She can barely get the words out as tears roll down her cheeks.

I sweep my arms around her, wrapping her up as if I can protect her. I want to calm her panic and fears, but I can't. It's the one thing I can't do because I don't know this man. But from what Sarah just described, I'd sure as hell like to get to know him. Up close.

Her head rests against my chest, her body shaking with a hushed cry. I hold her tight, feeling completely helpless, and I hate it.

"It's gonna be ok." I don't know how, but it has to be.

She shakes her head, not believing.

My jaw clenches tight with the only thing I know to do that might help. I force the words out. "You need to talk to Macavoy. He'll help you."

She pulls away, swiping at her cheeks. "He's my boss. I can't get him involved even if I could afford it." Her frustration is apparent. "Miles knows I can't fight this. It's been his plan all along. He's been saving up for when he needs it. Using Ollie and Frankie because he knows I'll do *anything* for them."

She tears the envelope open and drops the paper to the side in defeat.

I move to her, wrapping my arms around her again, and she leans into me. "We'll figure something out."

She buries her head in my chest, her trembling body sagging against me.

I may not be good at many things, but I'll do anything to protect the people I care about. There's only one way I might be able to help Sarah, but it will require a visit to the man who never offered me a damn thing.

CHAPTER 35

SLADE

I pull into the dark parking lot, hoping he's here this early. I grip the steering wheel tightly, feeling the slick coating of sweat on my palms. I never wanted to do this again, but I will. The momentary discomfort and angst will be worth it.

I vowed long ago to never ask this man for anything, but I've resigned to the fact that sometimes we have to lay our pride aside to do what's best for the ones we care about. And I care about Sarah and those kids more than I think I'm ready to admit.

I stayed with her the other night while she gave the kids baths. Once Ollie was finished, I read books to him when it was Frankie's turn. Then I went home, carrying Sarah's fear of losing her kids with me.

It can't happen. She can't lose them to a man who would throw his wife and kids to the wolves to protect himself and manipulate others. When Sarah told me he'd made people question whether Frankie was his, I wanted to hunt him down and help him forget he ever had a wife and kids. No child deserves to be used like that. I can hardly imagine what that did to Sarah.

My gut rolls as I pull open the glass door and head straight to the back, as I did long ago. I was just a kid watching life slip from my grasp.

I step into his office, and his head snaps up, his light eyes meeting mine.

I shove my sweaty hands into my coat pockets.

"This. . .is a surprise." Macavoy sets his pen down and pulls off his reading glasses.

I clear my dry throat. "Yeah, for me, too."

The tall man straightens in his chair. "Have a seat." He extends a hand to one of the leather chairs.

"No thanks." I stare at the aging man, who should mean something to me but doesn't. "I want to pay a retainer."

He frowns. "You need representation?" There's a slight tinge of concern in his tone, but I ignore it.

This conversation is business. It needs to be brief and to the point.

"Not for me. A friend."

He rests his arms on his desk, eyeing me. "I need specifics to determine if I can—"

"You can help." I cut him off, not needing any excuses. "You're the best at what you do. Believe me, otherwise I wouldn't be here."

He clasps his hands, his spine elongating. "So, you want to pay a retainer for a friend, and then what?"

"If they come to you or Kat seeking help, you do it pro bono. This stays between you and me." Sarah would never let me do this.

"And you'll foot the bill?" One dark gray eyebrow raises. "Son, you don't need to pay—"

"I'm not your son." I have no doubt he didn't mean it that way, but he needs to reserve that word for when it fits. "I asked for your help once, and you hid behind your job and family instead. I'm long past wanting anything from you. This is a business arrangement, that's it."

He exhales, leaning back in his chair, his gaze dropping to his desk. "I tried to help her. I offered to pay medical bills, give her money for groceries, for your school, make arrangements for Krissy—"

"Stop." My fists squeeze tight, not wanting to hear it. He didn't do shit but let my mom spend her short life pining after a man who'd only loved her in the dark.

His eyes meet mine. "I cared about your mother very much."

"Not even close to enough," I spit back. "I'm not here to talk about her or whatever kind of messed-up arrangement the two of you had. You chose your family. I'll do whatever it takes to protect mine."

"Does Krissy know?"

I shake my head. "It'd only break her heart more than it already has been."

"What if I'd like to—"

I scoff. "If you think for one second I will let you near her when we both know she'd just be another secret you'd have to figure out how to manipulate and control, you clearly don't know me and what you'd be risking." I don't give a fuck who he is. He'd better stay far away from Krissy. "She and Mom deserved so much better than you."

He nods, his jaw clenching, not liking my tone or the facts.

"Are you going to let me hire you or not?"

He crosses his arms over his chest. "Does this have to do with Sarah?"

I stare at him, unwilling to give him any more information than he needs until I know where we stand.

His eyes drop to his desk. "I saw you leave the pub with her the other night. Is she having trouble with her ex?"

"How do you know anything?"

He leans back in his chair. "I've been doing this a long time. I don't need specifics to know when someone has been pulled through the wringer."

"If she comes to you, you help her." I'm not asking this time. "I promised myself I'd never come to you for anything again, but Sarah needs your help."

"I tried to help your mom, but she refused. I would've done anything I could."

Except love her back. The truth is a hit square to the chest.

He inhales and lets it out. "I'll do whatever I can to help Sarah."

"I'll expect an invoice from your assistant."

He nods once, and that's all I need. I'm ready to get out of here as fast as I can.

"Slade."

I stop in his doorway, dragging my gaze to the man who chose his wife and other kids.

"Your mom did one hell of a job raising you. Far better than I ever could have." His gaze locks with mine. "I know you don't care, but I'm proud of the man you are. You've done an amazing job raising Krissy."

I'd like to ask him how the hell he knows, but I don't care enough. "You just stay on your side of the city, and we'll stay on ours."

I leave him and his words. There was a time when they might have mattered to me. Maybe they would have filled some portion of the empty space created by never having a father, but you have to respect someone for their words to carry weight—his float right past me and out the door.

CHAPTER 36

SARAH

I smile, blinking away tears as Ollie wiggles his hips and shakes his jingle bells, trying to stay in time with the song.

Frankie bounces on my lap, bracing one hand on Slade's shoulder so she can bob to the music.

The song ends, and the row of guys next to me whistle and cheer for Ollie, who grins and throws his bells in the air.

I put a hand over my face when they land at the teacher's feet, rather than placing them back in the basket like the rest of the kids.

"Look at that aim." Carson elbows Trig. "The kid's got an arm on him."

The room settles, and the kids finish the evening with "Up On The Rooftop," complete with all the hand motions. I soak in the smiles and joy that come with the season and the fact that Ollie has a row full of people here just for him. A year ago, I couldn't have imagined this was possible. But beyond the Christmas bliss, a new year awaits, and I worry about what it might bring.

I swallow the burning lump in my throat and glance up at the big guy next to me. The one who, despite all sound reasoning, has become my closest friend and someone I trust. The man I almost kissed.

I'm not sure I even contemplated what was happening, but I wanted to kiss him. I reeeaaally wanted to. Thankfully, a well-timed car alarm saved me from making a huge mistake.

This man has snuck in and flipped a switch inside me I thought was permanently disconnected. But the minute his hand slid around my back to guide me closer, I wanted everything that was about to happen.

Have I lain in bed every night since, wondering what it would have been like to feel his lips on mine? A million times yes. Have I let my mind wander further than that? You betcha. Do I need his friendship more than giving in to temptation, only to get slammed with reality? An overriding yes.

Slade told me the other night that "we'd" figure something out. I wanted to push him away and tell him I got it. But I don't got this. I cannot fight Miles alone this time. The thought of losing Ollie and Frankie, even only part-time, is gut-wrenching. If I'm going to make it through the next however long until I know what will happen, I need someone to hold my hand through it.

We stand and clap as the kids beam, bowing and waving.

I grip Frankie's hand, letting her toddle along as we gather in the atrium to wait for the little stars.

"That kid knows how to put on a show," Krissy says, taking Frankie's other hand.

"He gets it from his grandma," I say, knowing I'll never hear the end of it once I send her the video.

Ollie runs toward us and straight to Slade, who sweeps him up in his arms.

"Dude, that was awesome. Who knew you could rock out like that?" Trig says, extending his fist for a bump. Carson and Wind follow suit.

"Mama plays music and sings and d-d-dances every night when we eat."

One of Slade's dark eyebrows lifts.

I roll my shoulders back. "Dinner should be an experience. It's way more fun to eat your vegetables when you're dancing."

"It's true," Krissy says. "I can jam every night now that I don't live upstairs from the Grinch." She throws a thumb at Slade.

"Swade's, not the G-g-grinch. The Grinch gots red eyes until his heart grows bigger." Ollie holds Slade's face. "See, his eyes aren't r-r-red."

The guys snicker, but I smile at my boy, who knows a tender heart when he finds one.

"I don't know, Ol. He's been pre-tty growly this year." Carson crosses his arms. "I'm guessing there'll be a large rock under the tree for him."

Slade rolls his eyes. "Careful, or you'll find a pink slip."

Ollie's eyes grow wide. "S-s-santa is bringing me a train. I've been very good this year." He lifts his shoulder to his ear. "Except I p-p-peed in the trash can yesterday."

The guys' heads fall back with laughter, and Ollie grins.

I exhale, swinging Frankie to my hip. "All right, well, now that we know who's been naughty and nice, should we get cookies and punch?"

"Yeah!" Ollie throws his hands in the air. "I w-want a snowman."

We follow the snack line and find a table.

"You got your sled ready?" Trig asks as Slade helps Ollie with the folding chair. "It's supposed to snow tonight."

"We're going to see Grandma Susie," Ollie says, biting off the head of a snowman cookie.

The guys slide their phones from their pockets to check the predictions.

"You're going home?" Slade asks softly, and it almost sounds as if there's a hint of disappointment in his tone. It's probably more that I *want* there to be. *Dammit.* Things need to remain in the uncomplicated friend zone, which does not include hoping that he's a little bummed we're leaving.

I raise and lower my shoulder. "I can't just sit here and wait for a court date. It'll drive me crazy."

"But do you want to go?"

I inhale and let it out. "I don't want to face the barrage of questions about what I'll do if Miles wins. Everyone means well, and they care, but gossiping and drama are what they live on. I want the kids to have some Christmas magic, though. My mom is good at bringing the fun to avoid anxiety, so maybe we can just hide from the town. It's only two days."

We finish our cookies, and Ollie hugs everyone goodbye. "Merry Christmas, Kissy."

Krissy hugs him tightly. "I can't wait to see what Santa brings you. I'll be over to play. Ok?"

He nods and jumps to high-five all the guys.

Slade lifts him onto his shoulders and walks us to our car, helping Ollie buckle.

"Swade, do you think S-santa knows to bring my train t-t-to Grandma Susie's?"

Slade's eyes meet mine over the car seats, and I nod subtly. "Santa. . .has the best navigation system on his sleigh."

Thankfully, I was able to find a Thomas the Train set in amazing condition on the other side of town. It's not motorized, but Ollie will love laying the track in different formations.

"D-d-do you think you'll really get a rock?"

Slade groans, tickling his belly, and Ollie giggles.

I strap Frankie in and close the door. Slade rounds the back of my car, tucking his hands in his pockets.

"Were you able to get any more information on the petition?"

I shake my head. "I called my attorney and left a message. The receptionist said he'd get back to me after the holidays."

"You should talk to Macavoy. He'll help you."

My shoulders fall. "Slade, he's my boss. I don't want all of my past personal business to taint what I'm trying to build here."

His brow furrows. "Talk to Kat, then. She won't say anything."

I know he wants to help, but very few know Miles the way I do. I have first-hand experience of him manipulating even my closest friends. It's easy to do a lot of damage when you have a massive audience that believes what they see on a screen.

I smile. "You're awfully bossy." He rolls his eyes, and I move into him, wrapping my arms around his middle. "Thank you for caring and wanting to help me."

His arms slowly slide around me, pulling me close. "What time are you leaving tomorrow?"

I move to release him, but his arms stay locked, holding me to him. *All righty, then.* "You smell so good." Like cedar and car. I squeeze my eyes shut tight, having let that little bit slip out.

He huffs a laugh, his arms cinching me in a little tighter.

"In the morning, if it doesn't snow too much."

"I'll run over when we get home and check your oil and tire pressure."

I peer up at him. "You don't have to. I can do that."

"Will you have to Google it?"

I pinch him, and he flinches. "You know, Google has saved lives."

"It'll take me two minutes. It might take you all night."

I groan. "Fiiinnnne."

"You sure you want to go?"

I inhale his comforting scent and let it out, resting my head on his chest to stay warm, but also, it feels really nice. "Maybe it will snow three feet, and I'll be saved from having to perform a Christmas duet with my mom during karaoke."

"Is that really a thing?" He sounds mortified.

I rest my chin on his chest. "You've not met my mother."

"I'd like to see that."

"Oh, but everyone who attends has to sing. Now, *that* I would like to see."

"It'd be a cold day in hell before . . ."

I laugh, and he releases me. "Thank you for coming tonight. It was the highlight of Ollie's preschool experience. Make sure to tell the guys and Krissy, ok?"

He opens my door, waiting for me to climb in. "I'll follow you home."

I slide in. "See you in a few."

I watch him walk to his truck, wondering what it would be like if life were different. Different place. Different time. Different circumstances.

Slade is too good a man for me to allow him to get caught up in whatever I've got coming. It'll entail reliving the nightmare of what was, but if Miles wins, Ollie and Frankie won't be going anywhere without me. If I have to move to New York City, it will mean saying goodbye to Slade.

His brake lights flare along with my heart, and that's one more thing I'm not even close to being ready to think about.

CHAPTER 37

SARAH

"Honey, I don't know. They're working on clearing the highways, but Russ says the plows aren't even close to touching the county roads. It'll be dark by the time they get to them. I don't want you driving at night. It could be slick."

I run my fingers through Grover's soft, curly fur. "Ollie will be so bummed."

The snowstorm blew through, leaving behind six inches of snow and more back home. I'll be sad not to spend Christmas with my mom, but I can't say I won't be happy to avoid stirring the small-town gossip. I can definitely do without the questions about Miles's new gig and spending the next two days rehashing every worst-case scenario. Especially for Christmas.

"We'll FaceTime tomorrow, and maybe I can swing coming down for New Year's."

"Be careful when you go out to shovel." My mom will be out clearing a pathway through the trailer park to ensure the light show remains undeterred.

"Will do, honey. I'll send you pictures of the best decorations and a video of Agatha's drunken rendition of 'Santa Baby.'"

Agatha is eighty and lives two trailers over. She smokes like a chimney, and each Christmas Eve, she plants herself next to the punch bowl until it's her turn behind the mic. It's tradition.

"It'll be like I'm there." I laugh. "Love you, Mom."

"Kiss those babies for me."

I untuck myself from Ollie and Grover and shove my phone into the waist of my leggings. "I'm going to shovel part of the driveway while Frankie is still sleeping."

Ollie stares at the TV screen. "Are we leaving soon?"

"No." I run a hand over his head. "We got too much snow. I think it's best if we stay here."

He slumps. "But S-s-santa is bringing my train to Grandma Susie's."

"Are you kidding?" I squeeze him to my side. "Santa has special elves to track the weather. He's fully aware of the snowstorm and our change in plans."

"Will he have to fly through the snow?"

I shrug. "I don't know, but coming from the North Pole, I'm sure he's used to it."

He grins. "I b-bet Rudolph is good at finding the way."

I nod. "He won't let Santa down." I kiss his head, and Grover hops off the couch. "I'll be back."

"Can I play in the s-snow?"

"Not yet. Let me get some of it cleared first."

I slip on my shoes and open the back door. A whoosh of snow falls in, dusting the air. I sweep it out as Grover barrels past me and into the backyard.

I grab the shovel from the garage and scoop the snow away from the door and to the side of the driveway.

Movement catches my eye. I glance up and see the tall, muscular figure strolling down his neatly shoveled driveway, pulling on his Carhartt coat and stocking cap. His boots plow through the six inches of snow, and Grover barks, propping his front paws on the fence to greet him.

Slade scratches behind his ears before the dog runs off. I wrap my arms around myself as he stomps the snow off his boots.

"You can't travel in this. The roads up north are a mess."

I lean on the shovel, smiling up at him. "Well, good morning, Snow Leopard. I'm so glad to see you've put your bossy pants on today." I peer down at his long legs. "They're masculine, durable, annnnnddd mildly attractive." This man's jeans hug his legs and butt like they were made for him.

He shoves his hands in his coat pockets, staring down his nose at me, trying very hard not to crack his aloof stare with a smile. His light brown hair curls out from under his hat, and I wonder how many times I could twist it around my finger.

Crap.

I stab the ground with my shovel, along with that thought. Slade's amazing hair is not what I will spend Christmas thinking about.

"One might suspect that you, sir, were watching the road report and were concerned about us."

He only watches me, his eyes moving over my face.

"You can just settle down." I pat his chest. "We aren't going. They got even more snow, and it'll take forever to get the roads clear."

"So, you're staying here?"

"Yep." I glance around at the crisp white wonderland. "At least Ollie is excited to play in the snow."

Grover barks, plopping himself in a drift on the other side of the fence with his tongue hanging out.

"Mama." Ollie steps out of the house in his pajamas with his boots unfastened and on the wrong feet, his bear hat pulled over his ears.

Slade turns, taking two strides, and lifts him. "You're like your mom. Where's your coat?"

Ollie shrugs.

Slade tucks him inside his coat and carries him into the garage. "I was thinking about picking out a Christmas tree."

Ollie's eyes grow wide. "A real Christmas tree?"

Slade nods.

"You were gonna pick out a tree? In the snow?" I ask the man who just marched over here to tell me I wasn't going anywhere.

"It's the best time," he says matter-of-factly. "It doesn't feel like Christmas without snow."

Those green, green eyes stare back at me. "What do you say?" He nods his head toward his house. "Want to load up the kids and see if we can find the perfect tree?"

"Yeah!" Ollie throws his hands in the air. "Please, Mama. I want to g-go with Swade."

We have no Christmas decorations except for the little tabletop tree that Ollie picked out at the grocery store. Helping Slade find a tree will give him a slice of the Christmas experience.

I take in Ollie's bright eyes and full smile as he waits for my answer. "Is hot chocolate also involved?"

"And marshmallows?" Ollie twists like he's ready to jump out of Slade's arms to get going.

I glance at the big guy holding him.

"There's a sleigh ride, too."

Ollie grabs Slade's shoulders. "Can we g-go now?"

Slade waits for my answer.

"I have to get Frankie up," I say.

"Yes! Let's go." Ollie tugs on Slade's collar.

"All right, partner." Slade walks him back to the door and sets him down. "Find your clothes and switch your boots around while I shovel the driveway."

"Can I help shovel?" Ollie kicks his boots off.

Slade glances at me as Ollie scurries to get ready.

"Sure," I say. "Get dressed and go to the bathroom. I'll find your mittens. Make sure you aim for the toilet!" I holler after him, pulling the door closed.

Slade moves around me, grabbing the shovel. "You, too. You need a coat and a hat."

I reach to snatch the shovel back. "I can do that."

He ignores me, scooping the snow where I left off. "Unhook the car seats, and I'll pull my truck over." He looks at me over his shoulder. "Do you have boots?"

"Yes." I eye Mr. Fix-it.

He makes a path down the middle of the driveway. "Real snow boots, Sarah?"

I open the back passenger door. "As opposed to fake boots, Slade?"

"If you don't have any, I'll grab Krissy's out of the basement."

"Do you want to dress me, too?" I set Frankie's car seat on the garage floor.

The rhythmic scraping against the driveway halts, and that big body turns in my direction. Those deep green eyes find mine, one dark eyebrow raised. My entire body lights on fire with the intensity I see there.

I roll my lips, realizing what I just said. "You know, I think I can handle it."

"You sure?" His voice is low and sexy as hell.

Ohhhhhhh, shit. Shit. Shit. Shit!

I do not need to be thinking about Slade and any sort of clothing rearrangement or the gorgeous smirk curling at the corner of his mouth. Friend. This man is my friend. The one who cares enough to be sure we wouldn't attempt the treacherous drive home.

I exhale, calming the swirl of desire beginning to churn. "Yep. I'm just gonna go get myself ready."

I head inside to wake my sweet girl so we can help the Jolly Giant pick out a Christmas tree.

CHAPTER 38

SLADE

I slowly pull my truck into her driveway. In the rearview mirror, I see Ollie's sleepy head roll to the side, a ring of chocolate outlining his mouth.

"If you pull up to the back door. I'll carry them in," Sarah says, unbuckling.

After the sleigh ride, hiking through the snow to chop down the tree, and hot chocolate, these kids are spent.

I turn off the ignition, and Sarah jumps out, opening the back passenger door to get Frankie. "Let me lie her down, and I'll be back to get him." She throws the diaper bag over her shoulder and hurries around the front of the truck.

Sarah and I talked the whole way to the tree farm about holiday traditions. She told candid details about her neighbors in the trailer park and how her mom organized a Christmas light decorating competition. I told her about Krissy always searching for the saddest tree in the nursery because she felt bad that it was already cut down and would never get picked.

Sarah said this was the first time she'd ever been to a tree farm. Growing up, she and her mom decorated a silver tree strung with pink lights. I told her about my mom taking us to the grocery store to pick one out that had to have been a fire hazard since it had been sitting dry for so long.

I carefully pull Ollie from his seat. His head flops onto my shoulder, and his little arms squeeze my neck. This kid grinned ear to ear on the sleigh ride and begged to do it twice. So, we rode around the farm to ensure we could scout the perfect tree. Then he helped me saw it down.

I meet Sarah at the back door, and she stares up at me for only a second before holding out her arms. I shift Ollie to her.

"I'll lay him on the couch and then be back to get the car seats." She disappears into the house.

After finding the perfect tree, we rolled together a small snowman before sitting by a large fire with hot chocolate, and the kids played in the snow. We laughed when Frankie bit into a chunk of snow, her lip curling out, not expecting it to be cold.

I hear the door open and close.

"He seriously had the best time. Thank you so much for letting us—" Sarah stops beside me at the lowered tailgate. "What are you doing?"

I cut the plastic netting away with my pocket knife. "I'll run over and grab my drill. Once the stand is on, we'll carry it inside." I free the trunk and clip my knife to my pocket.

Sarah would never accept a tree from me, but she and the kids are getting one anyway.

"It'll just take a second to get the seats, then you can—"

I start down the driveway.

"Where are you going?" Her tone rises.

"I have to grab a few things. I'll be back."

"Slade."

I hear her confusion, but I keep moving, knowing what she'll say.

I get halfway down the driveway and—

Wham!

I stop, turning ever so slowly. Sarah stands, cupping another snowball in her hands. Her eyes are bright and playful, and I stare at her, wanting more of it.

"What did you just do?" I ask calmly.

She bites the corner of her lip. "You didn't answer me. *Where* are you going?"

The mischief in those beautiful, different-colored eyes sends my blood soaring through my veins. I have wanted to kiss this woman a thousand times since the other night, and I'm waiting for the perfect opportunity. Really, I need to be damn sure she's ready. But she's making it incredibly difficult for me to be patient.

"I'm getting my drill. Then you can help me make sure it's straight on the stand."

She rounds the snow in her hands, forming the perfect ball. "Annnndddd, why are you not taking your truck with you to do that over at your house?"

She's on to me, and I like it.

I tuck my hands in my coat pockets. "I don't think it will fit in my house."

Her eyelids droop just a little, her shoulders relaxing. There's stillness all around, except for the adrenaline building within me.

"Was this your plan all along?"

I'm not exactly sure what she's referring to, but falling for her was definitely not part of the plan. Getting the tree for them? Absolutely.

"Careful, Sarah." I gesture to the snowball, daring her.

Her sassy mouth creeps into a fearless smirk. Her eyes squint, contemplating the risk.

She goes for it just as I expected, pulling her arm back and releasing the snowball.

Bam!

It splatters square against my chest. I look at the broken clumps of white powder on my boots and then drag my gaze to hers.

This woman has no idea what she's just done.

Her smile fades as the silence falls around us again. There's nothing but the crunch of my boots as I charge up the driveway, scooping snow into my glove as I go. Her eyes grow wide, and she runs for cover.

I form the ball in my hands, and she laughs, ducking behind my truck. "I've never lost a snowball fight, and I don't care that you're a woman. I'll take your pretty ass down."

"Are you trying to scare me, Leo?" Her voice comes from the front end.

I inch closer. "Leo?"

"Really? The lion." Her voice retreats.

"You can't hide, Sarah." I move around the side.

Her head pops up across the hood, and she beams me in the shoulder with another snowball.

"You for sure can't hide, you big mountain lion." She laughs, and warm rays of joy explode in my chest.

I crouch low around the front of my truck, listening for her footsteps. I peek around the front and see her darting away. I hit her in the lower back, and she squeals, making a run for it.

I straighten, and she slips around the tail of my truck. "Surrender now, Sarah."

"Never!" she yells.

The top of her hat pops up over the hood of my truck, and my snowball crashes against the garage. The next one flies right past my head.

I crouch low, moving around the front again and reloading as I go. I peek around the corner expecting to see her, but—

"Pssst."

I twist and—

Splat!

A giant clump of snow hits me square in the face. I fall back into the pile along the side of the driveway.

"Oh my gosh." She laughs, but I can't see anything. "Are you ok?"

I wipe the icy flakes from my eyes and beard and blink away the cold specks. She stands over me with her hand over her mouth, trying not to laugh.

I'd take another hundred snowballs in the face if it made her this happy.

"I'm sorry. I meant to hit your back." She extends her hand to help me up, and I take it, yanking her down into the snow beside me.

Laughter spills from her, and I smile to the sky, knowing I definitely won in this game.

She rolls to her side and extends a handful of snow over my face. I turn to look at her, and she presses her lips together, withholding her joy.

"I'd be very careful, Sarah," I say, watching her contemplate it.

"Oh really? Or what?" she dares.

I grip her wrist, gently lowering it as I roll over her and pin it to her side. My chest rests against hers, and she watches me closely, her eyes staring into mine.

"Or this will turn into an entirely different kind of game."

Her eyes flick between mine. A red stocking cap covers her dark hair, but the long strands are splayed in the snow around her. She's stunning. An angel sent to save me from my self-sabotaging ways.

"Was this your plan all along? Getting a tree for us?" It's only a whisper, her breath moving over my lips.

I blink, wondering if she still tastes like chocolate and marshmallow.

"Slade, I can't accept the tree. You've already—"

"Yes, you can," I say softly.

Her gaze drops from mine, falling somewhere in the minimal space between us. "I can't. . .repay you."

"You already have." My stomach pinches tight with the absolute truth. "This is. . .the best day I've had. Ever."

Today was a gift. Just being with her and the kids.

Her gaze returns to mine, searching.

"It's something I've wanted to do and have never had anyone to do it with." My lungs burn with the honesty.

She reaches up, running her fingers over the icy droplets on my beard. "Thank you for watching out for us this morning and asking us to go with you. Ollie and I won't ever forget it." She blinks quickly.

I lower my forehead to hers. "Sarah," I breathe out, cupping her face with my cold fingers. I run my thumb over her parted lips.

"M-mama," Ollie whines, and I feel Sarah exhale beneath me. "Frankie is c-c-crying."

I roll off of her and stare at the gray sky as she stands, brushing herself off. "I'm coming, bud."

She extends her hand, and I take it.

"I'll be back in a few," I say, shaking the snow off my coat and pants.

She nods, heading into the house while I gather myself back from blissful anticipation.

She peeks her head out of the door. "Do you already have lights?"

"I hope you like multicolor."

She shakes her head, but I see her lips curl upward before she closes the door.

I shove my frozen hands into my gloves and smile as I walk across the street. Today was another risk, but it was totally worth it. I just really need to know that I'm going to get a lot more like it.

CHAPTER 39

SARAH

"I hope you're ok with the dino nuggets for dinner. Since we were gonna be gone, I didn't go to the store."

Slade is on his knees with Ollie next to him, stringing the colorful lights around the bottom of the tree.

"I'm pretty sure dino nuggets are the Christmas Eve meal of champions," he says, unwinding the end of a strand.

"Yeah. And you gots to b-bite the heads off first so they don't eat your veggies. Right, Mama?" Ollie says, watching him.

I shift Frankie to the other hip. "That's right."

Slade gently guides Ollie's little hands, looping the lights around the branches. A joyful peace I've forgotten spreads through my chest, dampened by the reality that this day has to end.

It's like a dream. The kind I had long ago. One I thought I'd have when I married Miles, but it never came to be.

This is what I've always wanted. The ultimate dream. A family. The ones who are my home, no matter where I am. It's not about a career or how much money you have. I think it's about being with the people who make you feel whole.

Slade glances over his shoulder at me, moving around the tree. I don't know what he sees, but he pauses. "You ok?"

He showed up unexpectedly this morning and took us on a grand adventure like none I've ever had. And this man is slowly making my heart ache for something I thought died along with my marriage. But it's also new. A kind of longing I didn't know existed—one filled with joy and anticipation and heat and trust.

I think, bit by bit, Slade might be putting back together the jaded, broken pieces of my heart, along with the hope blasted all to hell that a man could be true to his word, loving, kind, and. . .selfless.

I nod and smile as a burn crawls up my throat with a desire for more of this. But not only more of this. More of this with him.

I shove it down, knowing timing is everything, and my timing has always been off.

I carry Frankie to the closet and pull out an old quilt. "I think this calls for a dino nugget picnic in front of the tree."

"Yeah!" Ollie jumps as I spread the blanket.

"You guys finish with the lights, and I'll get dinner."

I set Frankie down, and she takes quick, wobbly steps to Slade's outstretched arms. He smiles at her and then places her on his knee.

I fill a cookie sheet with breaded dinosaurs, sweet potato fries, tiny oranges, and two small cups of applesauce.

We eat while Ollie bounces back and forth between his food and the tree, placing his airplanes in the branches while Frankie points to each colored light, mesmerized by their glow.

Slade and I rest back against the couch, watching them. Eventually, Frankie crawls into my lap and falls asleep against me, worn out from the excitement.

"She's a beaut, Clark." I bump his arm with my elbow.

His head swivels in my direction. "Did you, Miss USA, just quote *Christmas Vacation*?"

I twist, leaning away from him in mock offense. "First, it's former Miss USA. And second, it's a classic." I shrug, returning my gaze to the tree. "It's played every year in the community center on the cinderblock wall. I was watching it way before I understood everything that movie has to offer." I laugh.

"What do you mean by 'former?'" His tone is a little growly.

"I'm no longer the reigning Miss USA, but also . . ." I exhale, glancing at him, realizing he must not have Googled me. "All of my accomplishments, my sponsorship contracts, and community affiliations were negated when Miles fabricated stories about my. . .extracurriculars. He made sure everyone was informed. I'd cheated on the adored news personality who was gaining fans and attention faster than I could even register what was happening. I couldn't keep up with the lies."

"You didn't fight it?" he asks softly, but his question is filled with surprise.

I shake my head. "I was consumed with making sure I could feed these two and keep a safe roof over their heads. I couldn't fight the reach he had, especially when all my connections had already dropped me."

I gently rock Frankie back and forth, letting the shameful truth ease to the surface. The one it's taken me all this time to consider.

"Achieving the Miss USA title had consumed my life, and then after, I still lived in that world. Having a team to tell me what to do and where to be. Modeling and working with organizations that offered assistance to disadvantaged women and children. But I'd gotten lost in it all. It was as if I'd lost touch with real life. My true self. And then . . . suddenly, I crashed back into a reality I'd spent years hiding from."

His gaze shifts to me again, but I watch the kids, so thankful to be here, no matter how lonely or scary it's been.

"You're an amazing mom, Sarah." His voice is as tender as I've ever heard it.

I want it to be true. So badly. I want nothing more than to do right by them. "You do what you gotta do, ya know?"

He nods slowly, and I'm sure he gets it.

The silence settles around us, and the vulnerability has left me feeling raw.

"I should probably get him in bed," I say, knowing I could sit in front of the tree with Slade for the rest of the night. Just like this.

"I don't want to tell the tree goodnight." Ollie's excitement has turned to whining. "It's so b-b-beautiful."

"I know, bud, but Santa won't bring presents if you aren't asleep."

"Aww." That gets his attention, and he stands.

"What do you tell Slade?"

Ollie stops in front of him before throwing his arms around Slade's neck. "Thank you, Swade. This was my f-favorite day ever." Slade wraps his arms around him, hugging him tightly. "Can you come over t-t-tomorrow and watch me open my presents?"

Slade runs a hand over his hair. "I think you should do that with your mom and Frankie, but do you want to come over to my house for lunch?" Slade's eyes catch mine. "If it's ok with your mom. Krissy and the guys will be there."

"Are you watching f-football?" Ollie asks as if that's a deciding factor.

"You bet."

Ollie's head snaps in my direction. "Can we?"

I push my lips to the side as if I'm thinking hard about it. "Only if you get in bed really fast. Nobody wants a fussy party pooper for Christmas."

He giggles, releasing Slade, and darts back to the tree to snatch his fish.

"See you tomorrow, partner," Slade says as he zips past him and down the hall toward his room, with Grover following.

Slade helps me stand without waking Frankie and carries the cookie sheet and plates to the kitchen. I lay her in her crib and meet him back in the living room.

"It'd be great if you could come tomorrow," he says, slipping his arms into his coat.

I smile and nod, pulling in a breath and not really knowing what to say.

Slade is a gift I couldn't have expected. He said this was the best day he's ever had. This was a day I never knew existed, one filled with such happiness. The kind that is uninhibited and free.

But also, this man is stirring womanly things inside me that need to remain locked down tight. I cannot want things that could be hazardous to our friendship. The one I need to remain stable and uncomplicated.

Roxie said I needed him, and as much as I don't want to. . .I do. I need him and the comfort he provides, just with his presence, if I'm going to make it through this next round with Miles.

"Thank you so much. Today was. . .the best day." I twist to look at the colorful, flickering lights. I stare at the perfect tree, a lump forming in my throat.

I don't know how I'll ever repay him. "I can't—"

"Merry Christmas, Sarah." His deep green eyes linger between mine, the air around us swirling. Or maybe it's everything inside me that wants to grab him and kiss him and know what it feels like to be wrapped up in his arms, safe and secure, leaving all that's hard behind for only a moment. Because with Slade, it's just so easy.

I shake the thought, knowing it would change everything, and right now, I need his calm, protective strength.

"I'll head out the back, but make sure you lock your door."

I nod. "Ok."

He grabs his hat, and I can only watch him turn for the kitchen, feeling like so much remains unsaid. I run a hand over my face, reliving the moment in the snow, the weight of his body on top of mine, wondering what it would be like to move one inch and seal his mouth with—

"Mama! Come on!"

I inhale deeply and run a hand through my hair, getting a grip.

"Mama!"

I blow out a breath and head down the hall to Ollie's room. His clothes lay in a pile on the floor, but he's standing on his bed in his jammies, holding . . .

"What is that?"

Ollie extends the small, dark green metal car. "Swade gave it to me. It's a f-fastback. He said it's my Christmas present."

That. Big. Shit. Damn him.

"Climb into my bed. I'll be there in a minute."

Ollie jumps down, and the small car leads the way through the air.

I hurry to the kitchen and tug on my boots, not even attempting to tie them. I pull open the door and look down the driveway, seeing the broad shadow halfway to the street. I close the door and jog after him.

Hearing the crunch of my boots, he stops and turns, his face only visible by the dim glow of the street lights.

I break into a walk. The perpetually blunt man says nothing as I charge forth, knowing I might be making a seriously stupid mistake and ruining one of the very best things that has ever happened to me. But dammit, he gave my kid the very best day and his favorite car—the one his mom gave him.

I lunge for him, my body slamming into his as I throw my arms around his neck, hauling myself to his mouth. My lips crash into his as he stumbles back. His arm instantly comes around me, and he regains his footing, keeping us upright.

I press my lips to his, once, twice, wanting to feel everything.

I pull back, blinking as I second-guess my moment of complete insanity. Our breath clouds the inch between us. My feet dangle above the ground as he holds me to him.

Nose to nose, my eyes bounce between his, searching. If he puts me down, I'll run.

His soft lips press against mine tenderly as if he's testing, carefully exploring. His short beard brushes against my skin, and it feels freaking amazing.

My fingers dig into his neck, ignoring what is smart and safe territory, seeking more.

My boots touch the snow, and the warmth of his strong hold evaporates as his hands guide my head to just the right angle. I part my lips, and his tongue glides over mine as if he's savoring me.

I whimper, my body melting into him, and I fist his coat, pulling myself to him, needing him to do it again.

I nip at his lower lip, and he groans. I smile, and his mouth seeks sweet revenge, hot and slick, as his hands glide from my face down my neck and over my shoulders, making their way to my hips. His long fingers wrap around me, pulling me against him as if I might get away.

I slide my arms inside his coat and around him, pressing up on my toes and, taking my turn, tasting him.

He grunts and dives back in, stealing my breath. His fingers dig into my hips as his mouth consumes mine. His lips tug and pull, fast and then slow, as if he can't get enough. I never want him to stop.

He pulls away abruptly, our chests expanding and contracting in sync. The cold night air fills our lungs and shocks me to my senses.

His tight hold loosens only slightly as his forehead falls to mine. I stare back, afraid all words have taken flight for eternity.

I run my fingers over my puffy lips, the skin tingling in the best possible way. His fingers drag across my waist, as his hold slowly slips away.

I inhale a deep breath and take a step backward, unsure if a grin is about to break free or some kind of maniacal laughter because I'm not sure what in the ever-loving hell I just did.

I blink, retreating, and he watches me, his face partially masked by his moist breath.

I turn and charge back toward the house, wanting to run but maintaining steady strides.

I push open the door, step inside, and lock it.

Ho-ly shit.

My fingers run over my mouth again. I've been kissed before, but freaking hell, I've never been kissed like that. I smile, biting my lip, knowing with one hundred percent certainty I need that to happen again. Or maybe I don't. Maybe it can't happen again.

My body slumps, hearing Frankie's cries coming from her room as risky elation crashes into reality. I run a hand over my face, scrubbing it away.

All I know is I can't stand to screw this up or lose one more thing. Mainly the big man across the street, who's becoming insanely important to me. The kind of important I don't want to think about having to live without.

I blow air out of my cheeks.

Well, shit. What in the hell am I supposed to do now?

CHAPTER 40

SARAH

"You did what?!"

"I knnooooowww." I bury my face in my hands.

"Sarah, what the hell? Wait! Was it fantastic, or is this a call to tell me you'd been fantasizing about it only to find out it was like kissing a slimy, dead fish?"

I laugh. There was absolutely nothing dead about what happened in my driveway last night. I have never been kissed like that before, and I'm fairly certain I won't ever again. Unless it's Slade.

Heat creeps through my core just thinking about it, and I shiver. "Nope. It was so much better than I even imagined."

"Yes!" Roxie squeals.

"No!" I stop her celebration, bringing us both back to reality.

"No?! Why no?"

"Because," I whine, leaning back against the couch. I bend my legs, and Ollie lines wooden train track pieces underneath, using them as a tunnel.

"Sarah, it's a Christmas miracle. You just had the best kiss of your life with a man who's not only stealthy, sweet-as-pie but who looks like a bearded, flannelly-tattooed Superman. There is no room for nos here of any kind. You've needed this for sooooo long."

"But, Rox, Miles is suing me for custody, and if he wins like he does at everything else in life, I'll be moving to New York. There's no way Ollie and Frankie will go to the East Coast without me." I exhale. "And. . .I don't want to hurt Slade."

He told me about thinking he was going to be a father and wanting to get married, only to have that all ripped away at the same time his mom died. I can't fathom the wave of devastation and grief that hit him, then also having to care for and protect Krissy. I understand why he's closed off and distant. That kind of heartbreak would shut anyone down.

He's so kind and gentle under all that scowl, but that doesn't mean he's looking for anything more than a friendly hook-up. My body slumps with the possibility.

"Sarah." She says my name like I'm being overly cautious. "You have lived your life around Miles long enough. You cannot move to New York, and he cannot gain custody of the kids. You have to fight, not only for Ol and Frank but for yourself. You deserve to be happy and be able to say all the yeses to a guy like Slade."

"But I don't know how to do that when my weapons are limited." Frustration fills me for once again being a victim of Miles's egocentrism.

"Uh. . .don't you work for some of the best family law attorneys? And let's not forget this man has spent his career sleeping his way around the newsroom. I'm sure we can dig up a disgruntled one-time cleaning-closet buddy or two who'd be more than happy to spill those beans."

I lean back against the couch. "I've never wanted to put Ollie and Frankie through that."

"That's just it! Miles will say anything, and he did. He doesn't care and will do anything to paint himself as the poor, lonely dad who doesn't get to see his kids. Your boss and friends will find out anyway. Sarah, you need all the help you can get."

Rox is right. Miles will do whatever is necessary to cover his ass. Hell, he told the network executives that we're still a family and intends to pretend we are.

I need to consider discussing this with Kat or Griffin and assess the risk of bringing my personal issues into the office, which is my only source of income.

I change the subject, wanting Christmas Day to be about more than Miles and this. "Have you heard anything from Leo?"

I roll the Little People bus I found for Frankie in front of her so she can set the plastic figures inside.

"No, he said he's traveling overseas. We decided to hold off on breaking the big news until we can do it together."

"Rox, you haven't even seen him in years, and you're just going to announce you're getting married. Maybe you should go on a date first."

"Nah. It's best to just shock the shit right out of their stiff asses."

I can hear her grin. "I'm not sure Leo knows what he's getting into."

"He sure doesn't. I'm looking at it as the adventure of a lifetime. I'll make it my mission to keep the nerdy-by-nature genius on his quiet toes."

Ollie stands. "M-mama, I gotta poop."

"Ok. Go."

He jumps over the train.

"I'll have to wipe a butt in a minute."

"I'd rather be wiping butts. I'll be stuck at a table, wanting to pierce my eardrum with a fork so I don't have to listen to them drone on about the latest country club gossip with who's married and pregnant and doing due diligence to carry on the family line."

"Now, that's the Christmas Spirit!" I say, and she groans.

"Hey, listen, missy. One of us needs to Christmas the shit of this day. I'm nominating you as tribute. So, you march your cute, sassy butt over there and get more kissing action. Chop-chop. Maybe even go super wild and make out."

"Friends, Rox. I need friends."

"Ooohhhh, you need a lot more than that, sister."

I roll my eyes but smile. "Merry Christmas, Rox."

"I love you," she sings. "I'll be soaking in a bath to detox from misery, so I expect a detailed recount of all the delicious things."

"Love you, too."

My stomach swirls, thinking about kissing Slade again. I have no idea what to expect when I see him today, and I'm nervous. I threw myself at him last night, which might have been a mistake. I don't want it to be, but what I told Roxie is true. I won't hurt him or let anything screw up our friendship. The problem is my neighbor has snuck in and made me care about him far more than I realized.

I'll just go and pretend everything is normal. Like, launching myself at him in my driveway didn't happen. I can do that.

"Mom, I gots poop on my hand!" Ollie hollers.

"Hold on. Don't touch anything." I climb to my feet.

Slade is always telling me everything is fine. It has to be. At least for today, I'm going to believe that what I did last night will be ok.

Who am I kidding? It'll be a Christmas miracle if I can do anything other than think about needing that man to kiss me again.

CHAPTER 41

SLADE

Avoidance. Complete and utter avoidance is what's happening.

Sarah and the kids arrived thirty minutes ago, and she has spent each of those minutes averting all direct eye contact or being left alone with me. And I've about hit my limit.

When she met me in the driveway last night, I had no idea what she was doing until she made it very clear. I have thought about that kiss and every other thing I wanted it to turn into since. In fact, I've been planning how to make sure it happens again as soon as possible, but that won't be the case if she's unwilling to get within five feet of me.

I need to know why.

The day we spent together was like none other, and what was once hazy became crystal clear. I know what I want, and that's Sarah and the kids. She's going through a lot and might have a battle ahead, but I want to fight with her. I want her to want me to, but right now, it feels far from it, and it burns.

"All right, who's ready to exchange gifts?" Krissy clasps her hands, standing over an array of presents. "You all remember the rules. There are no exchanges, and you are required to be grateful for the time and effort put in."

"I will not be grateful for another year of finding tiny ducks everywhere, Krissy," Trig says.

She grins. "So much love was put into placing each one."

"Tell that to my foot when I stepped on them," he grumbles.

"Can we just get on with it?" I snap, wanting this over with so I can figure out how to get Sarah alone.

Sarah folds her legs under her on the floor as far from me as possible and pulls a few of Frankie's toys from the diaper bag.

"C-can I help?" Ollie stands beside Krissy.

"Sure," she grabs his hand, but stares the guys down. "There better not be anything inappropriate in here."

"I might need mine back, then." Trig laughs, and she glares at him.

My knee begins to bounce as my annoyance builds.

"Hold on. Kids go first." Carson hands a wrapped box to Ollie and then passes one to Sarah for Frankie."

"We all went in on these," Trig says.

Ollie plops on the floor and rips through the paper. He pulls out the tiniest baseball glove I've ever seen and a baseball.

His eyes grow wide as he grins from ear to ear. "Can we p-play catch right now?" He hops up.

"Maybe in a bit, bud," Sarah says, and his smile turns to a pout. "What do you say?"

He hugs the glove. "Thank you so much! Now I can play T-t-ball." He holds the glove in the air.

Sarah's eyes meet mine, but only for the briefest moment. "Thank you, guys. That's so thoughtful."

"We expect season tickets when he hits the major league." Wind says, holding his hands out for Ollie to lob him the ball.

Krissy sits beside Frankie. "Let's see what this little princess got?"

Sarah helps Frankie pull the snowman paper away to reveal her first tool bench."

"Alex would be so proud." Krissy smiles.

"Any little girl of ours will know how to change her oil and complete a tune-up." Carson leans back on the couch, rolling the baseball for Ollie to scoop up in his glove.

Sarah's shoulders fall, blinking back tears as Trig pulls out his pocket knife to open the box.

"You guys. Thank you so much. These are amazing," she says softly, still avoiding all direct eye contact with me.

I inhale and exhale slowly, needing this to move along..

One present is handed out, then another, slow as freaking molasses.

"What the hell is this?" Wind holds up a blue plastic dinosaur with a hole cut out of its back.

"Dat's a b-b-bronto-saurus," Ollie says, taking it from him and setting it on the floor to play with.

"It's a taco holder. Duh," Trig says.

"Who only eats one taco?" Carson asks.

"Shut up. Wind should," Trig says, and they all laugh, but I watch Sarah continue to ignore me.

"It's my turn," Krissy waves her hand and then pulls a pair of reindeer slippers out of a bag. Her mouth falls open. "These are amazing!" She slips them on and looks at the tag. "Thank you," she tells Carson softly, and he nods at her.

The rest of the gifts are handed out until there's one left, and Ollie brings it to me. "Dat's from Mama and me. I wicked the s-spatula," he says, smiling.

Sarah's eyes meet mine for the first time today.

Inside is a plastic container filled with perfectly round chocolate chip cookies. She raises an eyebrow with a slight smirk of pride, and I'd give anything to be able to kiss it right off her mouth.

"Hey, why didn't I get those?" Carson says. "I want a redo."

"There's no complaining." Krissy points at him.

"Those bath salts will make your skin feel like butter." Wind rubs a hand up and down his arm.

Luke lights up the Lightsaber I found at the grocery store and pretends to strike Ollie. He falls to the floor in exaggerated agony, with Carson dropping like a fly beside him. Millie steps over them to hand the box of chocolates to Krissy, who takes her sweet ass time selecting one.

"Mama, I gots to pee." Ollie hops up, holding himself.

"Ok. Let's go." Sarah leaves Frankie with Krissy and scoots him down the hall to the bathroom.

Seeing it as my opportunity, I stand, taking my homemade cookies to the kitchen. I set them on the counter and stalk after her.

The bathroom door opens, and Ollie flies past me back to the living room, but I block Sarah from escaping. I slip an arm around her waist and haul her directly to my room.

"Oh, hi. Hello. Ok."

I keep hold of her, closing the door.

She ignores me, surveying my room. "So, you're a make-the-bed kind of guy. I wondered—"

"What's going on?" It comes out as more of a bark than I intend.

Her eyes flick around the room. "What do you mean?"

My shoulders sag. "This. Why won't you look at me? You've spent the last hour ensuring you didn't have to talk to me."

Her spine stiffens. "I'm not—"

"Sarah." I might lose my fucking mind if she doesn't tell me what's happening inside her beautiful head.

She exhales, her gaze finally landing on mine. "I'm sorry about. . .last night."

My heart sinks to my gut, where it smacks it around for having hope. "Sorry about what part?"

There are some long moments of uncomfortable silence while she evaluates what exactly she's sorry about, and I use the opportunity to second-guess every single thing.

She shrugs. "I don't know." Her eyes flick between mine. "Look, we're friends, and you've helped me more times than I can count. I'm truly grateful. I just don't want to muddy anything up."

I blink, trying to stay calm. "Muddy things?" I ask as cooly as possible, needing her to clarify quickly.

She nods, and her eyes drop to the floor. "Yeah. I mean, if you can't tell my life is a mess, and you're my friend." It's a giant ass kick to the throat. "I need that more than I need. . .whatever happened last night." She pauses, dragging her chin up. "I don't want to lose you." She says it so matter-of-factly that it shocks my heart back into place.

I stare at her, trying to understand, but then I think I do. I'm no expert in healthy relationships, but I know the best ones are built around friendship.

I step into her, aching to pull her close and make her see, but hold back. For now. "It doesn't have to be one or the other."

She stares at me, her brow scrunching, but then it smooths. "I thought . . ." She pushes her hair behind her ear, shaking her head. "Never mind."

She twists, but I gently tug her back, keeping her between me and the door. She's not going anywhere. I brace my hand against it, needing her to tell me exactly what she thought.

I lean, getting eye-to-eye. "Tell me what you thought."

She presses her eyes closed. "I'm not . . . I can't do. . .casual. I need simple and stable and—"

I frown. "What?"

Her shoulders droop. "I can't be friends with benefits. My head doesn't work like that. I have all this stuff with Miles, and Ollie and Frankie to think about. I can't—"

"You think that's what this would be?" I try not to sound offended, but I hate that she would even think I would use her like that.

"I don't know," she whines, slapping a hand over her face, then dropping it. "I threw myself at you. Literally climbed you like a tree, and thank goodness you kissed me back because I might have just let myself be swallowed up by a giant pile of snow. But then, you pulled away, and I don't know what that meant. Maybe you realized what was happening and that it's not a good idea. Or you don't feel it, and we were just caught up in the most fantastic day that ever existed."

She pulls in air, and her panicked rush makes me feel so much better.

"And then I ran because I don't know what's happening or what's going to happen, and the absolute last thing I ever want to do is . . ."

She blinks, her gaze holding mine, and takes a moment as if she's finding the courage to say whatever it is. "Hurt you."

She stares at me, her fingers pressing against her lips as if she didn't intend to say all of that.

The tightness in my chest evaporates, and all my nerves stand down.

I grip her hips, needing her to hear me. "Sarah, I only pulled away because we were in the middle of your driveway, and if I didn't, the entire neighborhood would have gotten a show."

I inhale slowly and deeply as her eyes track mine. I back her into my door, wanting her like I've never wanted another.

"Soooo, it wasn't just a momentary lapse in judgment?" she asks, clarifying.

I shake my head, moving into her, and she watches me.

"You weren't just pity-kissing me back? You would've wanted. . .more?" Her cheeks flush, and I freaking love that I make that happen.

I slide my palm against her cheek, and her warmth radiates through me. "Yes. And it wouldn't have been just a one-time thing. Not with you."

"It. . .wouldn't?" Her words come out slowly and a little breathy.

This is what I've been waiting for since I pulled away from her last night.

Her eyes stay locked on mine.

"No. When I carry you to my bedroom, I want to be sure we're ready for that."

Her fingers grip my shirt, holding onto me.

"*I* won't be a one-time thing, Sarah. And it won't just be friendly."

She huffs out a laugh, and her breath whooshes over my lips. "You might change your mind."

I study her, not moving an inch except for my jaw clenching. "Did he put that thought there?" It's a bit of a growl.

Her eyes fall from mine. "When your husband spends his days and nights sleeping with other women, you can't help but think you are totally and completely unsatisfying."

I lift her chin. "It won't be one time, Sarah. It will be every night, and you will be the only one."

She whimpers, sliding her arms around my neck. "You cannot say stuff like that."

I smile, leaning closer.

"You big shit." She smiles. "And that damn dimple. Stoooopppp," she whines.

I brush her hair away from her face and run my lips over her cheek and jaw down to her neck. "You smell so fucking good."

She sucks in a breath, her body melting into mine. "Slade, I need to take this slow. I have to be sure Miles doesn't—"

I pull away to look at her.

She fists my shirt, yanking me back. "I have no idea what he's going to do or say. What if. . .I have to move to New York? This could be—"

"You're not moving to New York." It cannot happen.

Her head lolls to the side in disbelief. "I love that you're so confident, but history tells me not to put anything past him. I have no idea what he'll pull if I don't do what he wants."

Her using the word love in reference to me has my heart squeezing tight. I run my lips over her cheek, giving her the only thing I know for sure, and it surprises the shit out of me.

"Even if that were a possibility, I'd still kiss you. I'd still want you here. Just like this."

"I'm scared about what's coming," she whispers, and I hear her vulnerability.

I rest my forehead on hers. "It's going to be ok. We can take this slow and figure it out."

Her arms tighten around my neck, and she presses up on her toes. "Then you, sir, cannot say sexy things that make me *not* want to take this slow."

I suck her bottom lip between mine, and her body melts into me. I angle my head and kiss her like I've been wanting to all damn day.

Her tongue swipes mine, and I grunt, taking a handful of her perfect ass.

I feel her grin, and I kiss it away, making sure she understands I'm not going anywhere.

I know she's been hurt, and her trust isn't earned easily. I want her to feel that she can trust me with everything, and I won't betray it.

She pulls away, her chest moving in and out with mine. "We need to get back out there, or everyone will think we're doing things in here."

I nip at her neck, wanting to kick everyone out.

"We are doing things. Important things."

She smacks my arm. "It's a Christmas party, and this is your house."

"Yep. So I can tell them all to go home."

"Ok," she pries herself out of my arms. "How red and puffy are my lips?"

She lifts her chin and runs her hands through her hair.

I loop my arm around her, snatching her back. "Come here. Not puffy enough."

She laughs, and I hold her tightly. She rests her head against my chest. We stand like that for only a minute.

"Thank you for the cookies," I say.

"Better not thank me until you taste them." She peers up at me.

"I have something for you."

Her eyes droop into a playful glare. "Oh, really?"

Damn her. She's making it extremely difficult to control myself.

I nod, reluctantly releasing her to lift the wrapped box from the floor and set it on my bed.

She peeks at me, her lips turning up into a beautiful smile as she carefully unwraps it. When the paper is peeled back just enough, she stops.

"Nooooo." She spins to face me. "Slade Bennett. This is not fair. I cannot . . ."

I pull her to me again, linking my hands behind her back. "I'm not sure I should be supporting your addiction."

"Addiction?" she scoffs. "I'm a mom and have been surviving on sludge that might possibly be coating my insides with tar."

I drop my head to the side a quarter of an inch at her dramatics. "Why are you still drinking that stuff. I bought you a huge bag of grounds."

Her arms drop from my chest to her sides. "You said it was buy one, get one."

"I might've lied, but it was for a good cause."

Her shoulders droop. "Is that so?"

I nod. "That stuff makes you so damn happy."

Her mouth curls up, and she inhales like she can smell a fresh brew. "It really does. I've learned to savor the simple joys in life." Her arms slide around my neck. "So, I've been using them sparingly when I have a really shitty day."

"Well," I lean down, brushing my lips across her cheek. "This will make your coffee taste like it was brewed in one of those fancy coffee shops."

Her forehead presses against mine. "Slade, this is the most thoughtful gift I've ever been given, but I cannot accept this machine, no matter how badly I want to make a cup right now."

I press my lips to her. "Yes, you can."

She shakes her head. "No, I really can't." It's a bit of a whine.

"It's not just for you." I layer kisses down her neck. "I'll walk over and you can fill my travel mug in the mornings."

"That is not enough."

My teeth graze her neck. "Oh, don't worry. I plan on collecting payment in other forms."

"Is that a promise?"

I pull away to meet her gaze. "I've never made a promise I intend to keep more."

Her head tips back as she groans. "Fiiinnnee. I'll make you coffee and wait to pay up."

I stare into her eyes, imagining.

Her arms tighten around my neck. "Will you come over and sit in front of the tree with me tonight?"

"Can we go now?"

She rolls her eyes, grabbing my hand. "No. You are having a party with your friends first." She pulls open the door.

"I'm not playing any stupid ass games."

She twists back, pressing a quick kiss to my lips, and I'm tempted to haul her right back into my room, forgetting all thoughts of taking things slow.

"Fine, if there are games, you and Ollie can build a train track. I told him, you'd be an expert track layer."

I follow her to the living room, knowing this is the best Christmas I've ever had. We can take this as slowly as she wants, but I need to be sure she and the kids don't go anywhere.

I'm falling for Sarah. Shit. I've already fallen, not only for her but for her kids. They are what I want and everything I've been waiting for.

Somehow, I have to be sure her ex doesn't take them from me.

CHAPTER 42

SARAH

I hit send on the financial aid application for the speech therapy program, praying that Ollie qualifies for the next semester. Getting him back into a program to help him work on his speech patterns would be amazing.

I lift my phone and tap out a message.

> ME: Hi, Sunny Cat. Do you want to have dinner with us tonight?

I press send and wait for Slade's one-word reply. This man is killing me slowly.

We've spent almost every night together since Christmas, and two weeks later, the fresh tree is still up and glowing.

He's helped me put the kids to bed, and once books were read and the house was quiet, we snuggled on the couch in front of the tree and talked. It's been amazing.

I've told him more about my years with Miles and stories about my pageant days, and he's told me bits about what it was like to be twenty and raising a teen girl. But he'd still rather listen than share. I'm beginning to see that's who Slade is. He's a selfless protector, keeping things locked up where they don't hurt anyone else, but I want to be the one he lets in. I want him to let me be his protector—the one who keeps him and his heart safe.

For New Year's, we watched football at his house and spent the day with the guys and Krissy. Then, we rang in the New Year with a very long and satisfying make-out session that ended with Slade demanding I go to bed before things went further.

Did I want them to go further? Hell, yes. Are we ready for that? I'm not sure.

Miles has texted to remind me that I can make the custody petition go away if I agree to move to New York. As scared as I am, I can't do it. I cannot let my fear win. I've let him manipulate me long enough.

I've spoken with my attorney, and unfortunately, like with most things, you get what you pay for. I've documented Miles's complete lack of involvement in hopes that it'll somehow prove I'm the most fit to raise Ollie and Frankie, even though I don't have his clout and financial stability.

So Slade and I are taking things slow, but I have fallen for this man one hundred times over. I can't help but wonder if he feels that deeply, too.

I fell for a man who told me everything I wanted to hear and did all the right things that made me believe him, but I didn't see it—the truth. It feels unfair to even think about Slade in any comparison to Miles. But it's my ability to judge real, genuine affection and care that worries me. I'm scared of being wrong all over again and realizing I'm only a passing fancy or the object of someone's momentary desire.

I trust Slade. I'm still just a little hesitant to give him my heart when he hasn't quite trusted me with his.

"Oh, my goodness. Is it true?"

I twist in my chair, and Marcie and Robyn stand in my doorway, their eyes twinkling.

"Uh. . .is what true?" I set my phone on my desk.

"You were married to Miles Crawford?"

My breath catches in my throat. I stare at them. "Uh . . ."

"He is so hot. They just announced him as the new anchor on The Morning Show. His face is everywhere. Women are losing it, wondering where he's been hiding."

I want to gag, but first . . . "How. . .did you know we were married?" My heart starts to pick up the pace.

Marcie waves a hand. "Oh, Cory was talking about it in the kitchen this morning."

My brain splits in two. One half is sounding off relief signals that Miles isn't posting lies about us, while the other is firing rage that Cory has apparently spent time digging into my past. I'd like to know what he intends to do with the information he's gained.

"I can't believe we didn't know this," Robyn says. "So, you lived in Chicago? Wait, are you moving to New York?" Her eyes grow wide with excitement.

My stomach drops to the floor. This is always how it is. People find out about Miles, and it's as if I don't exist. There's not even a second of thought put into why we aren't married anymore. He can't possibly be anything but the good-looking, charismatic journalist who's breaking news one made-up story at a time.

This is what I've been avoiding. The thing I've been hiding from. They say the past always catches up with you. No matter how hard I've run, my tired ass just hit the wall.

Reality hits me under the chin in one quick, hard blow. It's only a matter of time before my name and our relationship hit the airwaves once again. The thing is, I'm not sure how Miles will address it. All the former ugly details will spread, but he's convinced the network we're still together.

I suck in air, holding it as the realization hits. This was his game plan. His way to sweep it under the rug and come out looking like the hero. The sweet man who rose above, forgave his unfaithful wife, and is now living happily ever after at the very top.

My stomach stirs, and my body breaks out in a cold sweat. I can't control any of it. *Fuck!*

My mind spins. What I can do is figure out what in the hell Cory is trying to do here.

I push out of my chair. "Will you guys excuse me for a second?" I stop in my doorway and face their confused expressions as my body warms with the force of blood pumping through me. "Be careful. Surface-level assumptions can be quite deceiving."

I walk two offices down and swing the door closed. Cory shifts his pointy nose away from his computer screens.

I cross my arms, trying to calm my raging anxiety, soaring fast and furious. "I heard you enlightened everyone this morning on my previous relationship."

He twists toward me, crossing his legs. "Is that a problem? I didn't realize it was a secret."

He knows damn well it's none of anyone's business.

"What the hell is your problem? I've done nothing but do what I've been asked and hired to do. I'm not trying to steal your work or your superiority. I'm just trying to pay my bills and make sure my kids are fed. *That's it*, Cory."

He shrugs one miserable shoulder. "I just wanted to understand why Griffin hired you."

"What's that supposed to mean?" My temperature spikes, and sweat pools in my armpits.

He links his skeleton hands in his lap. "We got tons of applicants. You were barely qualified. No experience. Hardly an education compared to everyone else." His head falls to the side, baiting me to see something I don't. "You're a beauty queen who can no longer live off her title, looking to fight social injustice. At least, that's what you built your platform around. I'm not sure how far that will get you now."

I press my eyes closed to keep from smacking him. I clench my jaw so tight it's possible my teeth shift.

When I open them, he sits there, socially inept as ever.

"Cory, whatever your point is, all I achieved has been hard-earned, including being here." My stomach pinches and rolls with his insinuation that I got this job for some other reason.

I inhale slowly, and his beady eyes only stare back. "I'm not sure what you aim to gain by wasting your time researching my past, but all damage to me personally has already been done. I have nowhere to go but up from here."

I turn, saying a silent prayer that's true, and haul the door open, not giving a single shit about anything he says or does. The only thing I have left to lose is Ollie and Frankie.

Cory can do his worst with old stories and lies. It no longer matters what these people or anyone else think. There it is. The swift kick of reality I've needed. My priority is to protect my kids, and that's what I will do.

I blow past Marcie and Robyn, who eagerly wait for the lowdown I won't be giving them. I stand in my office and yank my phone off my desk.

MILES: Don't drag this out, Sarah. You won't win. My move has been announced, and the welcome party is scheduled for next month. I expect you'll be there.

I squeeze my phone tightly, wishing I could throw it against the wall. Bile climbs up my throat with the realization that he's not wrong. I won't win. At least not the way I've been playing.

My eyes burn with tears, and I blink them away, knowing I need to get it together if I have any chance of keeping Ollie and Frankie from Miles's absurd and harmful expectations. And I want my life back.

I walk back down the hall all the way to Griffin's office. I knock on the door.

"Hey, Sarah."

"Do you have a few minutes?" I inhale a deep breath, needing it to slow my adrenaline.

He nods, peering at me over his reading glasses. "Sure. I was hoping you'd come to see me."

My shoulders drop. Of course Cory had a conversation with him. "Really? So, he's told you?"

He shakes his head. "No, he only told me you might seek my help."

I stare at him, completely confused. "He said I might need help?"

He pulls a legal pad out from underneath a stack of files. "Yes. He didn't give specifics. He said that was up to you, but I'm glad to help in any way I can. I'm honored." He gestures to a chair. "Why don't you tell me what's going on?"

I don't move. "What are you talking about?"

He straightens. "I assumed Slade was referring to issues with your ex, but if there's something else . . ."

My heart may no longer be beating, and the world stops turning. I hear nothing but the sound of my brain ticking at a zillion miles per hour.

"I'm sorry, what? Slade talked to you?" It comes out weak and a little breathy. I need oxygen, but my lungs aren't working.

He leans away from his desk and removes his glasses, running a hand over his face. I see him exhale.

"You didn't know." He closes his eyes, shifting in his chair.

My stomach muscles scream from holding myself together. "Would you be able to tell me. . .exactly what the two of you discussed?" I choke it out slowly and carefully.

He blinks a few times while my body instinctively roars with anger from the betrayal. I trusted him with private details of my life, and he came here behind my back to talk to my boss.

"He only wanted to be sure if you asked, I'd help you. I don't know anything more than that. He was just concerned and looking out for you."

I know damn well there's more to it than that. "And how exactly was he going to be assured of this?"

Griffin only stares back.

I blow out a breath, needing my stomach to settle before it launches itself up and out.

My gaze drops to the floor as my mind and heart shatter into a thousand pieces. I want to crumple to the floor right along with them, no longer able to bear the weight of it all.

I ease into his office and drop into a chair, closing my eyes.

"Sarah, let me help you." His words are soft and muted through the pressure building in my ears.

"Sarah."

I hear Griffin's voice, but I can't see my way out of the stabbing pain that Slade would do this.

Why? Why would he when he knows Miles betrayed me over and over again?

"Sarah."

My eyes snap open at my name this time, and Griffin's eyes are filled with concern.

I swallow the sob building in my throat. "Could I have the afternoon off?" I choke it out.

He nods slowly. "Sure."

I force myself out of the chair.

"Sarah." I stop in his doorway, needing to get the hell out of there. "He cares about you. He's. . .a good man. Better than so many of us."

Griffin's face fills with something resembling sadness. I don't understand it, but I can't think about that.

I grab my things from my office, bypassing Marcie and Robyn's stares as I exit and climb into my car.

I breathe through the burning ache in my throat so I can make it. I slump in my seat, wanting to fall apart. I want to cry and scream my head off. I want to text Miles to fuck off and never have to hear from him again. I want to know that my kids will be safe with me forever.

I grip my steering wheel, yanking on it as if it will help.

Fuck!

I can't do any of those things right now. The only thing I can do is find out why Slade, the man I was trusting with everything, went behind my back.

I want a partner and friend who will stand by my side, not do things around me. I thought maybe I'd found that. I rest my head on the steering wheel, terrified I was wrong once again.

One tear slips out and lands in my lap. I pull myself up and suck it all back, starting my car.

There's only so much one person can take, and I've had enough. No more hiding. It's time I get my life back, and it will be on my terms.

CHAPTER 43

SLADE

The cold air blows into the garage, and I press the button, lowering the door as Wind returns a car to the lot. I slip my phone from my pocket.

I responded to Sarah about dinner, and I'm waiting for her flirty, smartass reply.

"Are you skipping the gym again tonight?" Carson asks, hanging up his coveralls.

"Yeah. If we can get out of here early tomorrow, I'll go with you."

He smirks. "Sure you will."

"You need to get a life rather than go to the gym every night," Trig says, tossing a water bottle in the trash. "The racing expo is coming up. You should go with us."

"No offense, Trig, but I'm not really interested in partying with you and your friends."

"'Cause you have better stuff to do?" Trig grabs his keys.

"If you want a sponsor and to be taken seriously, you should consider this a business trip rather than going out there to chase women and score parts."

"Who says I can't do both?" Trig grins. "I'm out. See you all tomorrow."

"Me too." Wind waves. "Don't forget I'm bringing Millie's car in early to change the oil."

I nod, stacking the orders that still need to be input.

"You good here?" Carson asks, pulling on his coat.

"Yeah, I'm entering these and heading out."

The door opens, and Sarah steps inside.

"Hey, what are you . . ." I smile, but she doesn't.

Her eyes snag on Carson, and I can tell something is wrong.

"Hey, Sarah," Carson says, passing me. "I'm heading to the gym since this guy is slacking these days." He smiles, smacking me on the back. "I'll see you in the morning."

"See ya," I respond, but my eyes are stuck on Sarah. The door bangs closed, and I step around the counter. "What's wrong?" I reach for her, but she pulls away. My stomach hits the stained concrete floor.

Her intense gaze holds mine. "Did you talk to Griffin Macavoy about me and my issues with Miles?" There's a slight waver in her voice that's a direct hit in the chest.

"I did." I watch her. "But only to ensure he'd help you. He's the best, and I didn't want—"

"You had no right, Slade. This is my life and my kids."

The way she says the word "my" causes my lungs to deflate and stall.

My pulse rushes into my ears. "I only told him I would pay the retainer. I didn't tell him anything . . ."

Her head falls forward, her body sagging, and she closes her eyes.

I inch closer, my hands aching to grab hold of her. "Sarah, he can help you, and you can't afford to pay him. I didn't want—"

Her eyes harden. "You don't know anything." Her words are like a blast. "What I can afford and can't is just the beginning. I spent months watching my life implode. Everything I owned was gone." She snaps her fingers. "Just like that. Everyone I thought cared about me walked away disgusted for something I didn't even fucking do. It was him, and he used my daughter as a diversion. I was left with nothing but ten thousand dollars in an old bank account, which I fortunately never closed."

"This." She swings her arms out to the side. "This is all I have now. A job that allows me to feed my kids and hopefully build some kind of future for them and myself. I don't need everyone drawn into what I've tried to leave behind, or you going behind my back and talking to my boss about me or my situation."

My skin prickles at her accusation, which isn't totally inaccurate. "Sarah, he's a selfish bastard, which I'm pretty sure is what makes him so damn good at what he does. There's no way in hell I was going to let money or anything else stand in the way of him helping *if* you asked."

She pulls back at my words, her brow scrunching. "What are you talking about? He's been nothing but kind and generous to me. He gave me a chance when apparently I wasn't anywhere near qualified or even remotely capable."

"Who told you that?" I growl, my fists tightening.

She ignores me. "What is your deal with him? You clearly didn't have any problem strolling in there and asking for favors."

"I didn't ask him for anything." I spit it back, and I instantly regret it. I run a hand over my face, needing my panicked frustration to calm down.

She stares at me long and hard, then shakes her head. "I can't do this. I won't be with someone who won't talk to me or doesn't respect me enough to let me be a part of the decisions that impact my children and me."

My stomach bottoms out, and my heart might actually pound out of my chest. All words get caught in my throat as her eyes fill with tears.

Dammit! I need her to see that I was doing this *for* her. Only for her, Ollie, and Frankie.

Her shoulders fall, and she turns, defeated and giving up.

"He's my father."

She stops, slowly turning back.

There it is. The words I've only ever spoken out loud one other time. Both times, sending shrapnel soaring through all the wounds I've tried to bandage with minimal supplies.

Her eyes search mine, her brows tipping in. "What?" Her shaky voice is so soft.

"Krissy doesn't know. It's a long story that doesn't really matter." A fist grips my throat, and I force it out through my constricted airway. "Except I know he'll get you out of this."

She takes a tiny step forward. "It does matter. You matter." Her lips press together to keep them from quivering.

Those words tear through me, and I see the truth in her eyes. My throat is consumed by fire, restricting my ability to think or speak.

"But you can't fix everything, Slade." Her voice wavers again. "I know you want to, but whether you like it or not, I made this bed, and I have to lie in it. I married Miles and had children with him. I need to determine what's best for my kids. That includes knowing you aren't side-stepping me and taking a lead you have no right to."

There is so much to say, but I have no words. I go with the only thing I can at the moment. "I just wanted to help. I hated seeing you scared. I don't *ever* want you to be scared." It's the whole truth. Seeing her afraid made me react, and I did what I never thought I would—for her.

Her shoulders ease down with that admission.

"Then maybe. . .you need to try actually being scared *with* me." She pauses. "You can't always be the protector. Sometimes, you just have to be the partner. The one who sits and waits when there's nothing else to do. The one who holds my hand until we figure it out together."

She eases closer, her tone so gentle it rubs against every calloused and scarred place.

"You also can't remain closed off, sticking to the outside, standing guard."

"That's what I do. I fix things." It's what I'm good at, making sure those I care about are safe and cared for.

Her shoulders sag. "I know, but I need someone who wants to work on fixing things together."

Her eyes hold mine for only a moment longer before she turns and pushes out the door.

I stand there, unmoving, while my gut twists into a knot. I was only trying to help, but I also needed to be sure that she and the kids weren't going anywhere.

I yank my hat off my head and toss it on the counter. *Fuck!*

I rest my elbows on the edge and let my head fall into my hands, gripping my hair.

I'm so damn angry, but only at myself. All I wanted to do was make sure Macavoy helped this time. He could drive her ex into the ground like the piece of shit deserves.

I only wanted to protect her and make sure she never has to be afraid of him or what he might do again.

She trusted me, and I let her down. I could see it in her eyes. I grip the counter, wanting to rip it off. *Ahhhh!*

She said she couldn't do this, which meant she couldn't do this with me.

I blow out a breath, my eyes burning with anger and fear that I might have just fucked up the absolute best thing that's ever happened to me. The one person who sees right through me, even though I've given her so little.

I straighten, not having any idea how to make this better, but I have to. This one ignorant screw-up can't cost me what I'm not sure I'll ever fully deserve—Sarah and her kids. I have to show Sarah I want nothing more than to be her partner. I want to be the one who stands by her side through it all. I want to protect her and the kids, always.

But I'm going to have to figure out how to do that.

CHAPTER 44

SARAH

I kiss Ollie's cheek and tuck the covers around him, then check on Frankie before crawling into bed. I've held myself together all day, and I'm done now.

I curl into a ball, and my throat is consumed by a wildfire, raging to burn everything I've been containing. My body shakes with silent sobs that burst up and out of my eyes. I'm scared, alone, and so damn frustrated that the one place I want to go is across the street so Slade can tell me it will all be ok.

I'm mad that I want him to comfort me, but I do, and that's the worst of all. But what I told him was true. I can't be with him if he doesn't communicate or if he's going to do things behind my back.

I spent too many years with Miles treating me as if I were some kind of pet he'd take out when it suited him. We were never partners or equals. I was just the woman at home while he was out living his life like I didn't exist.

I know that's not Slade, but what he did felt all too familiar.

My mind is still reeling from what he told me—Griffin is his father. It only proves how little he has trusted me with himself, and it hurts all on its own when I've shared such personal details with him.

I pull my phone from my nightstand. It rings, and I hear her pick up.

"Mom." My voice quivers, and I try not to cry all over again.

"Honey, are you ok? What's wrong?"

Just her voice causes me to let loose, and I can't speak.

"Sarah, what's going on? Are the kids—"

"They're ok." I squeak. "I'm just . . ." I don't even know. I'm angry, sad, and so damn tired.

"Is this about Miles? I saw they announced his move." Her voice is filled with gentle worry.

Yes, it's about Miles. I'm exhausted from his demands and threats and the fear tied to them. But it's also about Slade and what I wanted that to be. It's freaking everything.

I hear frenzy and things banging and clanging. "Sarah, I'm getting in the car."

"No." I sit up a little, pulling myself together. I wipe my face with the hem of my shirt and suck back all of the snot. "I just need you to listen and help me figure out what to do."

"Sweet pea, then you need to tell me what's going on."

My mom may be full of show tunes and a good time, but she doesn't mess around when it's serious.

I blow my nose and get myself under control, filling my mom in. I start with the latest from Miles and his crusade to force us to appear as a family. Then I tell her about Slade and explain how we've become friends, slowly tipping into more. I include the cookies he brought for Ollie, staying at his house, the snowball fight, and Christmas, all the way through talking to Griffin.

My mom patiently waits on the other end of the line, listening with only the whistle of the kettle in the background.

I inhale long and slow, needing her to provide comfort and clarity when I have none.

"I've been waiting for you to tell me about this big hunk. Roxie said he's one tall drink of water." I hear the smile in her voice.

My mom cannot be Little-Miss-The-Sun-Will-Come-Out-Tomorrow right now. I need her in the gutter with me, sheltering from the storm spinning out of control.

"Mooooommmm!" I groan, wiping my nose on my sleeve.

"Ok, fine. You're angry and pissed, so who's ass is grass first?"

"Mom," I whine.

There's a pause, and I know she's getting to it.

My mom is dramatic and loud, but she has lived and survived and still finds beauty despite devastation and heartbreak.

"Slade's not wrong, sweetheart. You need help. Serious help. Someone to take Miles out at the knees. That man is already parading around as top dog, and we both know he'll yank every chain he can, snaking his way to the top."

I flop back against my pillows. "Mom, can we be team Sarah for a minute?"

"Babe, I am always team Sarah, and what he did sucks, but . . ."

I roll my eyes, not wanting to hear her defend him.

"Sometimes, people do shitty things that hurt us for the right reasons."

I want to put the pillow over my head and drown out her words.

"It's nowhere near the same, but your dad took off without a second glance, and I hated him for years. I was angry and brokenhearted that he didn't love me or you enough to stay. That he didn't see what we could be, but you know what? Leaving like that was the best thing he could have done for us. He knew he wasn't meant to be a father. Rather than make us be the misery that fed his addiction, he skidded out at the sight of two pink lines."

"Mom, how is it you always see the good?" This woman could find the silver lining in a pile of crap.

"Honey, there's plenty of bad all around. I just don't give it the power to hold me down. There's too much brightness to let the darkness crowd it out. We have to shine when we can."

I close my eyes, wishing I could see things the way she does, but . . . "Mom, what if I make the same mistake all over again? What if I don't see it like, I didn't with Miles? What if Miles wins, and I have to spend the rest of my life dealing with his narcissistic, belittling every damn day? I can't do that." My lungs ache with the possibility.

I sink into my bed again, wanting it to swallow me whole.

"Well, first, you aren't the same woman you were when you fell for Miles. You've lived, grown, and can spot a piece of shit a mile away. That's a gift, Sarah, that only comes with experience. But this means you already know Slade is nothing like him. Plus, he bought your baby cookies. What man does that?" My mom is swooning, and dammit, she's not wrong. "He held Frankie when she was sick and feverish."

He did the same with me.

Slade has shown me time and again that he's dependable and trustworthy, but I need him to actually talk to me.

"And Sarah." She shifts into that mom tone, and my muscles constrict. "You've got to gather up all your ammunition and fight Miles. He can't win this time. There's nothing weak about asking people for help when you need it. Why do you think I love it here in this small town so much? These people are insane, and they have nothing better to do than talk shit about each other, but when push comes to shove, they show up. Day or night. Whether they like you or not. All we've got is each other, and that's better than all the luxury of New York City or anywhere else."

I blow out a slow breath, resting back against my pillows. "So, just ask my boss to provide counsel, even though there's no way I'll ever be able to pay him back and have all my dirty laundry invade my workplace?" I never want to feel like I owe anyone anything.

Her voice softens. "What if this allows your boss an opportunity to help his child in a way he's never been able to? Sometimes, payment comes in the form of something so much greater than money."

I bite my lip hard, having never thought about it that way. "Ugh, this all feels so messed up."

She laughs. "Honey, this is life. Nothing is as simple as we'd like it to be. It's why I love this tiny trailer and the life I have. I have less to screw up."

I flop back on my bed, just wanting to live as carefree as my mom, but I know she wasn't always this way. She had to work for it, and so do I.

"With Slade, you have to decide if one momentary lapse in judgment done with good intentions will keep you from forgiving a man who might screw up again and again but always has your and Ollie and Frankie's best interest at heart." I can hear her smile. "I actually think that's all anyone can ask for."

I squeeze my eyes shut tight, already knowing the answer. "Mom, I miss you."

"I miss you, too, so much. I'll see when I can get down, ok?"

My throat tingles again, and I swallow it down. "Ok."

We hang up, and I stare into the dark space. Everything my mom said hits all my tender spots.

I have to lay my pride down to no longer be a victim of Miles's privilege. I need to do it for Ollie and Frankie. It's my best shot. And maybe, as my mom said, in some small way, it will allow a tiny bit of healing for Slade and Griffin, where I'm certain there is a mountain of pain and resentment.

My mom's not wrong. I know the kind of man Slade is, even if he hasn't shared his deep, dark secrets with me.

I couldn't love Miles. I wanted to, and I tried so hard. But you can't love someone who's never understood the meaning of it.

Slade loves big and hard. I've seen it in his relationship with Krissy. I heard it in the heartbreak he faced when he lost his mom and what he believed would be his family.

Slade is all quiet, selfless gestures. Nothing he does is for show or personal gain. But talking to Griffin without me felt like he was trying to take control of the situation, and it scared me.

He asked me to go easy on him, and I've been trying. The problem is I've fallen in love with the big, tattooed, tender-hearted lion. All the way.

But I'm terrified to be with someone who keeps me on the outside and holds me at arm's length. I want a partner who wants a relationship—one in which we work together. I need someone who doesn't just allow me to love them but will actually receive it.

CHAPTER 45

SLADE

"You wanna talk about it?"

I shake my head. "No." Carson sits in the chair across from my desk.

"Give her time to cool off, but not too much. You were trying to help. She'll see that once she gets past you going behind her back, which was stupid by the way."

I groan, letting my head fall back toward the ceiling. It's the same thing I did all night—stare at the ceiling, praying Sarah would see I was just trying to help.

"Dude, at some point, you're also going to have to tell her how you feel."

I slowly pull my head forward and glare at him. "We're not talking about this."

He crosses his arms. "Are you going to deny it? No man looks like this," he waves his hand at me. "Unless he's sunk."

I am not discussing my feelings about Sarah. That is for me to know, and I'm still figuring out what to do about it. I've tried showing her, and that only got me here—in deep shit.

I screwed up, but I'm navigating unchartered waters. I don't know how to care for someone this much and not do everything I can to protect them.

"Man, you've gotta have a plan. This sitting here feeling sorry for yourself isn't working for you."

"I don't feel sorry for myself," I spit. "I'm angry. I hurt her, and that's the last thing I wanted to do. I can't even blame her. I'd be fucking pissed if she'd done that to me. I acted without thinking, and I don't do that."

Carson's mouth creeps into a smirk. "You just proved my point. We can't stand it when the ones we love are hurting. You did the only thing you could to stop it. We don't always think rationally in those situations, so the best you can do now is apologize."

I have to quit being mad at myself and Sarah for not understanding that I did it *for* her. She said sometimes there isn't anything we can do, which might be true, but I'm not good at that. I didn't ask what she needed or how I could help. I just did what I thought I should. It's how I've operated.

But she's right. That's not how it should be in a relationship.

"She said she wants to be with someone who does things together." I drag my eyes to Carson's. "I've never done that before."

It feels ridiculous saying it out loud. I'm a grown-ass man, and I don't know how to be a partner. But that's what Sarah deserves, especially with everything she's been through.

"Dude, that's because you've never been one. You raised Krissy on your own. You had to be on top of everything and in charge at all times. You own this business, and we depend on you not to screw it up." He leans forward, resting his arms on his knees. "But think about what it would be like to have someone like Sarah to help carry a bit of the load and who'll walk through all the ups and downs with you. We need that. *You* need that."

He shakes his head. "You've got to let her, though."

I rest back in my chair, knowing he's one hundred percent right. If I want Sarah, I have to let her in. She has to see I'm in this *with* her. All the way. Even when I mess up.

The metal door bangs closed, and Krissy appears in her scrubs. "I tried calling you." Her eyes move to Carson and then back to me. "You all right?"

I nod. "Yeah. It's. . .just been a shitty day."

She steps into my office. "I uh. . .need to talk to you about something."

"I'm gonna clean up and put my tools away." Carson pushes out of the chair and slips past Krissy.

She stands on the other side of my desk. "Did you get your DNA results back yet?"

I shake my head. "Not yet."

"I looked online to see if I could check the status." She pulls a folded paper from her purse and lays it in front of me. "I did a little more research. You won't believe it." Her eyes grow wide with excitement. "Look!" She points to the paper.

I pick it up, running my eyes over it.

"There's someone in their database that matches my genome." Her eyes grow even wider as if she's willing me to catch up. "It's not exact, of course, but it means we have a half-sibling out there, I think. Who knows? Maybe more than one."

Her words rush at me a million miles an hour, but they hit a wall and explode.

"Can you even believe it? We could find out who our father is. I'm going to message them."

Our mom never told us who our father was, and once I found out, I understood why. It's why I've never told Krissy. I close my eyes, bracing for the impending blast from the cost of trying to protect someone.

"You can't do that," I say softly.

"I can. That's part of this. If they agree to put their information out there, you can contact them."

My heart begins to pound, and I feel like I could hurl. "No. You can't contact them."

She frowns, her head falling to the side. She stares at me, blinking a few times.

The silence is like the calm before the storm, eerie and imminent. I have no idea how to prepare her.

I want to kick myself in the face for not seeing this possibility.

She crosses her arms loosely as if she's shoring herself up. "Why can't I contact them?" Her question is soft, but demanding.

I drag my eyes to hers.

She straightens. "Slade, why can't I contact them?" Her tone hardens.

I lean forward, resting my arms on my desk as if somehow it will provide grounding. "It's not a good idea. It could impact. . .people."

"Like who?" she snaps, her arms wrapping tighter around herself.

"You, for one," I say, praying she'll let this go, but I know better.

Her eyes flick between mine. "Somehow, this feels like just the warning before the blow." Her eyes fall to the paper and then lift back to me. "We had a deal we'd never lie to each other, remember?"

"I haven't lied to you."

She huffs. "Then, you'd better tell me right now why I can't contact this person who very clearly looks to be genetically related to me." She points to the paper.

I run a hand over my face. "A lot of people."

Her lips press together. "You know who our father is."

I think it's more of a revelation than a question, so I stay quiet.

She stares at me. Her eyes are hard but full of hurt. I hate myself.

"Who is he? He clearly has other children."

She's right. I've never lied to her, and I won't now.

"It doesn't matter. You are—"

She lets out a small huff as if I hit her in the stomach. "Like hell, it doesn't. If it didn't matter, you would've told me. I begged Mom to tell me, but she wouldn't. How long have you known?"

"She never told me."

Her stance softens only slightly, and I see that helps a little.

I think about what Sarah said about sometimes having to sit and be quiet when there's nothing else to do. I can no longer protect Krissy, but I can sit with her in this.

"I overheard them talking when she was pregnant with you. I never knew who he was until then."

"Who is he?" It's only a whisper.

I push out a breath. "Griffin Macavoy."

She frowns, her eyes roaming. "The big shot lawyer?"

I nod slowly, giving her a second. "I don't know the details, but he and Mom were. . .involved for years, I guess."

"As evidence of me," she says, clarifying. "So, he has other kids now?"

I grip the pen, knowing this won't get any easier. "Then."

She stares at me.

"He had another child then and was. . .married. Still is."

She shakes her head in disbelief. "No." She laughs, and it's a bit hysterical. "No. There's no way."

I close my eyes. "He has two kids, actually." I give her all of it.

She huffs, and it's a whoosh of disbelief, her face falling into her hand. "She was protecting him."

I know what it feels like to be slammed with the truth about someone you love so dearly. To find out they made decisions you can't fathom or will never understand.

"Why didn't you tell me?" Her question is hard and accusatory. "All this time." Her arms fly out to the sides. "Why didn't you tell me?"

I give her the only truth I have. "It doesn't do any good."

Her eyes grow wide. "What? Not to know you are a product of a long-standing affair?!" She smiles, and it's wild and filled with pain.

"Kris." I don't know what to say. "I never wanted you to know."

She shakes her head and rips the paper off my desk, shoving it in her purse. "No, but you let me hope I was wanted and that somewhere out there was a man I could look up to."

It's a spear clear through that catches my breath and steals it.

She turns, storming out, and I pop out of my chair to follow her.

"Kris, wait."

She spins back, stopping in the middle of the shop. "No. You had years to tell me this. Years, Slade."

Carson stands at the workbench, his focus on Krissy.

My shoulders fall with so much regret, and my lungs try to recover from the piercing of her words. "I was trying to protect you." It sounds like the lamest excuse after everything these past few days, but it's what I thought I was doing.

She bites her lip to keep it from trembling. "All you did was protect their secret." One tear spills out, and my chest caves in. "I thought we were always in this together. You are all I've ever had." Her chin quivers as tears stream down her cheeks.

My throat might actually swell shut. "I didn't want what they did to hurt you."

She stares at me, struck by the truth.

This is exactly what I wanted to prevent. "I didn't want you to think of her differently." It's only a whisper.

She presses her eyes closed, and she shakes her head. "No, Slade. The only one you've been protecting is yourself."

It's a fast jab to a fresh wound.

She turns, and Carson hurries to follow her, but he stops. I tip my chin, telling him to go.

He runs, and the door bangs closed. It matches the pounding in my head and chest.

I stare at the door, knowing exactly what Krissy is feeling, but on top of that, she trusted me, and I let her down.

All we had for so long was each other, and she depended on me to be the one to keep her safe. In this case, I didn't do that.

The only one you've been protecting is yourself.

Her words stab me over and over again, and I wonder if they're true. Maybe that's all I've been doing this whole time, keeping myself from facing anything and everything where I risked being hurt. Maybe that's why I went to Macavoy without telling Sarah—I'm afraid of losing her.

I clench my fist and realize I'm still holding the pen. I throw it across the room, and the door swings open.

Carson steps in, shaking his head. "She's gone."

"She's not ok."

He runs a hand over his light scruff.

"I need you to check on her."

He nods. "I'll find her. You all right?"

Not even a little.

"Just make sure she's good for a while."

"You got it." He grabs his keys and takes off.

I stroll back to my office, wanting to rip the whole damn thing to pieces, but it won't help.

I drop into my chair, knowing I can't fix this. At least, not yet. I rest my elbows on my desk and let my head fall into my hands. My throat aches, and for the first time since my mom died, my eyes fill with tears while I drown in remorse.

I have no fucking clue what to do now.

CHAPTER 46

SLADE

I sit on the edge of my bed and run my hand through my damp hair. I dial Krissy again, but she doesn't answer. I squeeze my phone, wanting to throw it across my room.

I stare into the dark space. I can't stand sitting here, unable to do a damn thing. My stomach squeezes tight, and my forearms hit my knees, feeling like I might hurl.

I inhale and exhale. My chest is so tight that the pressure is painful. I rub at the spot in the center, thinking the same thing I've thought all evening—Sarah.

The minute Krissy stormed out, she's who I wanted to call. I wanted to hear her voice and have her hug me like only she does. The kind of hug that makes me think she might hang on and not let go.

I need her to tell me that Krissy will forgive me and that eventually, she'll understand why I didn't tell her about Macavoy and our mom.

But Sarah can't do that because I haven't shared any of it. I've not really told her anything.

Krissy is right. I've been protecting myself with Sarah, keeping her at arm's length to ensure she doesn't get close enough to hurt me. All that's done is push her away.

I press my fist to my forehead, wanting to yell. I want to walk across the street and tell her how sorry I am and beg her to forgive me.

I glance at the time on my phone and blow out a breath. It's after eleven.

Fuck it.

ME: Are you awake?

I wait for the three dots, hoping they'll appear. When they don't, I drop my phone on the bed beside me. I lie back, my throat burning with fear.

My phone vibrates. I roll up, blinking my eyes clear.

SARAH: Yeah.

My heart pounds, but this time with the tiniest bit of hope.

ME: Can I come over?

SARAH: Now?

ME: Yes.

She doesn't respond right away. My phone slips in my sweaty palm while my pulse echoes in the silence.

SARAH: Sure. See you at the back door.

I tug on a sweatshirt and slip on my tennis shoes. The freezing air stings my nose and lungs as I make my way down my driveway and up Sarah's.

I knock lightly on her back door, and she pulls it open. Her hair is a messy pile on top of her head, and she looks half asleep.

She wraps her arms around herself.

I suck in the icy air and hold it until my abs beg for relief. "Can you just. . .not be mad at me for a little while?" I choke out the vulnerability that dares to escape with desperation.

I want to grab her and never let her leave me.

Her brow scrunches, and her head falls to the side, staring at me. Then, she reaches out and grabs my hand, pulling me inside. Just her touch eases the grip of panic, choking me.

She closes the door and locks it. Grover sits at my feet, his tail thumping against the floor, and Sarah hushes him.

"Are you ok?" Her soft question ignites the wildfire in my throat and lungs all over again.

I shake my head. "Krissy—"

"Is she ok?" She steps closer, suddenly alert.

I nod. "She's ok. I just . . . She found out Macavoy is our father."

Sarah's shoulders fall, and I hear her exhale. "Did you tell her?'

I nod again. "She's. . .really angry. I've always done everything I could to protect her, but I kept this from her." The painful truth ricochets through me.

Her gaze drops from mine, taking it in. "She's hurting, and you're an easy target. She may not see it now, but you are protecting her. You're giving her the truth."

I drop my head, wondering if there's any possible way Sarah will eventually see that I was only trying to help her. "But I didn't tell her until I was forced to. It's not the same."

She moves into me, sliding her arms around my waist and pulling me close.

I'm so shocked it takes me a second to wrap mine around her, warming to the security I'm beginning to realize I only feel when I'm with her. Almost as if it's ok not to have to be strong every moment.

We stand in her dark kitchen for a long time, her holding me tightly. Eventually, her arms slip away, and I'm not ready to let her go. But instead of pulling completely away, her hand slips into mine. She turns, tugging me toward the living room.

'Sarah—"

She twists, pressing her finger to her lips. "It's late, and you need to sleep," she whispers.

I follow, not having the energy to argue, as she bypasses the couch and guides me down the hallway into her bedroom. Grover's nails click on the floor behind me.

I stop in the doorway. "Sarah."

She ignores me, lying down on the side of the bed closest to the door.

I stand there, knowing this is never how I wanted it.

"Slade, get in bed so Grover will settle down and not wake Ollie." It's a bit of an order, and at a different time, I'd smile.

I could go home, but I don't want to. All I want is to be near her.

"Slade." She says my name with more force.

I tug off my sweatshirt and lie down beside her, placing my hand behind my head. I stare at her ceiling with Sarah's scent wafting around me, and it's calming.

I search for the words I've longed to say.

"I'm. . .so sorry," I whisper, and it sounds ridiculously simple. It doesn't even begin to describe my remorse for making her feel like I didn't respect her.

Her hand finds mine, and her other wraps around my forearm.

I inhale, wanting to explain but not really knowing where to begin. "I'm not good at just sitting still when someone I care about needs help."

She inches a little closer, and her body presses against my side. I try to figure out how to give her a part of myself, wanting her to know me.

I don't know what to say, so I just start. "I wanted to be an engineer. I got accepted into an elite program, so Mom didn't tell me she was sick until it was too late."

I can still hear her voice on the other end of the phone. "I dropped out of school when she called and told me her time was limited. We brought her home from the hospital, and all I could do was watch her suffer and wither away. I couldn't do anything to make it better."

Sarah's fingers slip between mine, and she tucks our hands to her chest.

"Melissa was her nurse and was good with Krissy. Did her hair and made her laugh when she wouldn't even talk to me. She was. . .a distraction and a bright spot when everything else was dark and hard and scary. I felt less alone, facing everything that was coming."

The tightness in my chest eases a little. "When I told my mom Melissa was pregnant, she was so happy." I can still see her smile as she held my face and told me what an amazing father I'd be, wishing she'd be around to see it.

I take a moment to breathe through the memory, and as if Sarah senses it, her hand spreads flat across my heart. "She was getting a glimpse of what would be after she was gone. It was the only thing I could do to make any part of her dying even a tiny bit less terrifying. She knew we'd be ok." A giant lump forms in my throat, and I take a moment. "But it never came to be like I'd told her it would. I felt like I'd let her down."

It's the truth I've never admitted out loud. I felt like I'd lied to her about the one thing that brought her a final moment of joy.

I think about my mom and how she fought to be strong, not wanting Krissy or me to see her fear. She was always like that, never letting us see her struggle. But I heard her soft words at night on the phone with Macavoy and the hushed sound of her cries that followed, shielding us from her pain and disappointment. She sacrificed so that we always had what we needed and worked hard to love us enough for two parents.

"I miss her," I whisper the hidden truth. "She wasn't perfect, but she loved Krissy and me."

I take a deep breath and let it out. "Macavoy used her for so long. I didn't know until I overheard them when she was pregnant with Krissy. He was angry and told her she'd done it on purpose. I guess she was his receptionist before I was born. I never knew until then, and I didn't ask questions, hoping I could forget. I hated her for a while, knowing she'd been with him even though he had an entire family."

Her fingers pinch my shirt. "I spent years thinking about the women Miles had been with and how there was no way they didn't know I existed. He always told me it was just sex. It didn't mean anything. For him, that was probably true, even with me."

I can't stand to think about her with him.

"But I find it hard to believe that it didn't mean anything to any of those women. I almost hurt for them." Her voice is so soft. "They weren't doing it to cause me pain. They were satisfying a desire with a man they believed wanted them. I'm sure he told them as much, and it's painful to be rejected, especially when you're infatuated with the idea of who someone is and what could be."

I want to see the world the way Sarah does. To have enough insight and reflection to embrace the humanity inside things that cause heartache.

"I couldn't understand the hold he had over her, and then, it was just easier to hate him. I didn't want Krissy to see that part of her—the one who loved a man who would always choose someone else over her. I wanted to leave Krissy with all of the good and beautiful things. It's all I could give her."

"I think you've given her a lot more than that." Sarah's fingers draw across my forehead, brushing my hair away.

I close my eyes, wanting it to be true.

"She's angry and confused, and you have to let her be," she whispers. "That's a lot to absorb, and you can't rush it. She has a lot to grieve, and you need to be there when she's ready to talk to you or yell at you."

"I don't want her to hurt," I offer quietly.

"I know you were trying to protect me, too." Her soft words pinch that bruised place in the center of my chest that aches so damn bad it's all I can do to breathe.

I turn onto my side, facing her. "I was, but. . . I should have let you make that move if you wanted to. I didn't think. I just acted. Did the one thing I could."

She curls into my chest, and I slide my arm around her, holding her close. I press my lips to her forehead, and it gives me hope that at least this will be ok.

"Slade, I need you to be in this with me. We have to work through things together."

"I know. I'm not used to that, but I'm trying."

"I'm still a little mad. I was so angry at you, and yet I wanted to talk to you at the same time."

My aching heart stutters, and I pull away to look at her. "You did?"

Her chin lifts, and I can barely make out her eyes.

She nods. "Yeah. You kind of suck. You know that?"

I huff a laugh and pull her back to me. She buries her face in my chest, and I just listen to her breathe.

"Everything is going to be ok," she whispers.

My throat burns, and I close my eyes. I need that to be true. I have to know that she and the kids aren't going anywhere and that, at some point, Krissy will forgive me.

Eventually, I feel her relax and listen to her soft, sleepy breaths, willing them to drown out the noise inside me.

I lie there, hoping that if I give Krissy time, she'll see that it doesn't matter. She and I are still the same, and I will always be here.

And this, holding Sarah, I never want to be without it again. So, I'll try my damnedest to do this working together thing, no matter how foreign it is.

Like Alex said, if there's anyone I want to be scared with, it's Sarah. Maybe this is the first step in showing her I can do that.

CHAPTER 47

SARAH

"So, what else is there?" Kat taps her pen on her legal pad.

I fill my cheeks with air and blow it out. "Do you think that's enough?"

She smiles, raising her eyebrows. "Sarah, I'm not sure how you've kept your shit together all this time."

I woke up this morning and knew what I had to do. After all Slade shared with me about his mom, it didn't feel right to talk to Griffin. But I thought about my first day, when Kat dropped into the chair beside my desk. I want to believe we're friends, and she'd told me to let her know if I ever needed help. Well, I do. My mom and Slade are right. I need her to help me keep my kids.

I also want to permanently separate from Miles's constant narcissistic ways. But after sleeping beside Slade all night, I want the security to be able to do that every night.

I've fallen in love with Slade. I already knew that. That's why his talking to Griffin without me was so devastating. But I didn't know I could fall even harder.

When I woke up this morning, he wasn't there. Instead, there was a note I will keep forever. Just like Slade, it was short and to the point.

Didn't want Ollie to find me in your bed and confuse him. If you could give me a heads-up if you're back to being mad at me today, I'd appreciate it. Thank you for being there when I needed you. Slade

This man is always thinking of others. There's never been a time he hasn't had the best of intentions, caring for everyone else. Now, all I want is to take care of him. I just need him to let me, and last night seemed like a giant leap in that direction. I want more of it, so I'm here. Finally, brave enough to fight Miles with everything I've got.

"This is good, Sarah. From what you've told me, I'm sure he's working with a fantastic lawyer, but even the best can't argue against facts. Do you have names of the women he's been with? I'll need bank statements, bills, documentation of the things the kids have needed but you couldn't afford, emails, texts, any communication you've had."

I nod. "I can send you everything I've given to my lawyer. He's not doing anything productive."

"Clearly," she scoffs. "Don't worry. He may be fooling everyone in New York, but his lying ass will pay up and leave you alone for good. Plus, we're gonna get everything he owes you and then some." She winks.

"Thank you. It'll take me time, but I'll pay you. I—"

"Sarah, I'd take these kinds of cases for free." She leans back in her chair. "This is the fun part. Going after the bastards who like to push women around. You don't owe me anything. When we win, you can buy a round of drinks, and I'm not the only one drinking this time."

I want to hug her, and I will, but I'll save it for later. I push out of the chair. "I'll email you everything today."

She nods. "Oh."

I stop, turning back.

"Robyn and Marcie gave me the lowdown on Cory spilling your personal matters. He has no business trying to be intimidating or just a dickwad. His ass is fired."

I shake my head. "No, don't do that unless he violated policy." I shrug. "He wasn't mean, just. . .laid out the facts. Things I didn't want anyone to know. But I'm over that now." I smile. "You can only hide for so long."

She smiles back.

"Plus, he's one of those people who are just miserable. He's good at what he does, and that's important. This job might be the only thing he has."

"That and Harry Pooter," she snorts. "You're too nice, Sarah."

"Nah. I know what it's like to have nothing."

"Well, we're going to change that."

I take a deep breath and return to my office, hopeful for the first time in so long it's almost foreign. A positive outlook isn't something I'm familiar with, but I think I could get used to it.

I check my phone.

SLADE: Are you still speaking to me today?
SLADE: You know, just so I can be prepared.

I smile. The big lion is insecure. That I can handle as long as he talks to me.

> ME: Good morning, Snuggle Cub.

SLADE: Is that a yes?

> ME: Are you worried?

SLADE: Sarah.

> ME: Hmm.
> ME: I think I liked sleeping with you a little too much to stay mad at you.

SLADE: Maybe we'll do it again sometime.

> ME: That'd be convenient. Then, keeping the thermostat so low wouldn't be an issue.

SLADE: I'll need earplugs. You snore like a freight train.

I laugh out loud and cover my mouth.

"Something funny?"

I twist in my chair, surprised by the amused tone.

Junior leans against my doorway. "Marcie was just telling me once upon a time, you were Miss America." His head tips in the direction of their desks.

Marcie and Robyn are like two cute little mice. When they find the cheese, they can't wait to scurry about and tell all their friends. I'm not mad at them. They're young and filled with dreams about what life will be like. They should have that for as long as possible.

"Miss USA, actually. It was a beautiful dream while it lasted."

He nods, a smirk appearing. "Beautiful is right."

I want to roll my eyes, and it takes effort to refrain.

"That guy the other night. You knew him, didn't you?"

I stare at him—Slade's brother. It's so shocking, I'm dumbfounded. Two men who couldn't be so absolutely and completely different.

With what I know now, I understand Junior better. Kids aren't as resilient as people like to assume. I have no doubt the home he grew up in was full of conflict. He's a little kid starving for attention.

I smile. "Is that important to you, Junior? That I knew him."

He shrugs one shoulder. "I saw you leave with him." He rubs his clean-shaven chin. "Not quite what I would've expected to follow up Miles Crawford."

Taking a dig at Slade has him tripping into knee in the balls territory.

"You're right. I'm smart enough to only make that mistake once."

I force a smile, making myself clear.

He huffs a laugh.

"Let's go, Junior. I have to be in court in an hour," Griffin says, passing him in the hallway.

He turns. "I'll be around, Sarah." That sly grin creeps across his mouth, and he winks.

I laugh. I mean, what more can I do?

I check my email quickly to see if I've received anything from my professors. I hope this semester will go more smoothly than the last, and maybe I'll actually enjoy what I'm learning.

I get to work on my latest work assignment, sorting through records to summarize a report for a long-standing custody case where neglect and addiction are involved. It's only a small peek into the mental toll this job would take.

There's a rush of air, and Robyn and Marcie squeeze into my office, wearing contagious smiles.

"Hey," I say, turning and giving them my full attention.

Marcie drops down into the chair beside my desk. "We've been dying to ask." She glances at Robyn. "You've got to tell us everything about winning Miss USA."

"We're talking reality TV level detail on all of the backstabbing, bitch-slapping, hairspray-on-your-butt-cheeks goods." Robyn inches closer, her eyes growing wide.

I laugh. "I love you guys."

"Was it filled with as much drama as the girls on The Bachelor but with a crown?" Marcie asks.

"Anytime you have women vying for the same thing, there's drama," I say.

"Tell us everything. We need all the beauty hacks, too," Robyn clarifies, inching closer.

I lean back in my chair, my mind returning to that time in my life and all of the things I did to make myself stand out—to be exceptional amongst others. I learned a lot about presenting myself and what I stood for.

I realize it wasn't all a waste. I worked my ass off to make it happen, and no matter what anyone else thinks, I earned it. That is something to be proud of.

I cross my legs and rest back in my chair. "Well, as with most things, it all starts with training."

CHAPTER 48

SLADE

"This is not acceptable. She's denying all calls, and we have nothing to do with this." Trig cuts a hand through the air. "We're guilty by association."

"Yeah, and we like her better. If we have to choose sides, we pick hers." Wind puts his hands on his hips.

I roll my neck, not needing this *again*. It's constant with these idiots. They're worried about Krissy, and I appreciate that, but I can't handle their drama on top of my own feelings.

"I'm renting one of those planes with the banner that says, 'We choose you, Krissy.'" Trig moves his hand through the air.

I groan.

"I went by her townhouse this morning and waited for her until she got home. She told me to get lost." Carson tosses a rag on the workbench.

I shake my head. "Thanks for checking on her."

"She's talking to Millie. At least that's good," Wind offers.

"Maybe she'll talk to me," Luke says.

We all turn to look at him.

He shrugs. "I'm new. I don't have anything to do with whatever is going on."

Carson glares at him. "She won't talk to you. You're just a kid."

"Thanks," I tell Luke. "I'm the one who needs to talk to her."

"Yeah. We see how well that worked out," Trig grumbles.

"Well, she texted me and told me to tell you all to back the hell off." Luke holds a hand up. "Her words, not mine."

We stare at him.

"She messaged you?" Carson's question is full of irritation.

"Yeah. She said she knows the rest of you don't listen." Luke says it so innocently that it almost makes me laugh.

Krissy is as stubborn as they come. She's angry and hurt, but I really need her to talk to me. It's been a week. She'll let me have it, and we can move on. Sarah keeps telling me to give her time, but I need to know how long that will be.

Thankfully, she hasn't removed me from tracking her location, so I can be sure she makes it home each morning and night.

"I'm taking her some pot roast and vegetables to be sure she's eating," Wind says.

The guys scoff.

"What? Millie hasn't asked her that, and women stop eating when they're in an emotional state."

"No, asshole. She eats ice cream and sugary cereal," Carson says as if his last nerve is spent.

I look at him, wondering how in the hell he knows what Krissy eats when she's upset.

"Well, even better. She needs a nutritious meal and to know we still love her."

"I bet she's fully aware you still love her with all the smothering," Luke says dryly.

"We aren't smothering her. We just have to be sure she's ok. It's how we operate here," Carson says, crossing his arms.

"Call it what you want." Luke waves. "I'll see you all tomorrow. Let me know if I can help."

"I'm heading out. The Crock-Pot's been simmering all day, and I'm taking it over tonight. She needs more than sugar." Wind is a force to be reckoned with.

"Thanks," I say, and he salutes.

Trig follows him out.

Carson drops his screwdriver. "Shit!"

"I can't make her talk to me." I cross my arms.

"I know. I just hate that she's hurting alone," he says softly, but it feels like more than that.

"When are you going home?"

His gaze meets mine. "In a few minutes."

I stare at him, knowing he spoke to his brother, but I don't know exactly what they discussed. "That's not what I mean. It's time, man. Rip off the Band-Aid and face the fear."

He points at me. "You worry about your mess, and I'll worry about mine. I'll go when I'm good and ready." Carson's calm, cool state is ruffled.

"It sucks when the shoe is on the other foot, doesn't it?" I smile, and he flips me off as I head to my office. "Let me know if you want to talk about it."

I hear him grumble something on his way out the door.

I shut the computer down and lock up, ready to spend the evening with Sarah and the kids.

"Swade, wook!"

Ollie stands on his chair with a red, plastic fire hat on his head.

I shrug my coat off and untie my boots.

"N-nick's dad came to school today. He's a f-firefighter."

"That's cool, partner." I adjust the hat falling over his eyes. "Did you learn about safety and what to do if there's a fire?"

He grins and nods. "Yep. We gots to make sure our p-protectors are working."

Sarah smiles at me, turning back to the counter to shred chicken. She's wearing those damn skin-tight black leggings and a cropped sweatshirt that hangs off her shoulder. It takes everything in me not to slide my arm around her, haul her to the other room, and kiss her until she melts into me.

I've waited all day to be here with them. I've spent every evening here for the last week, and each night after the kids are in bed, we sit on the couch and talk. Sarah curls into my side, and thoughts of making good on my promise to carry her to bed consume me. I want Sarah desperately, but I won't rush it or her. I want forever, so I'll take all the nights on the couch, just talking and her teasing me until we get there.

She glances over her shoulder, catching my eyes running over her body. That flirty smile appears, making those thoughts roar to life and heat shoot through my veins. She turns away, her cheeks turning the tiniest bit pink as if she knows exactly what I'm thinking.

Sarah sets a plate in front of Ollie. "They're actually called detectors."

Ollie stutters it out, trying a few times. Sarah has been working with him and enrolled him in a speech program for the spring. It's slow, but he's making progress.

Frankie smacks her tray, wiggling to get my attention. I run my hand over her head as she shoves a fistful of mac and cheese into her mouth.

"How was your day?" Sarah hands me a plate.

"The guys are going to drive me to a firing spree. It's nonstop about Krissy."

She laughs. "She's still not talking to anyone?"

"No, and their frustration isn't helping anything."

Her arms slide around me, and I pull her close with my free arm. Her head rests against my chest. "Patience, big guy."

I groan. "I don't have that."

"Me either," Ollie says with a mouthful.

Sarah laughs, releasing me.

"Me. Me. Me," Frankie says, agreeing.

"Sounds like you three need to read *Caps for Sale* again tonight. That peddler wasn't getting his hats back, yelling at those silly monkeys."

Ollie giggles. "The monkeys are sn-sneaky."

Frankie shakes her fist, mimicking the angry peddler.

"See, Frankie gets it," I say.

"And yet, look how far that got him." Sarah smiles that beautiful smile, spreading pure joy through my chest. The kind so radiant it's almost painful.

We eat dinner, and the kids take turns in the bath. I help Ollie find his pajamas, and he tugs his shirt over his head, plopping down on his butt and bouncing when he's finished.

"Nick's dad was really c-cool," he says softly. His eyes lift to mine. "My dad doesn't like how I t-talk. He thinks I'm dumb."

I pause. Ollie hasn't ever mentioned his dad before, and Sarah has only said he doesn't ask about him. I know from experience that just because you don't say it doesn't mean you aren't thinking about them.

I kneel beside his bed. "You know you're not, right?" His sad eyes meet mine, and a rage ignites for whatever his dad has said to make him feel that way.

"I have to be slow with my words." He tries really hard not to stutter, meticulously pronouncing each one.

"Yeah. So." I shrug. "It's like tying your shoes. You know how long it took me to be able to do it."

He shakes his head.

"Forever. All the other kids could, but I still had to have help. They made fun of me for having to ask the teacher to tie my shoes because I couldn't. Said I was a baby."

"I can't t-tie my shoes."

"Not yet, but you will. And the more you practice talking slowly and carefully, the better you'll get at it."

"I'm already getting b-better."

"Just think where you'll be a month from now."

His head dips to his shoulder. "How long is dat?"

I huff a laugh, and he settles his hands in his crossed legs.

"Can you come t-t-talk to my class about c-cars?" His shy eyes focus on his hands. "My dad doesn't wive here. He wouldn't want to."

I still, knowing this is important, and do not want to screw it up. "Definitely, but let me talk to your mom about it. Ok?"

He nods, grinning. "Mama wikes you."

I ruffle his hair, and he pops up, jumping off the bed. Grover barks, following him to the living room.

"I hope she more than likes me," I mumble.

I sit in the recliner, and Ollie digs through the basket of books. Frankie toddles over in her soft footie jammies and tries to climb up my legs. I breathe in her clean baby scent, lifting her over my head, and she giggles.

I set Frankie on one leg, and Ollie climbs up on the other.

"Not the crabby peddler again," I groan, and Ollie scrunches into a ball, grinning ear to ear.

We've read this book the past three nights while Sarah sits on the couch working on schoolwork.

I growl as the peddler yells at the monkeys, and the kids join in. Frankie waves her fist in the air, chanting gibberish.

I glance at Sarah, and she's watching me. She smiles, but it's not the full deal. She blinks, and whatever is in her eyes is gone, but my stomach squeezes tight.

Once she's asleep, Sarah carries Frankie to her crib, and I take Ollie, whose head bobbed as we finished the last book.

I lie him in his bed, and he grips my neck, hugging me.

"Can we go to the p-p-park tomorrow?" His sleepy voice whispers.

I want to say yes, even in the cold and snow. I want to tell him I'll come to his school and that I'll be there for every other thing as long as he wants me there. I want to give him what I never had, but I'm not in a place to do that.

"I think you should get some sleep."

He hugs my neck tightly. "I wove you, Swade."

I close my eyes, sealing his words up tight, wanting to hold onto them. "Good night, partner."

I straighten and turn to find Sarah in the doorway, her head resting against it. Her gaze holds mine, and it's that look again. My gut pinches, but I shove it away, dismissing the worry building.

She grabs my hand, and I follow her to the couch. She drops down onto it, and I sit beside her just as we have each night.

She rests her head on my shoulder, and I link her hand with mine, needing the closeness.

"Did Kat have any news today?"

She shakes her head. "She sent the letter responding to the petition. She's hoping it will scare Miles off, but he's not easily intimidated."

I just need five minutes alone with that asshole. I know there's so much more than what Sarah has told me, but Ollie saying that his dad thinks he's dumb was enough. Kids don't just come up with stuff like that on their own. He must have said something, and that alone makes me want to rip his damn head off.

"Ollie asked if I could visit class." I lay it out there carefully, not wanting to disappoint him but also needing to know what Sarah thinks about it.

She lifts her head. "He did?"

I nod, and she doesn't say anything.

"What did you tell him?" Her question is soft.

"I told him I needed to check with you."

She exhales, and that nugget of worry resurfaces. "We need to be careful."

"About what?" It comes out a little bluntly, but I can't help it.

"I don't want him to get confused or . . "

I'm not sure what there is to be confused about. I shift, sliding my hand from hers, all defenses locking into place.

She stares at me. "Hey." She snatches my hand back. "I just want to be sure we're on the same page with all of this."

The same page. I don't know what in the hell that means, but I know I can't take one more thing right now.

"Sarah, what does that mean?" I ask straight up.

She frowns, most likely at my tone. "You and me is one thing, but Ollie and Frankie don't know anything other than you being here. They'll begin to expect it and . . ."

She trails off as if waiting for me to say something.

"I am here."

She nods slowly. "Yes, but this is a big deal."

Hell yes, this is a big deal, but I'm here. I've been here. Why is she pushing me away?

"We just . . ." She starts but stops. "I have to know what Miles is going to do, and then we can figure out what's best."

What's best is that asshole falls off the face of the earth, and Sarah and the kids stay here with me. Always.

I nod slowly, but my body goes rigid. I do my best not to be a jerk, but frustration fills me when she's shielding herself and the kids from me. At least that's what it feels like, and fear rears its ugly head.

I try not to be completely distracted, but for the next thirty minutes, I can do nothing but battle the worry taking hold. I need to sort it out before it sucks me under.

"I should go." I push off the couch, but she doesn't move.

She stares up at me and then slowly follows me to the door. I reach for my coat, but she grabs my arm.

"What's wrong? Tell me."

I shake my head. "Nothing." I won't push Sarah to be ready for something she's not. Her job is to protect her kids. I just never wanted her to feel like she had to protect them from me.

She slides her arms around my waist, and I pull her close, wanting her to tell me what she's afraid of. The annoying thing is. . .I'm scared, too.

I rest my chin on top of her head. Miles put her through hell. I can't blame her for being wary.

I inhale, taking in the feel of her as she's trying to reassure me. I need patience, but I'm no fucking good at that.

"I'll see you tomorrow, ok?" I need a minute to get my head straight and try to figure out how to be afraid in all of this *with* her.

She lifts her head, her chin resting against my chest. "You sure you're ok?"

I stare into her eyes, so incredibly extraordinary, I'm not sure I'll ever fully be used to them.

Three words I never thought I'd say again are on the verge of spilling out. I hold them back, protecting myself from not hearing her say them in return.

"Yeah, I'm sure."

I lean down and kiss her lips lightly, then pull on my coat to go home. I carry myself through my house to the shower. It's not where I want to be. I want to be back with Sarah on her couch or, better yet, in her bed.

I rest my hands against the shower wall, hearing the guys call me out for not telling her straight up that I love her. I do. So incredibly much.

But what if her hesitation is because she isn't quite ready to love me back?

CHAPTER 49

SARAH

My phone buzzes. I blink my eyes open to the early morning light, surprised not to have a small leg draped over me. I snatch it off the nightstand and swipe to answer.

"Shouldn't you still be sleeping?"

"I haven't gone to bed yet." Roxie's excited voice fills my ear, and I pull the phone away to turn the volume down. "Did you see?!"

I run a hand over my face. "See what?" I groan, not having any idea what's so urgent this early.

I roll onto my side and close my eyes, remembering Slade's abrupt goodbye last night. He said he was fine, but I know better.

I watched the big, gruff man read and be silly with my kids, and then I heard Ollie tell him he loved him. My stomach soared, and my throat ached. Whatever is happening between Slade and me is one thing, but I have two small, vulnerable hearts that could get broken.

Slade hasn't said how he feels, and I hope he's falling in love with me right back. But asking him to love and be a constant in two kids' lives is another thing entirely. I can't stand to see Ollie's heart broken by another man.

Roxie huffs, and I'm pulled back from dozing off.

"Seriously, have you not been paying attention? Miles." She grounds out his name.

I yawn. "Rox. I love you, but I don't care what Miles is doing at the moment." I'm in love with the gentle beast across the street. I've just got to be sure he loves me and will love my kids, too, before I throw myself at him again. And this time, it won't be in my driveway.

I caught him looking at me in the kitchen last night. I know what he was thinking. I've been having lots of the same tempting thoughts, and my body is ready. But my heart needs to be certain it's just as safe.

She groans. "Sarah, get up. Right now!"

"Rox, whaaaatt?" I whine, rolling myself.

"There are Two. Women. Talking," she enunciates clearly.

My eyes pop open, and I sit up straight. "What?"

"They're saying Miles slept with them while they were interns. He hit it and quit it, and they're coming for him."

I remain perfectly still. Evaluating this news.

Is this a good thing? I'm not sure. Regardless of how much I despise Miles, he's Ollie and Frankie's father, and I've never wanted them to be affected by this side of him. But if I've learned anything recently, it's that I can't protect them from everything.

I try to sort through all my questions. "When did this happen?"

"Uh. . .when did he sleep with them, or when did they come forward?" She doesn't wait for my answer. "They reported it when he was announced as the new anchor on The Morning Show. Apparently, text messages and details were just leaked. My guess is they're either looking for their five minutes of fame or payback for being used and dismissed."

I put her on speaker and Google it. My screen fills with the two young women's faces. I could be angry at them, but I'm not. They were likely lured and manipulated just as I was. I wonder if there will be more.

My empty stomach rolls and swirls. I blow out a slow breath.

"You know what this means?" Roxie sings as I scroll through another article. "His lying, cheating ass is sunk. Bullseye, baby. Those executives are seeing him for who he is. They must know that he was intentionally misleading them about your relationship. I'd like to see him stand before a judge and claim parental superiority now. Ha!"

My finger stalls on the screen.

What if this is it? What if this is the end, and he no longer has the power he's always held? What if I can finally be free?

"Hey, you ok?"

I don't know. I'm shocked and feel a little queasy. I stare at the wall across the room.

I've always just let everyone assume the worst of me, but now they'll know the truth.

I let out a little laugh. "I don't even care anymore." I don't care if people know the truth. The damage was done long ago, and I'm still standing.

"Sarah, what are you talking about?" Roxie's tone is serious.

"All I wanted was to start over. I wanted stability for Ollie and Frankie and a chance to be happy. It seemed so far out of reach every time I turned around, and Miles was there holding something over my head. Rox . . ." My heart beats faster, and my eyes sting with tears. "I'm not sure I really believed it was possible for it to ever be different."

I rest a hand on my chest. The enormous weight of years' worth of fear and anguish lifts, and a hope I haven't allowed blooms and spreads in its place.

"It should never have been this way," she says softly. "But you made it. You did it, and this is just the beginning." Her voice quivers, and a tear slips out and rolls down my cheek.

"Do you really think this is it?" I hold my breath, unsure if I should let myself look toward the light shining at the end of the tunnel.

Slade. I have to tell him.

I swallow my emotions, and the urgency to see him shoves me out of bed. I want to run across the street and jump into his arms and tell him that I'm not going anywhere.

I pull clothes from my drawers.

She sniffs, and her sassy voice returns. "Sarah, they're filing lawsuits. I can't imagine any lawyer would advise him to move forward with suing you for custody. He'll be too busy trying to save his own ass."

"I have to call Kat and tell her." I hold the phone between my ear and shoulder, trying to tug on my leggings.

"Yes, and then you have to tell me what she says."

I pull on a sweatshirt.

"Rox, I love you."

"I love you, too!" she squeals.

"Call you later."

"You better."

We hang up, and I use my fingers to pull my hair up into a ponytail, not giving a crap what I look like. Slade has seen me at my worst.

I sit on the edge of my bed and type out a message to Kat. It's still early, but she'll message me when she gets it.

There's a knock on my front door, and Grover barks. I rush to open it, ready to fling myself at him.

"Grover, shhh. No barking." I hush him, hoping he doesn't wake the kids.

I swing open the door. My lungs stall as my stomach hits the floor.

CHAPTER 50

SLADE

I park in front of Krissy's townhouse. The street light reflects off my windshield while I watch the sunrise, waiting for her to get home from work.

I could have continued to lie in bed and think about Sarah telling me that we need to be careful, but I did that all night, and I'd had enough.

So, I wait for the other most important woman in my life to tell me if she's ever going to forgive me.

Headlights flash in my rearview and slow as they get closer. She pulls into the short one-lane drive.

I climb out of my truck as she gathers her stuff from her car.

"Seriously, Slade. It's been a long night, and I'm tired." She shoves her car door closed with her hip.

I tuck my hands in my pockets. "Just five minutes, Kris."

She heads to her door, not even glancing at me. "Slade, I don't have anything to say right now." She twists the lock and steps inside.

I follow her in as she sets her things down and finally turns toward me.

"Just what? Say what you need to say so I can go to bed." She crosses her arms, looking as tired as I feel.

I should have prepared for this. I should know what I want to say, but I don't. Telling her I need her forgiveness seems like one more selfish request.

My stomach clenches tight, and I exhale, admitting the thing that's stuck with me since she stormed out of the shop. "I think you were right."

She stares at me.

"Part of the reason I didn't tell you was because I didn't want to face it all over again. But. . .I also couldn't stand to take anything away from how you remember Mom." I pause. "I knew it would hurt you."

"Hurt?" She scoffs and shakes her head. "It's all one big fat lie. I was such an idiot." She huffs a laugh. "No wonder she always avoided questions." Her eyes meet mine. "But *you* could have told me. *You* made the rule that we never lie to each other."

The force of her words slams into me.

"I didn't lie."

She rolls her eyes. "Keeping the truth from me is equivalent."

I can't even defend myself.

"It was him that day at the shop, wasn't it? He brought Sarah to get her car."

I nod, having no doubt she's spent hours researching Griffin Macavoy. "She works for him."

She shakes her head as it falls forward. "I'm so stupid. I just thought you were pissed another man was helping her."

Krissy stares at the floor. "Does she know?"

"Yes." I look at my boots, knowing I am about to make things even worse. "I went to see him," I admit softly.

Her gaze locks on mine.

"Once, after I found out Mom was sick. I wanted him to talk to her. See if she'd continue treatment. Then again, recently. Sarah's ex is petitioning for custody of Ollie and Frankie. Macavoy has seen us together. I had to be sure he'd help her if she asked. Not refuse because of me."

She lifts her chin. "And what? We're still nothing more than their dirty little secrets?"

I'm not sure how to answer that.

"You helped them hide it." Her tone is sharp.

I shake my head, stating the truth inside it all. "No. We're still you and me." My throat swells with the way I've always seen us, and my eyes sting, needing her to feel it.

She blinks, swallowing, and her gaze drops from mine.

I try to choke it all down, but it's difficult. "I don't know why they did what they did or why Mom allowed him in her life for all those years, but I know she loved you like crazy. I'll never understand it, Kris. I tried, but all it did . . ."

She won't look at me.

"For a long time, I was angry and confused and wondered how she could be with someone who only used her while he was building a family with someone else."

"Slade, he had two fucking kids and a wife!" Her voice charges forth with heartache that's so familiar it flares in my chest.

I nod, hearing the fresh anger and grief. "I know, but what they did has nothing to do with us. We have our own family. You and me and the guys."

The urge to claim Sarah and the kids as part of it is so great that it overwhelms me again. I run a hand under my nose.

Her lip quivers, and she sniffs. "I can't do this right now."

Sarah said I'm the target. Kris can take this out on me as long as she needs. I can handle it.

"Ok," I whisper, swiping at my cheek. "Kris, I'm not going anywhere. Be mad at me. Hate me. Get it out."

Her watery gaze drifts to mine.

"I let the hurt fester and steal. It wasn't ever mine to own. It's not yours either. Then Melissa . . ." I pause, remembering, and I find it's not as painful as it once was. "I shut everyone and everything out. Don't do that. Let the guys in. They love you."

Tears spill from her eyes, and she wipes her cheeks. I want to hug her, but I know that's not what she needs right now.

I grip the door knob but stop. "You know how they say beauty comes from ashes?" She blinks her glossy eyes, trying so damn hard to hold it all back. "Krissy, you are the beauty inside a messed-up situation. I was terrified to take on raising you, but so far, it's the best damn thing I've ever done. I screwed up a lot, but we did ok, didn't we?"

My nose burns, wanting to believe we did all right.

She nods, blinking so fast, but one more tear sneaks out of the corner of my eye.

"I love you. Always. Remember that."

I leave her for now, but I know we'll be ok. We have to be. All we have is each other.

I climb into my truck and drive home so I can talk to Sarah. I can't handle another sleepless night or let fear steal one more day. What I told Krissy was true. I closed myself off out of anger and fear for what others did, but I never should've allowed their actions to have that kind of impact on my life.

I take a long, hot shower, hoping it will help me figure out exactly what I want to say. I know Sarah's worried about what will happen with the custody case, but I can't see my life without her. She and the kids turned my sad, miserable existence upside down, and I can't go back to that.

She's like a wrecking ball, taking down one protective wall at a time. She, Ollie, and Frankie have stolen my sealed-off heart.

I pull on jeans, a T-shirt, and a flannel. I leave my room, rolling up my sleeves, wondering if she's up yet.

A rapid knock comes from my front door, and I tug it open.

Brandon stands there with his wiener shoved under his arm.

"Uh . . ." His gaze travels across the street, and mine follows.

I slide my feet into my boots, taking two steps at a time.

"Don't kill him!" Brandon hollers.

CHAPTER 51

SARAH

"You did this, didn't you?" he snarls.

I step out onto the porch with Grover and close the door. My dog sits at my feet, huffing out short little warning barks.

"Miles, what are you doing here?" I wrap my arms around myself, trying not to shake from the cold and my anxiety bouncing around like a ping-pong ball.

His eyes are wild and filled with rage. "You have no idea what you've done. You think you'll gain something from this?" he scoffs.

"Miles, what are you talking about?" I assume he's referring to the women coming forward, but I'm not sure.

"Don't play dumb, Sarah. We both know how desperate you are."

I shake my head, willing myself to remain calm. "Miles, everything you've done will only come back to haunt our kids. Don't think for one second I'd ever wish that on them. Whatever is happening, you did that."

I slide around him and descend the porch steps, leading him away from the house to his car.

"Where are you going?" His voice is raised, but I don't care.

I've spent enough time fearing a man who is nothing more than a coward.

"Sorry you made the trip, but it's time for you to go. Whatever mess your actions have led you to, that's your problem." I stop at his sedan, needing him to get in and never return.

"You just couldn't handle seeing me make it to the top. You're pathetic. If this is your attempt to spew some sob story, it won't work. Everyone already thinks you slept your way to the crown and beyond, but I forgave you even when they thought I wasn't the one who got you pregnant."

This man is seriously delusional. My gut fills with anger from the weight of his lies.

"You won't get away with trying to defame me." He snorts a laugh.

I cross my arms, tension screaming throughout my body, so completely sick of him and his ego.

The sound of my pulse fills my ears. "Miles, I don't care where you are or what you're doing. If I gave a shit enough to plan revenge, believe me, it wouldn't have taken this long."

His nostrils flare. "You seriously expect me to believe you or that bitch of a lawyer didn't contact these women and pay them to talk?"

I laugh, and my skin crawls with fire as sweat collects under my arms. "Pay someone? What? With my Mega Pot winnings. Miles, I'm lucky if I can buy something other than Folgers to survive on. And let me tell you, coffee is way more important to me than spending time or money scrounging up just a few of the women you did wrong."

"You think this is funny?" He grits his teeth, leaning and getting in my face.

"Hey!"

I twist at the sound.

Oh, man. Slade is a soldier charging into battle. His boots are unlaced, his sleeves are rolled up, revealing the beautiful artwork down to his balled fists. The fierce scowl on his face makes my stomach roll and flip into a backward somersault.

My lungs expand at just the sight of him.

Miles takes a quick step back. "I told you last time this doesn't involve you. You need to head back to your—"

"And I told you I don't give a fuck what you have to say. This involved me the second you rolled into this neighborhood." The warning in his ground-out words is loud and clear. "You touch her, and you'll spend years learning how to talk again."

I watch Slade's dominant posture grow three sizes as he stops beside me. I stare at him, his chest heaving, and there might be subtle growls rolling out.

Grover bounces at his feet as if he's happy to have back up.

Miles releases a little laugh that's filled with condescending arrogance.

The toes of Slade's boots inch forward, daring him. I shift, and the back of my hand presses into the solid muscle underneath his shirt to keep the Goliath in place.

"You need to go," I tell Miles, bracing myself against my protector.

"You've made a huge mistake, Sarah. The only thing you're doing is sending yourself and our kids back to the shithole you grew up in."

It should sting, but it doesn't. Growing up the way I did taught me how to work and appreciate every single thing I've earned. My mom is right. Small and simple leaves you with less to screw up.

"They are *not* your kids. No father lets his children starve." Slade's tone is so tense, I expect fire to shoot forth.

"They're only starving if she's not feeding them." Miles's arrogant, dark eyes run over Slade. "This is a joke. You think you have some place here?"

Slade takes a step closer, his nostrils flaring. "They're mine. All of them. It's up to Sarah if you're ever involved in their lives and to what capacity, but to be clear, it won't be because they need you."

My entire body goes still. Silence ensues as Miles pulls open his door. He says something, but I don't hear whatever garbage he spews.

I lift my gaze to peer up at the big man who just said. . .something.

My heart doesn't know what to do. It's fluttering all around. Speed up. Slow down. Speed up. Slow down.

I put a hand on my chest. *Did Slade just say that we are. . .his?*

I'm lost in some kind of momentary time warp. Slade watches Miles back out of the drive, but I can only stare at him. This man, who sat with me and held my kids while we were sick. The one who took us in when we needed it. He's been showing up day after day. Could he have possibly meant what I think he just said?

I need a second to wrap my head around it. Where the hell is a doorbell camera when you need one? I need proof. Evidence that this solid, solitary, overtly blunt, and semi-emotionless man just said that *we* are his.

My mind can't keep up, and it's a little hard to breathe. Ollie, squeezing his neck and whispering that he loves him, slams into me all over again.

Slade turns to me. "Are you ok?" His voice is low and gentle.

I don't know. What the hell is it with this driveway and things happening in it?

"Y'all ok?" Brandon's distant voice snaps me from my wonder.

Slade waves a hand, but his eyes don't leave mine.

I need a freaking moment. I turn, taking the porch steps two at a time, my heart hammering in my chest. I continue on toward the kitchen, but stop when I hear the front door click shut. I spin, and the man who I think just said what he said stands inside the door.

"Sarah, what happened?" His hands move to his hips while I feel like I might actually hyperventilate. "Did he—"

"What the hell was that?" It comes out breathy, and my throat might actually be closing up.

"He won't talk to you—"

I hold up my hand, reminding myself to inhale and exhale. I'm in love with him. Totally and completely, and I've only just realized how badly I need him to love me back. But not just me. Ollie and Frankie, too.

I've never been claimed or wanted for me. The messy, raw version that Slade should have grown tired of. The me who cries into his shirt and drools when she sleeps, so freaking tired from life screwing with me. The one who hides behind sarcasm and poise to shield me from the pain and shame that lies beneath.

I've been terrified this whole time, believing there's no way a man like *this* could ever want. . .me.

My eyes burn as I remind myself to breathe. "No. Not that." I shake my head.

He stares at me. He cannot go and say something like that without explaining himself.

My heart pounds and my throat narrows to the size of a straw. I rotate my finger, needing him to get with it and explain himself. Right now.

"Sarah." His weight shifts from one big foot to the other, his shoulders holding strong. "I seriously suck at charades. They weren't lying."

Is he trying to be funny? Now!

"I'm just a little. . ." I place a hand on my forehead.

He takes a tiny step closer. "I'm talking about the whole 'they're mine' thing." I choke it out. "What the hell was that?"

He doesn't move, his large hands falling to his sides as I watch his chest expand and deflate. I'm glad to know I'm not the only one who's having a little trouble with oxygen.

"I meant what I said." It's that clear, blunt tone that tells me he means it.

He told me he would never lie to me, so I know it wasn't just to scare Miles off. But does it really mean what I need it to mean? Because I need Slade.

A portion of the pressure eases off my chest. "Were you. . .ever going to say something?"

His lips twitch. "I was thinking about it."

I huff, my head falling toward the floor, my breath coming a little easier. "You were thinking about it?"

He remains silent, and my frustration climbs, needing him to tell me straight up what that meant.

"Slade, tell me exactly what you meant when you called us yours because I'm about one millisecond from coming over there and doing something that will change everything. If I do that and you push me away, I promise you I will not be ok."

Those green eyes flick between mine, and all I hear is the pounding of my own heart while I await his direct response.

"Get over here." It's that low, commanding tone, but gentle.

I stare at him, not moving, feeling like I'm standing on the edge of a cliff. I want to jump, but I'm scared.

"Sarah." The sound of my name rolling off his tongue brings me back from the ledge. "Come. Here."

I know him and the losses he's endured. He's just as afraid as I am and is asking me to meet him halfway.

I inhale and cross the room, standing before him.

"Sarah." His voice is even softer.

I meet his gaze, and all I see is earnestness.

"I meant everything I said. I want you to be mine. All three of you. I don't want you to need him. Ever."

I let those words soak in and through me.

His large, rough hands cup my face. "I wouldn't push you away. Not ever."

I blink, staring up at him. "You wouldn't?"

He shakes his head. "But I'm not really good at this, so I still need you to go easy on me."

A little laugh escapes as my heart rate begins to ease back into a normal pace, and my eyes fill with tears.

"Ok." I breathe out, knowing I can do that. "But are you sure? This. The three of us. It's a lot, and if we do this, you're going to be stuck with us."

He releases my face, linking his arms around my lower back. "I never thought I could do this with anyone. . .until you. And Ollie and Frankie. I didn't want to." He swallows, but his eyes never leave mine. "I *want* to be stuck with you. Forever."

I. Am. Done. I throw my arms around his neck and haul myself up, my mouth crashing into his.

I tilt my head, needing more, and his tongue tangles with mine. I kiss him like I've needed to every day since I kissed him for the first time.

His shoulders dip, and his large hands grip the back of my thighs, hoisting me up. I wrap my legs around him, and his fingers dig into my ass, pulling me against him.

I tug away, seeking air, and his mouth glides down my neck, kissing and nipping. I need this, and I need him. Always.

"Slade," I breathe out.

I lift his face to mine, and his emerald eyes tell me he needs me, too. I smile, leaning in and taking his lower lip between my teeth.

He groans a guttural sound, and I squeeze my legs around his waist, sparks shooting straight to my core. I chase his growl with a kiss as one rough palm slips under my shirt, skimming up my spine. He takes two steps—

"Mama."

I jerk away, but Slade keeps a firm hold on me. He doesn't even flinch, his chest moving in and out against mine.

I twist, and Ollie stands at the edge of the hallway with his bloated, sad, blue fish tucked under his arm, grinning.

I turn back to Slade. A confident smirk slides across his lips as if he knows exactly what he's doing. I release my breath and drop my forehead to his shoulder.

"Frankie was crying, so I took her b-bus to her. She's p-playing in her crib."

Slade releases my legs slowly, allowing me to stand on my own two feet again, and for the blaring need begins to dwindle.

He grabs my face and presses a quick kiss to my lips. "Later."

I sag, my body roaring at the sound of his promise as he steps around me.

Ollie snickers, and I let out a little laugh.

This man has completely undone me. Stripped me bare of all of my defenses and desire to be fully self-reliant.

"Morning, partner." He scoops Ollie from the floor and into his arms. "What do you think about making breakfast while your mom changes Frankie?"

"Can we make p-pancakes?" Ollie's hand rests on Slade's cheek.

"And eggs to build muscle?"

Ollie nods quickly.

"Deal."

"All right, you boys make breakfast, and we girls will. . .pull ourselves together." I glare at Slade for seeming so completely unaffected as I move around them.

His arm jets out, hooking my waist, but he looks at Ollie. "Is it ok if I kiss your mom sometimes?"

Ollie's face scrunches. "Wike on the wips?"

Slade nods. "Yeah."

"Eww. I guess." He shrugs his small shoulder but smiles.

"Good." Slade presses his lips to my forehead and then releases me.

I head to Frankie's room and hear them talking.

"How about pancakes with chocolate chips?" It's Slade's deep voice.

Followed by Ollie's, "Yes!"

Frankie sees me and stands in her crib. "Ma-ma."

"Hi, Love Bug. Did Ol bring your toys in here?"

She points to her bus and the little princesses around it.

"He's a pretty good big brother, isn't he?"

She smiles.

"Should we change your dipe?"

She reaches for me, and I lift her, smothering her with kisses as she giggles. I take my time, letting the emotions from the last hour roll from my body.

We join the boys in the kitchen, the scent of coffee in the air. Ollie sits on the counter, stirring the batter while Slade cracks eggs in a skillet.

"Ade. Ade. Ade." Frankie bobs on my hip toward him.

Slade looks over his shoulder at her. He rinses his hands, and she leans for him.

"Smells good in here." I smile at him.

"We're making ch-chocolate chip pancakes." Ollie lifts a spatula in the air.

"Think you can flip them and not let them burn?" Slade raises an eyebrow.

I dip a shoulder, taking the spatula from Ollie. "It was one moment of baking weakness. Are you ever going to let that go?"

He shakes his head slowly, but I see the mischievous smirk behind his stare.

I point the plastic tool at him. "Careful, Desert Kitty. Two can play at that game."

"I hope so."

I stare at him, holding my sweet girl and looking way too sexy and confident.

Well, shit. I squint one eye at him as I move to the stove, knowing this might be one very long day.

CHAPTER 52

SLADE

I carry Ollie to his bed—complete dead weight.

We spent the day building train yards and throwing sticks to Grover in the snow. Sarah pulled Frankie around in the sled, and she squealed each time it ran over a small drift.

It was a day full of the kids' giggles and Sarah's beautiful, relaxed smile. It all caused something to shift inside me. It was like joy breaking free that had been hidden inside a dark cave, afraid to peek its head out.

I've feared this kind of happiness. Scared to desire love and a family because, at any moment, it could disappear. I couldn't allow myself to be this close to someone only to find out they'd never really be mine.

But over these past few months, I have discovered something with Sarah that I didn't know existed. I've fallen in love with her—the drive-me-insane, all-consuming kind. But that love is built on friendship and trust that slowly morphed into an undeniable need. I need Sarah. She sets me off guard and breaks through all the protective layers I enclose myself in.

When I claimed her, Ollie, and Frankie, it just tumbled out in a moment of rage, but it's the truth. I want nothing more than this every day. I want all the messy, crazy, hard days with Sarah. She makes me a better person, and I've realized I'm not afraid to love her because, whether she said it or not, I know she loves me back.

For the first time, I've been my whole self with someone. No pretense or barrier. I screwed up, and she still invited me in. She held me, forgave me, and trusted me enough to know my error in judgment was never meant to hurt her. It's how love should be. She believed in me and saw through my mistake. That means more to me than she'll ever know.

I peek in on Frankie, her floppy lamb squeezed to her chest. I run my finger over her soft, chubby cheek, wanting this every night—rocking them by the fire and reading stories. Holding them until they fall asleep.

I blink, not believing I might actually have it.

I find Sarah at the kitchen sink with her back to me, drying the pan from dinner. Her tight black leggings hug her butt and waist. Those damn things are about to drive me mad.

I know what I want, and I think I know what Sarah wants, but nothing will happen until she's good and ready.

I slip my arm around her and tug her against me.

"Oh, hi."

I hear the smile in her voice as I run my lips down the side of her neck. "What did Kat say?"

Kat called with an update while I was reading to the kids. Sarah messaged her this morning about Miles's visit and the women coming forward.

She tips her head to the side, giving me better access to her soft skin. "I can't really think when you're doing that." It comes out slowly in a bit of a whine.

I straighten, and she twists in my arms, taking hold of my shirt.

"She said I should consider the case closed. His attorney has already dropped him as a client. Plus, he can't risk me going public with his threats to force me into appearing as a family. We have a witness, so he's screwed."

"We do?"

She smiles. "Brandon. His constant invasive nosiness did good this time."

Relief attempts to flood through me, crumbling my only remaining defenses. "So, that's it?" I have to be sure they aren't going anywhere without me.

She inhales and lets it out. "She'll give it a little time and then make it clear he's not welcome here again."

"How do you feel?" I watch her, needing to know.

"I'm. . .kind of scared to believe it." She huffs out a little laugh. "It feels too good to be true." She glances up at me, a sly smile appearing. Her hands slide over my shoulders and around my neck, her fingers pushing into my hair as she presses up on her toes. "But you know what this means?"

I link my arms around her lower back, bringing her slim body to mine. "What?" I peer down at her as the exhilaration that's been on hold since this morning reawakens.

"You're really stuck with us now." She bites her bottom lip, trying her damndest to hide that sassy grin, the one that turns my belly into a raging ball of fire.

I've been waiting for this all day. I release her, sliding my hands into her hair and guiding her head to the side. I steal her mouth, and it only takes a second for her lips to part. I sweep my tongue across hers, tasting and savoring her. She whimpers, her fingers digging into my neck, and I do it again.

She nips at my lip, teasing, and I groan. I feel her smile, and I kiss it away, stealing her breath with it. She melts into me, her heart hammering against mine.

I release her mouth, and her chest moves in and out quickly as she slowly opens her eyes. My teeth graze over her skin as her head falls back toward the ceiling.

"Are you finally gonna make good on that promise?" She's breathless, and I love it.

"What promise is that?" I'm messing with her. Sarah, lit up with flirty irritation, is sexy as hell.

Her hold on me loosens a little, and those dazed, tantalizing, opposite eyes flick between mine with a superficial glare.

"You, sir, know exactly what I'm talking about, but ya know. . ." Her arms drop from my neck, and she pulls away. "It's been one hell of a day. I should probably—"

I grab her and scoop her into my arms. She laughs, holding on to me.

"First, you hit on me. Now, you're demanding I make love to you."

She holds my face, brushing her lips over mine. "Nothing wrong with a girl knowing what she wants and going after it."

This woman is going to kill me, and I'll enjoy every second. "Is that so?"

Her lips move over my jaw to my neck. "Mmm hmm. And you cannot tell me you haven't been wanting the same." She kisses my neck. "Exact." Her teeth nip my skin, and my body flares with desire. "Thing."

I turn, twisting through the doorway to the hall, needing her room.

"Wait!" Her arm flies out, hitting the wall.

"Sarah." It comes out more like a growl. I take another step. "I've already seen your room."

"No. Stop. We need protection," she whispers, holding my face. "I'm not on birth control. If you take me in there, Slade, I'm not going to be able to control myself."

I grin.

"Put that dimple away. That's not helping." She presses her finger over the indent in my cheek.

I lean in, sucking her bottom lip between mine, and she makes a pouting noise. "We're covered." I proceed forward.

Her arm flies out again. "Wait. What? How old is it because—"

I kiss her hard, stealing her mouth in a hot, slick kiss. Her body goes limp.

I'm unsure if this panic is nerves or anticipation, but I'm promising her that no matter what, everything will be ok.

CHAPTER 53

SARAH

I cling to him, desperate for more. Slade quietly kicks the door shut and lowers my legs. My toes touch the floor, but his large, muscular arms wrap around me, keeping me close and making me feel so safe. Even in the dark, his green eyes find mine. Attentive. Gentle. Sure.

My heart beats fast with anticipation of sharing everything with him. I'm nervous, but it's the best kind of anxious tension.

I wasn't sure I'd ever find myself with a man I care about and trust so much I can't stand not being with him.

"This can happen now or months from now. My promise isn't going anywhere." His voice is soft but ragged.

I fist his shirt, choking out the truth. "This. . .is new for me." My gaze finds his again. "Being so cared for and allowed to care for you the same way. I didn't know love could be like this."

The back of his fingers grazes my cheek.

"I love you," I whisper. "And as hard as I tried not to, I need you. All the time."

His forehead falls to mine. "I'm pretty sure I fell in love with all three of you the moment you set foot in my house. I never wanted you to leave. I wanted to be around you all the time. The noise, chaos, and mess. I don't ever want to be without it."

I huff a quiet laugh. "You might change your mind when you're thrown up on, or the kids are screaming because you don't have the right snack."

He shakes his head. "No. There's no changing this, Sarah. I want it all. Maybe someday we'll add to the chaos."

I pull away just a little to look at him. "Yeah?"

He nods, and the intensity I see in his eyes burns through me, sending waves of heat soaring.

I undo one button on his shirt and then another until I reach the end. I push it over his shoulders, and it drops to the floor.

I smile, gripping the hem of his white T-shirt and tugging it up. He pulls it over his head, and I gape at the defined muscle underneath, marked with an intricate. . .lion head that spills over his shoulder onto his chest. It's beautiful and so entirely fitting.

He stands completely still, watching me take it in. I raise my eyebrows, my tongue pressing to the corner of my mouth. This man has no idea how incredibly gorgeous he is.

I trail my fingers up his inked arms, rippled with veins. "I've wondered how far these stretch."

His hands grip my waist, and he walks me back toward the bed.

"Will you tell me about them?"

"Not right now." It's that commanding tone, and it makes me smile.

The back of my legs hit the edge of the bed. "Fine, Bossy Pants."

He grunts, his hands sliding underneath my cropped shirt and pulling it over my head. He wastes no time stealing my bra with it.

His gaze pours over me, and I spread my hand over his heart, feeling it pound against my palm.

Those long, permanently stained, calloused fingers skim my stomach, moving carefully over each rib.

I suck in a breath, and he watches me.

"I've wanted you like this for far too long." The fierce focus of his gaze tells me just how much he means that.

I sit on the bed, pulling the waist of his jeans that sit low on his hips to bring him with me. The weight of his body settles on top of mine. His blazing skin surrounds me, and his hand glides up my thigh, gripping my hip, his finger slipping under the waist of my leggings.

His mouth hovers over mine, the ends of his hair falling against my face. "You cannot wear these if you want to do anything other than this."

I run my fingers through his hair, which is as wild as it is sexy. "That so?" I use his words, guiding his mouth to mine. "Seems you've been prepared."

"I only make promises I intend to keep."

My fingers trace over each defined ab, feeling them flex, but stop before undoing the button on his jeans. "You know, you told me once that at some point, I was going to have to trust you."

He kisses me achingly slow, moving down my neck to my collarbone, and then swirls his tongue around the most sensitive skin. I whimper as it catches my breath, and he pulls away.

That dimple that has taunted me for months appears, winking at me.

"I think I won you over." His mouth roams my stomach. "Despite my cold." Kiss. "Hard." Kiss. "Bitterness."

I laugh. "Listen, King of the Jungle." His gaze lifts to mine. "We'll have to see how these next few minutes go before the full ruling is in on that."

"A few minutes, my ass," he grumbles, but it's playful and sounds a heck of a lot like love.

I bite my bottom lip as those rough hands climb up my body. He wraps around me, and he rolls, flipping me on top of him. I straddle his hips, and he stares up at me. The intensity and heat I see there send pulses through me.

I lean down and take his mouth, pressing the tip of my tongue to his but pulling away, and he tries to chase me.

I grin. "You're sure about this, Wildcat? It might be a lot."

He nudges me with his nose, forcing my gaze to his. "Sarah, you can drive me crazy and run your sassy mouth all you want. I only want to be stuck with you. Just you." His eyes wander between mine.

I unbutton his jeans as his hands grip my ass. "Well, fair warning, you're gonna want to be extra careful with how often you wear your bossy pants."

I lay with my head on his bare chest, listening to his slow, steady breaths. I slide my leg over his, wanting to be as close as possible. I've never felt more at peace—just lying next to him, actually believing it all might really be ok.

I trail my finger over Newton's Law, scrolled across his forearm.

For every action, there is an equal and opposite reaction.

The law might only apply to the physical world, but there was a time when it felt true about my life.

With every stroke I took, it seemed there was an opposing force pushing against me, holding me down to keep me from taking another. All I wanted was to reach the shore, where the storm wasn't raging. I was so tired of living in survival mode, barely holding my head above water, lost and so damn tired of treading, never getting closer.

But I think I see now that, sometimes, we just have to keep fighting the current and pushing through, no matter what stands in our way or how difficult that next thrust forward might be. We have to keep believing that eventually, we'll hit the sand where we can bathe in the sunshine. If we're lucky, we might find someone there to lie beside us and soak up all the goodness that's been waiting.

Maybe it's just like Slade said, it's the hard road I had to take so that it would lead me here. To him.

"So, you got this one when you were accepted into the engineering program, but what about this one?" I move on, tracing the dark vine that crawls and wraps around his forearm.

His chest rises with an inhale and falls. "My mom's name was Ivy. She was. . .beautiful and smart, but she had a difficult life. Her love was suffocating at times, but she sacrificed everything for Krissy and me. Always put herself last." He pauses. "I wish she could've seen herself the way I did."

I set my chin on his chest to look at him. "Sometimes, we can be so desperate for love we'll spend our whole lives begging someone to love us back, just settling for what little they'll give us."

He brushes the hair out of my face, his fingers tracing through it and down my back. "You didn't."

"I could have. It's easy to be convinced you can't live without someone when you have nothing. Slade, I was so scared. I spent years thinking that's all I deserved, blaming myself for the choices I made."

"You were never to blame."

"No, but sometimes, life just sweeps in and leaves behind a person you no longer recognize, and the only thing you're left with is a load of lies you can't help but believe are true."

I spread my hand flat across his chest, feeling his heartbeat. "Your mom loved hard and well." I press up on my elbow to look at him. "It's the only way you turned out like this. Beautiful. Smart." I inch closer. "Kind. Gentle." I brush my lips against his. "With a scowl that is ridiculously appealing."

His hand cups the back of my head, and his mouth captures mine. He kisses me long and slow, my body sliding on top of his.

When I need air, I pull away, pressing my lips to the intricate lion head. "I want to know about Mufasa."

"You can't name him." His soft, deep voice rumbles.

I glare at him. "That's not fair. I knew you were all roaring lion."

He rolls his eyes, and I smile, resting between his legs with my cheek on the exquisite artwork. "I got it right after she died, when everything fell apart. It represented what I vowed to be. Brave, strong, loyal. . .wise. I never wanted to be blindsided again."

I stare at him, recognizing the scars of remorse in his green eyes. The same ones I bear.

"You know, I've wondered if maybe we have to go through hell in order to actually appreciate what comes after."

His eyes linger between mine. "It's taken me a long time to get to the appreciative part."

I squint one eye at him. "Yeah, but if you hadn't taken so long, we wouldn't be here."

His mouth runs over my cheek. "I've been thinking the lion needs an update."

I twirl the end of his hair around my finger. Twice. It can curl around the tip of my finger twice, and it feels like a privilege to get to be the only one who knows that.

"Oh, yeah. I think he's pretty perfect." I kiss the skin covered by the exquisite lion that represents everything he is.

His teeth graze my jaw and neck. "His eyes." I feel a little nip.

I pull away, tilting my head to inspect the fierce animal.

Slade's rough fingers run up and down my spine, making me shiver. "One brown and one blue."

My gaze snaps to his.

"I've never seen anything more beautiful in my entire life. I couldn't look away. Not that day you walked into the shop. Not now."

I blink, my eyes filling with so much love I can't breathe.

"Sarah, you see me the way no one else ever has."

I crawl forward, wrapping my arms around his neck. My throat burns, but I smile through it. "That's pretty permanent."

His eyes travel between my watery ones. "Yes. I promise to love you the best I know how."

I nod, unable to speak. "Me, too."

He kisses me lightly, rolling us. He stares down at me. "Just go easy on me." A sexy smirk curls at his lips, and I laugh.

I shake my head, hooking my legs around his back. "Never."

CHAPTER 54

SLADE

My phone buzzes rapidly in my pocket. I wipe my hands on a rag and pull it out to check it.

SARAH: Hey, Scowly Kitty.
SARAH: If you grab milk from the store on your way home, I'll make dinner.
SARAH: Oh, and two heads of broccoli.
SARAH: Wait, maybe three.
SARAH: I know how much you love it.

I smile.

ME: I'll get milk.
ME: Anything else?

SARAH: Hmmm. Let me think.

I roll my eyes, knowing whatever comes next will be good.

SARAH: If you have a crowbar lying around, I could use it to pry the stick out of Cory's ass. We all might feel better.

ME: How about I drop by? I'd like to chat with him.

SARAH: Nah. I'll let you save all that protective aggression for someone who won't cower at the sound of your growl.

I chuckle. Sarah knows I will take out anyone who even thinks about messing with her.

"What the hell is this? What's going on?" Carson wags a finger at me.

I raise my eyes to his, knowing at some point, these gossip queens will find out. I've kept Sarah and me taking things to a serious level to myself. I've wanted to enjoy it as long as possible before these nags insert their nonsense where it's unwelcome.

I've spent every night with her since I told her I loved her, and I plan to continue. I have promises to keep.

Carson crosses his arms. "You want to finally tell us why watching football at your house was canceled, and *why* there have been multiple sightings of your smile over the past week?"

"Krissy still isn't talking to him," Trig says. "There should be nothing but 'fuck offs' and 'get your asses back to work.'" He lowers his voice to mimic me.

"I talked to Krissy, so you can mind your own damn business." I spoke with her only that one morning, but I've texted her, and she's responded. It's progress. I'm giving her the space and time Sarah keeps reminding me to allow her.

"How the hell do you know Krissy still isn't talking to him?" Carson barks at Trig.

I want to smile. I'll sit back and let these idiots and their drama spin.

"What's it to you?" Trig snaps back. "Wind has been taking her food. Why aren't you jumping all over his ass?"

Carson grumbles something and tosses a socket into his tool chest.

"Seriously, Slade, what's going on?" Wind sets his hands on his hips. "The level of unexplainable tension in the place is miserable. These two are at each other's throats." He points at Carson and Trig. "Luke is trying to adjust to whatever this new mood is you're confusing us all with, and my gastrointestinal system can't handle this kind of stress. We can't fall apart like this."

"No shit." Trig turns to him. "We've been dealing with the second-hand repercussions of your ass bombs for far longer than a week."

He shrugs, his cheeks turning a little pink above his beard. "I had a little gluten. It was a mistake."

"It's kind of nice that he doesn't yell so much." Luke offers his two cents. "Have you all ever thought about family therapy?"

We stare at the naive kid.

"No. This is how we deal with stuff," Carson says.

"Yeah. We verbally beat it out of each other like normal men," Trig scoffs.

"With y'all's pissy attitudes, it doesn't appear to be working." Luke shrugs. "Except for Slade. He actually seems. . .happy."

All eyes slowly return to me. *Damn.*

I shove my phone in my pocket, staring at these morons and all of their pent-up feelings. "You all need to settle the hell down."

They cross their arms, looking glum and pathetic.

"Not until you tell us what you're doing being. . .happy." Carson has been unusually snappy.

I point at him. "Is this about your family requesting you to come home?"

He points back. "Don't change the subject."

It's my turn to cross my arms. "Fine. Sarah and I are—"

"I knew it! I told your asses!" Trig pumps a fist in the air.

"Sure as hell took you long enough," Carson says, a small smile appearing as he grips my hand and leans in for a hug.

I can't help but smile.

"I don't know if I like this," Trig says. "It feels strange when you smile like that."

I hear a sniff and look up to see Wind wiping his eyes. "Our giant grouch is growing up. He's fallen in love and understands what joy feels like."

I flip him off, and he sniffs some more while the guys laugh. "Don't think this changes things. Your asses better knock off these sour attitudes. It's affecting productivity."

"You just keep all that joy to yourself, and everything will be fine," Trig says, getting back to work.

"Wait, what's this about you going home?" Wind asks Carson, and all the guys turn to look at him.

I grin, heading to my office.

"You'll pay for this, jackass," he hollers at me.

I love these guys.

I'm so tired, and my brain is fried. It's midnight, and Sarah crawls into bed.

I extend my arm, and she tucks in beside me, resting her head on my chest. "How'd it go?"

"I read through each question twice to be sure I selected the correct answer." She throws her leg over mine.

"And?"

"I passed."

"Sarah."

"Fine. I got an A."

I slide my finger under her chin to lift her face to mine. I lean down and kiss her, taking my time, and it only takes a second for her to reciprocate, her body rolling on top of me.

She smiles. "Well, I think I need to make sure I get an A every time."

"I'm proud of you."

She rests her hands on my chest with her chin on top. "I hope it pays off. I applied for a new job today."

My eyes roam her face. "You did?"

She nods. "Yeah. Krissy told me months ago about a bookkeeping job at the women's clinic, and they still haven't filled the position. I think I'd really like it, but the pay has to be right."

I slip my hand under her shirt and drag my fingers up and down her spine. "Are you sure about giving up on the lawyer thing? I don't want my issues with Macavoy to—"

She presses her finger to my lips. "Slade, I wanted to be a lawyer based on what I thought it would be like long before kids. The reality isn't so great, at least for me. I've enjoyed the work, but a lot of it has to do with financial information."

She shrugs. "I'm good at it. Finding a new job is about moving forward, but also, I can't work with Griffin knowing he's your father. It's just. . .I love you and Krissy. I can't separate that. Besides, if this job at the clinic works out, in a way, I'll be helping women like I've always wanted to."

I stare at her, so damn lucky to be here. "I love you."

She presses a quick kiss to my lips. "I know." She lays her head on my chest. "Thank you for putting the kids to bed."

"Ollie wanted me to sleep with him tonight."

"I can't blame him." I feel her smile. "You're cuddly and warm and safe. He's nervous about his T-Ball game." Her head pops up. "You guys have to be chill tomorrow. You can't intimidate the shit out of these little guys."

I grunt. "We wouldn't intimidate them. At least not the kids." That asswipe of a coach is fair game.

She looks at me. "I saw you talking to the coach the other night at practice, all arms crossed and broody."

"Just making sure we were on the same page."

"Oh, really. What page is that?"

"He gives Ollie time to get his words out. If I catch him talking over him again or yelling, I make no promises."

Her shoulders slump. "Fiiinnnne. You can intimidate the shit out of the coach, but only on Ollie's behalf."

I wrap my arms around her. "Don't pretend you don't like it."

"Oh, I like it." She smirks. "If you stand at the fence with Frankie on your shoulders again and growl a few times, all the other moms will like it, too."

I roll my eyes. "You're ridiculous."

"Am I?" She looks toward the ceiling like she's contemplating it. "You know what else I like?" She pushes her fingers through my hair.

I glare at her, waiting for me to take the bait. "What?"

"The fact that I know you can be anywhere, with all your blunt grouchiness, and you're all mine."

"Damn straight, but that coach better not look at your ass one more time, or he won't see well enough again to pee in a straight line."

She laughs and rolls off me.

She's not going anywhere. I slide on top of her.

She grins. "And you call me ridiculous."

"Just protecting what's mine." I tug her shirt up and over her head.

Her hands glide up my back. "Now, don't go all Scar and end up in jail. I need you out here."

I groan, trailing kisses down her neck. "Someday, you're gonna run out of lion references."

She pushes her lips to the side as I find her collarbone. "Maybe. I'm just testing them all out to see which one fits." I nip at her skin. "Although Slade is pretty liony sounding."

"Good. Let's stick with that."

She hooks me with her legs. "Don't worry, you big beast. I am definitely sticking with you."

EPILOGUE

Six Months Later

SLADE

"Where in the hell is this supposed to go?" Trig holds up a six-inch bolt.

Carson snatches it from his hand and shoves it into his back pocket. "Would you go find something else to do?"

"You don't have to ask me twice." Trig heads toward the house and grabs a beer from the cooler. He plops down in a lawn chair beside Wind, who's manning the grill amongst an array of balloons and a Happy Birthday banner.

"Swade, catch." Ollie throws a ball, and I extend my arm above me to keep it from going over my head. He holds his mitt out, and I lob it back. It bounces off the edge of his glove, and Grover snatches it.

"No, Gro-ver. Drop," he says, carefully enunciating each word.

Over the past months, Ollie has made amazing progress with his speech. He still stutters when he gets excited or tired, but he's doing so well.

"Are you finally going to get the balls and do it? It would be an excellent birthday gift to yourself." Carson pulls the drill from his tool belt and screws in one side of a plank.

I start on the latter. "I'm getting to it. Just shut your yap and worry about your plans." He's not wrong. It would be a nice distraction from my birthday altogether.

"G-getting to what?" Ollie asks, tossing the ball with one hand and trying to catch it with the other.

I glare at Carson.

"Now is a good time," he says around a screw between his lips.

I'll wipe that smartass look off his face as soon as we are alone.

I take a deep breath, setting my drill down. "Toss me that ball. Let me see what you got."

Ollie takes a few steps back, and he throws it, using his whole body. I have to stretch, but I catch it.

"Love Bug incoming!" Sarah sticks her head out the back door and sets Frankie down.

Frankie takes off toward us, holding a large tube of bubbles.

"Aww. We're playing catch. I don't want to d-do bubbles."

"Bubbles. Bubbles." Frankie waves the tube at me, and I squat, taking it.

"Come here, partner. Let's see how big we can make these," I say, and Grover barks, ready to bite them.

I pull the sticky wand out and gently wave it in the air. Grover prances as Frankie tries to grab the mass of bubbles.

"These are small," Ollie pouts, plopping down in the grass.

"Hey, can I ask you something, man to man?"

He looks up at me. "Yeah."

I inhale, my stomach squeezing tight. I've been looking for the right moment to have this conversation, but I'm beginning to think there'll never be a perfect time.

"How would you feel about me marrying your mom?"

He blinks a couple of times, and I dip the wand into the bubbles, waiting. My heart pounds, knowing I need this little boy to want this as much as I do.

One side of his face scrunches. "Can you move all your stuff to our house?"

My shoulders stiffen, realizing I didn't think through all the questions that might be tossed at me. "Maybe. We'll live together here or wherever your mom and I think is best."

His eyes fall to the ground, and I can't interpret the look on his downturned face. I sit beside him, and Frankie scoots backward, falling into my lap and blowing on the dripping wand.

Carson's drill zips another screw into the playset while Ollie picks at the green grass.

"Does that mean you'll be our d-dad?" His voice is soft and tentative.

My body relaxes a little. "If you want, or I'll be whatever you want me to be. I'm not going anywhere. I just want to make it official with your mom. We'll be a family."

"Daddy," Frankie says, trying to stick the wand in the tube. "Daddy, bwow." She looks up at me and grins, her little nose curling up.

My chest swells with her words.

Ollie giggles. "She called you Daddy."

I watch him, so undeserving of that title, but I will never take it for granted. "What do you think, partner?"

He shrugs, climbing to his feet. "You can be my dad. I want to be a f-family." He says it so nonchalantly.

My body sags, clearly seeing I've been stressing about nothing. Now, I just need Sarah to marry me.

"Can we play catch now?" Ollie pats the ball into his glove.

"Ol, throw me that ball," Trig hollers. "Maybe those two can actually get your swings up sometime today."

"Wait, Ol." I stop him, and he turns. "What we talked about is just between us for now, ok?"

He frowns, and his head drops to the side. "Is this like Mama's s-secret about the baby?"

I stare at him as his eyes grow wide.

"Oopsie." He grins, his shoulders hunching up to his ears. "S-s-sorry." He turns, running toward Trig and throwing the ball.

I can't move. My heart might have stopped beating. I look around, wondering if anyone else heard what I just heard. *Baby?*

"Looked pretty serious over here. How did it go?" Carson's boots stop beside me.

I glance down at Frankie, who is blowing spit more than bubbles.

She twists, holding it up to my lips. "Daddy, bwow." That word strikes me square in the chest as her cheeks puff out with air.

"Not good?" Carson asks, sounding concerned.

My heart finally kicks back into rhythm, and my skin prickles with heat. I lift Frankie, handing her to Carson and climbing to my feet.

He scoops her up. "Well, hey, little darlin'. You want to help me hang these swings?"

I charge toward the house. *Baby.* What the hell? Maybe this is a joke, or he misunderstood.

My heart pounds with each step, and I rip the back door open, stepping inside.

My eyes roam over Sarah, looking for any clue. I inhale and hold it, needing to squash all hope and possible elation.

Sarah glances at me and returns to rinsing something. "Oh, hey. Krissy will be late. She got called in to work."

Millie steps around me with a giant bowl of fruit. "I'll check with Wind to see how much longer for the ribs."

Sarah scrubs a pan. "Can you get the—"

I move toward her, hitting the water off and pulling her to the side.

"Hey! What are you—"

I grab her waist and set her on the counter.

"Ok. Hello. What's happening? We have a house full of people. We cannot—"

I stand between her legs, bracing both hands on the counter, getting eye level. "Is there something you need to tell me?" It comes out a little ragged and growly. I don't mean for it to, but dammit, I need to know.

Her chin tips up a little, her eyes avoiding mine. "Umm."

"Sarah, you know I hate secrets."

Her eyes meet mine as she twirls a finger through the end of my hair, flipping out from under my hat. "But what if this is a good one?" she whispers.

"Sarah."

Her head tilts to the side, her eyelids dropping. "What specifically are you asking me?"

My head falls forward, and I groan.

Her hands lift my face back up to hers. "Fine. I might have something to tell you, but your birthday is still a couple of days away, and I—"

My heart starts pounding again. "I need you to tell me now. Are we having a baby?"

Her shoulders sag. "That little stinker. I knew he heard me talking to Roxie."

I straighten as hope explodes from my heart through my body. "When did this happen?"

"Well, you were definitely there. Could have been that one time in the shower, or maybe when you didn't—"

"How sure are you?"

She pushes her lips to the side, thinking as adrenaline soars through my body. I need a fan and an answer.

"I'm late. It's. . .a maybe." Her eyes flick between mine. "But my boobs are sore and growing, I've puked a few times at work, and I can't stand the smell of cheese." She shivers as if she got a whiff of it.

"What do we need to do to be sure?"

She slides her arms around my neck, pulling me close. "How about patience?" She tries to distract me, nipping at my bottom lip.

"I have none of that," I growl.

She laughs, her head falling to my shoulder. "I grabbed a test from the clinic on my way out yesterday, but I was waiting for your birthday. So it would be great if you could forget this little conversation for just a few days."

"No, let's go." I scoop her off the counter, and she wraps her legs around me.

"Slade Bennett, you are a total party pooper."

"I let you put balloons outside."

She laughs. "You're so generous."

I set her down just outside the bathroom door, and she peers up at me with those eyes that see straight through me. "Are you suuurrrre you don't want to wait?" she pleads.

I pull her close, angling my head and kissing her. Her arms swing around my neck, tugging me closer. She hangs onto me, but I pull away.

"Fine," she says breathlessly and slips into the bathroom.

Thirty seconds later, the door swings open, and she sits on the edge of the bed.

"Five minutes, you wild beast. So much for my surprise." She sets the timer on her phone.

I look down at her, knowing I'm already the luckiest man. I hear Frankie's sweet voice calling me daddy, and Ollie hugging me tight and making sure I'll be here when he wakes up.

My throat swells as my chest fills with awe at somehow getting to be a part of their lives.

I move in front of her and drop to my knees.

I wait for her gaze to meet mine. "You, Sarah, are the absolute best surprise of my life. Every day I get to be here with you and Ollie and Frankie, it's a gift I'll never take for granted. I want nothing more than just this. The three of you."

She blinks quickly, her head falling to the side.

I spread my hand over her stomach. "If there's a little life in here, my love will only stretch that much further."

She sniffs as her eyes well with tears, and my throat grows dry.

"I need you to marry me," I say clearly. "I don't care what the test shows, and if you don't want to do that again, I'm still going to be here. I'm already yours in every way that matters, and all three of you are mine. I need you all the time, but I'd really like for you to also be my wife."

Her lip quivers, and she smiles as tears roll down her cheeks. "I don't know what to say."

"Please say yes." I brush her cheeks with my thumbs. "I already told Ollie we'd be a family, and Frankie just called me daddy. And regardless of whether we made a baby or not, I can't be without you. Ever."

She leans forward, bringing her forehead to mine. "There was no question in there, Bossy Pants."

The timer goes off, and I smile.

"Sarah, will you marry me? Please." I whisper.

Her salty lips brush against mine. "I'd marry you this very minute."

The timer continues to chime.

My chest inflates with hope, joy, and wonder for all that will be.

"You ready?" she asks, holding my face.

"I'm always ready with you."

She grins and releases me, then goes into the bathroom and returns with the little stick.

I push to my feet.

Those different-colored eyes meet mine, and she bites her bottom lip. I hook an arm around her and snatch her off the floor. Her arms squeeze my neck, and my eyes burn with tears.

"I love you," I whisper.

She sniffs. "I love you, too. So much."

We stay wrapped together for a long moment before she pulls away, wiping her face.

"Did Frankie really call you daddy?"

I nod.

"I missed it," she whines.

"I asked Ollie about marrying you, but this is not how I planned it," I admit.

"You planned something?" Her mouth turns downward.

I exhale. "Yes. I wanted to ask you at the shop."

She swipes at her eyes. "Wait, was this going to include you calling me an asshole again? If so, I would have definitely said yes." There's a twinkle in that blue eye that makes my heart swell with pride that this woman will be mine. Forever.

I kiss her, unable to believe this will be the rest of my life.

"We should probably get back to your party," she says against my lips.

"Do we have to?" I slide my hands to her butt.

She pulls away, swatting me. "Yes. They're probably already thinking we're doing other things in here."

"So." I stay put, needing a second to be sure this is all real, but she grabs my hand.

"Come on." She tugs me. "We have lots to celebrate, but just so you know, we're going to the courthouse as soon as possible to make this legit."

I smile, so ready for this.

"Now, since you got your surprise early, you have to have a good attitude when we play birthday games later."

"I'm not playing any games, Sarah."

She links her fingers with mine, ignoring me. "Hey, if it's a boy, how do you feel about the name Simba?"

ACKNOWLEDGMENTS

Here we go again. How do I possibly thank all of the special people I’m somehow lucky enough to have in my life who help me be able to tell these stories? All I can do is try.

Brian, you are it, babe. The reason I get to continue to fulfill this dream and tell stories that make me laugh and cry and think about us.

To my kiddos, you guys are the best things I’ll ever do. Your love and encouragement make me believe I can. Thanks for the inspiration. Yeeessss, even the whole peeing on the wall thing.

Mom, for showing me that hell can be temporary. That sometimes, we just have to keep climbing, and eventually, we’ll find ourselves on the other side to see the beauty of all that comes after. Thanks for reading and cheering me on through the hard days.

Jordan, girl, we did it. Thanks for reading, for the love and encouragement, and for reminding me of the value of words. Here we go. F.O.R.W.A.R.D.

Natalie, your constant love and support and hours spent reading mean more to me than you’ll ever know. Thank you for helping make Slade and Sarah’s story the best it can be.

Cait, your thoughts on this one still bring a smile to my face. I can’t wait to do it again. Love you to the moon and back. Always.

Lauren, your love and encouragement are everything. Thank you for always being my cheerleader and having all the confidence in me when I have none.

Lizzie, it was just in the nick of time, but seriously, what I needed to hear in that exact moment. Thank you for making time for me and these characters.

To those having to start over. Fresh starts suck ass. It’s scary, intimidating, exhausting, and you will spend days wondering if it's worth it. Keep going. Don’t look back. You are braver than you will ever know. Someday, you’ll turn around and see how far you’ve come. The journey is what makes us truly appreciate all there is in the after.

ABOUT THE AUTHOR

Stacy Williams lives with her husband and children in Illinois. She writes in five-minute increments between homeschooling and extracurricular activities. She's spent years dreaming about writing love stories that, in a worn and broken world, remind us of what we're truly made for.

authorstacywilliams.com

@stacywilliams.writes

stacywilliams.writes

www.ingramcontent.com/pod-product-compliance
Lightning Source LLC
LaVergne TN
LVHW100502110826
845146LV00002B/492

* 9 7 9 8 9 8 9 0 4 4 9 8 6 *